WIZARDS

Edited by Jack Dann and Gardner Dozois

WIZARDS

EDITED BY
Jack Dann and Gardner Dozois

BERKLEY BOOKS, NEW YORK

THE BERKLEY PUBLISHING GROUP
Published by the Penguin Group
Penguin Group (USA) Inc.
375 Hudson Street, New York, New York 10014, USA
Penguin Group (Canada), 90 Eglinton Avenue East, Suite 700, Toronto, Ontario M4P 2Y3, Canada
(a division of Pearson Penguin Canada Inc.)
Penguin Books Ltd., 80 Strand, London WC2R 0RL, England
Penguin Group Ireland, 25 St. Stephen's Green, Dublin 2, Ireland
(a division of Penguin Books Ltd.)
Penguin Group (Australia), 250 Camberwell Road, Camberwell, Victoria 3124, Australia
(a division of Pearson Australia Group Pty. Ltd.)
Penguin Books India Pvt. Ltd., 11 Community Centre, Panchsheel Park, New Delhi—110 017,
India
Penguin Group (NZ), 67 Apollo Drive, Mairangi Bay, Auckland 1311, New Zealand
(a division of Pearson New Zealand Ltd.)
Penguin Books (South Africa) (Pty.) Ltd., 24 Sturdee Avenue, Rosebank, Johannesburg 2196,
South Africa

Penguin Books Ltd., Registered Offices: 80 Strand, London WC2R 0RL, England

This is an original publication of The Berkley Publishing Group.

This is a work of fiction. Names, characters, places, and incidents either are the product of the authors' imaginations or are used fictitiously, and any resemblance to actual persons, living or dead, business establishments, events, or locales is entirely coincidental. The publisher does not have any control over and does not assume any responsibility for author or third-party websites or their content.

First edition: May 2007

Library of Congress Cataloging-in-Publication Data

Wizards : magical tales from the masters of modern fantasy / edited by Jack Dann and Gardner Dozois.—1st ed.
p. cm.
ISBN 978-0-425-21518-0
1. Fantasy fiction, American. 2. Wizards—Fiction. I. Dann, Jack. II. Dozois, Gardner R.

PS648.F3W59 2007
813'.0876608377—dc22

2006101534

PRINTED IN THE UNITED STATES OF AMERICA

10 9 8 7 6 5 4 3 2 1

For Merrilee Heifetz, who saw it through

CONTENTS

Contents

Preface

Wizards have stalked through the human imagination for thousands and thousands of years, perhaps even from a time before we were fully human. Traces of Neanderthal magic have been found at prehistoric sites: a low-walled stone enclosure containing seven bear heads, all facing forward; a human skull on a stake in a ring of stones. A few tens of thousands of years later, in the deep caves of Lascaux and Altamira and Rouffignac, the Cro-Magnons were practicing magic too, perhaps learned from the vanishing Neanderthals, filling wall after wall in the most remote and isolated depths of hidden caverns with vivid, emblematic paintings of Ice Age animals and the abstract and interlacing paint-outlined human handprints known as "Macaronis" (there's little doubt that these paintings were used in sorcerous rites, especially as many of the paintings seem to have been ritually "killed," perhaps to ensure success in the hunt). These ancient walls also give us what may be the very first representation of a wizard in human history, a hulking, shaggy, mysterious, deer-headed figure watching over the bright, flat, painted animals as they caper across the stone.

Wizards, sorcerers, shamans, witches, medicine men, seers, root women, conjure men—every age and every culture from prehistoric times on has had its own version of the magic-user, the-one-who-intercedes-with-the-spirits, the one who knows the ancient secrets and can call upon the hidden powers, the one who can see both the spirit world and the physical world, and who can mediate between them. Sometimes they're benevolent and wise, sometimes evil and malign, sometimes—ambiguously—both. Even here in the twenty-first century, where space stations and satellites whirl overhead, you can communicate instantly with someone on the other side of the world, and you can cross a continent from one coast to the other in a matter of hours (things that would themselves have seemed like the most extreme magic only a few hundred years ago), the figure of the wizard is still a deeply significant one, an archetype that haunts art, advertising, literature, folklore, cartoons, movies, and even our very dreams.

We asked some of the very best modern fantasists—Neil Gaiman, Garth Nix, Elizabeth Hand, Eoin Colfer, Jane Yolen, Peter S. Beagle, Kage Baker, Tad Williams, Orson Scott Card, Gene Wolfe, Patricia A. McKillip, Terry Bisson, Nancy Kress, Andy Duncan, Mary Rosenblum, Jeff Ford, Tanith Lee, Terry Dowling—to write stories about that most potent of fantasy archetypes, The Wizard. The book you hold in your hands is the result, and here you will find wizards young and old, evil and benign, male and female, living in the ancient world and in the modern world and in fantasy worlds that never were . . . children who can talk to animals, and animals who are willing to give up their lives to fight evil magic, boys who are raised by the dead, and girls who make friends with ghosts in haunted houses, boys who find the Devil ruffling through magazines in their garage or who secretly have the power of gods, and women of deep secret knowledge who marry Winter, young men and women who fight Iron Magic with Holly Magic through the deep forests of Arthurian Britain, or who fight deadly magical conspiracies in their own backyards, talking chickens and monstrous manticores, stone men, mysterious strangers, and a ruby incomparable, wizards as blackly evil as night or as bright and gentle as a summer's day . . . plus a few wizards who just can't make up their minds!

We hope you enjoy them.

WIZARDS

The Witch's Headstone

Neil Gaiman

One of the hottest stars in science fiction, fantasy, and horror today, Neil Gaiman has won three Hugo Awards, two Nebula Awards, one World Fantasy Award, six Locus Awards, four Stoker Awards, three Geffens, and two Mythopoeic Fantasy Awards. Gaiman first came to wide public attention as the creator of the graphic novel series The Sandman, *still one of the most acclaimed graphic novel series of all time. Gaiman remains a superstar in the graphic novel field; his graphic novels, many in collaboration with Dave McKean, in-clude* Black Orchid, Violent Cases, Signal to Noise, The Tragical Comedy or Comical Tragedy of Mr. Punch, *and the children's books* The Wolves in the Walls *and* The Day I Swapped My Dad for Two Goldfish.

In recent years he's enjoyed equal success in the science fiction and fantasy fields as well, with his bestselling novel American Gods *winning the 2002 Hugo, Nebula, and Bram Stoker Awards,* Coraline *winning both Hugo and Nebula in 2003, and his story "A Study in Emerald" winning the Hugo in 2004. He also won the World Fantasy Award for his story with Charles Vess, "A Midsummer Night's Dream," and won the International Horror Critics Guild Award for his collection* Angels & Visitations: A Miscellany. *Gaiman's other novels include* Good Omens *(written with Terry Pratchett),* Neverwhere, *and, most recently,* Anansi Boys. *In addition to* Angels & Visitations, *his short fiction has been collected in* Smoke & Mirrors: Short Fictions & Illusions. *He's also written* Don't Panic: The Official Hitchhiker's Guide to the Galaxy Companion, A Walking Tour of the Shambles *(with Gene Wolfe), and edited* Ghastly Beyond Belief *(with Kim Newman),* Book of Dreams *(with Edward Kramer), and* Now We Are Sick: An Anthology of Nasty Verse *(with Stephen Jones). Coming up is a new collection,* Fragile Things.

In the lyrical tale that follows, he blurs the distinction between the quick and the dead—and shows us that what really counts is kindness, no matter which side of the grave you're on . . .

✳

T HERE was a witch buried at the edge of the graveyard; it was common knowledge. Bod had been told to keep away from that corner of the world by Mrs. Owens as far back as he could remember.

"Why?" he asked.

"T'ain't healthy for a living body," said Mrs. Owens. "There's damp down that end of things. It's practically a marsh. You'll catch your death."

Mr. Owens himself was more evasive and less imaginative. "It's not a good place," was all he said.

The graveyard proper ended at the edge of the hill, beneath the old apple tree, with a fence of rust-brown iron railings, each topped with a small, rusting spear-head, but there was a wasteland beyond that, a mass of nettles and weeds, of brambles and autumnal rubbish, and Bod, who was a good boy, on the whole, and obedient, did not push between the railings, but he went down there and looked through. He knew he wasn't being told the whole story, and it irritated him.

Bod went back up the hill, to the abandoned church in the middle of the graveyard, and he waited until it got dark. As twilight edged from grey to purple there was a noise in the spire, like a fluttering of heavy velvet, and Silas left his resting-place in the belfry and clambered headfirst down the spire.

"What's in the far corner of the graveyard?" asked Bod. "Past Harrison Westwood, Baker of this Parish, and his wives, Marion and Joan?"

"Why do you ask?" said his guardian, brushing the dust from his black suit with ivory fingers.

Bod shrugged. "Just wondered."

"It's unconsecrated ground," said Silas. "Do you know what that means?"

"Not really," said Bod.

Silas walked across the path without disturbing a fallen leaf and sat down on the stone bench, beside Bod. "There are those," he said, in his silken voice, "who believe that all land is sacred. That it is sacred before we come to it, and sacred after. But here, in your land, they bless the churches and the ground they set aside to bury people in, to make it holy. But they leave land unconsecrated beside the sacred ground, Potter's

Fields to bury the criminals and the suicides or those who were not of the faith."

"So the people buried in the ground on the other side of the fence are bad people?"

Silas raised one perfect eyebrow. "Mm? Oh, not at all. Let's see, it's been a while since I've been down that way. But I don't remember any one particularly evil. Remember, in days gone by you could be hanged for stealing a shilling. And there are always people who find their lives have become so unsupportable they believe the best thing they could do would be to hasten their transition to another plane of existence."

"They kill themselves, you mean?" said Bod. He was about eight years old, wide-eyed and inquisitive, and he was not stupid.

"Indeed."

"Does it work? Are they happier dead?"

Silas grinned so wide and sudden that he showed his fangs. "Sometimes. Mostly, no. It's like the people who believe they'll be happy if they go and live somewhere else, but who learn it doesn't work that way. Wherever you go, you take yourself with you. If you see what I mean."

"Sort of," said Bod.

Silas reached down and ruffled the boy's hair.

Bod said, "What about the witch?"

"Yes. Exactly," said Silas. "Suicides, criminals, and witches. Those who died unshriven." He stood up, a midnight shadow in the twilight. "All this talking," he said, "and I have not even had my breakfast. While you will be late for lessons." In the twilight of the graveyard there was a silent implosion, a flutter of velvet darkness, and Silas was gone.

The moon had begun to rise by the time Bod reached Mr. Pennyworth's mausoleum, and Thomes Pennyworth (*here he lyes in the certainty of the moft glorious refurrection*) was already waiting, and was not in the best of moods.

"You are late," he said.

"Sorry, Mr. Pennyworth."

Pennyworth tutted. The previous week Mr. Pennyworth had been teaching Bod about Elements and Humours, and Bod had kept forgetting which was which. He was expecting a test, but instead Mr. Pennyworth said, "I think it is time to spend a few days on practical matters. Time is passing, after all."

"Is it?" asked Bod.

"I am afraid so, young master Owens. Now, how is your Fading?"

Bod had hoped he would not be asked that question.

"It's all right," he said. "I mean. You know."

"No, Master Owens. I do not know. Why do you not demonstrate for me?"

Bod's heart sank. He took a deep breath and did his best, squinching up his eyes and trying to fade away.

Mr. Pennyworth was not impressed.

"Pah. That's not the kind of thing. Not the kind of thing at all. Slipping and fading, boy, the way of the dead. Slip through shadows. Fade from awareness. Try again."

Bod tried harder.

"You're as plain as the nose on your face," said Mr. Pennyworth. "And your nose is remarkably obvious. As is the rest of your face, young man. As are you. For the sake of all that is holy, empty your mind. Now. You are an empty alleyway. You are a vacant doorway. You are nothing. Eyes will not see you. Minds will not hold you. Where you are is nothing and nobody."

Bod tried again. He closed his eyes and imagined himself fading into the stained stonework of the mausoleum wall, becoming a shadow on the night and nothing more. He sneezed.

"Dreadful," said Mr. Pennyworth, with a sigh. "Quite dreadful. I believe I shall have a word with your guardian about this." He shook his head. "So. The humours. List them."

"Um. Sanguine. Choleric. Phlegmatic. And the other one. Um, Melancholic, I think."

And so it went, until it was time for Grammar and Composition with Miss Letitia Borrows, Spinster of this Parish (*Who Did No Harm to No Man All the Dais of Her Life. Reader, Can You Say Lykewise?*). Bod liked Miss Borrows, and the cosiness of her little crypt, and could all-too-easily be led off the subject.

"They say there's a witch in uncons—unconsecrated ground," he said.

"Yes, dear. But you don't want to go over there."

"Why not?"

Miss Borrows smiled the guileless smile of the dead. "They aren't our sort of people," she said.

"But it is the graveyard, isn't it? I mean, I'm allowed to go there if I want to?"

"That," said Miss Borrows, "would not be advisable."

Bod was obedient, but curious, and so, when lessons were done for the night, he walked past Harrison Westwood, Baker, and family's memorial, a broken-headed angel, but did not climb down the hill to the Potter's Field. Instead he walked up the side of the hill to where a picnic some thirty years before had left its mark in the shape of a large apple tree.

There were some lessons that Bod had mastered. He had eaten a bellyful of unripe apples, sour and white-pipped, from the tree some years before, and had regretted it for days, his guts cramping and painful while Mistress Owens lectured him on what not to eat. Now he waited until the apples were ripe before eating them and never ate more than two or three a night. He had finished the last of the apples the week before, but he liked the apple tree as a place to think.

He edged up the trunk, to his favourite place in the crook of two branches, and looked down at the Potter's Field below him, a brambly patch of weeds and unmown grass in the moonlight. He wondered whether the witch would be old and iron-toothed and travel in a house on chicken legs, or whether she would be thin and carry a broomstick.

And then he was hungry. He wished he had not devoured all the apples on the tree. That he had left just one . . .

He glanced up, and thought he saw something. He looked once, looked twice to be certain. An apple, red and ripe.

Bod prided himself on his tree-climbing skills. He swung himself up, branch by branch, and imagined he was Silas, swarming smoothly up a sheer brick wall. The apple, the red of it almost black in the moonlight, hung just out of reach. Bod moved slowly forward along the branch, until he was just below the apple. Then he stretched up, and the tips of his fingers touched the perfect apple.

He was never to taste it.

A snap, loud as a hunter's gun, as the branch gave way beneath him.

A flash of pain woke him, sharp as ice, the colour of slow thunder, down in the weeds that summer's night.

The ground beneath him seemed relatively soft, and oddly warm. He pushed a hand down and felt something like warm fur. He had landed on the grass-pile, where the graveyard's gardener threw the cuttings from the mower, and it had broken his fall. Still, there was a pain in his chest, and his leg hurt as if he had landed on it first, and twisted it.

Bod moaned.

"Hush-a-you-hush-a-boy," said a voice from behind him. "Where did you come from? Dropping like a thunderstone. What way is that to carry on?"

"I was in the apple tree," said Bod.

"Ah. Let me see your leg. Broken like the tree's limb, I'll be bound." Cool fingers prodded his left leg. "Not broken. Twisted, yes, sprained per-haps. You have the Devil's own luck, boy, falling into the compost. 'Tain't the end of the world."

"Oh, good," said Bod. "Hurts, though."

He turned his head, looked up and behind him. She was older than he, but not a grown-up, and she looked neither friendly nor unfriendly. Wary, mostly. She had a face that was intelligent and not even a little bit beautiful.

"I'm Bod," he said.

"The live boy?" she asked.

Bod nodded.

"I thought you must be," she said. "We've heard of you, even over here, in the Potter's Field. What do they call you?"

"Owens," he said. "Nobody Owens. Bod, for short."

"How-de-do, young master Bod."

Bod looked her up and down. She wore a plain white shift. Her hair was mousy and long, and there was something of the goblin in her face—a sideways hint of a smile that seemed to linger, no matter what the rest of her face was doing.

"Were you a suicide?" he asked. "Did you steal a shilling?"

"Never stole nuffink," she said. "Not even a handkerchief. Anyway," she said, pertly, "the suicides is all over there, on the other side of that hawthorn, and the gallows-birds are in the blackberry-patch, both of them. One was a coiner, t'other a highwayman, or so he says, although if you ask me I doubt he was more than a common footpad and nightwalker."

"Ah," said Bod. Then, suspicion forming, tentatively, he said, "They say a witch is buried here."

She nodded. "Drownded and burnded and buried here without as much as a stone to mark the spot."

"You were drowned *and* burned?"

She settled down on the hill of grass-cuttings beside him, and held his throbbing leg with her chilly hands. "They come to my little cottage at dawn, before I'm proper awake, and drags me out onto the Green. 'You're a witch!' they shouts, fat and fresh-scrubbed all pink in the morning, like so many pigwiggins fresh-scrubbed for market day. One by one they gets up beneath the sky and tells of milk gone sour and horses gone lame, and finally Mistress Jemima gets up, the fattest, pinkest, best-scrubbed of them all, and tells how as Solomon Porritt now cuts her dead and instead hangs around the washhouse like a wasp about a honeypot, and it's all my magic, says she, that made him so and the poor young man must be bespelled. So they strap me to the cucking-stool and forces it under the water of the duck-pond, saying if I'm a witch, I'll neither drown nor care, but if I am not a witch, I'll feel it. And Mistress Jemima's father gives them each a silver groat to hold the stool down under the foul green water for a long time, to see if I'd choke on it."

"And did you?"

"Oh yes. Got a lungful of water. It done for me."

"Oh," said Bod. "Then you weren't a witch after all."

The girl fixed him with her beady ghost-eyes and smiled a lopsided smile. She still looked like a goblin, but now she looked like a pretty goblin, and Bod didn't think she would have needed magic to attract Solomon Porritt, not with a smile like that. "What nonsense. Of course I was a witch. They learned that when they untied me from the cucking-stool and stretched me on the green, nine parts dead and all covered with duckweed and stinking pond-muck. I rolled my eyes back in my head, and I cursed each and every one of them there on the village green that morning, that none of them would ever rest easily in a grave. I was surprised at how easily it came, the cursing. Like dancing it was, when your feet pick up the steps of a new measure your ears have never heard and your head don't know, and they dance it till dawn." She stood, and twirled, and kicked, and her bare feet flashed in the moonlight. "That was how I cursed them, with my last gurgling pond-watery breath. And then I expired. They burned my body on the green until I was nothing but blackened charcoal, and they popped me in a hole in the Potter's Field without so much as a headstone to mark my name," and it was only then that she paused, and seemed, for a moment, wistful.

"Are any of them buried in the graveyard, then?" asked Bod.

"Not a one," said the girl, with a twinkle. "The Saturday after they drownded and toasted me, a carpet was delivered to Master Porringer, all the way from London Town, and it was a fine carpet. But it turned out there was more in that carpet than strong wool and good weaving, for it

carried the plague in its pattern, and by Monday five of them were cough-
ing blood, and their skins were gone as black as mine when they hauled me
from the fire. A week later and it had taken most of the village, and they
threw the bodies all promiscuous in a plague pit they dug outside of the
town that they filled in after."

"Was everyone in the village killed?"

She shrugged. "Everyone who watched me get drownded and burned.
How's your leg now?"

"Better," he said. "Thanks."

Bod stood up, slowly, and limped down from the grass-pile. He leaned
against the iron railings. "So were you always a witch?" he asked. "I mean,
before you cursed them all?"

"As if it would take witchcraft," she said with a sniff, "to get Solomon
Porritt mooning round my cottage."

Which, Bod thought, but did not say, was not actually an answer to the
question, not at all.

"What's your name?" he asked.

"Got no headstone," she said, turning down the corners of her mouth.
"Might be anybody. Mightn't I?"

"But you must have a name."

"Liza Hempstock, if you please," she said tartly. Then she said, "It's
not that much to ask, is it? Something to mark my grave. I'm just down
there, see? With nothing but nettles to mark where I rest." And she looked
so sad, just for a moment, that Bod wanted to hug her. And then it came to
him, as he squeezed between the railings of the fence. He would find Liza
Hempstock a headstone, with her name upon it. He would make her smile.

He turned to wave good-bye as he began to clamber up the hill, but she
was already gone.

THERE were broken lumps of other people's stones and statues in the
graveyard, but, Bod knew, that would have been entirely the wrong sort of
thing to bring to the grey-eyed witch in the Potter's Field. It was going to
take more than that. He decided not to tell any one what he was planning,
on the not entirely unreasonable basis that they would have told him not
to do it.

Over the next few days his mind filled with plans, each more complicated and extravagant than the last. Mr. Pennyworth despaired.

"I do believe," he announced, scratching his dusty moustache, "that you are getting, if anything, worse. You are not Fading. You are *obvious*, boy. You are difficult to miss. If you came to me in company with a purple lion, a green elephant, and a scarlet unicorn astride which was the King of England in his Royal Robes, I do believe that it is you and you alone that people would stare at, dismissing the others as minor irrelevancies."

Bod simply stared at him, and said nothing. He was wondering whether there were special shops in the places where the living people gathered that sold only headstones, and if so how he could go about finding one, and Fading was the least of his problems.

He took advantage of Miss Borrow's willingness to be diverted from the subjects of grammar and composition to the subject of anything else at all to ask her about money—how exactly it worked, how one used it to get things one wanted. Bod had a number of coins he had found over the years (he had learned that the best place to find money was to go, afterwards, to wherever courting couples had used the grass of the graveyard as a place to cuddle and snuggle and kiss and roll about. He would often find metal coins on the ground, in the place where they had been), and he thought perhaps he could finally get some use from them.

"How much would a headstone be?" he asked Miss Borrows.

"In my time," she told him, "they were fifteen guineas. I do not know what they would be today. More, I imagine. Much, much more."

Bod had fifty-three pence. It would not be enough.

It had been four years, almost half a lifetime, since Bod had visited the Indigo Man's tomb. But he still remembered the way. He climbed to the top of the hill, until he was above the whole town, above even the top of the apple tree, above even the steeple of the ruined church, up where the Frobisher Vault stood like a rotten tooth. He slipped down into it, and down and down and still further down, down to the tiny stone steps cut into the center of the hill, and those he descended until he reached the stone chamber at the base of the hill. It was dark in that tomb, dark as a deep mine, but Bod saw as the dead see, and the room gave up its secrets to him.

The Sleer was coiled around the wall of the barrow. It was as he remembered it, all smoky tendrils and hate and greed. This time, however, he was not afraid of it.

FEAR ME, whispered the Sleer. FOR I GUARD THINGS PRECIOUS AND NEVER-LOST.

"I don't fear you," said Bod. "Remember? And I need to take something away from here."

NOTHING EVER LEAVES, came the reply from the coiled thing in the darkness. THE KNIFE, THE BROOCH, THE GOBLET. I GUARD THEM IN THE DARKNESS. I WAIT.

In the centre of the room was a slab of rock, and on it they lay: a stone knife, a brooch, and a goblet.

"Pardon me for asking," said Bod. "But was this your grave?"

MASTER SETS US HERE ON THE PLAIN TO GUARD, BURIES OUR SKULLS BENEATH THIS STONE, LEAVES US HERE KNOWING WHAT WE HAVE TO DO. WE GUARDS THE TREASURES UNTIL MASTER COMES BACK.

"I expect that he's forgotten all about you," pointed out Bod. "I'm sure he's been dead himself for ages."

WE ARE THE SLEER. WE GUARD.

Bod wondered just how long ago you had to go back before the deepest tomb inside the hill was on a plain, and he knew it must have been an extremely long time ago. He could feel the Sleer winding its waves of fear around him, like the tendrils of some carnivorous plant. He was beginning to feel cold, and slow, as if he had been bitten in the heart by some arctic viper and it was starting to pump its icy venom through his body.

He took a step forward, so he was standing against the stone slab, and he reached down and closed his fingers around the coldness of the brooch.

HISH! whispered the Sleer. WE GUARDS THAT FOR THE MASTER.

"He won't mind," said Bod. He took a step backward, walking toward the stone steps, avoiding the desiccated remains of people and animals on the floor.

The Sleer writhed angrily, twining around the tiny chamber like ghostsmoke. Then it slowed. IT COMES BACK, said the Sleer, in its tangled triple voice. ALWAYS COMES BACK.

Bod went up the stone steps inside the hill as fast as he could. At one point he imagined that there was something coming after him, but when he broke out of the top, into the Frobisher vault, and he could breathe the cool dawn air, nothing moved or followed.

Bod sat in the open air on the top of the hill and held the brooch. He thought it was all black, at first, but then the sun rose, and he could see that the stone in the centre of the black metal was a swirling red. It was the size of a robin's egg, and Bod stared into the stone, wondering if there were things moving in its heart, his eyes and soul deep in the crimson world. If Bod had been smaller, he would have wanted to put it into his mouth.

The stone was held in place by a black metal clasp, by something that looked like claws, with something else crawling around it. The something else looked almost snake-like, but it had too many heads. Bod wondered if that was what the Sleer looked like, in the daylight.

He wandered down the hill, taking all the short-cuts he knew, through the ivy tangle that covered the Bartlebys' family vault (and inside, the sound of the Bartlebys grumbling and readying for sleep) and on and over and through the railings and into the Potter's Field.

He called "Liza! Liza!" and looked around.

"Good morrow, young lummox," said Liza's voice. Bod could not see her, but there was an extra shadow beneath the hawthorn tree, and as he approached it, the shadow resolved itself into something pearlescent and translucent in the early-morning light. Something girl-like. Something grey-eyed. "I should be decently sleeping," she said. "What kind of carrying on is this?"

"Your headstone," he said. "I wanted to know what you want on it."

"My name," she said. "It must have my name on it, with a big E, for Elizabeth, like the old queen that died when I was born, and a big Haitch for Hempstock. More than that I care not, for I did never master my letters."

"What about dates?" asked Bod.

"Willyum the Conker ten sixty-six," she sang, in the whisper of the dawn-wind in the hawthorn bush. "A big E if you please. And a big Haitch."

"Did you have a job?" asked Bod. "I mean, when you weren't being a witch?"

"I done laundry," said the dead girl, and then the morning sunlight flooded the wasteland, and Bod was alone.

It was nine in the morning, when all the world is sleeping. Bod was determined to stay awake. He was, after all, on a mission. He was eight years old, and the world beyond the graveyard held no terrors for him.

Clothes. He would need clothes. His usual dress, of a grey winding-sheet, was, he knew, quite wrong. It was good in the graveyard, the same colour as stone and as shadows. But if he was going to dare the world beyond the graveyard walls, he would need to blend in there.

There were some clothes in the crypt beneath the ruined church, but

Bod did not want to go there, even in daylight. While Bod was prepared to justify himself to Master and Mistress Owens, he was not about to explain himself to Silas; the very thought of those dark eyes angry, or worse still, disappointed, filled him with shame.

There was a gardener's hut at the far end of the graveyard, a small green building that smelled like motor oil, and in which the old mower sat and rusted, unused, along with an assortment of ancient garden tools. The hut had been abandoned when the last gardener had retired, before Bod was born, and the task of keeping the graveyard had been shared between the council (who sent in a man to cut the grass, once a month from April to September) and local volunteers.

A huge padlock on the door protected the contents of the hut, but Bod had long ago discovered the loose wooden board in the back. Sometimes he would go to the gardener's hut, and sit, and think, when he wanted to be by himself.

As long as he had been going to the hut there had been a brown working-man's jacket hanging on the back of the door, forgotten or abandoned years before, along with a green-stained pair of gardening jeans. The jeans were much too big for him, but he rolled up the cuffs until his feet showed, then he made a belt out of brown garden-twine, and tied it around his waist. There were boots in one corner, and he tried putting them on, but they were so big and encrusted with mud and concrete that he could barely shuffle them, and, if he took a step, the boots remained on the floor of the shed. He pushed the jacket out through the space in the loose board, squeezed himself out, then put it on. If he rolled up the sleeves, he decided, it worked quite well. It had big pockets, and he thrust his hands into them and felt quite the dandy.

Bod walked down to the main gate of the graveyard and looked out through the bars. A bus rattled past, in the street; there were cars there and noise and shops. Behind him, a cool green shade, overgrown with trees and ivy: home.

His heart pounding, Bod walked out into the world.

ABANAZER Bolger had seen some odd types in his time; if you owned a shop like Abanazer's, you'd see them, too. The shop, in the warren of streets in the Old Town—a little bit antique shop, a little bit junk shop, a little bit pawnbroker's (and not even Abanazer himself was entirely certain which bit was which)—brought odd types and strange people, some of them wanting to buy, some of them needing to sell. Abanazer Bolger traded over the counter, buying and selling, and he did a better trade behind the counter and in the back room, accepting objects that may not have been acquired entirely honestly, and then quietly shifting them on. His business was an iceberg. Only the dusty little shop was visible on the surface. The rest of it was underneath, and that was just how Abanazer Bolger wanted it.

Abanazer Bolger had thick spectacles and a permanent expression of mild distaste, as if he had just realised that the milk in his tea had been on the turn, and he could not get the sour taste of it out of his mouth. The expression served him well when people tried to sell him things. "Honestly," he would tell them, sour-faced, "it's not really worth anything at all. I'll give you what I can, though, as it has sentimental value." You were lucky to get anything like what you thought you wanted from Abanazer Bolger.

A business like Abanazer Bolger's brought in strange people, but the boy who came in that morning was one of the strangest Abanazer could remember in a lifetime of cheating strange people out of their valuables. He looked to be about seven years old, and dressed in his grandfather's clothes. He smelled like a shed. His hair was long and shaggy, and he looked extremely grave. His hands were deep in the pockets of a dusty brown jacket, but even with the hands out of sight, Abanazer could see that something was clutched extremely tightly—protectively—in the boy's right hand.

"Excuse me," said the boy.

"Aye-aye, Sonny-Jim," said Abanazer Bolger warily. *Kids,* he thought. *Either they've nicked something, or they're trying to sell their toys.* Either way, he usually said no. Buy stolen property from a kid, and next thing you knew you'd an enraged adult accusing you of having given little Johnnie or Matilda a tenner for their wedding ring. More trouble than they was worth, kids.

"I need something for a friend of mine," said the boy. "And I thought maybe you could buy something I've got."

"I don't buy stuff from kids," said Abanazer Bolger flatly.

Bod took his hand out of his pocket and put the brooch down on the grimy counter-top. Bolger glanced down at it, then he looked at it. He removed his spectacles, took an eyepiece from the counter-top and screwed it into his eye. He turned on a little light on the counter and examined the brooch through the eyeglass. "Snakestone?" he said to himself, not to the boy. Then he took the eyepiece out, replaced his glasses, and fixed the boy with a sour and suspicious look.

"Where did you get this?" Abanazer Bolger asked.

Bod said, "Do you want to buy it?"

"You stole it. You've nicked this from a museum or somewhere, didn't you?"

"No," said Bod flatly. "Are you going to buy it, or shall I go and find somebody who will?"

Abanazer Bolger's sour mood changed then. Suddenly he was all affability. He smiled broadly. "I'm sorry," he said. "It's just you don't see many pieces like this. Not in a shop like this. Not outside of a museum. But I would certainly like it. Tell you what. Why don't we sit down over tea and biscuits—I've got a packet of chocolate chip cookies in the back room—and decide how much something like this is worth? Eh?"

Bod was relieved that the man was finally being friendly. "I need enough to buy a stone," he said. "A headstone for a friend of mine. Well, she's not really my friend. Just someone I know. I think she helped make my leg better, you see."

Abanazer Bolger, paying little attention to the boy's prattle, led him behind the counter and opened the door to the storeroom, a windowless little space, every inch of which was crammed high with teetering cardboard boxes, each filled with junk. There was a safe in there, in the corner, a big old one. There was a box filled with violins, an accumulation of stuffed dead animals, chairs without seats, books and prints.

There was a small desk beside the door, and Abanazer Bolger pulled up the only chair and sat down, letting Bod stand. Abanazer rummaged in a drawer, in which Bod could see a half-empty bottle of whisky, and pulled out an almost-finished packet of chocolate chip cookies, and he offered one to the boy; he turned on the desk-light, looked at the brooch again, the swirls of red and orange in the stone, and he examined the black metal band that encircled it, suppressing a little shiver at the expression on the heads of the snake-things. "This is old," he said. "It's"—*priceless*, he thought—"probably not really worth much, but you never know." Bod's face fell. Abanazer Bolger tried to look reassuring. "I just need to know that it's not stolen, though, before I can give you a penny. Did you take it from your mum's dresser? Nick it from a museum? You can tell me. I'll not get you into trouble. I just need to know."

Bod shook his head. He munched on his cookie.

"Then where did you get it?"

Bod said nothing.

Abanazer Bolger did not want to put down the brooch, but he pushed it across the desk to the boy. "If you can't tell me," he said, "you'd better take it back. There has to be trust on both sides, after all. Nice doing business with you. Sorry it couldn't go any further."

Bod looked worried. Then he said, "I found it in an old grave. But I can't say where." And he stopped, because naked greed and excitement had replaced the friendliness on Abanazer Bolger's face.

"And there's more like this there?"

Bod said, "If you don't want to buy it, I'll find someone else. Thank you for the biscuit."

Bolger said, "You're in a hurry, eh? Mum and Dad waiting for you, I expect?"

The boy shook his head, then wished he had nodded.

"Nobody waiting. Good." Abanazer Bolger closed his hands around the brooch. "Now, you tell me exactly where you found this. Eh?"

"I don't remember," said Bod.

"Too late for that," said Abanazer Bolger. "Suppose you have a little think for a bit about where it came from. Then, when you've thought, we'll have a little chat, and you'll tell me."

He got up and walked out of the room, closing the door behind him. He locked it, with a large metal key.

He opened his hand and looked at the brooch and smiled, hungrily.

There was a *ding* from the bell above the shop door, to let him know someone had entered, and he looked up, guiltily, but there was nobody there. The door was slightly ajar though, and Bolger pushed it shut, and then for good measure, he turned around the sign in the window, so it said CLOSED. He pushed the bolt closed. Didn't want any busybodies turning up today.

The autumn day had turned from sunny to grey, and a light patter of rain ran down the grubby shop window.

Abanazer Bolger picked up the telephone from the counter and pushed at the buttons with fingers that barely shook.

"Pay-dirt, Tom," he said. "Get over here, soon as you can."

BOD realised that he was trapped when he heard the lock turn in the door. He pulled on the door, but it held fast. He felt stupid for having been lured

15

inside, foolish for not trusting his first impulses, to get as far away from the sour-faced man as possible. He had broken all the rules of the graveyard, and everything had gone wrong. What would Silas say? Or the Owenses? He could feel himself beginning to panic, and he suppressed it, pushing the worry back down inside him. It would all be good. He knew that. Of course, he needed to get out . . .

He examined the room he was trapped in. It was little more than a store-room with a desk in it. The only entrance was the door.

He opened the desk drawer, finding nothing but small pots of paint (used for brightening up antiques) and a paint-brush. He wondered if he would be able to throw paint in the man's face and blind him for long enough to escape. He opened the top of a pot of paint and dipped in his finger.

"What're you doin'?" asked a voice close to his ear.

"Nothing," said Bod, screwing the top on the paint-pot and dropping it into one of the jacket's enormous pockets.

Liza Hempstock looked at him, unimpressed. "Why are you in here?" she asked. "And who's old bag-of-lard out there?"

"It's his shop. I was trying to sell him something."

"Why?"

"None of your bees-wax."

She sniffed. "Well," she said, "you should get on back to the graveyard."

"I can't. He's locked me in."

" 'Course you can. Just slip through the wall—"

He shook his head. "I can't. I can only do it at home because they gave me the freedom of the graveyard when I was a baby." He looked up at her, under the electric light. It was hard to see her properly, but Bod had spent his life talking to dead people. "Anyway, what are you doing here? What are you doing out from the graveyard? It's day-time. And you're not like Silas. You're meant to stay in the graveyard."

She said, "There's rules for those in graveyards, but not for those as was buried in unhallowed ground. Nobody tells *me* what to do, or where to go." She glared at the door. "I don't like that man," she said. "I'm going to see what he's doing."

A flicker, and Bod was alone in the room once more. He heard a rumble of distant thunder.

In the cluttered darkness of Bolger's Antiquities, Abanazer Bolger looked up suspiciously, certain that someone was watching him, then realised he was being foolish. "The boy's locked in the room," he told himself. "The front door's locked." He was polishing the metal clasp surrounding the snakestone, as gently and as carefully as an archaeologist on a dig, taking off the black and revealing the glittering silver beneath it.

He was beginning to regret calling Tom Hustings over, although Hustings was big and good for scaring people. He was also beginning to regret that he was going to have to sell the brooch when he was done. It was special. The more it glittered under the tiny light on his counter, the more he wanted it to be his, and only his.

There was more where this came from, though. The boy would tell him. The boy would lead him to it . . .

A knocking on the outer door of the shop.

Bolger walked over to the door, peering out into the wet afternoon.

"Hurry up," called Tom Hustings. "It's miserable out here. Dismal. I'm getting soaked."

Bolger unlocked the door, and Tom Hustings pushed his way in, his raincoat and hair dripping. "What's so important that you can't talk about it over the phone, then?"

"Our fortune," said Abanazer Bolger, with his sour face. "That's what."

Hustings took off his raincoat and hung it on the back of the shop-door. "What is it? Something good fell off the back of a lorry?"

"Treasure," said Abanazer Bolger. He took his friend over to the counter, showed him the brooch under the little light.

"It's old, isn't it?"

"From pagan times," said Abanazer. "Before. From Druid times. Before the Romans came. It's called a snakestone. Seen 'em in museums. I've never seen metalwork like that, or one so fine. Must have belonged to a king. The lad who found it says it come from a grave—think of a barrow filled with stuff like this."

"Might be worth doing it legit," said Hustings, thoughtfully. "Declare it as treasure trove. They have to pay us market value for it, and we could make them name it for us. The Hustings-Bolger Bequest."

"Bolger-Hustings," said Abanazer, automatically. Then he said, "There's a few people I know of, people with real money, would pay more than market value, if they could hold it as you are"—for Tom Hustings was fingering the brooch, gently, like a man stroking a kitten—"and there'd be no questions asked." He reached out his hand, and, reluctantly, Tom Hustings passed him the brooch.

And the two men went back and forth on it, weighing the merits and disadvantages of declaring the brooch as a treasure trove or of forcing the boy to show them the treasure, which had grown in their minds to a huge underground cavern filled with precious things, and as they debated Abanazer pulled a bottle of sloe gin from beneath the counter and poured them both a generous tot, "to assist the cerebrations."

Liza was soon bored with their discussions, which went back and forth and around like a whirligig, getting nowhere, and so she went back into the store-room to find Bod standing in the middle of the room with his eyes tightly closed and his fists clenched and his face all screwed up as if he had a toothache, almost purple from holding his breath.

"What you a-doin' of now?" she asked, unimpressed.

He opened his eyes and relaxed. "Trying to Fade," he said.

Liza sniffed. "Try again," she said.

He did, holding his breath even longer this time.

"Stop that," she told him. "Or you'll pop."

Bod took a deep breath and then sighed. "It doesn't work," he said. "Maybe I could hit him with a rock and just run for it." There wasn't a rock, so he picked up a coloured-glass paper-weight, hefted it in his hand, wondering if he could throw it hard enough to stop Abanazer Bolger in his tracks.

"There's two of them out there now," said Liza. "And if the one don't get you, t'other one will. They say they want to get you to show them where you got the brooch, and then dig up the grave and take the treasure." She shook her head. "Why did you do something as stupid as this anyway? You know the rules about leaving the graveyard. Just asking for trouble, it was."

Bod felt very insignificant, and very foolish. "I wanted to get you a headstone," he admitted, in a small voice. "And I thought it would cost more money. So I was going to sell him the brooch, to buy you one."

She didn't say anything.

"Are you angry?"

She shook her head. "It's the first nice thing any one's done for me in five hundred years," she said, with a hint of a goblin smile. "Why would I be angry?" Then she said, "What do you do, when you try to Fade?"

"What Mr. Pennyworth told me. *I am an empty doorway, I am a vacant alley, I am nothing. Eyes will not see me, glances slip over me.* But it never works."

"It's because you're alive," said Liza, with a sniff. "There's stuff as works for us, the dead, who have to fight to be noticed at the best of times, that won't never work for you people."

She hugged herself tightly, moving her body back and forth, as if she was debating something. Then she said, "It's because of me you got into this . . . Come here, Nobody Owens."

He took a step toward her, in that tiny room, and she put her cold hand on his forehead. It felt like a wet silk scarf against his skin.

"Now," she said. "Perhaps I can do a good turn for you."

And with that, she began to mutter to herself, mumbling words that Bod could not make out. Then she said, clear and loud,

"Be hole, be dust, be dream, be wind,
Be night, be dark, be wish, be mind,
Now slip, now slide, now move unseen,
Above, beneath, betwixt, between."

Something huge touched him, brushed him from head to feet, and he shivered. His hair prickled, and his skin was all goose-flesh. Something had changed. "What did you do?" he asked.

"Just gived you a helping hand," she said. "I may be dead, but I'm a dead witch, remember. And we don't forget."

"But—"

"Hush up," she said. "They're coming back."

The key rattled in the store-room lock. "Now then, chummy," said a voice Bod had not heard clearly before, "I'm sure we're all going to be great friends," and with that Tom Hustings pushed open the door. Then he stood in the doorway looking around, looking puzzled. He was a big, big man, with foxy-red hair and a bottle-red nose. "Here. Abanazer? I thought you said he was in here?"

"I did," said Bolger, from behind him.

"Well, I can't see hide nor hair of him."

Bolger's face appeared behind the ruddy man's, and he peered into the room. "Hiding," he said, staring straight at where Bod was standing. "No use hiding," he announced, loudly. "I can see you there. Come on out."

The two men walked into the little room, and Bod stood stock still between them and thought of Mr. Pennyworth's lessons. He did not react, he did not move. He let the men's glances slide from him without seeing him.

19

"You're going to wish you'd come out when I called," said Bolger, and he shut the door. "Right," he said to Tom Hustings. "You block the door so he can't get past." And with that he walked around the room, peering behind things and bending awkwardly to look beneath the desk. He walked straight past Bod and opened the cupboard. "Now I see you!" he shouted. "Come out!"

Liza giggled.

"What was that?" asked Tom Hustings, spinning round.

"I didn't hear nothing," said Abanazer Bolger.

Liza giggled again. Then she put her lips together and blew, making a noise that began as a whistling and then sounded like a distant wind. The electric lights in the little room flickered and buzzed. Then they went out.

"Bloody fuses," said Abanazer Bolger. "Come on. This is a waste of time."

The key clicked in the lock, and Liza and Bod were left alone in the room.

"HE'S got away," said Abanazer Bolger. Bod could hear him now, through the door.

"Room like that. There wasn't anywhere he could have been hiding. We'd've seen him if he was."

A pause.

"Here. Tom Hustings. Where's the brooch gone?"

"Mm? That? Here. I was keeping it safe."

"Keeping it safe? In your pocket? Funny place to be keeping it safe, if you ask me. More like you were planning to make off with it—like you was planing to keep my brooch for your own."

"Your brooch, Abanazer? *Your* brooch? Our brooch, you mean."

"Ours, indeed. I don't remember you being here when I got it from that boy."

There was another long silence, then Abanazer Bolger said, "Well, look at that, we're almost out of sloe gin—how would you fancy a good Scotch? I've whisky in the back room. You just wait here a moment."

The store-room door was unlocked, and Abanazer entered, holding a walking-stick and an electric torch, looking even more sour of face than before.

"If you're still in here," he said, in a sour mutter, "don't even think of making a run for it. I've called the police on you, that's what I've done." A rummage in a drawer produced the half-filled bottle of whisky, and then a tiny black bottle. Abanazer poured several drops from the little bottle into the larger, then he pocketed the tiny bottle. "My brooch, and mine alone," he muttered, and followed it with a barked, "Just coming, Tom!"

He glared around the dark room, staring past Bod, then he left the store-room, carrying the whisky in front of him. He locked the door behind him.

"Here you go," came Abanazer Bolger's voice through the door. "Give us your glass then Tom. Nice drop of Scotch, put hairs on your chest. Say when."

Silence. "Cheap muck. Aren't you drinking?"

"That sloe gin's gone to my innards. Give it a minute for my stomach to settle . . ." Then, "Here—Tom! What have you done with my brooch?"

"*Your* brooch is it now? Whoa—what did you . . . you put something in my drink, you little grub!"

"What if I did? I could read on your face what you was planning, Tom Hustings. Thief."

And then there was shouting, and several crashes, and loud bangs, as if heavy items of furniture were being overturned . . .

. . . then silence.

Liza said, "Quickly now. Let's get you out of here."

"But the door's locked." He looked at her. "Is there something you can do?"

"Me? I don't have any magics will get you out of a locked room, boy."

Bod crouched and peered out through the keyhole. It was blocked; the key sat in the keyhole. Bod thought, then he smiled momentarily, and it lit his face like the flash of a light-bulb. He pulled a crumpled sheet of newspaper from a packing case, flattened it out as best he could, then pushed it underneath the door, leaving only a corner on his side of the doorway.

"What are you playing at?" asked Liza impatiently.

"I need something like a pencil. Only thinner . . ." he said. "Here we go." And he took a thin paint-brush from the top of the desk and pushed the brushless end into the lock, jiggled it, and pushed some more.

There was a muffled clunk as the key was pushed out, as it dropped from the lock onto the newspaper. Bod pulled the paper back under the door, now with the key sitting on it.

Liza laughed, delighted. "That's wit, young man," she said. "That's wisdom."

Bod put the key in the lock, turned it, and pushed open the store-room door.

There were two men on the floor in the middle of the crowded antique shop. Furniture had indeed fallen; the place was a chaos of wrecked clocks and chairs, and in the midst of it the bulk of Tom Hustings lay, fallen on the smaller figure of Abanazer Bolger. Neither of them was moving.

"Are they dead?" asked Bod.

"No such luck," said Liza.

On the floor beside the men was a brooch of glittering silver; a crimson-orange-banded stone, held in place with claws and with snake-heads, and the expression on the snake-heads was one of triumph and avarice and satisfaction.

Bod dropped the brooch into his pocket, where it sat beside the heavy glass paper-weight, the paint-brush, and the little pot of paint.

LIGHTNING illuminated the cobbled street.

Bod hurried through the rain through the Old Town, always heading up the hill toward the graveyard. The grey day had become an early night while he was inside the store-room, and it came as no surprise to him when a familiar shadow swirled beneath the street-lamps. Bod hesitated, and a flutter of night-black velvet resolved itself into a man-shape.

Silas stood in front of him, arms folded. He strode forward impatiently.

"Well?" he said.

Bod said, "I'm sorry, Silas."

"I'm disappointed in you, Bod," Silas said, and he shook his head. "I've been looking for you since I woke. You have the smell of trouble all around you. And you know you're not allowed to go out here, into the living world."

"I know. I'm sorry." There was rain on the boy's face, running down like tears.

"First of all, we need to get you back to safety." Silas reached down and enfolded the living child inside his cloak, and Bod felt the ground fall away beneath him.

"Silas," he said.

Silas did not answer.

"I was a bit scared," he said. "But I knew you'd come and get me if it got too bad. And Liza was there. She helped a lot."

"Liza?" Silas's voice was sharp.

"The witch. From the Potter's Field."

"And you say she helped you?"

"Yes. She especially helped me with my Fading. I think I can do it now."

Silas grunted. "You can tell me all about it when we're home." And Bod was quiet until they landed beside the church. They went inside, into the empty hall, as the rain redoubled, splashing up from the puddles that covered the ground.

"Tell me everything," he said.

Bod told him everything he could remember about the day. And at the end, Silas shook his head, slowly, thoughtfully.

"Am I in trouble?" asked Bod.

"Nobody Owens," said Silas, "you are indeed in trouble. However, I believe I shall leave it to your foster-parents to administer whatever discipline and reproach they believe to be needed."

And then, in the manner of his kind, Silas was gone.

Bod pulled the jacket up over his head and clambered up the slippery paths to the top of the hill, to the Frobisher vault, and then he went down, and down, and still further down.

He dropped the brooch beside the goblet and the knife.

"Here you go," he said. "All polished up. Looking pretty."

IT COMES BACK, said the Sleer, with satisfaction in its smoke-tendril voice. IT ALWAYS COMES BACK.

THE night had been long, but it was almost dawn.

Bod was walking, sleepily and a little gingerly, past the final resting-place of Harrison Westwood, Baker of this Parish, and his wives, Marion and Joan, to the Potter's Field. Mr. and Mrs. Owens had died several hundred years before it had been decided that beating children was wrong, and Mr. Owens had, regretfully, that night, done what he saw as his duty, and Bod's bottom stung like anything. Still, the look of worry on Mrs. Owens's face had hurt Bod worse than any beating could have done.

He reached the iron railings that bounded the Potter's Field and slipped between them.

"Hullo?" he called. There was no answer. Not even an extra shadow in the hawthorn bush. "I hope I didn't get you into trouble, too," he said.

Nothing.

He had replaced the jeans in the gardener's hut—he was more comfortable in just his grey winding-sheet—but he had kept the jacket. He liked having the pockets.

When he had gone to the shed to return the jeans, he had taken a small hand-scythe from the wall where it hung, and with it he attacked the nettle-patch in the Potter's Field, sending the nettles flying, slashing and gutting them till there was nothing but stinging stubble on the ground.

From his pocket he took the large glass paper-weight, its insides a multitude of bright colours, along with the paint-pot and the paint-brush.

He dipped the brush into the paint and carefully painted, in brown paint, on the surface of the paper-weight, the letters

E H

and beneath them he wrote

WE DON'T FORGET

It was almost daylight. Bedtime soon, and it would not be wise for him to be late to bed for some time to come.

He put the paper-weight down on the ground that had once been a nettle patch, placed it in the place that he estimated her head would have been, and, pausing only to look at his handiwork for a moment, went through the railings and made his way, rather less gingerly, back up the hill.

"Not bad," said a pert voice from the Potter's Field, behind him. "Not bad at all."

But when he turned to look, there was nobody there.

Holly and Iron

GARTH NIX

Here's a spooky, suspenseful, and exciting adventure set in a time when two worlds and two races, and two ancient systems of magic, have collided, one pitched in a deadly battle against the other—with some surprising results.

Australian writer Garth Nix has worked as a book publicist, editor, marketing consultant, public relations man, and literary agent while also writing books, including the bestselling Old Kingdom series, which consists of Sabriel, Lirael: Daughter of the Clayr, Abhorsen, *and* The Creature in the Case. *His other books include the Seventh Tower series, consisting of* The Fall, Castle, Aenir, Above the Veil, Into Battle, *and* The Violet Keystone; *the Keys to the Kingdom series, consisting of* Mister Monday, Grim Tuesday, Drowned Wednesday, Sir Thursday, Lady Friday *and two more titles yet to be published; as well as stand-alone novels such as* The Ragwitch *and* Shade's Children. *His most recent book is the collection* Across the Wall: A Tale of Abhorsen and Other Stories. *Born in Melbourne, he grew up in Canberra and now lives in Sydney, Australia.*

"SIX men-at-arms, all mounted," reported Jack. He paused to spit out some nutshells, a remnant of his transition from squirrel-shape to human form, before he added, "Three in front of the litter, three behind."

"And the litter-bearers?" asked Merewyn. She didn't look at Jack as he put his clothes back on, her sharp blue eyes intent on the party that was making its way along the old Roman road that cut straight through the valley, only a hundred yards below their hiding-place high on the densely wooded slope.

"Slaves," said Jack. "Our folk, from the look of them. They all wear braided holly-charms on their ankles. So there is no ironmaster hiding amongst them."

"An ironmaster can stand holly for a short time, longer if it is not against his skin," corrected Merewyn. "Or they might make false holly from paper or painted wood. You're absolutely sure?"

Jack nodded. He was a big man, six feet tall and very broad in the shoulder. Even in his smallest squirrel-form, he was almost two feet tall, and he could also shape himself as a large boar or bear. Even so, he was a head shorter and fifty pounds lighter than his younger brother, known as Doublejack, who stood silently by, awaiting Merewyn's instructions. Doublejack would probably take the shape of a *cralle* dog—a huge beast the size of a pony—if they were to attack the Norman in the litter and his guards.

Jack and Doublejack were the only shape-shifters in Merewyn's band. It was a very rare talent, not often used as shifters needed to eat a huge amount of fresh meat upon returning to their human form, something not easily obtained. Even now, Jack was eyeing the freshly dressed deer hanging by its hind leg from a nearby branch. Going down in size made him less hungry than going up, but he would still eat a haunch or two, leaving the rest for Doublejack to gorge on later.

"Six men-at-arms," mused Merewyn aloud. "A curious number. Why only six? Everyone knows we're in these woods. They look sun-dark too, maybe pullani mercenaries . . . not household troops, which is also curious. And there is something strange about that litter. I cannot truly say I sense it, but I suspect some Norman magic is at work. Something of cold iron . . . yet I cannot be sure . . . Robin?"

Robin shook her head impatiently, indicating she felt no Norman magic at work. She did not want to feel any, so she did not focus her full concentration on the litter.

"Do we attack or not?" asked Robin impatiently.

Like the men and her half-sister Merewyn, Robin was dressed in a heavy woollen tunic over leather-booted hose, but apart from the clothes neither she nor Merewyn tried to disguise their femininity. Both had long hair, braided back and pinned with silver and amber, offering some protection against Norman magic workings and helpful for their own Inglish magic.

Silver and amber looked perfectly normal against Merewyn's blonde hair. She was all Inglish, tall and muscular, a fair-faced warrior woman who could wrestle down a stag and stab it in the neck, or send a cloth-yard shaft from her longbow two hundred yards through a Norman man-at-arms, brigantine and all.

Robin, to her eternal embarrassment and shame, looked more Norman than Inglish herself. She was shorter and stockier than her sister, dark-haired and grey-eyed, and always very brown from their outdoor life. She took after her mother, her father's second wife. The one he had stolen from her Norman father, unwittingly setting in train not only his own death but also the loss of his kingdom to that selfsame Norman, and the chain of events that led to his two daughters lurking in the fringe of trees above a valley, the elder leading a band of what could variously be described as bandits, rebels, or the last remnants of the army of the true King of Ingland.

"I am uneasy," said Merewyn. She looked up at the sky. The sun was still a full disc, but low and near the western hills. Two ravens circled overhead, black shapes against the darkening sky. "We will lose the light very soon, and we do not know who is in the litter."

"Only six guards," said Robin. "It can't be any one important . . . or dangerous."

"It could be someone confident enough to need no larger escort," said Merewyn. "An ironmaster hiding his charms and devices until the last."

"Let's attack before it *is* dark," urged Robin. "We haven't had a chance like this for weeks."

Merewyn didn't answer. Robin frowned, then tugged at her sister's sleeve.

"This'll be the third Norman we've let go if you don't give the order! What's wrong with you?"

"There is nothing wrong, Robin," said Merewyn softly. "Knowing when not to attack is as important to a leader as being up front swinging a sword."

"That's not leading!" snapped Robin. "*This* is leading!"

She snatched the horn from Merewyn's shoulder and, before her sister could stop her, blew a ringing peal that echoed across the valley. That done, she darted forward, drawing her sword as she ran.

The horn blast set the well-prepared ambush in motion. The heavy reverberation of axes on wood sounded ahead of the Norman's party. A few seconds later, a great tree came twisting down across the path, testament to the wood-cutters' skill in keeping it balanced all afternoon on the thinnest spire of uncut trunk.

As the tree crashed, archers stepped out from their hiding places on the edge of the cleared area on the side of the path and began to shoot at the guards' horses. The guards responded by charging the archers, bellowing oaths and cursing. Unusually, the litter-bearers didn't simply run away, toppling the litter, but set it down carefully before sprinting off between the trees.

Robin ran on the heels of a shaggy, slavering dog that stood higher than her shoulder. Merewyn and Jack came behind her, with a dozen of their band, all armed with swords, spears, or bill-hooks. They were the blocking force, to prevent an escape back along the path, as the fallen tree prevented any escape the other way.

But there was no attempt to flee. One of the guards was dead on the ground, killed instantly by an arrow that found a chink in his mail coif. Two more were trapped under dead or dying horses. The remaining three had realised the impossibility of riding down archers hiding in the forest fringe and had turned back.

"Surrender!" called Robin. She was out of breath from the mad charge down the slope and had to repeat the call. "Surrender!"

The three men-at-arms looked at the archers, who were once again stepping out of the green shadows, at the huge *cralle* dog that chose that moment to howl, and at the fifteen armed bandits approaching.

"You will die if you try to charge through," said Merewyn loudly, correctly observing the intention announced by the tensing of the men's arms and the flick of their horses' heads. "We will give quarter."

Two of the men-at-arms looked at the third, who nodded and threw down his sword. His companions did likewise. Then they dismounted and stood by their horses' heads, casting dark looks at Robin and Merewyn and nervous glances at Doublejack, who was sniffing around the litter.

Merewyn made a signal, and the archers moved closer, arrows still nocked and ready to loose. Six of her men raced forward and threw the men-at-arms to the ground, binding their hands as they also removed their daggers, boot-knives, and, in the case of the leader, a tiny knife scabbarded in the back of his gauntlet.

"Who is in the litter?" asked Robin. There had been no movement from it, not even the twitch of a curtain pulled aside. Doublejack was still sidling around it, his huge nose wrinkled much as a human forehead might frown in thought.

"An old Norman merchant," said one of the men-at-arms, the one the others had looked to. He had the faded, crescent scar of a slave tattoo on his cheek. "Going to the baths at Aquae Sulis."

"Not until he's paid his toll, he's not," said Robin. She strode over to the litter, hacked off the knots that held the curtain to the frame, pulled the rich but travel-stained velvet drapes aside, and trampled them under her heels.

There was a man inside the litter, sitting upright, wrapped in a thick cloak of blue felt, the hood pulled up and forward, so his face was shadowed. He had a chess-table set before him, of dark mahogany and ivory. There was a game in progress, though no one sat opposite him, slate-grey pieces in movement against softer, smaller ones of cherry-wood.

"You are our prisoner," said Robin. She extended her sword-arm, the point hovering a few inches from the man's hooded face. "And we will want a suitable ransom. What is your name?"

Instead of answering, the man lifted one of the slate-grey knights from the chess-board. Robin had only a moment to register that *all* the grey pieces were knights before she suddenly felt her sword twist violently out of her hand and hurtle up and behind her, almost impaling Doublejack.

Robin immediately snatched her necklace-garrote of holly-beads from her belt, but before she could do anything with it, the Norman flung down the grey knight. As it hit the ground, there was a clap of thunder, strange and terrible in the still air. Heat washed over Robin, as if she'd stepped into a forge, and there was no longer a chess piece between her and the palanquin, but an eight-foot-tall warrior, made entirely of iron, bearing a sword of blue-edged star-steel and a kite shield green with verdigris.

The iron warrior pushed his green shield at Robin, a blow that would have knocked her to the ground if she had not flung herself backward. Losing her garrote in the fall, she rolled and wriggled away as the iron warrior stomped towards her, its feet leaving deep impressions in the soft forest soil.

Robin heard Merewyn shouting "Flee!" but her sister did not follow her own orders. Instead, she rushed forward to help Robin up. The ground was damp and the leaf mulch slippery, and they slid apart as Robin got to her feet, with Merewyn behind her.

In that instant, the iron warrior was upon them. Merewyn tried to pivot on guard as it slammed its iron shield towards her, but it was too quick. The iron rim of its shield caught her full in the neck. There was a sickening crack, all too like a snapping branch, and Merewyn was hurled to the ground. She lay there, her head at an impossible angle.

Robin could do nothing but run. There were thunder-claps all around as the ironmaster threw out his chess pieces, iron warriors rising up where the knights fell. Robin ducked, weaved, and zigzagged to the tree-line, with iron warriors smashing their way through saplings, shrubs, and bushes towards her.

She paused when she reached the trees, twisting back to take a look. The nearest iron warrior was a dozen paces away, allowing Robin a few seconds' grace to take in the scene before she had to run again.

A full dozen iron warriors stalked the clearing, and there were two more standing in front of the palanquin, their shields raised to protect the ironmaster from archery. Not that there was any one shooting at him. Merewyn's band had vanished like a summer shower. The only signs that they had ever been there were the men-at-arms working away at their bonds—and Merewyn's body, a dozen paces from the palanquin.

Robin waited another second she couldn't afford, hoping that she would see Merewyn move, that her sister would suddenly get up and sprint away. But she didn't move. Deep inside, beneath the barrier of hope, Robin knew that Merewyn wouldn't get up, now or ever. She'd been hit too hard.

The iron warrior struck at the tree in front of Robin, its sword shearing through the wrist-thick branches she was sheltering behind, a spray of woodchips chasing Robin as she fled deeper into the forest.

NOT long after dawn the next morning, with the inexplicably insistent and enduring iron warriors left behind only a few hours before (and at least one of them struggling in one of the forest's more extensive bogs) Robin wearily climbed up on to the broad, ground-sweeping branch of an ancient oak and used it as a bridge over the narrow ravine known to locals as Hammerbite.

She looked for the two sentinels on the upper branches, but no one was there. There didn't seem to be any one in the camp either, when she rounded the trunk and looked out through the lesser trees at the row of leather tents, carefully pitched under the overhang of a huge ledge of shale, an outcrop from the grey hill whose bare crown poked out of the forest a hundred yards above the camp.

Robin whistled dispiritedly, not really expecting an answer, and so was not surprised when there wasn't one. She trudged over to the fire pit and looked down into it. The fire was emplaced about three feet down to disguise the smoke, and it was fed only good, dry wood, so it would burn clean. It was always kept alight, for there was never any knowing when fire might be needed.

But it was not burning now. Robin picked up the bent iron rod that doubled as poker and pot-hanger and stirred the ashes, but not one bright coal emerged.

She kept poking it long after this was clear, for want of anything better to do. It seemed symbolic to be stirring dead ashes, the ruins of a once-bright fire. Merewyn was dead, and it was all Robin's fault. She had got her own sister killed. The fact that none of the band had returned to the camp indicated that they thought so too, perhaps coupled with the distrust of her Norman heritage that had always simmered beneath the surface, kept in check only by Merewyn's authority.

She stabbed the poker hard into the ashes, wishing that it were the heart of the Norman ironmaster. Flames suddenly erupted from the dead ashes, and Robin jumped back. Not in fear of the flames, but of what she had just done, without thinking.

"That's a right Norman trick. Iron magic," said Jack, making Robin jump again, this time almost into the fire.

"I . . . I didn't . . ."

Jack shook his head and crouched down to pick up a gnarled knot of ancient beech, which he threw down on to the fire.

"You needn't fear, lass," he said. "I always knew you had the iron magic from your mother. There's no one here to see but me and Double-jack, and he's across the Hammerbite, eating up a gobbet of something I didn't care to look at."

"Did you see . . ." asked Robin quietly. "Is Merewyn . . ."

Jack took the poker and made sparks fly. He didn't look at Robin.

"The Princess is dead," he said finally. "I took the squirrel-shape and went back to be sure, though the *Ferramenta* chased me anyway. Her neck was broken. They took the body."

"I killed her," whispered Robin. She picked up handfuls of dry dirt and smeared them across her face, then she stood up and screamed, her words flying back at her, reflected by the overhanging shale. "I killed my sister!"

She reached for the hot coals of the fire and would have taken two handfuls, but Jack caught her in a bear hug and lifted her away, with her still kicking and screaming and quite out of her head with shock and grief and exhaustion. He carried her to the tent that was their makeshift surgery and hospice, patting her on the head and crooning the nonsense words he'd used long ago to calm young dogs when he was the King of Ingland's master of hounds.

When her threshing stopped and the screaming subsided into a dull, inward keening, he laid her down, and, taking up a small leather bottle, poured a cordial of *dwale* down her throat. Within a few minutes, the potent combination of hemlock, Italian mandragora, poppy-juice, henbane, and wine quieted her and only a little later sent her into a dreamless sleep.

When she awoke, Robin felt strangely calm and distant, as if a veil of many months lay between her and Merewyn's death. But she knew that the dusk she could see outside was the partner of the *Ferramenta*-haunted dawn. Even *dwale*-sleep could not hold someone for more than nine or ten hours.

The taste of the herbal brew was still in her mouth, and her breath stank as if she had vomited, though she was clean enough. Her hands had been washed, and the scratches smeared with yarrow paste. Robin stared at the scratches and for a few seconds couldn't remember how she had got them. She sat for a minute or two, thinking, then she slowly unfastened her dark Norman hair and hacked it short with her dagger, so short that her scalp bled and had to be staunched with cloth.

Jack and Doublejack were sitting by the fire, occasionally passing a wine-skin between them, with an even more occasional word or two. They looked around as Robin emerged from her tent, started at her changed appearance, then got up and bowed as she approached. Deep, courtly bows, out of place for outlaws in a wild woodland den.

"Don't," said Robin. "Not to me."

"You are the Princess Royal now," said Jack. "Heir of Ingland."

"Ruler of all I survey," muttered Robin, gesturing at the empty camp. She held out her hand for the wine-skin, and poured a long draught down her throat before handing it back.

"You are King Harold's daughter," said Jack. Doublejack nodded in emphasis, almost spilling the wine. "You are the rightful Queen of Ingland."

Robin laughed bitterly.

"Queen of nothing," she said. "We should have found another way, not this bandit life, skulking in the trees, while Duke William's rule grows ever stronger."

"We have been biding our time," said Jack. The words came easily to his lips, the familiar speech he had made to doubters before. "The Duke is old and has no sons. The Normans will fight each other when he dies, and we shall have our chance. The true Inglish will flock to your banner—"

"No," said Robin. "They won't. They might have come to serve Merewyn. They won't serve me. Besides, Duke William looked well enough yesterday eve. He might live for years, even beget himself new sons."

"It was the Duke?" asked Jack. "I wondered—"

"It must have been," said Robin. "Fourteen *Ferramenta*, walking for hours, never wavering in their purpose. Duke William is the only living ironmaster who wields such power. It was him. My grandfather was my sister's bane. Though I also must bear the fault—"

"Nay," interrupted Jack quickly, as he saw the grief begin to twist Robin's face. "None can escape their doom. The Princess was fated to fall as she did."

Robin did not answer for a full minute, her gaze locked on the fire. When she at last lifted her chin, her eyes were red, but there were no tears. A plan . . . or at this stage just a notion . . . was already swimming up from the dark depths of her mind.

"Who stands to inherit from the Duke should he die now?" she asked. Merewyn had always kept up with the many machinations, plots, counter-plots, and deaths among the Norman nobility, but Robin chose not to know, as part of her repudiation of that side of her heritage.

"I think three of the eight grand-nephews still live, his sister's son's sons," replied Jack. "And the son of his brother's leman, the Bastard of Aurillac, has something of a claim to Normandy alone."

He hesitated, then added, "None of your cousins has as good a claim to the Duke's lands as you do, Highness."

"I am not a Norman heir!" protested Robin. "My claim flows from my father, the true and Inglish King! Besides, the Duke has already tried to slay me, as his iron servants slew Merewyn!"

Jack tilted his head just a fraction, indicating his doubt that the *Ferramenta* had actually tried to kill Robin. But she did not see it, her eyes on the fire and her mind on other things.

"If I die, Jack, who stands next in the true line?"

Jack looked at her, trying to fathom what she was thinking. He had known her since she was born, but even as a little girl it had been hard to gauge her thoughts or predict her actions. She was always headstrong, a fault usually tempered by intelligence. She never did the same stupid, impetuous thing twice. Though sometimes once was all it took for lifelong regrets.

"None stand clear," replied Jack slowly. "The kin of your father's brother's wife in Jutland. King Sven would claim by that right, I think. But he would gather no following amongst our people here—"

"Is there no other Inglish heir?"

"There are distant cousins of your family, but none with the name or blood to stir the hearts of the people. Even fewer could wield the holly-magic or the rowan, as you do."

The fact that Robin could also wield the iron magic was left unsaid between them. The magics of holly and rowan were Inglish, born of the land, bred true in the royal line. Iron magic was not native to the island kingdom; it was an alien power, like the Norman invaders themselves. It was also magic much more suited to war and conquest.

"What do you intend, Highness?" asked Jack.

Robin did not answer.

"I know . . . I suppose . . . you will wish to see the rites conducted for Princess Merewyn. But we cannot bring a priest here, or linger ourselves. The *Ferramenta* may not cross the Hammerbite, but men-at-arms could, and this place is known . . . and the local folk may not hold out against questioning."

"Not now they know Merewyn is dead," said Robin bitterly. "Tell me, does that fat priest still haunt the cave near the whitestone glade?"

Jack looked at Doublejack.

"Aye, he does," said the huge man.

"Which god does he serve?"

Doublejack shrugged. "He keeps to himself. I would guess the All-father."

"Not the best—" said Jack.

"Can he sing a death?" interrupted Robin.

"He sang for Wat the miller's son," said Doublejack. "Not at the cave, though."

"Her death should be sung at the High Chapel in Winchester," said Robin bitterly. "But we cannot go there, or to any temple or church that I can think of. So we will go to the fat priest, no matter which god he worships."

Jack and Doublejack bowed, though it was clear Jack would have argued more if Robin had allowed it.

"We should take what we can from here, Highness," said Jack. "We will not be able to come back."

"I will gather what is needed from our . . . my tent," said Robin. She walked the little way over to the small leather tent she had shared for so many years with Merewyn. There was little enough inside to pack. She took Merewyn's second-best bow, which was better than her own, but left everything else. Of her own stuff, she took a quiver, amongst its dozen arrows one ivory-tipped, black-fletched shaft, made for killing Norman iron-masters; a small purse of silver pennies; and more hunting-clothes.

Then she reached under her straw-stuffed bed and retrieved a leather case. It contained two books. One, bound in bright blue calf-skin, was a primer for the Inglish magics of holly, rowan, and oak. The other, bound in dull bronze and black leather, was her mother's *grimoire*, an ironmaster's compendium of spells and lore.

Robin took everything outside to pack and sort. She could feel grief and raw emotion rising up in her again, overcoming the numbing dregs of *dwale* that still coursed through her blood. But she forced the complex mix of guilt, rage, and sorrow back down and concentrated on balancing her case, bow, quiver, and sack of clothes. It took her only a very few minutes, for quick departures had been part of her life for four years. Even so, Jack and Doublejack were already ahead of her, the hawker's baskets on their backs full of everything of worth that needed to be carried away.

IT was a long walk, via the most hidden paths in the deep forest. The night was light enough for travel, with the moon waxing and near full, and the stars bright save for a single long wisp of cloud on the horizon. Robin gave little thought to where she put her feet or to the green world around her. She simply followed Jack, with Doublejack behind, her mind mostly stuck on a narrow path of its own, a constant repetition of those fateful seconds when the *Ferramenta* stepped forward and swung its shield at Merewyn.

To try to break out of this pattern, Robin began to focus on a plan that was slowly gathering momentum in her mind. An act that, if successful, might make some small amends to Merewyn's shade, to her father, and to the people of Ingland.

It was near midnight when they reached the cave. Though they were quiet and came so late, the priest was waiting for them on the high ledge outside the cave-mouth.

Merewyn's band knew him as the fat priest, for he had carried much excess flesh when he'd first arrived in the forest. But that was two years past, and he was now gaunt, great folds of skin around his cheeks and neck the only signs of his previous corpulence. It was unlikely any one from his past, before he came to the cave, would recognise him. Particularly since, in addition to being a much reduced man, he had also chosen to cut out his left eye in honour of his god.

The priest went down on one knee as Robin climbed up the stone steps to the cave entrance, Jack pushing past him to make sure no one lurked inside.

"I welcome you, Highness, in the Allfather's name," the priest intoned quietly.

"I am honoured," replied Robin. It was best to be civil to priests and particularly to those who served the Allfather. "I suppose since you know who I am you also know what I wish of you."

"To sing Princess Merewyn beyond this world," replied the priest. "A raven came to me with the dawn, with the news of her death and what would be required of me. But come, set down your burdens. I have prepared ale and oat-cakes within."

"We do not worship the Allfather," said Robin. "And do not wish to be beholden to him. We will set our packs down here, sit on these steps, and sup on our bread and water, while you sing."

"As you wish," said the priest. He got to his feet creakily and went into the cave, emerging a few minutes later with a harp that only had four strings, a cup of ale, an oat-cake, and a silver-bound ox-horn. He set all but the harp upon the ground. Taking the instrument under his arm, the priest looked to the starry sky and slowly began to pick out a tune. It began simply, but grew more complex, and Robin felt sure she could hear the strings that weren't there.

Then the priest began to sing as well. His voice was hoarse, but strong, and after the first few words, it echoed strangely, almost as if someone far distant had joined in the singing.

Robin shivered as the song grew louder and stranger, with the unseen voice beginning to drown out the priest. Then suddenly Robin heard Merewyn, clear through the layers of song, in between the harp notes.

"Robin! Seek new beginnings!"

Robin sprang to her feet and rushed towards the priest, but even as she gripped him, screaming "Merewyn! Merewyn!" her sister's voice was gone, as were the others. There was only the priest, silent now himself, plucking one last note.

"She is gone," said the priest. He stepped back out of Robin's grasp. She did not try to restrain him. "You had best begone yourself, Highness, before your men wake."

Robin looked behind her. Jack and Doublejack were sprawled against the steps, chests slowly rising and falling in the rhythm of deep sleep.

"Duke William is at Winchester," said the priest. His single eye reflected the moonlight with a red glint, as if there was also fire in the sky. "You wish to kill him, do you not? Have your revenge?"

"Yes," said Robin warily. She was not entirely sure who she was talking to now, whether it be the priest or the one he served. She could feel the sudden attention of the oaks in the forest. They would not bend themselves to listen to a mortal. But it was not safe to seek the Allfather's favour. He was a god who loved battle and dissent, and delighted in sudden treachery.

"Your servants would try to prevent you going to Winchester," said the priest. "But they will sleep here till the dawn, and by then you will be at the gates of Winchester, with your black arrow."

"I do not want your aid, whoever or whatever you are," snapped Robin. "Wake my men!"

"I only wish to be of service," wheedled the priest. "Duke William is a powerful adversary. How will you strike at him, without more powerful allies?"

"I asked only for what any kin may ask of any priest, to sing my sister's death," said Robin. "I will take nothing else, and owe no debt. Wake my men!"

"Very well," said the priest. "I will wake them."

He snatched up the ox-horn and blew it mightily, its peal echoing out across the forest. It was answered not just by Jack and Doublejack's sudden, surprised oaths, but by many voices on the forest path below, accompanied by the jangle of arms, armour, and harness.

Robin looked down and saw a column of men-at-arms stretching back along the path, their helmets glinting in the moonlight. They were leading their horses and there were at least two score of them, perhaps more.

When Robin turned back, the priest was gone, as were horn, cup, and oat-cake. Shouts from below showed that she had been seen. Within a few seconds there would be Norman men-at-arms charging up the steps.

"Into the cave, Highness!" exclaimed Jack. He pushed Robin out of the moonlight, into the dark entrance. "You must escape!"

Robin knew there was a wide, natural chimney at the rear of the cave, but she couldn't see it, and she didn't even try to find it. Instead, she turned back towards Jack and Doublejack. Two silhouettes, etched in moonlight, standing in the cave entrance with drawn swords. From beyond them came the crash of soldiers charging up the steps, and sudden war-cries that echoed and danced around the cave.

"Go!" shouted Jack. He didn't turn around. A moment later, he and Doublejack were beset by three men-at-arms, all that could attack the cave-mouth at one time. But many more waited their turn on the steps or the forest-floor below.

Robin tried to think of some magic she could do, something that might hold the soldiers off long enough for Jack and Doublejack to disengage. But no Inglish spell came to mind, not one that would work in a cold stone cave. And she had none of the apparatus or the prepared objects that would let her work any serious Norman magic.

But she had her sword. She ran forward and, crouching between her two housecarls, stabbed out at the knee of one of the attacking men-at-arms. Her thrust struck home, sliding under the skirts of the man's mail byrnie. He stumbled back, teetered on the edge of the cave's natural porch, was helped along by a sword-thrust from Jack, and fell over the edge.

One of the other men-at-arms was already dead on the ground. The third backed towards the steps. A commanding voice from the forest-floor below bellowed out, "Bring up the archers!"

"Take the Princess and flee!" ordered Jack to his brother. Doublejack shook his head. It started as a human head-shake but ended up as a dog's. His shredded clothes and basket fell to the ground and a huge *cralle* dog crouched, ready to spring. With a deep bass howl that Robin felt from her feet up through her breastbone, the huge beast leapt forward, straight at the terrified men-at-arms, who tried to jump back, beginning a mass fall down the steps.

Jack watched for two long seconds, then whirled around, gripping Robin's arm with considerable force.

"To the chimney!"

Robin tried to wriggle out of his grasp as they ran into the cave. She couldn't see a thing, but Jack obviously could, for they didn't run into anything.

"We have to go back! Doublejack—"

"They'll shoot us down. Don't waste his gift!"

Robin stopped struggling. Jack dragged her along another half-dozen steps, then abruptly picked her up. Tilting her head back, Robin could see a faint circle of lighter darkness above her.

"There are iron staples," said Jack. "I hope."

"There are," said Robin. She knew where they were without having to see them. Iron called to her; she could feel its resonance deep in her bones. She reached out blindly, her fingers closed around the first staple, and she started to climb.

The chimney was about fifty feet high. Robin emerged on the side of a steep slope, between stunted trees that clung to the rock with gnarled, exposed roots. Jack climbed out behind her.

Both of them looked down the slope. The cave-mouth was hidden from them, but they could see at least forty Norman men-at-arms standing ready on the path below it, including half-a-dozen archers who stood in a semi-circle, laughing and joking. From their triumphant demeanour, and the snatches of talk that drifted up the hill, it was clear Doublejack's furious attack had ended under a hail of arrows.

"Doublejack—"

"He's dead," said Jack. "Come on. Some brave fool will try the chimney, sooner or later, and the wiser will come up the easy side of the hill."

Using the exposed roots as handholds, Jack started to make his way diagonally across and up the slope. Robin followed more slowly. Jack no longer had his basket to weigh him down, but Robin had managed to keep her leather bag and quiver, though Merewyn's bow lay on the cave steps below.

It was a hard scramble to the top of the hill, followed by a frantic, dipping, ducking run between, under, and around the trees and bushes that followed the ridge-line, as the Normans had already raced up the easier side of the hill. Fortunately, they were much slower and clumsier in the forest than Jack and Robin and could not simply bull their way through the undergrowth like the *Ferramenta*.

At last, when the noise of their pursuers faded and there was only the expected sounds of the night forest, Jack stopped before a vast, lightning-struck remnant of a royal oak. It was split in several places, revealing a hollow chamber within, but none of the holes were large enough to allow even a child passage.

"Highness, can you make us a way?"

Robin touched the oak, her palm flat on the ancient trunk. If the tree had been alive, she would have felt its green spark at once. But this oak was long dead. Only its shade remained, contained within the collective memory of the forest.

Robin stopped breathing and stood as still as she could. She felt the forest mind slowly drift into her head, like a fog gliding across the moor. She felt what it was to be a sapling reaching for the sun, to have leaves trembling under heavy raindrops, branches reaching out and dividing many times, a trunk thickening its girth for year after year, century after century.

She became the oak, took its place in the memory of the forest. Green shoots sprang out around her palm. Old, dry bark quickened under her skin. One of the holes in the trunk groaned and split farther, a tiny twig growing out from one side. The split expanded, and the twig became a branch, tiny shoots forming on its edges, leaves unrolling from the green buds a few moments later.

"Enough," said Jack.

Robin heard him from far away. But she did not want to let go, did not want to leave the forest. She was the oak, and all her human pain and guilt and fear were somewhere else, far away and alien.

More branches grew around the split, questing outward.

"Enough!" said Jack again, more strongly.

Robin shuddered and withdrew her hand, tearing the skin where the bark had grown around the fleshy mound between thumb and wrist.

She sucked at the graze as she ducked through the split and into the warm, dry, and remarkably roomy chamber that occupied perhaps a quarter of the royal oak's broken stump. The interior was lined with thick moss, on which Robin gratefully lay down, letting the exhaustion she'd held back flow through her limbs.

After a few minutes, Jack, who was propped up near the split, said, "We'll be safe enough here till the dawn. After that, it might be best to make for the convent at Avington. You could claim sanctuary there."

"No," said Robin. "I'll not run from the Allfather to Christ Godsson."

"What shall you do then, Highness?" asked Jack. His voice was weary, so weary that he stumbled on his words. Robin looked at him, and for the first time in her young life, saw that Jack was old. Forty at least, perhaps even older. She hadn't noticed that he was grey with fatigue, for Robin had been thinking only of herself.

"I'm sorry, Jack," she said quietly. "For everything. If I hadn't been so impatient to attack, none of this . . . Merewyn . . . Doublejack . . ."

"If not then, it would have been soon anyway," said Jack. All his usual confidence was gone, his tone strange to Robin. "Princess Merewyn knew it. We had more than two thousand men in the months after Senlac Hill. How many stood with us two days ago? Four-and-thirty! I fear to say it, Highness, but I think the time has come for you to treat with your grandfather."

"What?" snapped Robin.

Jack closed his eyes for several seconds before forcing them open again with obvious effort.

"Let us speak of this in daylight, Highness," he whispered. "I am weary, so weary . . . perhaps it is weariness and despair that speaks. Let us talk on the morrow . . ."

His voice trailed off, his head slumped to one side, and his breathing slowly changed, clear indication that he had fallen into an exhausted sleep.

Robin stayed awake, anger frothing about inside her, but she could not maintain her rage. Jack had served her father and her sister faithfully for far longer than Robin had lived. He was mistaken, of course. It might seem as if the Inglish were defeated, but Robin had no intention of falling on her knees before her grandfather and begging forgiveness. She had other plans.

Other plans which meant forcing herself to wake before the dawn and creep from the hollow oak, leaving Jack still asleep. She looked down at him for a few moments, wondering if she was doing the right thing, and found herself reaching out to wake him. But she stopped, her hand wavering a few inches from his shoulder. Jack would not allow her to do what she intended.

Even so, she felt she could not leave him without a word or sign to show that she had gone of her own free will and not been taken by enemies. So she took the silver-set amber hairpin that no longer had a place to go on her shorn head, and stuck it in the ground by Jack.

BY the time the sun was well up and warming the air, Robin was hidden amidst long grass, watching the Roman road that ran down from Newbury to Winchester. A lone rider had passed by just after the dawn, but Robin was looking for a large group of travellers, or better yet, a train of merchants that she could join and mingle with. To better do so, she had thrown away her quiver, keeping only the ivory-tipped arrow, which was uncomfortably tied to her waist under her tunic. She had cut it short, throwing away the flight end, for Robin did not intend to shoot this arrow.

A small group of broad-hatted, staff-wielding pilgrims followed the lone rider an hour after the dawn had yielded to the bright sunshine of a summer day. Robin ignored them too. She would stand out like a dark toadstool in a basket of mushrooms amidst the pilgrims.

The next group was much more promising. It looked like the whole population of a village, going to the fair at Winchester to sell their produce. More than thirty men and women, with half a dozen hand-carts and three ox-hauled wagons.

Robin stepped out of the trees, pulling her tunic down and hose up, as if she were returning to the road after modestly finding a more private toilet than the roadside ditch.

Thirty pairs of suspicious eyes watched her approach. But when they saw that she had neither sword nor bow, and was not the precursor of a throng of armed bandits, some called out a greeting, the words unclear but the intention friendly.

They were from two villages, Robin found as she walked and talked amongst them. She had thought they might be wary of her, with her Norman looks, but if they were, they didn't show it. Towards mid-morning, a grandmother even invited Robin to ride with her on an ox-wagon, making one of her grand-daughters step down. Robin accepted gratefully, for she was very weary.

They did not talk at first. But after a mile of silence, save for the rumble of the wheels, the creak of the cart, and the occasional snuffling bellow from the oxen, the woman asked a question. Her dialect was thick, but Robin understood her well enough.

"Where are you from, boy? Who is your master?"

"Winchester," said Robin, glad that as she hoped, she had been taken for a boy. "I am a freeman. My name is . . . Wulf."

The woman nodded three times, as if impressing the information into her head.

"I am Aelva," she said. "Widow. My sons are also freemen, holding a hide of land from Henry Molyneux."

"Is he a good lord?" asked Robin.

"Aye, better than the last."

"The Normans have many bad lords," said Robin. She saw the woman's gaze slide across her shorn hair, and added, "My father was Inglish. My mother Norman."

"The last lord before Sir Henry was Inglish. We danced when the tidings came of his end at Senlac Hill."

Robin glared at her and stood, ready to jump off the cart. But the woman caught her elbow.

"I meant no harm, lad. Inglish or Norman lords, it matters not to me, but I'll say no more."

Robin slowly sat back down. They did not talk again, but after a while settled into a companionable silence, the moment of tension between them left on the road behind.

Instead of talking, Robin watched the country-side, enjoying the fresh air and the sunshine. It was years since she'd been out of the forest in daylight. The land looked more prosperous than she remembered. There were more sheep on the hill-sides, and more farm buildings, and the road was well mended.

The villagers stopped to rest the oxen and themselves when the sun was high. Robin thanked Aelva and wished them all well, and continued on her way. She felt much more rested in body, but her mind was besieged by new thoughts, brought on by the peaceful road, the contentment of the villagers, and the wealth of the country around her. She tried to tell herself that it was fattened as a lamb was fattened for the slaughter, but this did not agree with what she could see, or with the demeanour of the people.

A mile farther on, she caught her first look at the city of Winchester, the ancient royal capital of Ingland. Once it had been her home, but she had not seen it for more than three years. She had expected it to look exactly the same, for it had not changed in the first twelve years of her life. But it was different, very different, and Robin stopped on the road and stared.

The old wooden palisade was gone, replaced by a much higher one of white-faced stone that incorporated the three old stone watch-towers and had four new towers as well. At first she thought nothing remained of the old royal palace, a large hall, which used to perch atop a low hill, then she realised it had been incorporated into the fabric of a new castle, a fortification that would completely dominate the city were it not balanced by the abbey, whose bell-tower was as tall, if not so martial. The abbey had also been extended and rebuilt since Robin had seen it last. Harold had not favoured the followers of Christ Godsson, but William was said to hold their priests in high esteem.

Entering the city through a new gate of freshly worked stone with masons still finishing the façade, Robin found herself in a crowd and for a few moments was struck with a sudden, nameless fear. She wasn't used to the noise, to the bustle, to the accidental touches as people moved all around her. But she kept pushing forward, making for the market square, where there would be more room. Surely, she told herself, that would not have changed overmuch.

Yet, when she came to it, she found the square also completely different to her expectations, as it was neither an empty field, as it used to be seven days out of fourteen, nor awash with buyers and sellers, goods, and smaller livestock as it would be on the seven fair days.

Instead, the whole field was roped off with muddy red cord fixed to iron pickets driven into the ground. Small groups of men-at-arms lingered at each corner of the field, and right in the middle there was a huge roughly hewn lump of sandstone lying on its side like a toppled sarsen-stone. It had a sword stuck right in the middle of it. Even sixty feet away, Robin could feel the iron magic involved. The sword had been plunged into the stone by some great magic.

But there was also a hint of Inglish magic there. Robin couldn't make it out, but there was something on the stone next to the sword. A pile of sticks, perhaps a bird's-nest, or something like that, only it emanated a strong sense of holly magic, and rowan too. It gave her a strange, slightly nauseating sensation to feel the two magics so close together.

"Strange, ain't it?" whispered a voice near her elbow. "Kiss my hand with silver, and I'll tell you the tale."

Robin looked down and stepped back. A crippled man, both of his legs lost at the knee, was grinning up at her and holding out his hand. He would have been tall and strong once, Robin could see, a handsome Inglishman. Now he was a beggar, though she guessed he must be a successful one, for he had decent-enough clothes and good padding on his stumps.

"Did you lose your legs at Senlac?" she asked. If he were one of her father's men, she thought to give him a coin.

"Nay," smiled the man. "It was an accident, building the castle. The King's reeve paid me leg money, but that's long gone. Go on, give me a scratch of silver, and I'll tell you about the sword."

"No," said Robin. She turned away and headed back towards the busy, closed-in streets. The cripple shouted after her, but in good-nature. Something about it being a story worth hearing but only if told well.

The crowd swallowed Robin up and buffeted her. It took a while for her to get her bearings again and try to find the human currents that would carry her in the direction she chose, rather than force her back or push her into the more dubious side streets.

Her destination was always visible to Robin, no matter how the streets turned or the people thronged about her. The castle was a constant landmark, its towers looming above the roof-tops.

Finally, she reached the gate and stood alone between the commercial hurly-burly of the city and the guards who glanced at her with casual disinterest. The gatehouse was new, of the same white-faced stone as the city wall. But the twin leaves of the gate were the old ones, the palace gates of ancient oak, etched with the names of all the Kings and ruling Queens of Ingland back to Alfred.

Robin found her father's name there. Duke William had not removed it, as she thought he might. But his own name was there too, clear-cut and bright on the old wood, above Harold's and the Edwards, Edgars, Edmunds and others fading into illegibility below.

Robin coughed to clear her throat, and the guards looked at her again. She stared back, suddenly aware that this was a moment just like when she had snatched Merewyn's horn. If she stepped forward and spoke, her plan would be put irrevocably in motion. Her fate would be decided by its success or failure, and the fate of Duke William, and the fate of the whole kingdom of Ingland and perhaps the world.

If she stepped forward and spoke.

One of the guards let his hand drop to the hilt of his sword. Three of them were watching her now, wondering why she did not finish her gawping and turn away, as so many did.

Robin stepped forward. At the same time, she reached out to the iron in the guards' swords, helmets, and mail, feeling the weight of it, the currents of attraction and repulsion that moved in the metal. She made a ritual gesture with her hand, closing her fist and shaking it, and, as her hand moved, everything of iron on or about the guards let out a keening wail, a crescendoing shriek that was loud enough to make the youngest guard screw his face up and move a little out of position.

It was the iron cry, the announcement of the arrival of a Norman noble ironmaster. Everyone in the castle would have heard it. But even the iron-masters would not recognize this particular cry, because Robin had never used it. From the Duke down, they would be wondering who could have summoned such a loud, pure call.

The guards reacted instinctively, bracing to attention. Robin might look like a vagrant boy, but there was no denying the iron cry. She walked towards them, stopped under the gate, and spoke.

"I am Princess Robin. I wish to be escorted to my grandfather, Duke . . . King William."

More guards ran out to stand at attention, lining both sides of the gate passage. A knight, busy buckling on his sword, followed them, marching up to Robin. He bent his knee briefly and smiled, a cheery, honest smile that had no hint of the Norman duplicity Robin always suspected.

"Greetings, Your Highness. I am Geoffrey of Manduc. The King has been expecting you, and awaits you in the Great Hall. This way."

"Expecting . . . me?" asked Robin, confusion and fear suddenly gripping her throat, so the words came out hoarse and broken.

"Indeed, all the King's heirs are here," said Geoffrey happily as he bounced along one step behind, still fumbling with his sword-belt. He reminded Robin of a hunting-dog she'd had, long ago when her father had been alive. Or rather it was a dog supposed to be a hunter, but despite its enthusiasm it kept tripping over its own paws and running around in cheerful, ever-decreasing spirals. "When the King returned from the forest yestereve he told the court that you had chosen to end your self-imposed exile. You are very welcome, Highness."

"That's not . . ." said Robin. She was already trying to work out what the Duke was up to, and how it might affect what she planned. "Never mind. You said all the King's heirs are here?"

"Yes, they have all been summoned here, though none know why," burbled Geoffrey. "The King has not spoken, though many believe it has something to do with his sword, which he set in a stone down in the market field last settling-day."

"A beggar said he could tell me the story of the sword," said Robin, though she felt like someone else was speaking. Most of her attention was on the passage through the gatehouse, and then on the clear space of the outer bailey beyond. She noted the guards' positions and looked for a postern gate or any other way out of the castle.

"I'm sure he did!" laughed Geoffrey. "Stories being the stock of beggars.

But surely, Highness, you have better stories of your own. To live as a priestess of the Easterner's Moon Goddess must have given you many stories—"

"What?" asked Robin. "I haven't been a priestess for any god, let alone the Easterner's Moon mistress. I've been . . ."

Geoffrey leaned in, intent on her words, and Robin realized that he was probably not the fool he appeared. He was some sort of functionary, but at a royal court, and already he was trying to gain some advantage, some secret knowledge of the King's granddaughter.

"Is it not known where I have been these last four years?" she asked quietly, as they rounded the base of the motte hill, heading towards the Great Hall rather than climbing the steps to the Keep.

"No, Highness," said Geoffrey. "But there have been many tales."

"What of . . . what of my sister, the Princess Merewyn? What do these tales tell of her?"

Geoffrey looked surprised.

"The Princess Merewyn? She died of a fever only three days after Senlac Hill, did she not?"

Robin shook her head, unable to speak. It was becoming clear to her that her life of the last four years had been largely irrelevant to the Normans, to the people, to . . . everyone in the world outside the forest. They had just been another band of robbers, hiding in the greenwood as robbers so often did. Not even a big enough nuisance for proper tales to be told about them.

The huge doors of the Great Hall were open. As they approached, Robin could hear voices raised in uproar, immediately followed by the harsh clang of *Ferramenta* beating their swords on their shields.

"I suspect the King has explained the matter of his sword," said Geoffrey. He lengthened his stride and began to hurry. Despite the booming bell-noise of the *Ferramenta*, the shouts and impassioned voices inside had not subsided.

It was much louder inside the Hall. A vast, high-roofed building, it was a sea of shouting men and a smaller number of equally loud women. Down the far end, a line of twenty *Ferramenta* held the crowd back from a dais with a simple wooden throne on it. Only four of them were striking their shields, the insistent clangour slowly quietening the crowd. Behind the *Ferramenta* were a score of archers who wore the black surcoat of Duke William's guard.

The Duke himself stood in front of the throne, calmly waiting for quiet. If he saw Robin, he did not show it. As Geoffrey led her through the crowd towards the throne, Robin realised that nearly everyone around her was a follower of one or the other of William's heirs. The Hall was packed with Norman nobility and the most important knights and ladies of William's realm. Most of them either angry, shocked, or excited, the end result being a lot of noise.

Robin didn't speak to any one of them, but every few yards, Geoffrey would grab an elbow and exchange a few words and there would be a bit of space for Robin to squeeze through.

They were only halfway through the crowd when Robin suddenly felt a cold, biting pain behind her right eye. It only lasted a moment, but it also made a strange and sudden anger well up inside her. Anger that was directed at Duke William. He had slain her father, and her sister, and usurped the crown that was rightfully hers. He had to die!

Robin stopped. She had certainly felt anger towards the Duke. She planned to kill him, it was true, but that had been a cold decision, not born of anger. This sudden fury felt strangely out of place, as if it had come from somewhere else. She looked around and saw only Normans looking to the throne.

Then she looked up and saw a raven staring down at her from the rafters. Its beady black eye was fixed upon her, but its gaze was not that of a bird. She felt it almost like a wind, something invisible but powerful and cold.

Robin shook her head and looked at the floor, mud and rushes overlaying the white flagstones. The fury was still there, but she knew it was not hers. It was the Allfather, trying to force her to play her hand too early.

"Are you well, Highness?" whispered Geoffrey. Robin jerked her head up, suddenly aware that the *Ferramenta* had stopped their clanging, the people their shouting, and that the Hall was growing quiet. She took a slow breath, forcing out the anger that would not help her.

"Yes," she answered. "But before we go on, tell me, what has caused this commotion?"

"The King has announced that his heir will be—"

Geoffrey stopped as the King suddenly spoke, his voice strong and penetrating, echoing above Robin's head.

"I have spoken. It is as it is. Who will be the first of my blood to try the test?"

Silence greeted the King's words for several seconds. Then a short but very broad-shouldered man with the back of his head shaved to the crown pushed to the front and walked between the *Ferramenta*. The iron knights let him pass, and the black-clad archers merely watched as he strode to the foot of the dais. He did not bow, but did incline his head a fraction.

"Aurillac," whispered Geoffrey to Robin.

"I protest, Uncle!" snorted the Bastard of Aurillac. "There should be no test! I claim to be your heir by right of blood. There is no need for this foolery with swords—"

"There are others with an equal or better right of blood," said William. "More is needed from one who would be heir to the King of Ingland and Normandy both. I have proclaimed the manner of my choosing. If you do not dare attempt it—"

Aurillac snorted like a bull.

"I am a greater ironmaster than any here save you, Uncle. I will go now and take your sword from the stone!"

He did not wait for permission, but bent his head a little once more, then turned and strode towards the doors. His lesser barons and knights, perhaps a quarter of all those present in the Hall, turned to follow him. Shouting and scuffling broke out again, intensified as the *Ferramenta* suddenly tromped into a wedge formation and began to march for the doors, with the King and his archers within the wedge.

Geoffrey gingerly pinched Robin's sleeve, being careful not to touch her, and tried to draw her back.

"Best we hold back and follow the King," he said. "This crowd is too great to draw near to him."

Robin nodded and followed his twisting, winding progress between people to the side of the Hall. She could feel the ivory-tipped arrow at her side and her hand ached to draw it out and plunge it into William's chest. But she could not get close enough now. Later, she would have her chance.

She would be slain soon after, Robin knew, but at least she would die knowing that she had avenged her sister's and father's deaths, and that William's heirs would plunge Ingland and Normandy into war. Though from the look of things, the Bastard of Aurillac might well win that struggle quickly, for his entourage was by far the largest and most warlike. He would also be here, in the capital . . .

A shadow of doubt slowly slid into Robin's mind. If she slew William, then she might be giving Ingland to Aurillac, who by all accounts would be a far worse master than the Duke. And did she really want Ingland to be stricken by yet another war? These thoughts felt disloyal, and were slipperier and harder to grapple with than the pure anger she felt towards William. But they were also persistent, and they stuck with Robin as she followed the crowd out of the castle and down through the town to the market field.

The commotion from the castle, with the sudden parade of the King, the *Ferramenta*, and over four hundred Norman notables, caused an even greater sensation in the town. It seemed to Robin that absolutely everyone within the city walls was streaming towards the market field, townsfolk and country visitors mingling with the outer edges of the procession from the castle.

With Geoffrey's deft help, whispered words to barons and knights ahead of her, and directions via her sleeve, Robin found herself only just behind the wedge of *Ferramenta* when they reached the field. There, the iron knights and the bowmen, reinforced by the men-at-arms already at the field, formed a cordon thirty yards out from the sword in the stone, holding back the crowd, which to Robin now seemed to number in the thousands.

Within the cordon, William stood alone with Aurillac. Geoffrey tugged at Robin's sleeve and gently manoeuvred her to a position at the very front, so she could see clearly between two *Ferramenta*. She shivered as she stood up close to them, blinking as she felt the hot spirits contained within the metal bodies reach out to touch her mind. She was both repulsed by and attracted to that mental touch. She had not felt it for many years, not since her lessons with her mother. She had been too busy fleeing from the iron warriors two days before.

Aurillac was shouting something at William. Robin forced her attention away from the iron knights in order to listen to the Bastard.

"—the commoners away! I shall not be tricked, Uncle, in front of the mob!"

William said something Robin couldn't hear, and gestured at the sword. Aurillac snarled and strode over to it. He climbed up on the stone and planted his feet on either side of the sword, grasping it with both hands. His muscles tensed, and at the same time, Robin felt a surge of iron magic emanating from him. He was trying to manipulate both the metal of the sword and the more unyielding stone, which William had melded together.

"You must also wear the crown!" called out William. He indicated what Robin had thought was a bird's-nest, an irregular ring of sticks and berries, before she'd sensed its magic.

"What?" shouted Aurillac, his nose and cheekbones bright with fury and exertion. "You push me too far! I'll not wear some fool's cast-off casque—"

"It is King Alfred's crown," William said, and though he did not shout, his voice penetrated through the crowd and Aurillac's anger, quietening both. "Lost these two centuries, now found again. Wear the crown of holly, Aurillac, and draw the sword of iron, and you shall succeed me as King of Ingland and Normandy."

"Is this yet another insult?" asked Aurillac. "I am pure Norman, no matter that my parents were not wed. I cannot wear a crown of holly!"

"That is nonsense, born of tales and fancy," said William. He walked over to the stone and reverently picked up the ancient crown. He held it aloft for a few moments, then gently placed it on his head. There was a collective gasp from the crowd, but William neither sweated blood, nor fainted, nor showed any of the other signs Norman ironmasters were supposed to when touched by good Inglish holly.

Aurillac stared at William, then a slow smile crept across his face. It was obvious to Robin that he thought the crown some kind of trick, a thing of paper berries and painted sticks. But she could feel its power too, like a cool and separate pool, riven by currents of hot iron magic that flowed between the *Ferramenta*, William, Aurillac, and . . . herself.

"Give me the crown!" Aurillac demanded. He stretched out his hand, but William stepped back and held the crown aloft.

"Let the crown of King Alfred choose my successor!" he intoned. Aurillac grunted and climbed down from the stone. He bent his head slightly to allow William to place the crown on his head, then he stood up.

The smile faded from his flushed face as thorns suddenly grew from the holly, long thorns that scraped and scratched like claws towards his eyes. Blood suddenly gushed from his nose, and his breath came in harsh, wheezing gasps. He fell to his knees, with his hands pressed over his eyes to protect them from the thorns. William stepped forward and lifted the crown from his head, the thorns retreating.

Robin stared. She had felt the holly magic surge, its calm replaced by a sudden chill blast, like a freezing wind off the sea. But she had also sensed that the crown had not reacted to Aurillac's Norman blood, but to some other sense of wrongness. She vaguely remembered her mother saying too much was made of the Norman antipathy to holly and oak, but it was widely believed—and that belief had its own power. There were rare people—even rarer than shape-changers—who did not believe in magic at all, and they were extremely resistant to spells, and sometimes could even prevent magic being done at all. Savants speculated that this was a type of magic in itself.

Two of Aurillac's knights helped him up. The Bastard wiped his bloody face, stared at William, then turned on his heel and strode to join his followers. There he held a quick conversation, and his men began to turn around and start pushing the common folk, to create a path away from the field.

"Aurillac!" William called out. "I have not given you leave to go. There are others of my blood here. If one succeeds, all must swear allegiance to my chosen heir."

Four *Ferramenta* moved as William spoke, the iron knights lumbering closer to where Aurillac paused, fury expressed in his clenched fists and caution in his twisting torso, as he turned back to face the sword in the stone.

William looked at another knot of knights and men-at-arms behind three young men who all stood scowling at the stone. Unlike Aurillac, they were not in mail, and their bright garb was in stark contrast to most of the other men.

"Well, nephews?"

"We will wait till you're dead, Great-uncle," said the one with the bright blue tunic and the silver-tipped cap. He looked over at Aurillac and added, "Then split everything between us equally."

William laughed.

"Honest as ever, Jean. But I do not intend to die for some time. I think I will find my heir today—and you will swear allegiance."

"Who?" asked Jean. "Aurillac could not draw your sword, and my brothers and I know better than to attempt it. There is no one else."

William smiled again and turned to face the crowd. He didn't speak, but stood waiting. A hush fell upon the crowd, the silence spreading till the only sound Robin could hear was the thumping of her heart, the blood vessels in her neck hammering like a drum.

"The iron call outside the castle," Jean said suddenly, his voice strange and reedy in the silence of the crowd. "Who was that?"

A raven cawed its lonely cry and flew over the field. A one-eyed man pushed to the front of the crowd, right behind Robin and Geoffrey.

52

She reached inside her tunic to grasp the broken end of her ivory-tipped arrow, but still hesitated. She would never have such an opportunity again to kill William, but still—

The one-eyed man touched Geoffrey on the small of the back with his little finger, a touch that would not have crushed a fly. But the Norman courtier fell and would have hit Robin, but she had already started forward, bursting into the clearing, where she appeared like a sprung child's toy from between the two *Ferramenta*.

There was a collective gasp from the crowd as Robin slowly walked towards William. To them it looked like a poor Norman boy, a peasant, was approaching the King of Ingland and Normandy—with head held high.

"Princess Robin," said William.

"Grandfather."

A shriek came from the crowd as she spoke, and nervous laughter, followed by many voices calling for quiet. Aurillac started forward, and the *Ferramenta* moved fast, blocking his way. William made a sign and his black-clad archers moved closer, their eyes on the Bastard and his entourage.

"What is to be, then?" asked William softly, so no one else could hear. "What do you hold there? A wooden stake? Will you hear me first?"

Robin nodded, though instantly she felt that this was a mistake. Her courage and fury, pulled taut as a bow-string, could not be held so long. She gripped the arrow more tightly and told herself that a minute more would not matter. William would merely die a little later.

"Kill me, and you will die," said the King. "Ingland will be riven by war. Everything your father held dear will be lost—"

"You slew my father!" Robin whispered hoarsely, while all the crowd leaned forward, desperate to hear what was being said.

"He died in battle, with a sword in his hand, as did your sister. I regret their deaths, particularly Merewyn's. My death will not return them to the living, Robin. *Your* death will serve no purpose. Wear the crown and take my sword, and within a year or two at most, you will be Queen of Ingland and Normandy!"

William spoke fiercely and reached out to grip Robin's shoulders. She shuddered under his touch and half-drew the arrow. He was so close, it would be so easy to punch the arrow up through his old ribs and into his heart. All the charms and protections every ironmaster wrapped himself in would be as nothing to the sharp ivory point.

Robin raised her elbow and began to draw the arrow out through the fold in the front of her tunic.

"You are my granddaughter," whispered William. He closed his eyes and leaned forward, as if seeking an embrace. "Do what you will."

"Seek new beginnings," whispered Merewyn. Though her voice was nearly drowned by the sudden cawing of ravens overhead, it sounded to Robin like her sister was just behind her.

But she wasn't. There was only her old grandfather, his eyes still closed, his hands on her shoulders. There was the crowd beyond, a great mass of excited expectation, aware that they were witnesses to a great and strange event. The three grandnephews, staring at her as if she were some strange creature. Aurillac, his stare that of an enemy, held in check only by temporary weakness.

Robin remembered grabbing the horn from Merewyn. Remembered charging down the slope. Remembered the sound of Merewyn being struck by the iron knight.

Knowing when not to attack . . . seeking new beginnings . . . Merewyn's voice echoed in her head, as it would probably echo for as long as Robin lived.

Slowly, she pushed the arrow back under her tunic, through her belt, and pulled her hand free.

"I will never forgive you," she whispered. "But I will take your sword."

Then she spoke loud enough for the crowd to hear.

"Give me the crown."

A cheer rippled through the mass of onlookers, though Robin wasn't sure whether they were cheering her on or hoping to see a repeat of what had happened to Aurillac.

William held the crown high, and Robin felt the magic within it. It was like a seed, a container of potent force waiting for the right conditions to burgeon forth.

Robin bent her head and felt the rough touch of the holly leaves scrape through her hair. She tensed, waiting for the sharper stab of thorns, or for a sudden, shocking attack of nausea. But the crown sat comfortably on her near-shaven head, and her stomach was no more stricken with anxiety than it had been before.

"The sword!" someone shouted from the crowd, a cry that was taken up in seconds, to become a chant, several thousand voices all calling at once.

"The sword! The sword!"

Robin reached up to steady the crown and was startled to find her fingers touching flowers and green shoots rather than dried sticks and wizened berries. She was even more startled to find that the stubble on her scalp was no longer harsh and fuzzy. Her hair was growing back impossibly fast, and was already as long as the first two knuckles on her little finger.

"The sword," said William. Robin couldn't hear him, the chanting was so loud, but she knew what he was saying. She dropped her hands from her new-found hair and the flowering crown, flexed her fingers, and stepped up on to the stone.

The sword radiated iron magic like a miniature sun. Robin felt the heat wash across her face and breathed hot air through her mouth. But she knew this was not real heat, and it would not burn her unless she feared it would.

Without hesitation, she gripped the hilt of the sword with both hands, accepting the heat and the magic, letting them flow through her body, taking in the strength of the iron to add to her own.

She felt no conflict from the crown, but rather an acceptance that this too was part of her. Her heritage was of both the green forest and the hot stone that lay deep beneath the earth, and they did not clash within her.

The chant grew louder and more frenzied as Robin bent her knees and focused both her strength and her will upon the sword in the stone. She could feel how William had meshed blade and rock, but it was no easy matter to undo what he had done. But slowly she compelled sword and stone to separate, and with a screech like some tormented beast of legend, the weapon came free, an inch at a time.

Sweat poured from Robin's face, and pain coursed through her lower back and forearms, but with one last outpouring of strength and determination, the stone gave up its prize. Robin whipped the sword around and held it aloft, too breathless to shout or even speak. Not that even her shouts would be heard above the noise of the crowd.

William held up his hands for silence, the *Ferramenta* booming and clanging to punctuate his demand. As the crowd stilled, William turned to the stone and started to walk the few paces over to Robin.

At that moment, Aurillac and his men suddenly charged, the Bastard himself leaping up on the stone, sweeping his great sword out of its scabbard as he jumped.

Robin ducked under his first blow, Aurillac's sword-point skittering off the stone in a spray of sparks. She parried the next, but the blow was so strong that William's sword was smashed out of her hand, and her fingers were suddenly numbed and useless.

Three arrows bounced off the Bastard, repelled by his charms, as he struck again. Robin jumped backward off the stone, landed well, and backed away, the crowd receding like the tide.

A sweeping glance showed Robin that William, his bowmen, and *Ferramenta* were wreaking bloody havoc amongst Aurillac's men, and that this stupid battle would not last more than a few minutes.

But that was all the Bastard would need to kill her.

He jumped from the stone and charged towards her as Robin tried to pull out the black arrow with her left hand. She tensed, ready to try and dodge, the arrow still stuck in her clothes. But as Aurillac raised his sword, he was suddenly struck from behind by a huge lump of snarling brown fur that was either a dog or a small bear that had jumped from the fringes of the crowd straight on his back.

At the same time, more than a dozen unarmed men—townsfolk or simple peasants—charged in front of Robin. One fell beneath Aurillac's sword, but the others leaped on him as the bear brought the Bastard bellowing down. More men and women surged from the crowd to form a human shield-ring around Robin.

All were shouting the same thing.

"Ingland! Ingland! Ingland!"

Then Robin was being lifted up, onto the shoulders of the taller men of those about her. Aurillac lay dead nearby, or good as dead, as eight or nine people hacked at him with small knives, hatchets, and even their hands. The bear that had felled him sat up on its haunches, the crowd giving it space as it licked its paw and muzzle clean of blood.

Robin looked at the bear and it met her gaze with a human understanding.

"I thank you, Jack," said Robin softly.

The bear got up and stood on his hind legs. Then he slowly sank onto one knee and bowed his head. All around him, the people followed suit. It was like the wind pressing down a field of corn, as heads suddenly lowered and men, women, and children all sank to one knee. The peasants and townsfolk were first, but then the Norman men-at-arms followed suit, then the knights and lords and ladies, into the bloodied mud where Aurillac's followers lay dead or wounded.

Only William still stood. Even the men who carried Robin had sunk to their knees, so she was seated on their shoulders. Her hair had grown long and now framed her face, and the holly flowers of her crown had grown and spread too, to make a mantle that fell down her back like a rich, royal cloak.

William walked to her. Halfway, he held out his hand, and his sword flew into it. He reversed it to hold the blade. Then he proffered the hilt to Robin, and she took it in her left hand and held it high.

So the Princess Robin came into the inheritance she had never sought; amidst blood, but not of her choosing; welcomed by a grandfather she had always feared and hated; hailed by the Normans she looked like and the Inglish that she felt were her true people.

Overhead, two ravens cawed once in disgust and flew north-east, biting and snapping at each other as they flew. As they fled, a one-eyed man coughed and died where he lay on the ground between two of Aurillac's dead men, the arrow that had chance-hit him buried deep in his chest.

Color Vision

MARY ROSENBLUM

When wizards are involved, sometimes a lot more than beauty can be in the eye of the beholder . . .

One of the most popular and prolific of the new writers of the nineties, Mary Rosen-blum made her first sale, to Asimov's Science Fiction, *in 1990, and has since become a mainstay of that magazine and one of its most frequent contributors, with almost thirty sales there to her credit. She has also sold to* The Magazine of Fantasy & Science Fiction, Sci Fiction, Science Fiction Age, Pulphouse, New Legends, *and elsewhere. Rosenblum produced some of the most colorful, exciting, and emotionally powerful stories of the nineties with titles such as "The Stone Garden," "Synthesis," "Flight," "California Dreamer," "Casting at Pegasus," "Entrada," "Rat," "The Centaur Garden," "Skin Deep," "Songs the Sirens Sing," and many, many others. Her novella "Gas Fish" won the Asimov's Readers Award Poll in 1996 and was a Finalist for that year's Hugo Award. Her first novel,* The Drylands, *appeared in 1993 to wide critical acclaim, winning the prestigious Compton Crook Award for Best First Novel of the year; it was followed in short order by her second novel,* Chimera, *and her third,* The Stone Garden. *Her first short story collection,* Synthesis and Other Virtual Realities, *was widely hailed by critics as one of the best collections of 1996. Her most recent books are a trilogy of mystery novels written under the name Mary Freeman, and a major new science fiction novel,* Horizons. *A graduate of Clarion West, Mary Rosenblum lives in Portland, Oregon.*

I'M staring at Mr. Beasley while Mrs. Banks drones on about fractions. He's some sort of python, I can't remember what kind. Mrs. Banks is my teacher. Her words come out a dull, dirty sort of blue-green, like the ocean right before a storm comes in. Fits the fractions. Mr. Beasley hisses purple at me. I don't think he likes me. But then, I don't like him either. He has *fun* when he squeezes the poor little mice Mrs. Banks feeds him. Snakes aren't supposed to have fun.

"Hey, what color am I now?" Jeremy's leaning across the aisle. "I'm trying to talk green."

Jeremy's mom is the school counselor. But I like Jeremy anyway. "Shut up," I tell him, because Mrs. B is just looking for a reason to stick us both with detention. It occurs to me that she has fun, too, when Mr. Beasley squeezes those mice. "You're always yellow," I whisper to Jeremy to shut him up. Which he knows, because I told him how synesthesia works about a hundred times. But he thinks it's cool, so I don't care. It scares my dad, I'm not sure why. I think he worries that I'm like my mother. But this doctor said it was just a brain thing, that I'm kind of cross-wired and sound turns into color for me. But it still scares him. I liked the doctor, but his voice was a yucky, puke green color, and we moved again right after. We move a lot. Even if I don't talk about synesthesia.

"You can put your books away now." Mrs. B is staring at the clock, and her hands are kind of fluttering. "We're going to have a special visit from the new principal. Mr. Teleomara ran a very successful private school in New York and we're incredibly lucky to have him." She pats her hair and glances at her reflection in the glass of Mr. Beasley's aquarium. Is that lipstick? I can't believe it, but yeah, she's smearing it on, real sneaky, with her back to us like we can't see. And she has to be a hundred years old. Well, fifty anyway.

"I want you on your best behavior," she says, and pins Jeremy and me with the Death Eye. "Any disturbance and we'll have a quiz on fractions every single day for the next week."

Great, now everybody's looking at us. Jeremy makes this innocent face that makes everybody laugh and I just look at my book. Trying real hard to look real well behaved. Nobody's seen the new principal. He's supposed to be real strict and probably eats babies. You know. I keep pretending to be really into my fractions as Mrs. B goes all high-pitched and breathy at the door, welcoming him.

"Hello, class. I'm delighted to meet you." Deep voice.

Silver?

I blink. It kind of sparkles in the air, like glitter. Never seen *that* before. So I look up and he's tall and looks like a movie star, which is why the lipstick on Mrs. B, I guess. She's patting her hair again and smirking and her voice has this greenish tinge now. Even Mr. Beasley gets into the act, hissing purple all over the place. And I look, and then I look again. He's now got a bright blue jewel right in the center of his head and he's got human eyes, you know, with an iris and pupil.

And yeah, he does *not* like me.

Something is wrong here.

"Ah, a reptile lover."

Mr. Beasley hisses real purple and I look back quick at my book, but it's too late. The new principal comes over to stand right next to my desk. He's smiling, and you know what? His smile makes me think of Mr. Beasley's. I don't think he likes me, either.

"Melanie has an attention problem," Mrs. B twitters. "She's a special ed student."

Catherine Summers, head of the In Crowd, kind of snickers, and I can feel my face getting hot. But then I notice this ugly old dish on Mrs. B's desk, the one she puts paper clips in.

It's gold. With like . . . rubies in it.

Yeah . . . something is *really* wrong.

"I am so looking forward to working with everyone in the school." Mr. Teleomara's glittery silver words are kind of hanging in the air. Like fog. And that's not how synesthesia works either. They're drifting around me and I can *feel* 'em, like powdered razor blades or something. They make me itch.

Mr. Teleomara smiles even more like Mr. Beasley. "Melanie Dreyling, it has been a long time."

Uh-oh. Dreyling is my *real* name.

He can't know that. But he's smiling right at me and that razor-dust silver is so thick I can barely see Jeremy's surprised look. I got to get out of here. I got to tell Dad. Better yet, I got to tell Cris. He'll know what happened to Mr. Beasley and the dish.

But I can't move. Can't breathe. The silver stuff is clogging up the air.

"I know your mother," he says. "You look just like her."

There's this buzzing in my ears, and I think of Mr. Beasley grabbing the poor mice and how they scream one little mousey scream before he squeezes them. There's this buzzing in my ears and my stomach kind of turns inside out, maybe from breathing the razor-dust air. And Mrs. B is clucking about my name and I'm going to faint or . . .

. . . throw up.

All over my math book. And the desk. And the floor.

The silver goes away. Then Mrs. B is scolding ugly, storm-colored words and everybody is making *yuck* noises and the colors are all off and sick. I'm going to puke again, so I just bolt. Out the door, down the hall; no way I'm going back in there again.

Mr. Teleomara is having just as much fun as Mr. Beasley does with his mice.

"Hey, wait up!" Jeremy catches up to me as I duck out the fire door at the end of the hall. "Are you okay?" His voice is worried, kind of this off-orange.

"No. Yes. I'm okay." Which I'm not. I look back but nobody comes charging out after us. "I'm going home. You better get back in there before you get detention."

"What happened?" He doesn't go. "How come he called you Dreyling? How come you threw up?"

"Food poisoning." I head across the playground, waiting for somebody to start yelling. I guess maybe I could tell myself that I was imagining a weird silver voice like that . . . but I *felt* it and it hurt. And then there was Mr. Beasley and the gold dish.

And Mr. Teleomara.

I gotta talk to Cris.

"I ate in the cafeteria, too." Jeremy catches up to me. "And I'm not puking. And what about your mom? My mom told me she was dead. She said not to talk about her because you were in denial."

"She's not dead." I really snap at him, then I feel bad. Jeremy stuck up for me when I first came here, last winter. He talks to me when the In Crowd won't. "Sorry." I sigh. "Look, I gotta go talk to somebody. It's really important." We're across the playground now, still nobody yelling. I can't believe how easy it is to skip school. I duck through the hedge beyond the swings and monkey bars, into the yard where the yappy little dog lives, but he must be inside. Jeremy's still following me.

I should tell him to get lost. So what if I hurt his feelings? But I don't want to. He thinks hearing color is cool, even if his mom is a counselor and thinks I'm in denial. And I wonder if maybe, just maybe, he'd be okay with Cris. So I don't say anything and he climbs over the old board fence with me and we cut through the weedy lot and head down Fir Street, which turns into the rutted gravel road that leads way back into the woods to the dump we rented. I'm not going home, though. I need to talk to Cris first, because as soon as I tell Dad about Mr. Teleomara, we're gonna be in the car and heading for another state.

And that hits me, all of a sudden. That we'll leave. I mean we always do, but I'll really miss Cris, because before Cris I didn't really have a clue. And my throat starts hurting because we've only been here a few months and I like Jeremy and I don't usually make friends. And now I have two and I have to leave. A mower's buzzing out hot red-orange and spring birdsong sparkles blue and pink and gold in the trees, and it would be a really pretty day if Mr. Stinking Teleomara hadn't walked in.

It's all dark and quiet now, all thick Sitka spruce and salal thickets, and it's almost dark as twilight. The old bullfrog is thumping in the scummy pond.

"Hey, what color is that?" Jeremy asks. "I bet it's dark purple."

He always asks and it makes me smile. "Wrong," I say. "It's dark brown, like chocolate."

"Okay, want to tell me what's wrong?" He's walking right next to me now. "What's with you and the new principal. Mr. Teleo-whatever?"

"I don't know." I shrug. "Something weird happened. I think it was the color of his voice."

"What color was it?"

"Silver. But not . . . not like color usually is. When I hear words, I just see blue or yellow or whatever. It doesn't really get in the *way* of anything else I'm looking at. You know what I mean?"

"So this did?"

"Yeah, it did." I'm watching him from the corner of my eye . . . waiting for him to stop believing me. "I felt it . . . and it kind of hurt. And it made me sick." Never mind Mr. Beasley and the dish.

"So how come?" And he's frowning, but not like he doesn't believe me.

What have I got to lose? We're gonna hit the road as soon as I tell my dad, so if Jeremy thinks I'm crazy, who cares?

Well, I care, I guess.

So I don't say anything and just walk faster so he has to catch up.

"You mean you walk this far every day?" He's panting now. "Geez that's bad. Why won't the bus come pick you up?"

The bus would, but buses are worse than class: I found that out a long time ago. "I don't mind walking." I cut through the woods before we get close to the house. Dad might be home and he'll know in a second that something's wrong. I've never lied to my dad, so I just head for the path I made back when I first found Cris.

"Where are we going?" Jeremy looks around. "Want to come over to my house? This is Mom's day at the high school and she won't be home until five. We can go play that new Xbox game I got. Before Mom tries it out and takes it away from me. It's real cool so it has to be psychologically damaging."

"We're almost there," I say. I guess I really do want him to meet Cris. "I . . . I've got this friend. I need to talk to him is all."

"Okay." Jeremy shrugs. "Then can we go to my house? He can come, too."

"He can't. He's in a wheelchair and . . . he just can't. This way." The path takes us left, closer to the ocean. I can smell it and hear the surf in the distance. I'll miss that, too.

"Nobody lives out here." Jeremy yelps as a blackberry cane snags him. "There aren't any houses out here. I'm bleeding."

"No, you're not." I work the thorns out of the back of his shirt. Well, not much. "It's just ahead."

"This better be . . ." He shuts up as we push through this thick wall of salal and some kind of creeper. "Wow!" He just stares for a moment. "How the heck did *this* get out here?"

Well, yeah, it sort of looks like Sleeping Beauty's castle with the gray stone wall and all the blackberry canes. Actually, it looks a *lot* like Sleeping Beauty's castle. I'm bleeding, too, and I suck at the scratch on my wrist.

"Melanie, hold on." Jeremy's words have gone dark yellow. "I know what this place is. The guy who built the lumber mill . . . the one that's shut down . . . He built this mansion out here on the point. But that was forever ago and it's all falling down, now. My cousin and his friends came out here last Halloween. On a dare. He said the roof had fallen in and it was all grown over with blackberries and stuff. They couldn't even get inside. He said it was a waste of time." He stared at the big stone wall. "He didn't say anything about a wall. Or a castle. It isn't like *this*."

"How do you know?" I smile at him.

" 'Cause my cousin . . ." He looks at the wall again. Touches it like he expects it to bite him. It doesn't. "He would have told me. If it was here."

I'm waiting. To see if he gets it. He probably won't, but you know something? I really really *want* him to get it.

"And where's a road?" He's looking around. "How would they get groceries here? Go to church? Melanie, nobody can live out here like this."

I quit waiting and head for the old apple tree, the one that kind of leans on the wall like the old guys you can see through the doors of taverns at noontime, leaning against the bar. I start climbing up.

"Hold on. Wait for me." Jeremy scrambles up behind me and he's better at climbing than I am. And you know what? I don't care.

I'm glad he didn't turn around and go home.

The apple tree's branches sort of make this leafy cave at the top of the wall and one thick, knobby branch sticks out like an arm to keep you from falling over. Funny. I probably never would have met Cris if this apple tree hadn't been here. But I climbed it and there Cris was. Jeremy leans over the apple-arm like he's done it a hundred times.

"How did a castle get out here? There isn't any road." He's still fussing. "Hey look!" He points. "Is that your friend? In the wheelchair?"

"Yeah, that's Cris." I grab the apple branches and kind of let myself down, kind of slide down the wall.

"Hi, Melanie." Cris tries to push the wheelchair closer, but the vines that grow all over the ground always seem to tangle up in the wheels. They remind me of skinny, green Mr. Beasleys, and I don't think they like me any more than he does. At least they're always trying to wrap around my ankles and trip me. I don't know how he gets into the castle at night. Maybe his uncle carries him. I wonder why they don't just get a Weed Eater and chop all those vines down.

Cris doesn't look good. His brown arms are real skinny and his black hair is stuck to his forehead today, like he's been sweating, but it's only May and not very warm at all. His words are the color of dog poop.

"I can't make these vines let go." He gives up and slumps in his chair. "Hi," he says, as Jeremy kind of falls down the wall. "Nice to meet you. I'm Cris."

"Hi, I'm Jeremy." Jeremy shakes what looks like a bird's nest out of his hair. "I've lived here all my life and never heard of a castle back in here." He looks around. "This is so *cool.*"

"Oh, it's a true-shape." Cris shrugs. "You probably saw something else here is all. You know . . . a house or a barn or something."

Jeremy looks real blank. Okay, here goes.

"He's magic, Jeremy," I say. "There's this whole world around us and we don't even know it's there." You know, I used to think I'd maybe made it up, like my teachers said, all the stuff I used to see when my mom was around. But then I found Cris and he told me I wasn't making it all up. "You just don't usually see it," I tell Jeremy. "Unless you're around somebody magic."

"Ooookay," Jeremy finally says, real slow. He gives me this look, like he thinks I'm jerking him around. And I could get Cris to show him, but I'm too worried.

"We got a new principal today," I blurt out. "Cris, he's like you. Weird stuff happened when he walked in the room."

"Puking is weird?" Jeremy gives me another look.

"I saw true-shapes, Cris. And Mr. Teleomara knew my name. My mom's name, I mean. My real one."

"Zoroan." Cris looks scared. "Your mom has to have been one of the First Born. That means he's after you, too. You're her firstborn, right?"

"Yeah, but . . ."

"Okay, this is a cool club." Jeremy's words are pill yellow. "But I don't speak the language. I'm going home to play with my Xbox." And he starts for the wall.

"Wait a minute," I say, because I really want him to stay. But all of a sudden those stupid vines start really wrapping around my ankles.

"Go hide!" Cris looks over his shoulder at the castle. "My uncle is coming. I'm not supposed to have any visitors."

Jeremy's already on top of the wall and I scramble up after him. I don't know why his uncle is so paranoid about visitors. Cris says it's because his uncle thinks this Zoroan is prowling around. I catch up with Jeremy at the top and grab his leg as he starts to climb over. "Lie down flat," I whisper. "Cris's uncle is coming and we're not supposed to be here."

"Oh, thanks." Jeremy is *really* pissed now. "Get me arrested for trespassing, why don't you?"

"Just shut *up*." And I shove him and he sprawls flat on top of the wall under the apple branch that hangs over it and I'm on top of him and there's no time to do anything else because all of a sudden, I see this silver sparkly shimmer at the other end of the garden and all the vines just kind of curl aside, like Sunday school pictures of Moses parting the Red Sea, you know?

Oh, shit.

"Let's just climb down and get out of here," Jeremy grumbles.

"Shut up." I whisper it this time and pinch him. Hard. The silver stuff flows along that parted-Red-Sea path and coils around Cris's wheelchair like Mr. Beasley might. If he was *really* big. And I don't think Cris even sees it, he's just kind of looking at the door at the end of the vine's path. And I don't know if I should yell or go back or what. I start to sit up but the apple limb gets caught in my shirt or something and I can't get loose.

The door opens.

"That's Mr. Teleomara," Jeremy hisses. "What's *he* doing here?"

And I look at Cris, and it's like he got turned to stone in his chair. He just sits there, doesn't move, doesn't say anything. Mr. Teleomara walks down that path, and the vines kind of cringe away from him, and then he bends over Cris. And I want to scream and I think I'm maybe going to throw up again, and the apple limb is squashing me, and even Jeremy is quiet, because there's something really nasty about the way he's looking at Cris.

Then he puts his hand on Cris's throat and Cris screams.

It's not real loud, it's like how you scream in a nightmare when you want to scream really loud and it just comes out little and breathy. But it's an awful scream, and his eyes are closed, and he's kind of twitching, like he's trying to struggle or wake up or something. And all the time he's screaming.

And I *really* want to puke.

And Jeremy looks like he does, too.

"Not much longer," Mr. Teleomara says quietly and that razor-blade mist starts forming around Cris. "A few more sessions and I'm done with you. You'll be a husk. Empty. A few more First Born and I'll have it all." Then he strokes Cris's face, like real tenderly, and that makes my skin crawl. "Sleep well, child," he says. "We don't want anything to happen to you. Yet." Then he laughs and walks away, back through the door, past the shivering vines.

And the door closes.

"Holy shit, what was that all about?" Jeremy's voice is sort of lemony. "What did he do to Cris?"

"Nothing good." I start scrambling down the wall.

"Are you crazy?" Jeremy leans down. "What if he comes back? This is right out of a late-night vampire movie."

"He didn't bite Cris." But yeah, he's kind of right. And I keep one eye on that door as I scramble through the stupid vines, which leave me alone for once. "Cris, Cris, wake up." I shake him, really scared now.

"Is he okay?" Jeremy leans over my shoulder.

I thought he'd be on his way home by now. "I don't know."

But then Cris blinks, yawns, and smiles at us. "Sorry. Guess I fell asleep waiting for you. How was school today? Did you see that weird principal again?"

Jeremy and I look at each other. "It's still today," Jeremy says. "We didn't leave."

He doesn't sound like he's going to go home and play with his Xbox anymore. "Mr. Teleomara was here," I tell Cris. "The weird principal."

"He couldn't be." Cris looks kind of confused, like he just woke up. "My uncle was just here. He would have seen him. He won't let anyone in. Because of Zoroan."

"We just saw the new principal here with you," I tell him.

"My uncle was here." Cris is really confused now. "And . . ."

"What did you and your uncle do while he was here?" Jeremy interrupts. "What did you have for dinner last night? What did you talk about?"

"Oh, we . . ." Cris gets this weird look on his face. "I . . . I can't remember. I mean I know . . . I know I live here with my uncle. That he keeps me safe here. But I just . . ." He's looking really confused now. "I just can't remember what . . . what we did last night. That's all."

Jeremy and I look at each other again.

"I think your 'uncle' *is* Zoroan, Cris." I'm guessing, but the image of Teleomara bending over Cris as he struggled and screamed still makes my stomach twist. "Cris, you need to come with us." I go around and grab the handles of the wheelchair. "You can't stay here. He'll be back."

"But my uncle . . ."

"He was *hurting* you, whoever he is." I lean on the handles of the chair, but the vines are all wrapped through the spokes. And I have this scary vision of Cris sitting in this chair in the middle of the night, in the rain, frozen in silver fog.

"I think this is called kidnapping," Jeremy says. And he starts kicking at the vines, tearing them loose from the wheels with both hands.

I start tearing at 'em, too, and I swear they wrap back around the chair as fast as we tear 'em loose. But finally we get the chair moving, with Jeremy pushing and me stomping on the vines in front of the wheels. "How do we get out of here?" Jeremy pants.

Not through the door Mr. Teleomara went through, that's for sure. "Is there any other way out, Cris?" I ask.

He shakes his head, still looking like he's not really all there yet. We just push the chair over to where the apple branch leans over the wall.

"You climb up," Jeremy tells me. "I'll boost Cris up and he can grab your hand. Then I'll climb up and help you pull him up. We did this in Scouts once. Okay, Cris?"

"Sure," Cris says, but he sounds scared.

I never did this in Scouts, and I look at the wall. It's real high. But I scramble up. I don't know if we can pull Cris up, skinny or not. But I can't think of anything else to try, so I brace my feet and lean way over the apple branch.

"Come on, Cris, I'm going to boost you up." Jeremy lifts Cris out of his wheelchair. "Man, you don't weigh any more than my little sister. Hang on. I'm going to try and step up on your chair."

Jeremy grunts as he climbs very slowly and carefully up onto the seat of the wheelchair. It's not gonna work. "Ready, Melanie?" He wobbles a little and I hold my breath. "Okay, Cris, just reach up. Grab Melanie's wrists. You grab Cris's, Mel."

I can't reach him.

"Lean out as far as you can," Jeremy gasps, his words hot yellow. "Can you stretch up farther, Cris?"

I can't . . . quite . . . reach him. Zoroan, Mr. Teleomara, will be back any second.

The limb falls out from under me. I yelp, grabbing at the limb, then Cris's face is right in front of mine.

"Grab him, grab his wrists," Jeremy is yelling. And I do, and Cris's hands close around my wrists. And then we're swinging *up* and my arms are coming out of their sockets, and then we're falling and my ribs hurt and I see leaves, sky, leaves, and then . . .

. . . I land flat on the grass on my back and I can't catch my breath. Sky. Leaves. Sky. I sit up and nothing hurts *too* much and Cris is lying on his back, giggling softly.

"What the heck happened?" Jeremy's head pops up at the top of the wall and a second later he scrambles down. "You guys okay? I swear that tree just boosted you right over the wall. I'm not kidding! You should have *seen* it."

"It's an apple." Cris sits up. "That's my birth tree. We've got to get out of here. That was a trap. Zoroan's trap. He had me imprisoned in it and was draining my First Born power."

"Right now, I believe that." Jeremy looks back at the castle. "Wow, look."

I look, and it's not a castle anymore. It's this big, old, fallen-down house, just like Jeremy said it would be.

"So what's a First Born power and why does he want to drain it?" Jeremy asks.

"You know, we could maybe talk about this later," I snap. "Like after we get a long way away from here?"

"Yeah, we need to get out of here," Cris says. "I think . . . I think maybe I can walk. The wheelchair thing . . . that was just part of the trap. I think."

We both have to help him up, but yeah, he can walk. Not very well and he's really weak and almost falls down a lot even with us helping him. He looks better, though. And older, I realize. I thought he was younger than us, but now I think he's more like fifteen or sixteen. And his words aren't dog-poop-colored anymore. They're gold and glittery . . . sort of like Mr. Teleomara's, but they don't hurt. He's still real skinny. I guess you would be if someone was draining your life out of you. "Where should we go?" I'm not really asking, I'm just wondering.

"The police?" Jeremy says.

I give him a look. "Hello, Officer," I say sweetly. "Here's this kid whose life force is being sucked out by the school principal. Could you go arrest the principal, please?"

"I get the point," Jeremy says, sour-lemon yellow. "What about your dad?"

I want to look away. "I don't know." I swallow. "I . . . don't think we can take Cris there." And they're both looking at me and I just can't say anything else.

"Okay. We better figure something out." Jeremy sighs. "If Mr. Teleomara is like your guardian or something in the real world, they'll just give you right back to him." He frowns, thinking hard. "My dad's a lawyer, so I know how this kind of thing works. They don't take a kid's word for stuff over a grown-up's. Cris, what about your family?"

"They were both First Borns." He says it so softly that I can hardly hear him. "Zoroan got them."

We're all real quiet for a minute. It's getting dark under the trees. An owl hoots dark green and suddenly flits down to land in the path in front of us. Its eyes glow with yellow light, and I never saw an owl like that before.

It hoots softly green, and Cris says something to it in a language I don't know. "Zoroan knows I escaped." Cris leans on us like he's about to fall down.

"We can go to my tree fort," Jeremy says, kind of doubtfully. "I can sneak you in there and nobody'll know we're there. Maybe he'll be afraid to do anything right in someone's backyard. Man, will I get in trouble if I get caught."

And I don't think he really wants us to go there, but we can't think of any other place. And maybe he's right and Zoroan will be afraid to do anything so close to houses and people. I don't think that's going to matter to him, but like I say, we can't think of anything better. So we go.

It's kind of a weird walk. Some trees, mostly the really old ones, you can almost see this person inside. It's like they're made of see-through glass and someone is inside the trunk, only the glass isn't really clear, so you can't make out a face. And I'm pretty sure I see the little people I used to see with my mother . . . the Shy Folk, she called 'em. And Jeremy is seeing 'em, too; I can tell by the way he looks quick, then stares. I guess it's because we're with Cris.

I'm kind of sorry when we get to Jeremy's house. It's in one of those nice developments, all nice houses and neat yards with swing sets and flowers. Jeremy's house is at the edge, and the backyard comes right to the woods. His fort is back here, kind of out of sight. I bet it embarrasses his mom because it's a mess of plywood and stuff and he built it himself. We sit out there sometimes and talk about school and listen to CDs that his mom says are bad for us.

It sure doesn't look real safe from Zoroan. But the owl with the glowing eyes flits down to settle on a limb of the old apple tree it's built in, so maybe it's better than nothing. We help Cris up into the fort and scramble up after, and I'm looking around everywhere for silver glitter, but I don't see any.

I like it, inside. Clean plywood floor, even if it's gray and weathered, shelves made out of old apple crates turned on their sides, full of CDs, books, and stuff like that. I like it better than some of the dumps we've rented. Cris kind of falls down on the old sofa cushions against the wall.

"You okay?" Jeremy asks.

"I guess so," Cris says. "Just tired."

"Look, I'd better get in the house." Jeremy glances over his shoulder. "I'm gonna be in trouble for being late, even if the school didn't call about me skipping out. I'll see if I can sleep out here tonight. It's a weeknight, but sometimes Mom lets me anyway. I'll sneak you out some food and stuff."

"Water, too, okay?" Soon as I say that, I'm dying of thirst. I bet Cris is, too.

"There's some pop out here. I hid a couple of cans here last week so Mom wouldn't know." Jeremy rummages in the apple crates, brings out a can of Coke. "Here's a flashlight, in case I can't come back out right away. Don't shine it out the window or Mom might see. I'll be back as quick as I can." And Jeremy jumps down from the fort and heads for the house.

It's starting to get kind of cold. I open the Coke and sit down by Cris. I hand it to him and he drinks some and sits up. That warm Coke is the best thing I've ever tasted and we finish the can in about a minute. Birds are making night noises; soft pink and blue and green, little bursts of light, like the fireflies I remember from when we lived in Ohio once.

"How can you be a First Born and not know about magic?" Cris asks after a while.

I think about that for a while. "I never really knew it was magic, I guess." I shrug. "That's just how the world was . . . there were Shy Folk, and unicorns, and some animals talked to her and some didn't." I shrug.

"How did . . . how did Zoroan take her?"

I swallow. I still dream about it. Nightmares. "She . . . fell through a door that just opened up one day. We were walking in the woods. I was pretty little." I shrug, although I can still see that door and the *nothingness* behind it, and the look on her face as she fell backward through it. "Dad said never ever talk about it. And I don't. Until I met you," I tell him. "And I don't know . . ." I look down at the empty Coke can. "I guess I was starting to think that . . . you know . . . it maybe didn't happen the way I remember." No sign of Jeremy. His mom found out, probably, and he's in real trouble. I wonder if he'll rat on us. Maybe, if he's in too much trouble. He didn't really want us to come here. Will they call the police? Give Cris back to Mr. Teleomara, like Jeremy thinks? I watch for the muddy gray sound of a police car, and I watch for silver, and what does it matter if I see 'em? What are we gonna do about it? And I think of Cris screaming and it all of a sudden hits me that Zoroan did that to my *mom*, too. And then I realize Cris is crying, real soft, a dark gold sound that makes me even sadder.

And I put my arm around him because I know he's thinking the same thing.

"Hey, you guys there?"

Jeremy's whisper sounds so *good*. "Yeah, we're here," I say, and I want to hug him as he scrambles into the fort, lugging a backpack. "You didn't tell."

"What d'you mean? Did you really think I would? Thanks, Melanie. I don't run out on my friends." His words come out an ugly orange.

"I'm sorry." And I mean it. "I guess . . . I never really had a real friend before. I kind of don't know the rules. Did you get into trouble?"

"Oh, tons. Gimme that flashlight." He sets the backpack down on the floor, clicks on the light. "I'm grounded *forever* for skipping school, and your dad called the police, I guess. When you didn't come home. And somebody saw us leave together. I said you were really upset and I was just trying to counsel you and you wouldn't talk to me, so then I figured as long as I was already outside, I might as well enjoy the skip. My mom liked the trying-to-counsel-you part, so I think she sort of believes me. Maybe. I brought you guys some water—filled up an empty milk jug—and I snuck some stuff out of the pantry in the garage. I didn't dare go into the kitchen . . . I have to go right past Mom and Dad's bedroom. They're having a fight right now about whose fault I am." He grins, but it's kind of weak. "I think Mom's winning and I'm Dad's fault."

The water tastes a little like sour milk, but I'm not complaining and neither is Cris. Jeremy brought peanut butter and a box of Saltines, too. "This is the best I could do." He makes a face. "Everything else is in cans. So okay." He digs a battered old table knife out of an apple crate and starts slathering peanut butter on crackers. "You want to tell me what's going on, Cris? Before the police show up and we all get arrested or something?"

"Don't worry about the police." Cris starts stuffing crackers into his mouth and I think again about him maybe stuck in his chair, night and day, in those vines. "Worry about Zoroan," Cris says, with his mouth full. "He wants all the First Born power." He swallows, gulps more water. "It's getting more concentrated. The First Born power. Used to be a lot of First Born. But some people don't have kids before they die, you know? So fewer and fewer share it. If he ever got it all . . ." Cris shrugs. "I think . . . our world would just go away or something. Or maybe Zoroan would turn it into something different or use the power to mess with you all. I just . . . don't know. But he's been secretly kidnapping the First Born for, oh . . . maybe a thousand years or so. People figured it out after a while, so we're real careful. But he has so much of the power now that you can't really fight

him. It's more a matter of staying out of his traps. Like the one I was in."
Cris looks away. "It takes him a while to empty all the First Born power out
of one of us."

I shiver and Jeremy's looking real wide-eyed. "What happens when
he . . . takes it all out of you?" he finally asks.

"I don't know." Cris looks down at the cracker in his hand. "I guess you
just die. I mean . . . nobody has ever come back. There's this prophecy . . .
that he can be destroyed only by a First Born using a true-shape weapon.
And I guessed . . . it was a trap." He stares at the cracker, all squashed to
crumbs in his hand. "I guess . . . I just hoped . . . I thought . . . What did I
have to lose?" His voice is dull, like old metal now. "I thought . . . it might
bring them back."

I'd have tried it, too. If I thought maybe it would bring my mom back.

"Okay, okay, time-out here." Jeremy starts waving his hands. "I now
believe in magic. I am grounded for the rest of my life for skipping school.
I am probably going to get arrested for kidnapping. For that, I want to hear
what is going on in *English* please." He glares at Cris. "What is all this
First Born stuff. What did we see when we were coming over here . . . the
weird trees and stuff? Where *is* your world?"

"Right here." Cris shrugs. "I guess you maybe saw true-shapes because
you were with me. It's like this . . . what if you could only see red and blue
and green, and anything yellow was invisible to you?"

"We'd bump into a lot of school buses."

"But you couldn't *feel* yellow things, either. You just wouldn't know
they were there. You'd walk right through yellow things."

"World would sure look funny." Jeremy's frowning.

"No sun, just light. No sunflowers, no buttercups, no yellow M&Ms."
I'm thinking about those Shy Folk and the unicorns I used to see sometimes
with my mom. "So we don't know yellow is there?"

"Oh, that was just an example." Cris shrugs. "Nah, it's more like you
can see yellow. Just not all the *other* colors." He picks up the old knife that
Jeremy was using to glop peanut butter on the crackers.

It turns into a cool dagger with blue jewels in the handle.

"Wow!" Jeremy's eyes really do bug out. Well, it *is* pretty cool.

"How'd you do that?" Jeremy touches the knife, yelps, and sucks on
his finger. "It's just something I found out in the old dump, way out in the
woods. I cleaned it up before I used it, honest."

"I guess you guys can see true-shapes when you're close to one of us."

Cris looks at the knife. "I don't know what you saw . . . or didn't see . . . on our way here, but that's probably why. Because you're with me."

I'm thinking about Mr. Beasley with that jewel in his forehead. I wonder if he told Mr. Teleomara that I was in Mrs. Banks's class? Cris is looking at me. "I still don't get it why you can't see everything, Melanie. You're a First Born."

"Uh . . ." They're both looking at me. "I guess it's because . . . my dad's not magic." And doesn't ever ever want to talk about it.

Cris looks shocked. "That's not supposed to happen."

"Well, I'm here. And what's so wrong about it?" I'm glaring.

"So hey . . . how come this fort isn't a castle or something?" Jeremy breaks in. "How come it looks like always?"

"It's made out of dead trees." Cris's lip kind of curls. "This *is* its true-shape."

"Okay." Jeremy's frowning. "But how come I could skin my elbows sliding down that rock wall and then, when we all climbed over, I look back and yeah, it's the old haunted house, same as I thought it was?"

"Because I wasn't there anymore and neither was Zoroan." Cris frowns. "I don't know why you saw it in the first place, Melanie. If you can't see the true-world?"

I shrug, still a little mad at him. Actually, I saw the apple tree first, I remember now. And then I noticed the wall. Which is kind of weird, because the tree is leaning *on* the wall. I remember that I went for a walk in the woods that day, feeling pretty sorry for myself. The In Crowd again. And I was walking along and thinking about my mother and the fun stuff that had happened when she took me for walks in the woods, and how I wished my dad would talk about her. And I saw the apple tree and wanted to pick some of the blossoms on it. And I was still thinking about her when I noticed the wall and climbed it and . . . well, you know the rest.

And you know . . . I wonder if maybe . . . maybe the world hasn't changed. Maybe it's *me*. That it isn't that I *can't* see the Shy Folk and the unicorns and the people in the trees that I remember. Maybe . . . I just *don't*. I mean, you tell people about meeting a unicorn or one of the Shy Folk, they think you're lying or crazy. I wonder if maybe I started, well . . . *believing* them? That I was crazy? Like deep down inside?

And that makes me sad, like I'm betraying my mom or something. And it's not like Dad ever said that it wasn't real. He just said not to talk about it. But maybe that made me listen too much. To the people who said it didn't happen. Jeremy's going on about magic and what Cris sees that he doesn't, and I'm not really paying attention. I'm just feeling sad and looking out into the darkness of Jeremy's yard.

Only . . . it's not darkness.

Oh, crap.

"Look." I grab Cris's arm. "Look there. Can you see it? No . . . there!" Silver. Powdered razor blades. The owl we saw before suddenly darts down through the darkness, hooting urgent green, circling the tree.

"Look at what?" Jeremy blinks. "The bird?"

Cris looks blank, too.

"Mr. Teleomara . . . Zoroan." All of a sudden I'm freezing, shivering. "Can't you see that silvery stuff over there by the house? He's out there."

"Zoroan's umbra?" Cris is staring at me, and I never noticed before that his eyes are green, and they glow like the owl's eyes glowed. "I can sense him," he says. "He's close. You mean you can *see* it?"

"I don't know. What's an umbra? I can see when he talks. Like you talk gold and Jeremy talks yellow. Maybe we ought to get out of here?"

Too late. A river of silver, razor-dust fog snakes across the yard, circling the swing set and disappearing under the fort where I can't see it. The owl drops like a stone. With a glittery flash, the silver strikes, wrapping the owl just like Mr. Beasley would. It lets out a single, high-pitched hoot, then pops like a bubble pops and just . . . disappears. Then . . . too fast to really see . . . the razor-fog is in the doorway, like a huge silver Mr. Beasley. Just like Mr. Beasley going after a mouse, it goes after Cris.

And I step in front of it.

It slaps into me like a hose turned on real hard. And it hurts. Like it *is* made out of razor blades, and I can't help it, I yell, and I'm trying to grab on to it, but it's like water, too, and my hands just kind of go through it. And it feels like it's burning my skin off and I close my eyes and I can't stand it any longer and . . .

. . . it stops. And Cris is standing in front of me with that gold dagger and a few wisps of mist are sort of trickling out of the fort.

"Yahoo, Cris, way to go!" Jeremy claps Cris on the back, and he staggers and it's like the dagger is real heavy for him, like it weighs a ton.

"What happened?" I look at myself. I'm okay. No burns, not even like a sunburn. "That hurt."

"He's really strong." Cris sits down on the floor all of a sudden. "Maybe

75

from all the First Born power he's taken. I . . . I don't think I can stand up to him."

And his words are kind of tinged with that dog-poop color again. I figure that is not good. He looks at me. "Melanie, it really helps that you can see it . . . his umbra. Tell me where it is. If I can cut through it, it doesn't have any power anymore."

"You're a First Born, maybe you destroyed him when you stabbed it with that dagger, huh?" Jeremy sits down beside Cris. "I couldn't see anything, but isn't that what the prophecy said?"

"I have to stab his body with a true-shape weapon, not just stab his umbra." Cris's head droops. "He won't let me get that close, and I don't think I'm strong enough to fight through." He looks at me. "That was really brave, Melanie. Trying to stop his umbra. It can kill you. You're lucky," he says. "As well as brave."

Lucky, yes. Not brave. Just stupid. I rub my arms. Jeremy's looking at me like he's impressed. I make a face at him. "What do we do now, Cris?" My voice comes out shaky. "Is there any way to keep it out?"

"There's nothing else I can use to stop it." He looks around the fort. "If I had another First Born, we might be strong enough to keep him at bay. Maybe."

Well, I can't help it if my dad isn't magic and I'm not magic.

"Come on, Cris." Jeremy is kind of hopping up and down. "Melanie can see this umbra thing. You have the dagger. We gotta work together on this. You can't just sit here and wait for him."

While Jeremy's going on, I'm looking out into the yard. It's real late now, the empty, cold part of the night like when you wake up and you feel like you're the only living thing in the world. And there he is. Walking into the yard just like he walked into class. And I can see him real easy, even though it's dark and there isn't even a moon. That silvery stuff kind of drifts around him, like he's walking in his own fogbank.

"Hello, Melanie." He looks up and smiles like a teacher smiles when you're doing something wrong, but he's not real upset by it. "Jeremy, you don't want to be here," he says. "You'll get into a lot of trouble and your parents won't ever really trust you again. They won't wake up if you sneak back in, now. I won't even give you detention for skipping. You were worried about a friend, and that's a good thing. Go to bed now, and I'll see you in the morning."

He sounds so warm. So *worried* about Jeremy. And I look at Jeremy, and he's squirming. And even I want to go inside and go to bed and see him in the morning.

"Melanie, you need to go home right now. Your father is really worried about you, you know. He might . . . well, you know that if he thought he had lost you, too, as well as your mother, he might do something terrible to himself."

And I'm on my feet. Dad. I haven't really thought about him, and Mr. Teleomara is right . . .

"Stop it, Zoroan." Cris's voice sounds like a frog croaking, but the gold is real bright, all sparkly. "Don't play your tricks on them."

And it's like someone dumped a bucket of water on my head.

"He's lying, Jeremy." My voice sounds ugly, too. "Don't listen to him."

"This is not your worry, children." He's still smiling. "It's not your world. Nothing that happens here has anything to do with you. Go home. Go to bed. Everything will be all right in the morning."

The silver words smell sweet. Words don't *smell*. Wrong, wrong, wrong. "Don't, Jeremy." I grab him as he makes a move toward the door. "It really is a trick or a spell or something." But he's not hearing me, and he pulls away, and I really want to do what Mr. Teleomara says, too.

And then . . . my dad walks out of the woods.

"Melanie?" he calls. He stops at the edge of the yard. What is he *doing* here? "Melanie?" he yells again. His green words sound . . . scared.

"Dad," I say, and it comes out like a mouse's squeak. But he hears.

"Are you okay?" He starts for the tree fort like Mr. Teleomara is invisible. "Are you all right, sweetheart?"

Mr. Teleomara steps in front of him and blocks his way. "Go home," he says, and that silver stuff gets thick all around my dad. "Go home now."

And I realize all of a sudden that he wasn't going to let me leave, that Cris is right, and he wants me, too.

"I see you. I know what you are." My dad doesn't move. "She doesn't belong to your world. Get out of my way."

I've never heard my dad talk like that, not to anyone.

"Too late." Mr. Teleomara smiles. "She's mine now, too."

My dad punches him.

Jeremy whoops and Mr. Teleomara falls on his butt and all the silver vanishes, and for a second I think it's going to be okay.

And then the silver stuff just sort of rises out of the grass and it wraps around my dad. He stumbles back, his mouth open like he's screaming, but

I can't hear anything, and he's all arched backward like he's going to fall, but he's frozen in place.

And he's going to die, any second now, pop like a bubble and just vanish. Like the owl. I know it like someone told me.

I'm firstborn. I'm my *mother's* firstborn. And I grab the dagger out of Cris's hand and he yells and I don't care. I jump down from the fort and land on my hands and knees. Zoroan doesn't notice, he's looking at my dad and having fun, just like Mr. Beasley with his mice. And I crawl over, and on my knees, holding the dagger with both hands, I stab him in the leg.

The dagger melts.

Just like that.

And Mr. Teleomara looks down at me and smiles. "Half-breed," he says. And something like a giant hand slaps me and I hit the trunk of the apple tree and end up on the ground.

Firstborn, but my *dad's* firstborn as well as my mom's. Maybe he's right. And maybe there's no true-world for me.

"Melanie, Melanie." Jeremy jumps down from the fort, pulls me to my feet. "Are you okay? What happened?"

And I get it. I hope I do. I look up at the fort and I see a place where the plywood has split. Grab it. A long splinter comes off, about as long as my finger. "Stab him with this." I shove the splinter at Jeremy. "You're a firstborn, right? Just do it, Jeremy. This is *your* true-shape weapon. Stab him!" And I don't wait for him to answer, I just throw myself on Zoroan, trying to scratch his eyes, pounding on him with my fists. And the silver stuff wraps around me like a burning hand and I can't breathe and I was wrong, and Zoroan is laughing and I'm going to die, too . . .

. . . and over his shoulder, through all the glitter and the hurting, I see Jeremy do this wild, crazy stab with the stupid little splinter and it sticks into Zoroan's back.

It goes right in, so easy that Jeremy trips and falls flat. Everything starts to shake, like an earthquake or something. And I'm on the ground looking up, and Cris falls out of the fort and nearly lands on top of me. The fort is falling apart. All the tree branches are waving. I roll over, and Zoroan is standing with his arms in the air, and the silver stuff is all gone. His face is changing, melting into another face, and another, young, old, men, women, even kids' faces, faster and faster, until his face is a kind of blur. Then this icy wind like the middle of winter starts blowing, and it smells like the dead possum I found under the porch of our house when we moved in.

And this hole opens. It goes down forever, and that's where the smell and the cold wind are coming from. The last of the fort shreds apart, books, CDs, and boards all falling into the hole, and I'm sliding toward it, like the wind is dragging me, and Jeremy's at the edge, going over, and I grab him, and Cris is sliding in, too, and . . .

. . . something hard wraps around my waist and yanks me back and all of a sudden I'm up in the apple tree. And the wind stops. And the hole is gone. Another limb is holding Jeremy, and Cris is sitting in the crotch of the tree where the fort used to be. There's nothing left of it.

My dad is lying on the grass like he's asleep, and all of a sudden the limb under me bends down and sort of dumps me on the grass. And I run over to my dad, who's starting to sit up, and I'm so glad that I can't talk and I'm crying and all I can do is sort of burrow into his arms. And he holds me so tight it hurts and that's fine.

"Wow." Jeremy's voice is a real pale yellow. He's still up in the tree. "That was cool." His laugh is kind of shaky. "Make a good end for a horror movie."

"He's gone. He's destroyed. Zoroan can't ever come back. You fulfilled the prophecy. How did you do that?" Cris slides to the ground looking confused. "You're not . . . you're not one of us. You can't have done that."

"He's a firstborn, too," I say, still hanging on to my dad. "And the prophecy said true-shape. You said the wood in the fort was a true-shape for us . . . for Jeremy. I think the dagger melted because I don't . . . belong in either world." The words are really hard to say and I don't look at my dad.

He gets to his feet, pulling me with him, then he turns me around so that I have to look at him. "You're part of *both* worlds," he says, real low. "That's what your mother and I wanted." He swallows hard. "When he . . . took her, I was afraid. I wanted you to . . . be safe." He kind of brushes my hair back from my face. "I was wrong," he said. "I should have taught you about her . . . your world. When the owl came, I saw it was one of the owls that your mother used to talk to. And I knew I'd made a mistake. So I followed it."

The owl with the glowing eyes? "Zoroan killed it," I whisper. "I didn't know . . ." I'm not really sure what I want to say.

"I know." He pulls me real close. "I'm sorry."

"Ouch." Jeremy yelps as the apple tree dumps him onto the ground. "Okay, I'm sorry I built a fort in you. Hey." He ducks as a twiggy branch swipes through his hair. "Now cut it out."

"I can't believe you really did that." Cris holds out a hand to Jeremy. "Every true-being owes you thanks. I'll never think that you people are less than us again. Just because you can't see the true-world. He could have killed you in a second."

"Glad I didn't know that." And Jeremy shoots me a look, but his words are sun yellow. "You're cool, Cris." He combs leaves and twigs out of his hair. "Hey, are you gonna stick around? For when I get done being grounded forever? I really want to see what your world looks like. Can you show me?"

That's Jeremy. I smile.

"Just give me a call. Whenever you're not grounded." Cris laughs. "I'll hear you." And he looks thoughtful. "Maybe I should find out more about your world. I don't know . . . I never thought it mattered. But maybe it does."

"Well, I think so." Jeremy makes a face. "Hey, you can come with us to a baseball game. I bet you'll like it."

"It's a deal." Cris smiles. "And I've got some friends who'll give us a ride and then you can really see a lot."

"Oh, cool, what kind of friends? I hope they can fly. Oh gosh, look." Jeremy points at the sky. "It's getting light. Oh, man, I'd better get inside. Or I'll get grounded for *two* forevers. You gonna come to school, Mel?" He's already heading for the house. "I bet they won't let me say I'm sick."

"I'll be there," I tell him. I guess I want to prove to myself that Mr. Teleomara isn't there, that we really did destroy him. "What about you, Cris?"

He shrugs. "I'm going to go find people . . . let them know what happened." He gives me a shy smile. "I'll tell 'em about you, Melanie. And Jeremy. I think we'll all feel a little different about you people from now on." And he holds out his hand to me. "Can I come back and visit?"

"You bet." And then I look up at my dad. "Uh . . . are we gonna stay here for a while?"

"Why not?" But his smile is kind of sad. "I don't think we have to run anymore. This is as good a place to live as any and you have friends here."

Cris turns and walks away and I notice that he doesn't leave any tracks in the dew-wet grass. Then he fades into the tree shadows. Jeremy is already inside. It's just Dad and me, and the sun comes up and makes the dew glitter like diamonds. And all of a sudden, I *see* diamonds hanging on the bushes and sprinkled on the grass. And then it's just dew again.

Dad's looking at me and he looks . . . well . . . shy. "It's okay," I tell him. "I get it. You were afraid someone was going to come after me. And he did."

"No." He puts his arm around me. "It's more than that. I was angry. At her world. Because it . . . took her."

He can't say it either . . . that she's dead. What did Jeremy's mom call it? "I guess I'd have been angry, too," I tell him, but he's shaking his head.

"It's *your* world, too. That apple tree that saved you all . . . the apple is your birth tree."

Mine, too? And I think how that old apple sort of helped me over the wall, back when I found Cris.

"I think you'll find that you're more a part of your mother's world than you realize." Dad sighs. "Maybe Cris can help you."

Lights are going on in the houses, people are letting dogs out, and a kid on a bike pedals up the street, tossing papers into yards from a bag on the handlebars. I know him. He's in the other sixth-grade class and put a green bean up his nose in the cafeteria last month. He talks bright pink. "Maybe I can be sort of in between," I say. I'm trying out the words, but they feel right. Half-breed. Maybe that's a *good* thing. I stop talking because there, back in the tree shadows, I see one of the Shy Folk. She notices me looking and waves one pale hand. Huh.

"Does it bother you?" Dad asks. "Being . . . between worlds?"

"No." I say it first, for him, but then I think about it. It really doesn't. Cris seems so . . . well . . . alone. Why didn't the First Born get together to stop Zoroan? Why didn't someone help him or come looking for him when Zoroan trapped him? I think of Jeremy, and I think maybe I like my world. But the unicorns were cool. I smile up at Dad. "I like being part of both." And I really do.

"Your mother would be . . ." He clears his throat. "Your mother would be so proud of you." He looks around. "We'd better get home if you're really going to go to school. If we hang around here much longer, we'll get arrested for trespassing."

And we both laugh, and he keeps his arm around me, and we take the path through the woods back to the little rental dump where we're living. We can stay. That thought sort of feels like . . . well, like a birthday present. You know, the kind you don't really want to unwrap because you know what it has to be and it's gonna be so cool and you just don't want that feeling to be over yet.

Dad keeps his arm around me and that feels good, too.

I see a unicorn when we're almost home. Not close, just kind of drifting through the woods like a pale deer with a single horn. Wow. To quote Jeremy. Maybe, when Zoroan died he let loose all that First Born power. Or maybe it was me and I didn't want to see, before. I can just make out our house in the deep shadows of the tall Sitka spruce that sort of leans over it.

Dad left the lights on.

"I didn't leave the lights on," Dad says.

We both stop under the Sitka's branches. Dad is holding his breath and he's scared and so am I. The door opens. This woman comes out. Black hair, like mine, all curly around her face, and she's wearing a white dress. She's shorter than I remember. Well, I guess I'm taller. I look like her. That shocks me. I didn't know that.

Dad lets go of me and charges through the ferns that grow behind the house. She opens her arms to him and I can see diamonds that are probably tears in her eyes. Or maybe they are diamonds. She looks just like I remember.

Oh, Cris, I think. You, too, I hope. Then I stop thinking.

"Mom," I yell, and charge after Dad.

The Ruby Incomparable

KAGE BAKER

One of the most prolific new writers to appear in the late nineties, Kage Baker made her first sale in 1997, to Asimov's Science Fiction, and has since become one of that magazines most frequent and popular contributors with her sly and compelling stories of the adventures and misadventures of the time-traveling agents of the Company; of late, she's started two other linked sequences of stories there as well, one of them set in as lush and eccentric a High Fantasy milieu as any we've ever seen. Her stories have also appeared in Realms of Fantasy, Sci Fiction, Amazing, *and elsewhere. Her first Company novel,* In the Garden of Iden, *was also published in 1997 and immediately became one of the most acclaimed and widely reviewed first novels of the year. More Company novels quickly followed, including* Sky Coyote, Mendoza in Hollywood, The Graveyard Game, The Life of the World to Come, *as well as a chapbook novella,* The Empress of Mars, *and her first fantasy novel,* The Anvil of the World. *Her many stories have been collected in* Black Projects, White Knights, Mother Aegypt and Other Stories, Dark Mondays, *and a collection of Company stories,* The Children of the Company. *Her most recent Company novel is* The Machine's Child. *In addition to her writing, Baker has been an artist, actor, and director at the Living History Center and has taught Elizabethan English as a second language. She lives in Pismo Beach, California.*

When purest Evil and purest Good join in marriage, you can't expect the relationship to be a tranquil one—but sometimes it can produce unexpected consequences that surprise both.

*

THE girl surprised everyone.

To begin with, no one in the world below had thought her parents would have more children. Her parents' marriage had created quite a scandal, a profound clash of philosophical extremes; for her father was the Master of the Mountain, a brigand and sorcerer, who had carried the Saint of the World off to his high fortress. It's bad enough when a living goddess, who can heal the sick and raise the dead, takes up with a professional dark lord (black armor, monstrous armies, and all). But when they settle down together with every intention of raising a family, what are respectable people to think?

The Yendri in their forest villages groaned when they learned of the first boy. Even in his cradle, his fiendish tendencies were evident. He was beautiful as a little angel except in his screaming tempers, when he would morph himself into giant larvae, wolf cubs, or pools of bubbling slime.

The Yendri in their villages and the Children of the Sun in their stone cities all rejoiced when they heard of the second boy. He too was beautiful, but clearly good. A star was seen to shine from his brow on occasion. He was reported to have cured a nurse's toothache with a mere touch, and he never so much as cried while teething.

And the shamans of the Yendri, and the priests in the temples of the Children of the Sun, all nodded their heads and said: "Well, at least we have balance now. The two boys will obviously grow up, oppose each other, and fight to the death, because that's what generally happens."

Having decided all this, and settled down confidently to wait, imagine how shocked they were to hear that the Saint of the World had borne a third child! And a girl, at that. It threw all their calculations off and annoyed them a great deal.

The Master and his Lady were surprised, too, because their baby daughter popped into the world homely as a little potato, by contrast with the elfin beauty of her brothers. They did agree that she had lovely eyes, at least, dark as her father's, and she seemed to be sweet-tempered. They named her Svnae.

So the Master of the Mountain swaddled her in purple silk and took her out on a high balcony and held her up before his assembled troops, who roared, grunted, and howled their polite approval. And that night in the barracks and servants' hall, around the barrels of black wine that had been served out in celebration, the minions of the proud father agreed amongst themselves that the little maid might not turn out so ugly as all that, if the rest of her face grew to fit that nose and she didn't stay quite so bald.

And they at least were proved correct, for within a year Svnae had become a lovely child.

✳

ON the morning of Svnae's fifth birthday, the Master went to the nursery and fetched his little daughter. He took her out with him on his tour of the battlements, where all the world stretched away below. The guards, tusked and fanged, great and horrible in their armor, stood to attention and saluted him. Solemnly, he pulled a great red rose from thin air and presented it to Svnae.

"Today," he said, "my Dark-Eyed is five years old. What do you want most in all the world, daughter?"

Svnae looked up at him with her shining eyes. Very clearly she said: "Power."

He looked down at her, astounded; but she stood there looking patiently back at him, clutching her red rose. He knelt beside her. "Do you know what Power is?" he asked.

"Yes," she said. "Power is when you stand up here and make all the clouds come to you across the sky, and shoot lightning and make thunder crash. That's what I want."

"I can make magic for you," he said, and with a wave of his gauntleted hand produced three tiny fire elementals dressed in scarlet, blue, and yellow, who danced enchantingly for Svnae before vanishing in a puff of smoke.

"Thank you, Daddy," she said, "but no. I want *me* to be able to do it."

Slowly, he nodded his head. "Power you were born with; you're my child. But you must learn to use it, and that doesn't come easily, or quickly. Are you sure this is what you really want?"

"Yes," she said without hesitation.

"Not eldritch toys to play with? Not beautiful clothes? Not sweets?"

"If I learn Power, I can have all those things anyway," Svnae observed.

The Master was pleased with her answer. "Then you will learn to use your Power," he said. "What would you like to do first?"

"I want to learn to fly," she said. "Not like my brother Eyrdway. He just turns into birds. I want to stay me and fly."

"Watch my hands," her father said. In his right hand, he held out a stone; in his left, a paper dart. He put them both over the parapet and let go. The stone dropped; the paper dart drifted lazily down.

"Now, tell me," he said. "Why did the stone drop and the paper fly?"

"Because the stone is heavy, and the paper isn't," she said.

"Nearly so; and not so. Look." And he pulled from the air an egg. He held it out in his palm, and the egg cracked. A tiny thing crawled from it, and lay shivering there a moment; white down covered it like dandelion fluff, and it drew itself upright and shook tiny stubby wings. The down transformed to shining feathers, and the young bird beat its wide wings and flew off rejoicing.

"Now, tell me," said the Master, "was that magic?"

"No," said Svnae. "That's just what happens with birds."

"Nearly so; and not so. Look." And he took out another stone. He held it up and uttered a Word of Power; the stone sprouted bright wings and, improbably, flew away into the morning.

"How did you make it do that?" Svnae cried. Her father smiled at her.

"With Power; but Power is not enough. I was able to transform the stone because I understand that the bird and the stone, and even the paper dart, are all the same thing."

"But they're not," said Svnae.

"Aren't they?" said her father. "When you understand that the stone and the bird are one, the next step is convincing the *stone* that the bird and the stone are one. And then the stone can fly."

Svnae bit her lip. "This is hard, isn't it?" she said.

"Very," said the Master of the Mountain. "Are you sure you wouldn't like a set of paints instead?"

"Yes," said Svnae stubbornly. "I *will* understand."

"Then I'll give you books to study," he promised. He picked her up and folded her close, in his dark cloak. He carried her to the bower of her lady mother, the Saint of the World.

Now when the Lady had agreed to marry her dread Lord, she had won from him the concession of making a garden on his black basalt mountain-top, high and secret in the sunlit air. Ten years into their marriage, her orchards were a mass of white blossom, and her white-robed disciples tended green beds of herbs there. They bowed gracefully as Svnae ran to her mother, who embraced her child and gave her a white rose. And Svnae said proudly:

"I'm going to learn Power, Mama!"

The Lady looked questions at her Lord.

"It's what she wants," he said, no less proudly. "And if she has the talent, why shouldn't she learn?"

"But Power is not an end in itself, my child," the Lady said to her daughter. "To what purpose will you use it? Will you help others?"

"Ye-es," said Svnae, looking down at her feet. "But I have to learn first."

"Wouldn't you like to be a healer, like me?"

"I can heal people when I have Power," said Svnae confidently. Her mother looked a little sadly into her dark eyes but saw no shadow there. So she blessed her daughter and sent her off to play.

THE Master of the Mountain kept his promise and gave his daughter books to study, to help her decipher the Three Riddles of Flight. She had to learn to read first; with fiery determination she hurled herself on her letters and mastered them, and charged into the first of the Arcane texts.

So well she studied that by her sixth birthday she had solved all three riddles and was able at will to sprout little butterfly wings from her shoulders, wings as red as a rose. She couldn't fly much with them, only fluttering a few inches above the ground like a baby bird; but she was only six. One day she would soar.

Then it was the Speech of Animals she wanted to learn. Then it was how to move objects without touching them. Then she desired to know the names of all the stars in the sky: not only what men call them, but what they call themselves. And one interest led to another, as endlessly she found new things by which to be intrigued, new arts and sciences she wanted to learn. She spent whole days together in her father's library, and carried books back to her room, and sat up reading far into the night.

In this manner she learned to fly up to the clouds with her rose-red wings, there to ask an eagle what it had for breakfast, or gather pearls with her own hands from the bottom of the sea.

And so the years flowed by, as the Master throve on his mountain, and the Saint of the World brought more children into it to confound the expectations of priests and philosophers, who debated endlessly the question of whether these children were Good or Evil.

The Saint held privately that all her children were, at heart, Good. The Master of the Mountain held, privately and out loud too, that the priests and philosophers were all a bunch of idiots.

Svnae grew tall, with proud dark good looks she had from her father. But there were no black lightnings in her eyes, as there were in his. Neither were her eyes crystal and serene, like her mother's, but all afire with interest, eager to see how everything worked.

And then she grew taller still, until she overtopped her mother; and still taller than that, until she overtopped her brother Eyrdway. He was rather peevish about it and took to calling her The Giantess, until she punched him hard enough to knock out one of his teeth. He merely morphed into a version of himself without the missing tooth, but he stopped teasing her after that.

Now you might suppose that many a young guard might begin pining for Svnae, and saluting smartly as she passed by, and mourning under her window at night. You would be right. But she never noticed; she was too engrossed in her studies to hear serenades sung under her window. Still, they did not go to waste; her younger sisters could hear them perfectly well, and *they* noticed things like snappy salutes.

This was not to say that Svnae did not glory in being a woman. As soon as she was old enough, she chose her own gowns and jewelry. Her mother presented her with gauzes delicate as cobweb, in exquisite shades of lavender, sea mist, and bird-egg blue; fine-worked silver ornaments as well, set with white diamonds that glinted like starlight.

Alas, Svnae's tastes ran to crimson and purple and cloth of gold, even though the Saint of the World explained how well white set off her dusky skin. And though she thanked her mother for the fragile silver bangles, and dutifully wore them at family parties, she cherished massy gold set with emeralds and rubies. The more finery the better, in fact, though her mother gently indicated that perhaps it wasn't quite in the best of taste to wear the serpent bracelets with eyes of topaz *and* the peacock necklace of turquoise, jade, and lapis lazuli.

And though Svnae read voraciously and mastered the arts of Transmutation of Metals, Divination by Bones, and Summoning Rivers by their Secret Names, she did not learn to weave nor to sew; nor did she learn the healing properties of herbs. Her mother waited patiently for Svnae to become interested in these things, but somehow the flashing beam of her eye never turned to them.

One afternoon the Master of the Mountain looked up from the great black desk whereat he worked, hearing the guards announce the approach of his eldest daughter. A moment later she strode into his presence, resplendent in robes of scarlet and peacock blue, and slippers of vermilion with especially pointy toes that curled up at the ends.

"Daughter," he said, rising to his feet.

"Daddy," she replied, "I've just been reading in the Seventh Pomegranate Scroll about a distillation of violets that can be employed to lure dragons. Can you show me how to make it?"

"I've never done much distillation, my child," said the Master of the Mountain. "That's more in your mother's line of work. I'm certain she'd be delighted to teach you. Why don't you ask her?"

"Oh," said Svnae, and flushed, and bit her lip, and stared at the floor. "I think she's busy with some seminar with her disciples. Meditation Techniques or something."

And though the Master of the Mountain had never had any use for his lady wife's disciples, he spoke sternly. "Child, you know your mother has never ignored her own children for her followers."

"It's not that," said Svnae a little sullenly, twisting a lock of her raven hair. "Not at all. It's just that—well—we're bound to have an argument about it. She'll want to know what I want it for, for one thing, and she won't approve of my catching dragons, and she'll let me know it even if she doesn't say a word, she'll just *look* at me—"

"I know," said her dread father.

"As though it was a frivolous waste of time, when what I really ought to be doing is learning all her cures for fevers, which is all very well, but I have other things I want to be learning first, and in any case *I'm not Mother*, I'm my *own* person, and she has to understand that!"

"I'm certain she does, my child."

"Yes." Svnae tossed her head back. "So. Well. This brings up something else I'd wanted to ask you. I think I ought to go down into the world to study."

"But—" said the Master of the Mountain.

"I've always wanted to, and it turns out there's a sort of secret school in a place called Konen Feyy-in-the-Trees, where anybody can go to learn distillations. I need to learn more!"

"Mm. But—" said the Master of the Mountain.

She got her way. Not with temper, tears, or foot-stamping, but she got her way. No more than a week later she took a bag and her bow and quiver, and, climbing up on the parapet, she summoned her rose-red wings, which now swept from a yard above her dark head to her ankles. Spreading them on the wind, she soared aloft. Away she went like a queen of the air, to explore the world.

Her father and mother watched her go.

"Do you think she'll be safe?" said the Saint of the World.

"She'd better be," said the Master of the Mountain, looking over the edge and far down his mountain at the pair of ogre bodyguards who coursed like armored greyhounds, crashing through the trees, following desperately their young mistress while doing their best not to draw attention to themselves.

Svnae sailed off on the wind and discovered that, though her extraordinary heritage had given her many gifts, a sense of direction was not one of them. She cast about a long while, looking for any place that might be a city in the trees; at last she spotted a temple in a wooded valley, far below.

On landing, she discovered that the temple was deserted long since, and a great gray monster guarded it. She slew the creature with her arrows and went in to see what it might have been guarding. On the altar was a golden box that shone with protective spells. But she had the magic to unlock those spells, and found within a book that seemed to be a history of the lost race whose temple this was. She carried it outside and spent the next few hours seated on a block of stone in the ruins, intent with her chin on her fist, reading.

Within the book, she read of a certain crystal ring, the possession of which would enable the wearer to understand the Speech of Water. The book directed her to a certain fountain an hour's flight south of the temple, and fortunately the temple had a compass rose mosaic set in the floor; so she flew south at once, just as her bodyguards came panting up to the temple at last, and they watched her go with language that was dreadful even for ogres.

Exactly an hour's flight south, Svnae spotted the fountain, rising from a ruined courtyard of checkered tile. Here she landed and approached the fountain with caution; for there lurked within its bowl a scaled serpent of remarkable beauty and deadliest venom. She considered the jeweled serpent, undulating round and round within the bowl in a lazy sort of way. She considered the ring, a circle of clear crystal, hard to spot as it bobbed at the top of the fountain's jet, well beyond her reach even were she to risk the serpent. Backing away several paces, she drew an arrow and took aim. *Clink!*

Her arrow shuddered in the trunk of an oak thirty paces distant, with the ring still spinning on its shaft. Speedily she claimed it and put it on, and straightaway she could understand the Speech of Water.

Whereupon the fountain told her of a matter so interesting that she had to learn more about it. Details, however, were only to be had from a little blue man who lived in dubious hills far to the west. So away she flew, to find him . . .

She had several other adventures and it was only by chance that, soaring one morning above the world, deep in conversation with a sea eagle, she spotted what was clearly a city down below amongst great trees. To her inquiry, the sea eagle replied that the city was Konen Feyy. She thanked it and descended through the bright morning to a secluded grove where she could cast a glamour on herself and approach without attracting undue notice. Following unseen a league distant, her wheezing bodyguards threw themselves down and gave thanks to anyone who might be listening.

THE Children of the Sun dwelt generally in cities all of stone, where scarcely a blade of grass grew nor even so much as a potted geranium, preferring instead rock gardens with obelisks and statuary. But in all races there are those who defy the norm, and so it was in Konen Feyy. Here a colony of artists and craftsmen had founded a city in the green wilderness, without even building a comfortingly high wall around themselves. Accordingly, a lot of them had died from poisoned arrows and animal attacks in the early years, but this only seemed to make them more determined to stay there.

They painted the local landscapes, they made pots of the local clay, and wove textiles from the local plant fibers; and they even figured out that if they cut down the local trees to make charmingly rustic wooden furniture, sooner or later there wouldn't be any trees. For the Children of the Sun, who were ordinarily remarkably dense about ecological matters, this was a real breakthrough.

And so the other peoples of the world ventured up to Konen Feyy. The forest-dwelling Yendri, the Saint's own people, opened little shops where were sold herbs, or freshwater pearls, or willow baskets, or fresh produce. Other folk came, too: solitary survivors of lesser-known races, obscure revenants, searching for a quiet place to set up shop. This was how the Night School came to exist.

Svnae, wandering down Konen Feyy's high street and staring around her, found the place at once. Though it looked like an ordinary perfumer's shop, there were certain signs on the wall above the door, visible only to those who were familiar with the Arcane sciences. An extravagant green cursive explained the School's hours, where and how she might enroll, and where to find appropriate lodgings with other students.

In this last she was lucky, for it happened that there were three other daughters of magi who'd taken a place above a dollmaker's shop, and hadn't quite enough money between them to make the monthly rent, so they were looking for a fourth roommate, someone to be Earth to their Air, Fire, and Water. They were pleasant girls, though Svnae was somewhat taken aback to discover that she towered over them all three, and somewhat irritated to discover that they all held her mother in reverent awe.

"You're the daughter of *the* Saint of the World?" exclaimed Seela, whose father was Principal Thaumaturge for Mount Flame City. "What are you doing here, then? *She's* totally the best at distillations and essences. Everyone knows that! *I'd* give anything to learn from her."

Svnae was to hear this statement repeated, with only slight variations, over the next four years of her higher education. She learned not to mind, however; for her studies occupied half her attention, and the other half was all spent on discovering the strange new world in which she lived, where there were no bodyguards (of which she was aware, anyway), and only her height distinguished her from all the other young ladies she met.

It was tremendous fun. She chipped in money with her roommates to buy a couch for their sitting room, and the four of them pushed it up the steep flight of stairs with giggles and screams, though Svnae could have tucked it under one arm and carried it up herself with no effort. She dined with her roommates at the little fried-fish shop on the corner, where they had their particular booth in which they always sat, though Svnae found it rather cramped.

She listened sympathetically as first one and then another of her roommates fell in love with various handsome young seers and sorcerers, and she swept up after a number of riotous parties, and on one occasion broke a vase over the head of a young shapeshifter who, while nice enough when sober, turned into something fairly unpleasant when he became unwisely intoxicated. She had to throw him over her shoulder and pitch him down the stairs, and her roommates wept their thanks and all agreed they didn't know what they'd do without her.

But somehow Svnae never fell in love.

It wasn't because she had no suitors for her hand. There were several young gallants at the Night School, glittering with jewelry and strange habits, who sought to romance Svnae. One was an elemental fire-lord with burning hair; one was a lord of air with vast violet wings. One was a merlord, who had servants following him around with perfumed misting bottles to keep his skin from drying out.

But all of them made it pretty clear they desired to marry Svnae in order to forge dynastic unions with the Master of the Mountain. And Svnae had long since decided that love, real Love, was the only reason for getting involved in all the mess and distraction of romance. So she declined, gracefully, and the young lords sulked and found other wealthy girls to entreat.

Her course of study ended. The roommates all bid one another fond farewells and went their separate ways. Svnae returned home with a train of attendant spirits carrying presents for all her little nieces and nephews. But she did not stay long, for she had heard of a distant island where was written, in immense letters on cliffs of silver, the formula for reversing Time in small and manageable fields, and she desired to learn it . . .

"SVNAE'S turned out rather well," said the Master of the Mountain, as he retired one night. "I could wish she spent a little more time at home, all the same. I'd have thought she'd have married and settled down by now, like the boys."

"She's restless," said the Saint of the World, as she combed out her hair.

"Well, why should she be? A first-rate sorceress with a double degree? The Ruby Incomparable, they call her. What more does she want?"

"She doesn't know yet," said the Saint of the World, and blew out the light. "But she'll know when she finds it."

AND Svnae had many adventures.

But one day, following up an obscure reference in an ancient grimoire, it chanced that she desired to watch a storm in its rage over the wide ocean and listen to the wrath of all the waters. Out she flew upon a black night in the late year, when small craft huddled at their moorings, and found what she sought.

There had never in all the world been such a storm. The white foam was beaten into air, the white air was charged with water, the shrieking white gulls wheeled and screamed across the black sky, and the waves were as valleys and mountains.

Svnae floated in a bubble of her own devising, protected, watching it all with interest. Suddenly, far below in a trough of water, she saw a tiny figure clinging to a scrap of wood. The trough became a wall of water that rose up, towering high, until into her very eyes stared the drowning man. In his astonishment, he let go the shattered mast that supported him and sank out of sight like a stone.

She cried out and dove from her bubble into the wave. Down she went, through water like dark glass, and caught him by the hand; up she went, towing him with her, and got him into the air and wrapped her strong arms about him. She could not fly, not with wet wings in the storm, but she summoned sea-beasts to bear them to the nearest land.

This was merely an empty rock, white cliffs thrusting from the sea. By magic she raised a palace from the stones to shelter them, and she took the man within. Here there was a roaring fire; here there was hot food and wine. She put him to rest all unconscious in a deep bed and tended him with her own hands.

Days she watched and cared for him, until he was well enough to speak to her. By that time, he had her heart.

Now, he was not as handsome as a mage-lord, nor learned in any magic, nor born of ancient blood: he was only a toymaker from the cities of the Children of the Sun, named Kendach. But so long and anxiously had she watched his sleeping face that she saw it when she closed her eyes.

And of course when Kendach opened his, the first thing he saw was her face: and after that, it was love. How could it be otherwise?

They nested together, utterly content, until it occurred to them that their families might wonder where they were. So she took him home to meet her parents ("A *toymaker*?" hooted her brothers), and he took her home to meet his ("Very nice girl. A little tall, but nice," said his unsuspecting father. They chose not to enlighten him as to their in-laws).

They were married in a modest ceremony in Konen Feyy.

"I hope he's not going to have trouble with her brothers," fretted Kendach's father, that night in the inn room. "Did you see the way they glared? Particularly that good-looking one. It quite froze my blood."

"It's clear she gets her height from her father," said Kendach's mother, pouring tea for him. "*Very* distinguished businessman, as I understand it. Runs some kind of insurance firm. I do wonder why her mother wears that veil, though, don't you?"

Kendach opened a toy shop in Konen Feyy, where he made kites in the forms of insects, warships, and meteors. Svnae raised a modest palace among the trees, and they lived there in wedded bliss. And life was full for Svnae, with nothing else to be asked for.

And then . . .

One day she awoke and there was a gray stain on the face of the sun. She blinked and rubbed her eyes. It did not go away. It came and sat on top of her morning tea. It blotted the pages of the books she tried to read, and it lay like grime on her lover's face. She couldn't get rid of it, nor did she know from whence it had come.

Svnae took steps to find out. She went to a cabinet and got down a great black globe of crystal, which shone and swam with deep fires. She went to a quiet place and stroked the globe until it glowed with electric crackling fires. At last these words floated up out of the depths:

YOUR MOTHER DOES NOT UNDERSTAND YOU.

They rippled on the surface of the globe, pulsing softly. She stared at them, and they did not change.

So she pulled on her cloak that was made of peacock feathers, and yoked up a team of griffins to a sky chariot (useful when your lover has no wings, and flies only kites), and flew off to visit her mother.

The Saint of the World sat alone in her garden, by a quiet pool of reflecting water. She wore a plain white robe. White lilies glowed with light on the surface of the water; distantly a bird sang. She meditated, her crystal eyes serene.

There was a flash of color on the water. She looked up to see her eldest daughter charging across the sky. The griffin-chariot thundered to a landing nearby, and Svnae dismounted, pulling her vivid cloak about her. She went straight to her mother and knelt.

"Mother, I need to talk to you," she said. "Is it true that you don't understand me?"

The Saint of the World thought it over.

"Yes, it's true," she said at last. "I don't understand you. I'm sorry, dearest. Does it make a difference?"

"Have I disappointed you, Mother?" asked Svnae in distress.

The Lady thought very carefully about that one.

"No," she said finally. "I would have liked a daughter to be interested in the healing arts. It just seems like the sort of thing a mother ought to pass on to her daughter. But your brother Demaledon has been all I could have asked for in a pupil, and there are all my disciples. So why should your life be a reprise of mine?"

"None of the other girls became healers," said Svnae just a little petulantly.

"Quite true. They've followed their own paths: lovers and husbands and babies, gardens and dances."

"I have a husband too, you know," said Svnae.

"My child, my Dark-Eyed, I rejoice in your happiness. Isn't that enough?"

"But I want you to *understand* my life," cried Svnae.

"Do you understand mine?" asked the Saint of the World.

"Your life? Of course I do!"

Her mother looked at her, wryly amused.

"I have borne your father fourteen children. I have watched him march away to do terrible things, and I have bound up his wounds when he returned from doing them. I have managed the affairs of a household with over a thousand servants, most of them ogres. I have also kept up correspondence with my poor disciples, who are trying to carry on my work in my absence. What would you know of these things?"

Svnae was silent at that.

"You have always hunted for treasures, my dearest, and thrown open every door you saw, to know what lay beyond it," said the Saint of the World gently. "But there are still doors you have not opened. We can love each other, you and I, but how can we understand each other?"

"There must be a way," said Svnae.

"Now you look so much like your father, you make me laugh and cry at once. Don't let it trouble you, my Dark-Eyed; you are strong and happy and good, and I rejoice."

But Svnae went home that night to the room where Kendach sat, painting bright and intricate birds on kites. She took a chair opposite and stared at him.

"I want to have a child," she said.

He looked up, blinking in surprise. As her words sank in on him, he smiled and held out his arms to her.

Did she have a child? How else, when she had accomplished everything else she wanted to do?

A little girl came into the world. She was strong and healthy. She looked like her father, she looked like her mother; but mostly she looked like herself, and she surprised everyone.

Her father had also been one of many children, so there were no surprises for him. He knew how to bathe a baby, and could wrestle small squirming arms into sleeves like an expert.

Svnae, who had grown up in a nursery staffed by a dozen servants, proved to be rather inept at these things. She was shaken by her helplessness, and shaken by the helpless love she felt. Prior to this time she had found infants rather uninteresting, little blobs in swaddling to be briefly inspected and presented with silver cups that had their names and a good-fortune spell engraved on them.

But *her* infant—! She could lie for hours watching her child do no more than sleep, marveling at the tiny toothless yawn, the slow close of a little hand.

When the baby was old enough to travel, they wrapped her in a robe trimmed with pearls and took her to visit her maternal grandparents, laden with the usual gifts. Her lover went off to demonstrate the workings of his marvelous kites to her nieces and nephews. And Svnae bore her daughter to the Saint of the World in triumph.

"*Now* I've done something you understand," she said. The Saint of the World took up her little granddaughter and kissed her between the eyes.

"I hope that wasn't the only reason you bore her," she said.

"Well—no, of course not," Svnae protested, blushing. "I wanted to find out what motherhood was like."

"And what do you think it is like, my child?"

"It's awesome. It's holy. My entire life has been redefined by her existence," said Svnae fervently.

"Ah, yes," said the Saint of the World.

"I mean, this is creation at its roots. This is Power! I have brought an entirely new being into the world. A little mind that thinks! I can't wait to see what she thinks *about*, how she feels about things, what she'll say and do. What's ordinary magic to this?"

The baby began to fuss and the Lady rose to walk with her through the garden. Svnae followed close, groping for words.

"There's so much I can teach her, so much I can give her, so much I can share with her. Her first simple spells. Her first flight. Her first transformation. I'll teach her everything I know. We've got that house in Konen Feyy, and it'll be so convenient for Night School! She won't even have to find room and board. She can use all my old textbooks . . ."

But the baby kept crying, stretching out her little hands.

"Something she wants already," said the Lady. She picked a white flower and offered it to the child; but no, the little girl pointed beyond it. Svnae held out a crystal pendant, glittering with Power, throwing dancing lights; but the baby cried and reached upward. They looked up to see one of her father's kites, dancing merry and foolish on the wind.

The two women stood staring at it. They looked at the little girl. They looked at each other.

"Perhaps you shouldn't enroll her in Night School just yet," said the Saint of the World.

And Svnae realized, with dawning horror, that she might need to ask her mother for advice one day.

A Fowl Tale

EOIN COLFER

Irish author Eoin Colfer is the creator of the bestselling Artemis Fowl *series, which includes* Artemis Fowl, Artemis Fowl: The Arctic Incident, Artemis Fowl: The Eternity Code, *and, most recently,* Artemis Fowl: The Opal Deception. *His other books include* The Wish List, The Supernaturalist, Benny and Omar, Benny and Babe, The Legend of Spud Murphy, *three books for those age six and under,* Going Potty, Ed's Funny Feet, *and* Ed's Bed, *and a guide to his own series,* Artemis Fowl Files: The Ultimate Guide to the Best-selling Series. *His latest is the next Artemis book,* Artemis Fowl: The Lost Colony. *He grew up in Wexford, Ireland, where he still lives with his family.*

In the droll story that follows, he shows us that those prepared to sing for their supper must be careful just what they sing . . .

IN medieval Europe, travellers were always welcome to a bowl of stew on one condition—they were required to spin an interesting tale. On this occasion, an unusual traveller joins the queue of Erik the Boy King.

FINALLY, it was my turn to speak. And a good thing too because I was famished. I'll just spin them my yarn, I thought. Whatever it takes to get a bowl of stew, and maybe a good deal more.

"You there," said the boy king, pointing the sword at the knight below me. "Tell us a tale."

"Just a minute," I protested, swooping down to the table. "I believe I am next."

The assembly was surprised to hear a bird speak, but I didn't get the big reaction I usually get. Generally there are cries of aaarrgh! Witchcraft! And boil the demon chicken. But this time, just a few raised eyebrows. I suppose after the stories already told this day, the assembly has become accustomed to the fantastic.

I fluffed my feathers. "Well? Do I get my rightful turn? Will you deny a bird his feed?"

The boy king smiled. "Proceed, Master Chicken."

"I am not a chicken," I said, feeling slightly miffed. "I am a dove. It's a completely different thing. Chickens are dirty creatures who chatter incessantly and deposit their droppings on whatever patch of ground they happen to be inhabiting. We doves are far more discreet."

"Accept my humble apologies and pray proceed, Master Dove."

I bowed in thanks. Now for my story. Not mine, of course. There must be one I could drag up from childhood memories. I would make them drag mine from me.

"Ahem, yes. My story. Once there was a noble knight who searched far and wide for the holy grail."

A noble knight behind me in the queue raised a chain-mailed finger.

"That would be me, and that would be my story."

I changed tack hurriedly. "On a fine summer's day three little pigs decided to move out of their mother's house . . ."

"Heard it," said the boy king.

I tried again. "One morning, a lonely orphan received his invitation to attend wizard school."

The boy's sword quivered a hairbreadth from my beak. "The line is long, bird. Tell your tale or forfeit your meal."

I tried to make light of the situation. "There are only seven real stories anyway. What matter the tale, as long as it is well told?"

"There is only one story here and now, Master Dove," said the boy king, frowning. "And that is yours. Are you willing to share it?"

I snapped at an impertinent flea between my feathers. "The whole affair is a tad embarrassing. Not something one likes to talk about in polite society."

The knight chortled. "One talks about? Polite society? You're very well spoken, for a chicken."

"Dove!" I snapped. "And yes, polite society. I am, after all, royalty. Or I was, until I was transformed."

The knight elbowed a hermit beside him. "Don't tell me, you're the missing Prince Husnivarr."

I didn't answer, just clicked my beak modestly.

The knight drummed his fingers on an armoured forearm. "So, you're saying, little chicken, that you are Prince Husnivarr? Heir to the Mont Varr kingdom, not to mention the mountain of gold. But every one knows that the Husnivarr brat was transformed into a pig."

"That is so untrue," I chirped. "Well, perhaps I was something of a brat, but I was never a pig. Never. There was a pig in the vicinity when my transformation took place, and it caused some confusion, that's all."

"Whatever you say, porky," said the knight, winking at the assembly. I was really beginning to dislike that man.

"Speak, Prince," said the boy king, interrupting the general laughter. "Your own story this time."

It was time for my story. It was that or hunger.

"It is true," I began sadly. "I am Prince Husnivarr, or rather I was. This poor battered bird you see before you was once the heir to the richest kingdom on earth. I lived a privileged life in court. My duties were light and my comforts were many. I grew spoilt and petulant. My father, a noble king, decided that a good old-fashioned task would strengthen my character. One day he called me into his throne-room and sat me by his side.

" 'One day the big chair will be yours, Husni,' he said. 'And I don't think that you have the bottom to fill it. I've been watching lately, and you have no respect for your fellow man or beast. You need to learn that respect before you can be king.'

"There was a golden tray on his knee and on the tray rested a common grey rock. It was about the size of a rabbit's head and streaked with white.

" 'This is the Karma Stone,' my father explained. 'My magicians brought it back from Persia. We had to dig a large chunk from the mountain of gold to pay for it.'

" 'Very, eh, pretty,' I said, reaching to stroke the stone.

" 'Not so eager, Husnivarr,' said the king, grasping my wrist. 'The Karma Stone moves people who touch it through their circle of life. It accelerates their incarnations. Watch.'

"My father placed his hand on the stone and immediately transformed. He became a stoat, then a wolf, a tall shaggy beast that I could not identify, then, once more, himself. Finally, he removed his hand.

" 'You get what you deserve, you see. It only took me three incarnations to become a man. Strength of character, you see. And when I die, I will become a stoat once more. You, Husni, I suspect it will take you a thousand years to become human again. Would you like to know how many stages there will be for you?'

" 'No,' I replied.

" 'I insist,' said my father, placing my hand on the Karma Stone.

"My transformation was immediate. The world grew huge as I grew small, and only my human thought-process kept me from flying away. I was a mosquito.

" 'Aah,' said my gigantic father mournfully. 'It is worse than I thought. You will begin your next cycle as a mosquito. Very low on the reincarnation scale.'

"The urge to suck his blood quickly faded, as I transformed into a dung-beetle.

" 'Still an insect,' noted the king. 'I hope you become a mammal soon, for your mother's sake.'

"My shell popped and disappeared, fur sprouted along my back, and I became a rat. I could clearly see my own nose and the whiskers quivering like tiny foils at its tip.

" 'A mammal,' admitted my father. 'But not a very noble one.'

"Then disaster struck. A crazed pig, escaped from the kitchen, burst into the chamber, pursued by a trio of cleaver-wielding butchers. Pandemonium was immediate. I was in the throes of becoming a dove and could barely follow the sequence of events.

"The pig charged my father's chair, knocking him over backwards to the floor. His head cracked against the stone flags, knocking the life from his body. My contact with the Karma Stone was roughly broken before my human senses had asserted themselves. I had become a dove, with a dove's brain and vocabulary. The pig lunged, the butchers swiped their cleavers, and I flew. Oink, roar, and coo!

"I followed my dove's instincts and found an open window. In minutes, I was miles away, riding the tails of a west-bound wind. For two years I roamed the skies as a simple dove, with no inkling of what had befallen me. Until one summer, I made my home in the eaves of a cottage and heard human voices once more. These voices stirred something within me, waking memories and senses.

"I realised that I must return immediately to my grieving family and assure them that their son and heir is alive and well, if a little indisposed. Once they hear what my late father did to me, I feel sure that I will be welcomed with open wings, eh, arms. So that is my quest, and I have only stopped here for a much-needed meal."

I finished my tale, dipping my beak in a convenient water-jug. My story had been a success. Already the waiter was filling a bowl of stew.

The knight removed his helmet. "A fascinating story, chicken. Prince Husnivarr you say?"

"Alas, yes," I said. Sad yet noble.

"Amazing. The Karma Stone, you say?"

I snapped my beak. "Yes, yes. That's what happened."

The knight removed one gauntlet. "And tell me, chicken . . . I mean, Prince, about your famous family birth-mark."

Birth-mark? I had a famous birth-mark?

"Ah, yes. Of course. The heirs to the mountain of gold always have a birth-mark in the shape of a . . . birth-mark. The exact details escape me at the moment. Not all my memories have returned."

The knight peeled off his breastplate. "Let me refresh your memory. The birth-mark is in the shape of a peacock's fan. Rather like this one."

There was a birth-mark on the knight's side, in the shape of a peacock's fan.

I flapped my wings nervously. "So, that would mean that you would be . . ."

"Prince Husnivarr," completed the knight. "I've been away on a campaign. Not a pig or chicken in sight."

"This is ridiculous," I blustered. "I am Husnivarr, rightful heir to the . . ."

"Mountain of gold," completed the knight. "More of a molehill I'm afraid. Oh, it was a mountain once, but that was before empire tax and a few decades of war. I'd be surprised if there's a single sovereign left in the treasury now."

I felt like fainting. "No gold?"

"Not a penny."

"There's still the castle," I said, grasping at straws.

"There is that," agreed the knight. "A fine castle with portraits of me in every hall."

"Ah . . ." I could feel all eyes on me now. "Perhaps I exaggerated my story slightly . . ."

The boy king drew his sword again. "So, you're not a magical dove."

"No. A parrot actually. An albino parrot."

"And how did you learn to talk."

"I always knew how to talk. But I learned to understand in a magician's laboratory. Some chap called Marvin, I think."

"Merlin?" said the boy.

"That's the one. I think breathing in the gas from his potions boosted my parrot brain somewhat."

The knight broke the tension. He laughed until his armour rattled, and salty tears gathered in his beard.

"By God, a conniving parrot. I've heard it all now. I want to thank you, little chicken. I haven't laughed this much in a decade. Not since I was turned into a pig."

They were all laughing now, and I sensed that a meal might still be on offer. I waved a wing towards the steaming pot.

"I've told you a story, do I get a bowl? Just a small one. I eat like a bird."

The knight snatched a bowl from a passing steward. "Of course, young prince. Your lies are worth at least a few chunks of boiled meat."

I peered into the bowl. The soup was grey and unappealing.

"And what meat would that be?" I asked.

Prince Husnivarr winked maliciously.

"Chicken," he replied.

Slipping Sideways
Through Eternity

JANE YOLEN

Millions of devout Jews set a place for Elijah at the table every Passover—what would happen, though, if he actually showed up . . .

One of the most distinguished of modern fantasists, Jane Yolen has been compared to writers such as Oscar Wilde and Charles Perrault, and has been called "the Hans Christian Andersen of the Twentieth Century." Primarily known for her work for children and young adults, Yolen has produced over 270 books, including novels, collections of short stories, poetry collections, picture books, biographies, and a book of essays on folklore and fairy tales. She has received the World Fantasy Award, the Golden Kite Award, and the Caldecott Medal, and has been a finalist for the National Book Award, as well as winning two Nebula Awards, for her stories "Lost Girls" and "Sister Emily's Lightship." Her more adult-oriented fantasy has appeared in collections such as Tales of Wonder, Merlin's Booke, Sister Emily's Lightship, Storyteller, Dragonfield and Other Stories, *and* Once Upon a Time (She Said), *and in such novels as* Cards of Grief, Sister Light/Sister Dark, White Jenna, The One-Armed Queen, *and* Briar Rose. *Her children's fantasy collections include* Twelve Impossible Things, Here There Be Dragons, Here There Be Witches, Here There Be Angels, Here There Be Ghosts, Here There Be Unicorns, Dream Weaver, *and* The Girl Who Cried Flowers. *Her children's fantasy novels range from high fantasy like* The Magic Three of Solatia, *the Young Merlin Trilogy,* Sword of the Rightful King, Wizard's Hall, *and* Dragon's Boy *to time travel such as* The Devil's Arithmetic, *to urban fantasy like the Tartan Magic books:* Wizard's Map, The Pictish Child, *and* The Bagpiper's Ghost, *to science fiction fantasy, most notably the Pit Dragon trilogy. Her most recent fantasy novels are* Pay the Piper *and* Troll Bridge *both with Adam Stemple, and* The Year's Best Science Fiction and Fantasy for Teens, *coedited with Patrick Nielsen Hayden. She and her family live part of the year in Massachusetts and part in Scotland.*

SHANNA opened the door slowly and peered out. The lake surface ruffled in the wind but there was no one on it. She shrugged, came back to the seder table. "No one there," she said. She was only five after all, ten years younger than me. She got to ask the questions, open the door. I got to drink watered wine. It was some sort of trade-off.

Everyone laughed.

"Elijah is there, only you can't see him," Nonny said.

But she was wrong. I could see him.

Elijah stood in the doorway, tall, gaunt, somewhere between a concentration camp victim and a Beat poet. I read a lot of poetry. Then I paint the poems, the words singing their colors onto the page. Sometimes I think I was born in the wrong century. Actually, I *know* I was born in the wrong century.

Elijah saw me see him and nodded. His eyes were black, his beard black and wavy, like a Labrador's coat. When he smiled, his eyes nearly closed shut. His tongue came out of his mouth tentatively, licked his upper lip. It was the pink of my toe shoes. Not that I dance anymore. Pink toe shoes and *The Nutcracker*. That's for babies. Now I'm into horses. But his tongue was so pink against his black beard, it made me tremble. I'm not sure why.

I motioned to the chair. No one but Elijah noticed.

He shook his head, his mouth formed the words: "Not yet." Then he turned and left, slipping sideways through eternity.

"He's gone," I said.

"No," Nonny contradicted, shaking her head, the blue hair a helmet that never moved. "Elijah is never gone. He is always here." But she looked at me strangely, her black-button eyes shining.

I took another sip of the watered wine.

THE next time I saw Elijah was in shul. It's the only temple on the island so everyone Jewish goes there, even though it's a Reform temple. I was sitting snuggled up next to Shanna, more for the warmth than friendship. Shanna's okay, when she's quiet and cuddly. But little sisters can be a pain.

Especially when they're ten years younger, an embarrassment, and a sign that your parents—your parents, for G-d's sake—are still having sex.

We were in the middle of one of Rabbi Shiller's long, rambling book reports. He rarely says anything religious. My mother likes that. Thinks it's important. "Keeps us in touch with the greater world," she says. Meaning non-Jews. I get enough book reports in school in my AP classes, where we call them essays but they are really only high school book reports, though with bigger words. Besides, the rabbi was talking about *Maus*, which I'd just done an AP report on, and got an A, and my insights were better than his. So I snuggled close to Shanna and closed my eyes.

Or I almost closed my eyes.

And there, standing on the bima, finger on his lips, was Elijah, same black eyes, same black wavy beard, same pink tongue. I was not sure if he was shushing me or the rabbi but he was definitely shushing someone.

I sat up, pushed Shanna off me, looked around to see if anyone else had noticed him.

But the congregation was intent on the rabbi, who had just announced that in *Maus*, "The commentary should disrupt the facile linear progression of the narration, introduce alternative interpretations, question any partial conclusion, withstand the need for closure . . ." which I recognized immediately as a quote from Friedlander. The rabbi had been doing his research online. And he was not giving credit where credit was due, as my AP English teacher, V. Louise always reminds us. She would have had him gutted for breakfast.

I glanced back at Elijah, who was shaking his head, as if he, too, knew the rabbi was a plagiarist. But maybe if you had to give a sermon every Friday night for your entire life, plagiarism becomes a necessity.

To be certain I wasn't the only kid seeing things, I checked on my friends. Barry Goldblatt was picking boogers from his nose. Nothing new there. Marcia Damashek was whispering to her mother. They even dress alike. Carol Tropp had leaned forward, not to listen to the rabbi but to tap Gordon Berliner on the shoulder. She has a thing for him, though I can't imagine why. He may be funny—like a stand-up comic—but he's short and he smells.

I kept checking around. Every single one of the kids I knew was distracted. No one seemed to have seen Elijah but me. And this time I had no watered wine to blame.

Clearly, I thought, clearly I'm having a psychotic break. We studied psychotic breaks in our psychology class. They aren't pretty. Either that, or Elijah, that consummate time traveler, that tricky wizard of forever, was really standing behind the rabbi and snorting into a rather dirty handkerchief, the color of leaf mold. Couldn't he take some time out of his travels to go to a Laundromat? We've got several downtown I could tell him about.

I shook my head and Elijah looked up again, winked at me, and slipped sideways into some sort of time stream, and was gone. He didn't even disturb the motes of sunlight dusting the front of the ark.

Standing, I pushed past my sister and mother and father and walked out of the hall. I know they thought I had to pee, but that's not what I was doing. I went downstairs to wait in the religious center till the service was over. The door to the middle students' classroom was open and I went in. Turning on the light, I sighed, feeling safe. Here was where I'd studied Hebrew lessons with Mrs. Goldin for so many years. Where I'd learned about being Jewish. Where no one had ever said Elijah was real. I mean, we're Reform Jews, after all. We leave that sort of thing to the Chassids. Leaping in the air, having visions, wearing bad hats and worse wigs. Real nineteenth-century stuff.

I idled my way over to the kids' bookcase. Lots of books there. We Jews are big on books. The People of the Book and all. My father being a professor of literature at the university, we have a house filled with books. Even the bathrooms have bookshelves. We joke about the difference between litter-ature and literature. One to be used in the bathroom, the other to be read. Those sort of jokes.

My mom is a painter but even she reads. Not that I mind. I'm a big bookie myself, though I don't take bets on it. That's another family joke!

Finding a piece of gray poster paper, I began to doodle on it with a Magic Marker. Mom says that doodling concentrates the mind. I didn't draw my usual—horses. Instead I drew Elijah's head: the wavy hair, the dark beard, the tongue lolling out, like a dog's. A few more quick lines, and I turned him into a retriever.

"And what do you retrieve?" I asked my drawing. The drawing was silent. I guess the psychotic didn't break that far. Yeah—I have the family sense of humor.

I thought maybe there'd be a book or two in the classroom on Elijah. Squatting, I quickly scanned down the spines. I was right. Not one book but a whole bunch. A regular Jewish pop star.

Settling down to read the first one, I felt a tap on my shoulder that didn't make me jump as much as it set off a series of tremors running down my backbone.

I turned slowly and looked up into Elijah's long face. Close, he was younger than I'd thought, the beard disguising the fact that he was probably only in his twenties. A Jewish Captain Jack Sparrow with a yarmulke instead of a tricornered hat.

He crooked his finger at me, held out his hand.

Years of stranger-danger conversations flashed through my head. But who could be afraid of a figment of her imagination? Besides, he was cool-looking in a Goth beatnik kind of way.

I put my hand in his and stood. His hand seemed real enough.

We turned some sort of corner in the middle of the room, slid sideways, and found ourselves in a long gray corridor.

WAS I afraid?

I was fascinated. It was like being in a sci-fi movie. The corridor flickered with flashes of starlight. Meteors rushed by. And a strange wandering sun seemed to be moving counterclockwise.

"Where are we go . . . ?" I began, the words floating out of my mouth like the balloons in a comic strip.

He put a finger of his free hand on his lips and I ate the rest of my question. What did it matter? We were science-fictional wanderers on a metaphysical road.

The sound of wind got wilder and wilder until it felt as if we were in a tunnel with trains racing by us on all sides. And then suddenly everything went quiet. The gray lifted, the flashes were gone, and we stepped out of the corridor into . . . into an even grayer world, full of mud.

I craned my neck trying to see where we were.

Elijah put his hands on both sides of my head and drew me around till we were facing.

"Do not look yet, Rebecca," he said to me, his voice made soft by his accent.

Was I surprised that he knew my name? I was beyond surprise.

"Is this place . . . bad?" I asked.

"Very bad."

"Am I dead and in hell?"

"No, though this is a kind of hell." His face, always long, grew longer with sadness. Or anger. It was hard to tell.

"Why are we here?" I trembled as I spoke.

"Ah, Rebecca—that is always the most important question." His r's rattled like a teakettle left too long on the stove. "The question we all need to ask of the universe." He smiled at me. "You are here because I need you."

For a moment, the grayness around us seemed to lighten.

Then he added, "You are here because you saw me." He dropped his hands to my shoulders.

"I saw you?"

He smiled, and, for the first time, I realized there was a gap between his top front teeth. And that the teeth were very white. Okay, he might not hit the Laundromat often enough, but he knew a thing or three about brushing.

"I saw you? So why is that such a big deal?" I think I knew even before he told me.

Shrugging, he said, "Few see me, Rebecca. Fewer still can slip sideways through time with me."

"Through time?" Now I looked around. The place was a flat treeless plain, not so much gray as hopeless. "Where are we?" I asked again.

He laughed into my hair. " 'When are we?' is the question you should be asking."

I gulped, trying to swallow down something awful-tasting that seemed to have lodged in my throat. "Am I crazy?"

"No more than any great artist."

He knew I did art?

"You are a really fine artist. Remember, Rebecca, I travel through time. Past and future, they are all as one to me."

Even in that gray world, I felt a flutter in my breast. My cheeks grew hot with pleasure. A great artist. A fine artist. In the future. Then I shook my head. Now I knew I was dreaming. Too much watered wine at the seder. I was probably asleep with my cheek on Nonny's white tablecloth. Yet in my dream I painted a picture of Elijah brooding in that open door, dark and hungry, his lips slightly moist with secrets, his mouth framing an invitation in a language both dead and alive.

"You will paint that picture," he said, as if reading my mind. "And it will make the world notice you. It will make me notice you. But not now. Now we have work to do." He took my hand.

"What work?"

"Look closely."

This time when I looked I saw that the flat treeless plain was not empty. There were humans walking about, women, girls, all dressed in gray. Gray skirts, gray shirts, gray scarves on their heads, gray sandals or boots. Oh, I could see that the clothes they wore had not always been such a color, but had been worn thin and made old by terror and tragedy and hopelessness.

"You must bring them away," Elijah said. "Those who will go with you."

"You are the time traveler, the magician," I told him. "Why don't you do it?"

That long face looked down at me, his dark brown eyes softening. "They do not see me."

"Will they see me?" I asked. But I already knew. They were coming toward me, hands out.

"Elijah," I asked him, "how will I talk to them?"

He reached out a hand and touched my lips. "You will find a way, Rebecca. Now go. I can tell you no more." Then he disappeared, like the Cheshire cat, until there was only his mouth, and it wasn't smiling. Then he was gone entirely.

I turned to the women and let them gather me in.

They told me where we were, how they were there. I had read their stories in books so I had no reason to disbelieve them. We were in a camp.

Oh, not a summer camp with square dances and macramé projects and water sports. I'd been to those. Girl Scout camp, art camp, music camp. My parents, like all their friends, saw the summer as a time to ship-the-kids-off-to-camp. Some were like boot camp and some were like spas.

This was a Camp.

I asked the question that Elijah told me was the one I should be asking. "When are we?"

And when they told me—1943—I couldn't find the wherewithal to be surprised. I'd already seen a ghost out of time, traveled with him across a sci-fi landscape, been told about the future. Why not be landed in the past?

"Thanks for nothing, Elijah," I whispered.

Something—someone—whispered in my ear, the accent softening what he had to say. "Thanks for everything, Rebecca."

"I've done nothing," I whined.

"You will," he said.

And the women, hearing only me, answered, "None of us have done anything to put us in this place."

✳

SO my time in the Camp began. It was not Auschwitz or Dachau or Sobibor or Buchenwald or Treblinka, names I would have recognized at once.

"Where are we?"

"Near Lublin," one woman told me, her eyes a startling blue in that gray face.

I knew that name. Squinting my eyes, I tried to remember. And then I did. My great-grandmother had been born in Lublin.

"Do you know a . . ." I stopped. I only knew my great-grandmother's married name. Morewitz. What good would that do? Besides, she'd come over to America as a child anyway, and was dead long before I was born. I changed the sentence. "Do you know a good way to escape?"

They laughed, a gray kind of laugh. "And would we still be here if we did?" said the woman with the blue eyes. Her hand described a circle that took in the gray place.

I followed that circle with my eyes and saw a gray building, gray with settled ash. Ash. Something had been burned there. A lot of somethings. It was then I really understood what place Elijah had brought me to.

"So this a concentration camp?" I asked, though of course I already knew.

"There is nothing to concentrate on here, except putting one foot in front of the other," said the blue-eyed woman.

"And putting one bit of potato into your open mouth," said another.

"Not a concentration camp," said a third, "but a death camp."

"Hush," said the blue-eyed woman, looking over her shoulder.

I looked where she was looking but there was no one there to hear us.

"I have to get out of here," I said. Then bit my lip. "We all have to get out of here."

A gray child with eyes as black as buttons peeked from behind the skirts of the blue-eyed woman. She pointed to one of the buildings, which had an ominous metal door that was standing open. Like an open mouth waiting for those potatoes, I thought.

"That is the only way out," she said. Her face was a child's but her voice was old.

I took a deep breath, breathed in ash, and said, "We will not go that way. I promise."

The women moved away from me as one, leaving the child behind. One whispered hoarsely to me over her shoulder, "This is a place of broken promises. If you do not understand that, you will not live a moment longer." Then she said to the child, "Masha, it's time to go to bed. Morning comes too soon." But she was speaking to me as well.

The child slipped her cold gray hand in mind. "I believe your promise," she said. She looked up at me and smiled, as if smiling was something new that she needed to practice.

I smiled down at her and squeezed her hand. But I'd been a fool to promise her any such thing, and she was a fool to believe me.

"Elijah . . ." I began, "Elijah will help us." But he'd helped me into this mess, then disappeared. I realized with a sinking feeling that I was on my own here. Now. Whenever.

"Elijah the magician?" She scarcely seemed to breathe, staring at me with her black-button eyes.

I nodded, wondering what kind of magic could get us away from this terrible place and time.

FOLLOWING the women, like a lamb after old ewes, the girl led me into a building that was filled with wide triple bunk beds. There were no sheets or pillows or blankets on the beds, only hard slats to lie upon. The only warmth at night came from the people who slept on either side. I had read about this, seen movies. What Jewish kid hadn't?

The cold was no worse than a bad camping trip. The slats on the boards were like lying on the ground. But the smell—there were three hundred or more women squeezed into that building, with no bathing facilities but buckets of cold water. No one had a change of clothing; some must have been living in the same dresses for months. And those were the lucky ones, for they were still alive.

Masha snuggled next to me, her body now a little furnace, a warm spot against me. On the other side was the blue-eyed woman who introduced herself as Eva. But that first night my head raced with bizarre imaginings. Either I was crazy or dreaming. Maybe I'd had some kind of psychotic break—like my cousin Rachael, who one night after a rave party thought she was in prison and tried to escape through a window, which turned out to be on the third floor of their apartment building. I just couldn't stop from wondering and I didn't sleep at all. A mistake, it turned out. By morning I was exhausted. Besides, sleep was the one real escape from that place. It was why the women went to bed, side by side, as eagerly as if heading for a party. After that there was the work.

YES, there was work. That first morning they showed me. It wasn't difficult work—not as difficult as the work the men were doing, breaking stones on the other side of the barbed wire—but still it broke the heart and spirit. We were to take belongings from the suitcases inmates had brought with them, separating out all the shoes in one pile, clothing in another on long, wooden tables. Jewelry and money went into a third pile that was given to the blovoka—the head of the sorters—at day's end. She had to give it to the soldiers who ran the camp. Then there were family photographs and family Bibles and books of commentary and books of poetry. Piles of women's wigs and a huge pile of medicines, enough pills and potions for an army of hypochondriacs. There were packets of letters and stacks of documents, even official-looking contracts and certificates of graduation from law schools and medical schools. And then there was the pile of personal items: toothbrushes and hairbrushes and nail files and powder puffs. Everything that someone leaving home in a hurry and for the last time would carry.

I tried to think what I would have taken away with me had someone knocked on our door and said we had just minutes to pack up and leave for a resettlement camp, which is what all these people had been told. My diary and my iPod for sure, my underwear and several boxes of Tampax, toothbrush, hairbrush, blow-dryer, the book of poems my boyfriend had given me, a box of grease pencils and a sketchbook of course, and the latest Holly Black novel, which I hadn't had time to read yet. If that sounds pathetic, it's a whole lot less pathetic than the actual stuff we had to sort through.

And of course the entire time we were sorting, I alone knew what it all meant. That there were these same kinds of concentration camps throughout Poland and Germany. That six million Jews and six million other people were going to die in these awful places. And my having that knowledge was not going to help a single one of them.

Boy, it's going to be hard for me ever to go to a summer camp again, I thought. If I get out of here in one piece. That's when I began crying and calling out for Elijah.

"Who's Elijah?" a girl my age asked, putting an arm around me. "Your brother? Your boyfriend? Is he here? On the men's side?"

I turned, wiped my nose on my sleeve, and opened my mouth to tell her. When I realized how crazy it sounded, I said merely, "Something like that." And then I turned back to work.

The temptation to take a hairbrush or toothbrush or nail file back to our building was enormous.

But little Masha warned me that the guards searched everyone. "And if they find you with contraband," she said—without stumbling on the big word, so I knew it was one everyone used—"you go up in smoke."

The way she said that, so casually, but clearly understanding what it meant, made my entire backbone go cold. I nodded. I wasn't about to be cremated over a broken fingernail or messy hair. I left everything on the long tables.

THE days were long, the nights too short. I was a week at the camp and fell into a kind of daze. I walked, I worked, I ate when someone put a potato in my hand, but I had retreated somewhere inside myself.

Masha often took my hand and led me about, telling me what things to do. Saying, "Don't become a musselman." And one day—a day as gray as the ash covering the buildings, gray clouds scudding across the skies, I heard her.

"Musselman?" I asked.

She shrugged. A girl standing next to me in the work line explained. "They are the shadows in the shadows. The ones who give up. Who die before they are dead." She pointed out the grimed window to a woman who looked like a walking skeleton dressed in rags. "She is a mussleman and will not need to go up in smoke. She is already gone."

I shook my head vehemently. "I am not that."

Masha grabbed my hand and pulled. "Then wake up. You promised."

And I remembered my promise. My foolish promise. I looked out the window again and the woman was indeed gone. In her place stood Elijah, staring at me. He put a finger to the side of his nose and looked sad. The lines of his long face were repeated in the length of his nose. There were shadows, dark blue with streaks of brown, under his eyes. My hand sketched them.

"What are you doing?" Masha asked me.

"I need to paint something," I said.

"Foolishness," the girl next to me said.

"No—art is never foolish," I told her. "It is life-giving."

She laughed roughly and moved away from me as if I had something contagious.

I looked over the tables—the boxes of pills, the jewelry, the documents, the little baby shoes, the old women's handbags. And finally, I found a battered box of colored chalks some child must have carried with her. I picked the box up, grabbed up a marriage certificate, and went into a corner.

"What are you doing?" asked the blovoka. "Get back here or I will have to report you."

But I paid no attention to her. I sat down on the filthy floor, turned the certificate over, and started to draw. With black chalk I outlined Elijah's body and the long oval of his face. I overlayered the outline with white till it was gray as ash. Having no gum eraser, I was careful with what I drew, yet not too careful, knowing that a good painting had to look effortless. At home I would have worked with Conté pastels. I had a box of twenty-four. But I used what I had, a box of twelve chalks, most of them in pieces. To keep my drawing from smudging, at home I would have coated the whole thing with a light misting of hairspray. But home was a long way—and a long time—from here. And hairspray was, I guessed, a thing of the future.

The blovoka began to yell at me. "Get up! Get up!" And suddenly there was a flurry of legs around me, as some of the women were shouting the same.

Masha sneaked through the forest of legs and sat by me. "What are you doing?"

"I am making a picture of someone you need to see," I said. I sketched in the long nose, the black and wavy beard, and the closed-eye smile. I found a pink for his lips, then smudged them purposefully with fingers that still had black chalk on the tips.

The blovoka had stopped yelling at me and was now yelling at the women who had formed a wall around Masha and me.

I kept drawing, using my fingers, the flat of my hand, my right thumb. I spit onto my left fingers and rubbed them down the line of his body. With the black chalk I filled in his long black coat. I used the white chalk for highlights, and to fill in around his black eyes. Brown chalk buffed in skin tones, which I then layered on top with the ashy gray.

"I see him. I see him," Masha said to me. "Is it Elijah?" She put her hand on the black coat, and her palm and small fingers became black at the tips.

Two of the women standing guard above us drew in a quick breath, and one said to the other, "I see him, too." It was Eva's voice. She knelt down and touched the paper.

Someone suddenly called my name. A man. I looked up. Elijah stood there, in the midst of all the women, though none of them seemed to notice him.

"Masha," I said urgently, "do you see him there?" I took her head in my hands and gently turned it so she was looking up as well.

"How did he get here?" she asked, pointing right at him. "In the women's side?"

Eva gasped at the sight of him.

But Elijah smiled, holding out his hands. I stood and took his right hand and Masha took his left. Eva grabbed hold of Masha's waist as if to drag her from me.

"There they are!" came the blovoka's shrill voice. "There!" The rest of the women had scattered back to the sorting tables, and Masha, Eva, and I were in her line of sight. Beside the blovoka were two armed guards.

They pulled out their guns.

This time Elijah laughed. He dragged us toward him, and then we turned a corner in the middle of that room, sliding sideways into a familiar long gray corridor.

Eva gasped again, then was silent, as if nothing more could surprise her. She held tight to Masha's waist.

And then we were flying through the flickering starlight and rushing meteors. A strange sun stood still overhead. As suddenly as they'd begun, the lights and sounds stopped when we came to the other side.

Masha dropped Elijah's hand and looked around, but Eva never let go of her waist.

This time I knew to ask the right question. "When are we?"

Elijah said, "We are still in the same year but five thousand miles away. We are in America now."

"We are in America then," I said.

He nodded. "Then," and he touched my shoulder. "Kiss the child, Rebecca. Assure her that she will be well taken care of here." His face seemed no longer gray, but blanched, as if the traveling had taken much of his energy. "The woman, while not her own mother, will watch over her."

"Eva," I said. "First mother."

"Of course." We both nodded at the irony.

"But I can't just leave her," I said, though I saw the two of them had already found a table of food and were happily filching stuff and hiding it in their pockets.

"You must. The child will have a fine life, a good family."

"Will I ever see her again?"

"No, Rebecca, she will be dead before you are born. Besides, you have pictures to paint. Of me." He smile was seductive, as if he were already posing for me.

I think my jaw dropped open. But not for long. "Why . . . you . . . you." Suddenly I couldn't think of a word bad enough for him. Had this whole thing, this trip into the past, into that awful place, had it just been to satisfy his enormous ego? I stared at him. His face was positively gaunt, the eyes like a shark's, dead giving back no light. How could I ever have found him intriguing? My cheeks burned with shame. "I'll never paint that picture. Never."

He held up his hands as if to ward off the blow from my words. "Hush, hush, Rebecca. The picture has to be painted. This is not about me but about you. Not about you but about your people. For the children of the great Jewish diaspora. To remind them of who they are. It will begin a renaissance in Judaism that will last well beyond your life and the lives of your great-great-grandchildren and to the twentieth generation."

I don't know what stunned me more—that a picture I was to paint someday would have that power, or that I would have great-great-grandchildren. I mean—I was only fifteen after all; who could think that far?

"But why me? And why Masha? Why Eva?"

He glanced over his shoulder at where Masha was sitting, now surrounded by a group of children her own age. She seemed to be playing, all that lost innocence returned to her in a single moment. Eva stood with her back to the wall, watching carefully, already Masha's guardian, her angel, her mother. Elijah turned back and cocked his head to one side. "Surely you have figured it out by now."

I looked at Masha again. She looked over at me and smiled. It was my sister's smile. How could I have not known—except Masha had never smiled before. Not in the camp, where there was nothing to smile at. Of course. My sister had been named after our great-grandmother, Mashanna.

"If she'd died in the camp, you would never have been born," Elijah said, even as he started to fade. "The picture never would have been painted. The great renaissance never to happen."

"But I was born . . ." I began.

"Born to paint," he said, before grabbing my hand and dragging us both sideways into the future and home.

The Stranger's Hands

TAD WILLIAMS

Tad Williams became an international bestseller with his very first novel, Tailchaser's
Song, *and the high quality of his output and the devotion of his readers has kept him
on the top of the charts ever since. His other novels include the* Memory, Sorrow and
Thorn *series (* The Dragonbone Chair, Stone of Farewell, To Green Angel Tower*),
the* Otherland *series (* City of Golden Shadow, River of Blue Fire, Mountain of
Black Glass, Sea of Silver Light*),* Caliban's Hour, Child of an Ancient City
(with Nina Kiriki Hoffman), and The War of The Flowers. *He is currently finishing
the* Shadowmarch *series (* Shadowmarch, Shadowplay, *and* Shadowrise*). In addition to his novels, Williams writes comic books for DC Comics (* Aquaman, The
Next, Factory*) as well as film and television scripts. He lives with his family in the
San Francisco Bay Area.*

    *In the ingenious story that follows, he suggests that the problem with using magic to
get your Heart's Desire is that you might actually get it . . .*

PEOPLE in the village had been whispering for days about the two
    vagabonds in Squire's Wood, but the boy Tobias was the first to speak
to them.

    Tobias was a somewhat wayward lad, and the fact that he should have
been grazing his father's sheep on the hill above the forest at that hour more
or less assured the sheep in question would be wandering along the shady
edges of the wood instead, with Tobias wandering right behind them.

    It was not until he saw a drift of smoke twining like a gray scarf
through the trees that the boy remembered that strangers had been seen
in the wood. He felt a moment of fear: why would anyone live out of

doors in the cold nights and flurries of autumn rain if they were God-fearing folk? Only robbers and dangerous madmen dwelt under the un-sheltered sky. Everyone knew that.

If he had been a fraction less headstrong, Tobias would have turned around then and hurried back to the hillside, perhaps even remembering to take his father's sheep with him, but there was a part of him, a strong part, that hated *not knowing* things worse than anything. It was the part that had once caused him to pull the leg off a frog, just to find out what it would do. (It did very little, and died soon after with what Tobias felt guiltily certain was an accusatory look in its bulging eyes.) It was also the reason he had dented his father's best scythe when he had used it to try to cut down a tree, and why he had dumped the contents of his mother's precious sewing basket all over the ground—a search for knowledge that ended with Tobias spending all afternoon in the fading light on his hands and knees, locating every last needle and pin he had spilled. Once this rebel voice had even led him several miles out of the village, on a quest for the town of Eader's Church, which he had heard was so big that the streets actually had names. His father and two other men had caught up to him an hour after sunset as he sat exhausted and hungry by the side of the road. He had got a whipping for it, of course, but for young Tobias whippings were part of the cost of doing business.

So now, instead of turning and leaving the woods and its perilous in-habitants behind (for the sake of his father's livestock if nothing else), he followed the trail of smoke back to its source, a small cookfire in a clear-ing. A small man with a ratlike face was tending the flames, his wrinkles made so deep and dark by grime he looked like an apple-doll. His large companion, who sat on a stone beside the fire and did not look up even when Tobias stepped on a twig and made the little man jump, was so odd to look at that the boy could not help shivering. The large man's head was shaved, albeit poorly in some places, and the skull beneath the skin bulged in places that it should not. His bony jaw hung slack, the tongue visible in the space between top and bottom teeth, and although he did not seem blind, the eyes in the deep sockets were dull as dirty stones.

If the big man was paying no attention, the little man was. He stared at Tobias like a dog trying to decide whether to bark or run.

"Your wood's too wet," the boy told him.

"What?"

"You'll get mostly smoke and little fire from that. Do you want smoke?"

The small man frowned, but in dismay, not anger. "I want to cook this fish." He had the sound of a southerner, the words stretched and misshapen. Tobias wondered why they couldn't learn to speak properly. He squinted at the man's supper with the eye of an experienced angler. "It's small."

"It's better than starving," the man pointed out.

"Well, then, I'll show you." Tobias quickly found enough dry wood to rebuild the fire and within a short time the little man was cooking the fish over it on a long stick. His large companion still had not moved or spoken, had not even seemed to notice the newcomer in their camp.

"Thanks for your kindness," the small man said. "I am Feliks. We are new to this."

"My name's Tobias," the boy said, basking in the glow of his own helpfulness. "What does that mean, 'new'?"

"We have been living somewhere there was food." Feliks shrugged. "The food ran out."

Tobias stared at the other man, who still gazed at nothing, only the slow movement of his chest behind his dark, travel-worn robe showing that he was something other than a statue. "What's *his* name?"

Feliks hesitated for a moment. "Eli." He said it in the southern way, the last syllable rising like a shorebird's cry—Eh-*lee*. "He was my master, but he . . . something happened to him. He lost his wits."

Tobias now examined the big man with unhidden interest—if he had no wits, it couldn't be rude to stare, could it? "What happened?"

"The roof fell on him." Feliks took the fish from the stick, burning his fingers so that he almost dropped it—Tobias was amused by how many things the man didn't know how to do—and then cut it into two pieces with a knife, handing the larger piece to the silent giant. Eli moved for the first time; he took the fish without looking at it, put it in his mouth, and chewed with bovine patience. Feliks began to eat the other piece, then turned shamefacedly to Tobias. "I should offer some to you, for your kindness."

Tobias was old enough to understand this would not be a small sacrifice for Feliks. "No, I'll eat at home. And I'd better go now or Father will have the strap out." He looked through the trees to the angle of the sun, which was definitely lower than he would have liked. "He'll have the strap out, anyway." The boy stood. "I'll come back tomorrow, though. I can help you catch better fish than that one." He hesitated. "Have you been to other places? Other villages, even towns?"

Feliks nodded slowly. "Many places. Many cities all over the Middle Lands."

"Cities!" Tobias swayed a little, faint-headed at the thought. "Real cities? I'll be back!"

The tall man named Eli suddenly put out his hand, a gesture so startling after his hour of near immobility that Tobias recoiled as though from a snake.

"He . . . I think he wants to thank you," Feliks said. "Go ahead, boy—take his hand. He was a great man once."

Tobias slowly extended his own small hand, wondering if this might be the beginning of some cruel or even murderous trick—if he had been too trusting after all. Eli's hand was big, knob-knuckled, and smudged with dirt, and it closed on the boy's slim fingers like a church door swinging closed.

Then Tobias vanished.

✳

WHEN two days had passed with no sign of the boy, suspicion of course fell on the two strangers living in Squire's Wood. When the man named Feliks admitted that they had seen the child and spoken to him, the shireward and several local fellows dragged them out of the forest and chained them in wooden stocks beside the well in the center of the village, where everyone could see them and marvel at their infamy. Feliks tearfully continued to insist that they had done nothing to harm the boy, that they did not know where he had gone—both things true, as it turned out—but even if the two men had not been strangers and thus naturally suspect, the villagers could see that the big one was plainly touched, perhaps even demon-possessed, and almost no one felt anything for them but horror and disgust.

The lone exception was Father Bannity, the village priest, who felt that it was a troubling thing to imprison people simply because they were strangers, although he dared not say so aloud. He himself had been a stranger to the village when he had first arrived twenty years earlier (in fact, older villagers still referred to him as "the new priest"), and so he had a certain empathy for those who might find themselves judged harshly simply because their grandfathers and great-grandfathers were not buried in the local churchyard. Also, since in his middle life he had experienced a crisis of faith, leading him to doubt many of the most famous and popular tenets of his own religion, he was doubly unwilling to assume the guilt of someone else simply because they were not part of the familiar herd. So Father Bannity took it on himself to make sure the two prisoners had enough food and water to survive. It would be a long wait for the King's Prosecutor General to arrive—his circuit covered at least a dozen villages and lasted a full cycle of the moon—and even if the two were guilty of killing the poor child and hiding his body, Father Bannity did not want them to die before this could be discovered for certain.

As the small man, Feliks, grew to trust him, he at last told Bannity what he swore was the true story of what had happened that day, that the boy had touched big Eli's hand and then disappeared like a soap bubble popping. Father Bannity was not quite certain what to think, whether this was a true mystery or only the precursor to a confession, a man easing gradually into a guilty admission as into a scalding bath, but he stuck by his resolution to treat them as innocent until they told him otherwise, or events proved the worst to have happened.

One day, as he was holding a ladle of water to Eli's dry lips, the big man suddenly looked at him almost as if seeing him for the first time, a flash of life in the dull, bestial eyes that Bannity had not seen before. Startled, the priest dropped the ladle. The big man lifted his hand as far as he could with his wrist restrained by the stocks and spread his long fingers like some strange flower blooming.

"Don't," whispered Feliks. "That's what the boy did."

Father Bannity hesitated for only a moment. Something in the big man's strange gaze, something solemn and distant but not unkind, convinced him. He reached out and allowed Eli's hand to fold around his.

For a startling moment Bannity thought he had become a fish, jerked thrashing out of the river and up into the daylight, blinded by the sun and its prismatic colors, dazzled by the burning air. Then, a half instant later, he realized it was as though he had been out of the water for years, and now had suddenly been plunged back *into* it: everything that had withered in him suddenly sprang back to life, all the small losses of the passing days and months—color, feeling, ecstasy. The feeling was so strong, so overwhelming, that he could not even answer Feliks's worried questions as he staggered away.

Bannity *knew* again. He had forgotten what it felt like, but now he remembered, and the thunderous force of belief returning betrayed how much he had lost. God had sent him a miracle in the person of the silent giant, and with that single touch, a world that had slowly turned gray around him over the years had been kindled back into flaming life.

God was in everything again, just as He had been when Bannity was a child, when he had been able to imagine nothing better than to serve Him.

God was alive inside him. He had experienced a miracle.

It was only when the first surge of ecstatic happiness had become a little more ordinary, if no less pleasurable, that Father Bannity realized nothing tangible had actually changed. It wasn't so much that God had shown him a miracle, a sign, it was more as if touching the giant's hand had reawakened him to the love of God he had once had, but which had slipped away from him.

It was Eli, he realized, although undoubtedly acting as God's messenger, who had given him back his love of the Lord, his belief in a living Creation, and most of all, his certainty that what *was* was *meant to be.*

The silent, damaged man had given Bannity his heart's desire, even though the priest himself had not known what it was.

Grateful, renewed, the priest resolved to speak on behalf of the two prisoners when the Prosecutor General returned to the village, to tell the truth even if it meant admitting that he had, for a time, lost his own faith. Father Bannity would undoubtedly have been their only defender, except that on the day before the traveling lawspeaker rode into town, the boy named Tobias came back.

He had been, the boy told the villagers (and very gleefully too) in the town of Eader's Church, and it was just as big and wonderful as he had imagined. "They have lots of dogs!" he said, his eyes still bright with the spectacle he had seen. "And houses that go up and up! And people!" He seemed to feel that the whipping his father had just given him—on general principles, since the actual mechanics of the boy's disappearance were still a mystery— was a small price to pay for all he'd seen.

Tobias knew nothing about how he had got from the village to the far-off town—it had happened in an instant, he said, from clasping Eli's hand to finding himself in the middle of the Eader's Church marketplace—but unfortunately there had been no equally magical way of returning. It had taken him all the days since he'd been gone to walk home.

When the Prosecutor General arrived the next day, there was no longer a case for murder to be tried, although several of the villagers were talking darkly of witchcraft. The Prosecutor General, a small, round, self-important fellow with a beard on his chin as small and sharp as an arrowhead, insisted on being taken to see the two former prisoners, who had been released to their campsite in Squire's Wood, if not to their previous state of anonymity.

Holding out his rod of office, the lawspeaker approached Eli and said, "In the name of the State and its gracious Sovereign, His Majesty the King, you must tell me how you sent the boy to Eader's Church."

The big man only looked at him, unbothered. Then he extended his hand. The Prosecutor General, after a moment's hesitation, extended his own small plump hand and allowed it to be grasped.

When Father Bannity and the other men watching had finished blinking their eyes, they saw that instead of his prosecutor's tunic, the Prosecutor General was now unquestionably wearing a judge's robes, cowl, and wreath, and that a judge's huge, round, golden emblem of office now hung on a chain around his neck. (Some also suggested that he had a stronger chin as well, and more penetrating eyes than he had heretofore possessed.) The ex–Prosecutor General, now a full-fledged Adjudicator, blinked, ran his fingers over the leafy wreath on his head, then fell down on his knees and uttered a happy prayer.

"Twelve years I've waited!" he said, over and over. "Thank you, Lord! Passed over and passed over—but no more!"

He then rose, and, with fitting jurisprudential gravity, proclaimed, "These men have not practiced any unlicensed witchcraft. I rule that they are true messengers of God and should be treated with respect."

Finding that his pockets were now richer by several gold coins—the difference between his old salary and new—the new-minted Adjudicator promptly sold his cart and donkey to Pender the village blacksmith and left town in a covered carriage, with a newly hired driver and two new horses. Later rumors said that he arrived home to find he had been awarded the King's Fourteenth Judicial Circuit.

In the wake of the Prosecutor General's astonishing transformation, Squire's Wood began to fill with people from the village and even some of the surrounding villages—for news travels fast in these rural areas—turning the two men's camp into a site of pilgrimage. The size of the gathering grew so quickly that Father Bannity and some of the wood's nearer and soberer neighbors worried that the entire forest soon would be trampled flat, but the squireward could not turn the newcomers away any more than he could have held back the tide at Lands End.

125

Although none of this swarm of postulants was turned away, not all re-ceived their heart's desire, either—Eli's hand opened only to one in perhaps three or four, and it was impossible to force the issue. One man, a jar maker named Keely, tried to pry the big man's fingers apart and shove his own hand in, and although he succeeded, nothing magical happened to him except that he developed a painful boil in the middle of his forehead the fol-lowing day.

Some of the pilgrims' wishes turned out to be surprisingly small and domestic: a man whose sick cow suddenly recovered, a woman whose youngest son abruptly discovered he could hear as well as he had before the fever. Others were more predictable, like the man who after clasping Eli's hand discovered a pot of old coins buried under an ancient wall he was re-building.

To the astonishment of many, two blighted young folk who lived on neighboring farms, a young man with a shattered leg and a girl with a huge strawberry blotch on her face, both went to Eli, and both were gifted with a handclasp, but came out again looking just the same as they had be-fore. But within the next few days the young man's drunkard father died of a fit, leaving him the farm, and the girl's cruel, miserly uncle who treated her like a servant fell under the wheels of a cart and died also, leav-ing her free to marry if anyone would have her. The two young people did indeed marry each other, and seemed quite happy, although they both still bore the disfigurements that had made them so pitiable to the rest of the village.

The only apparent failure of Eli's magical touch was Pender, the black-smith, who went to the campsite a massive, strapping man with a beard that reached halfway down his chest, and went away again with the shape and voice and apparently all the working parts of a slender young woman. He left town the same night, trading the Prosecutor General's old cart for a pair of pretty dresses before setting off on the donkey toward the nearest city to start his life over (at least so he told his neighbors), so no one was ever able to find out exactly how such a strange thing had happened when others had been served so well.

Soon the lame youth and other grateful folk came and built a great tent in Squire's Wood for Eli and Feliks to shelter in, and began bringing them daily offerings of food and drink. People were coming to see the two strangers from all around, and even the villagers who had not obtained a supernatural gift from the silent giant came to realize how valuable his presence was: the village was full of pilgrims, including some quite well-to-do folk who were willing to pay exorbitant prices to be fed and housed near the miracle worker.

Father Bannity, still basking in the joyful light of his newly recovered faith, did not doubt that Eli and Feliks were gifts from God, but he had not lost all caution or good sense, either, and he was worried by what was happening to his quiet village. He sent a messenger describing recent events to Dondolan, the nearest accredited wizard, who had an eyrie near the top of Reaching Peak. The wizard had not passed through the village for years, but he and the priest had met several times. Bannity liked the mage and trusted his good sense, certainly beyond that of the village elders, who were growing as greedy of pilgrimage gold as children tumbled into a treacle vat, happily eating themselves to death.

DONDOLAN the Clear-Eyed, as he had been named back in his Academy days, took one look at the priest's letter, then leaped out of his chair and began packing (a task that takes a wizard a much shorter time than the average traveler). The messenger asked if there would be any reply, and Dondolan told him, "I will be there before you." Then, suiting deed to word, he promptly vanished.

He appeared again in the village at the base of the mountain and took his horse from the livery stable there—even an accomplished wizard will not travel by magic for twenty leagues, not knowing what he will find at the other end, for it is a fierce drain on the resources—and set out. Other than an ill-considered attempt by some local bandits to waylay him just outside Drunken Princes' Pass, an interaction that increased the frog population of the highlands but did not notably slow Dondolan's progress, it was a swift journey, and he reached the nameless village within two days. Spurning more ordinary couriers, he had sent a raven ahead, and as a result Father Bannity waited at the crossroads outside of town to meet him.

When they had greeted each other—fondly, for the respect was mutual, despite their differences on the theological practicalities—Bannity led Dondolan through the fields around the outskirts of the village, so as not to cause more ruckus and rumor than was necessary; already the village practically breathed the stuff, and the pilgrims arriving daily from all over only made things more frantic.

"Do you wish to speak to the two of them?" Bannity asked. "It will be difficult, but I might persuade the village elders to let us close off the camp, although it will not be easy to remove all the addled folk who are living there now—they have practically made a new town in the middle of the forest."

"We should decide nothing until I see these miracle men," Dondolan said. "Although I must say that the description of them in your letter gave me an unpleasant feeling in the pit of my stomach."

"Why?" asked Bannity with some alarm. "Do you think they mean harm? I worried mainly that so many pilgrims would jeopardize the safety of our little town, drawing thieves and confidence tricksters and such. But surely God has sent those two to us—they have done so much good!"

"Perhaps. That is why I will restrain my conjectures until I have seen them."

They made their way through the woods, between groups of revelers singing and praying, gathered around so many campfires it seemed more like the eve of a great battle than twilight in the woods outside a quiet village too unassuming even to have its own name. As they grew close to the great pale tent and the crowd of people waiting there—some patiently, others loudly demanding that they be allowed to be next to see the wonder-workers because their need was so great—Bannity found it increasingly difficult to make headway through the throng. It was a mark of how many of the people were strangers to the area that the village's well-respected priest almost got into two fights, and only Dondolan's discreet use of a quelling-charm got them past those at the front of the line without real violence.

They slipped through the tent's flap-door. Dondolan stared across the big tent at the miraculous pair sitting like minor potentates on high-backed chairs the villagers had built them, the small man Feliks and the big man with the misshapen skull. Feliks was scratching himself and laughing at something. Eli was staring down at one of the kneeling postulants before him, his expression as emptily self-absorbed as a bullfrog waiting for a fly of sufficient size to happen past. Dondolan swallowed, then stepped back out of the tent again, and Bannity followed him. Even by torchlight, the priest could see the wizard had gone quite pale.

"It is indeed as I feared, Bannity. That is no poor traveler, innocently touched by God—or at least that is not how he began. The large man is the dark wizard Elizar the Devourer, scourge of the southern lands, and greatest enemy of the archmage Kettil of Thundering Crag."

"Elizar?" Bannity suddenly found swallowing difficult. Even a village priest knew the Devourer, who had burned whole towns because he liked the gloomy skies their smoking ruins provided, who had performed vile rites to turn men into beasts and beasts into men, and whose campaign of violent conquest had only been stopped by Kettil himself, the greatest wizard of the age, who had come down from his great ice caverns atop Thundering Crag and helped the young King defeat Elizar's vast army of slavering beast-men at the field of Herredsburn. Kettil himself had dueled Elizar before the gathered forces of both armies—the skies above Herredsburn, everyone remembered, had lit up as if with half a dozen simultaneous thunderstorms, and although neither had managed definitively to best the other, it had been Elizar who had fled the field, his plans in ruins, and retreated into a dark obscurity that had covered him for years—an absence that had lasted until this very moment. "*That* Elizar?" murmured Father Bannity. "*Here?*"

"I would stake my life on it," said Dondolan, "and may be doing so. Even if his mindlessness is real, just seeing someone like me that he has known might shock him back to his prior self."

"But we cannot simply . . . leave it. We cannot leave things this way."

"No, but I dare not go near him. His miracles, you tell me, are real, so he still wields mighty powers. Even if he stays witless, I cannot afford the chance he might decide to give *me* my heart's desire." Dondolan shook his head, his white beard wagging. "The heart of a wizard, even a relatively decent one like myself, is full of dark crevices. It is the world we inhabit, the wisdoms we study, the powers we have learned to harness, if not always to understand." He smiled, but there was not much pleasure in it. "I truthfully do not know my heart's desire, and have no urge to discover it this way."

"I'm . . . I'm not certain what you mean."

"What if my heart's desire is to be the greatest wizard of my age? I felt that way once, when I was young and first entering the Academy. What if that desire has not gone, only hidden?" He shook his head again. "I dare not risk it."

"But what if an ordinary mortal—someone not a wizard—has the same thing as *his* heart's desire? Or something worse, asking for the end of the world or something."

Dondolan gave the priest a shrewd, sober look. "So far, that has not happened. In fact, the power Elizar wields seems not to have harmed much of anybody, except, by your account, a pair of nasty old folk who deliberately stood in the way of their children's happiness. And even there, we cannot prove that coincidence did not carry them away. Perhaps there is something to Elizar's magic that is self-limiting—something that prevents him from granting any but mostly benign wishes. I do not know." He looked up. "I *do* know that we must discover more before we can make up our minds. We cannot, as you said, simply leave things be, not with Elizar the Devourer here, surrounded by eager supplicants, busily creating miracles, however kindhearted those miracles may seem." Dondolan ran his fingers through his long beard. "Not to mention the evil chance that this is all some cruel trick of Elizar's— that he only shams at having lost his mind, and plots to seize the Middle Lands again." He frowned, thinking. "When do they stop for the night?"

"Soon. When my sexton rings the church bell for evening prayer."

"Wait until that bell rings, Father, then bring me the man Feliks."

THE small man seemed almost relieved to have been found out. "Yes, it is true. He was once Elizar, the greatest wizard of all."

"After Kettil the archmage, you mean," said Dondolan.

Feliks waved his hand. "My master poured his soul into five thousand beast-men at Herredsburn, animating them throughout the battle. Even so, he dueled Kettil Hawkface to a standstill."

"This is neither here nor there," said Father Bannity impatiently. "Why is he the way we see him? Is this some new plot of his, some evil device?"

"Tell the truth, minion, and do not think to trick me," Dondolan said harshly. "Even now, Kettil himself must be hearing news of this. He will not take longer than I did to deduce that your Eli is in fact his old archenemy."

Feliks sighed. "Then we must be moving on again. Sad, that is. I was enjoying it here."

"Damn it, man, one of the most dangerous men in the world sleeps twenty paces away! Talk to us!"

"Dangerous to you, perhaps." Feliks shook his head. "No, not even to you—not now. There is no trick, wizard. What you see is the truth. The old Elizar is gone, and dumb Eli is what remains.

"It was after Herredsburn, you see, when the King and your Wizard's Council turned us away. With all his beast-men dead or changed back to their former selves, my master left the field and retreated to his secret lair in the Darkslide Mountains."

"We suspected he had a bolt-hole there," murmured Dondolan, "but we could never find it."

"He was determined to have his revenge on Kettil and the others," continued Feliks. "I have never seen him thus. He was furious, but also weary, weary and distraught." The small man peered at the priest and the wizard for a moment. "Once, in middle-night when I was awakened from sleep by a strange noise, I found him weeping."

"I cannot believe that," said Dondolan. "Elizar? The Devourer?"

"Believe what you will. There was always more to him than you folk on the Council understood. Whatever the case, he became fixed on the idea of securing the Amulet of Desire, which can grant its possessor whatever gift he most wants. He spent many months—a year, almost—pursuing its legend down many forgotten roads, in old books and older scrolls. He spoke to creatures so fearsome I could not even be under the same roof while they were conversing." The memory still seemed to make Feliks fearful, and yet proud of his bold master. "At last the time came. Deep in our cavern home in the Darkslide Mountains, he prepared the spells. I helped him as best I could, but I am just a servant, not a necromancer. I stoked the fires, polished the alembics, brought the articles he needed from our reliquary. At last the hour came when the spheres were in alignment, and he began the Summoning of the Empty Gods.

"He had been nights on end without sleep, in the grip of a fever that I had never seen in him before, even on the night before Herredsburn, when dominion over all the world was still at his fingertips. Pale, wide-eyed, talking to himself as though I was not even present, he was like a prisoner desperate for release, whether that release came from the opening of the prison door or from the hangman's rope."

Feliks sighed and briefly wiped his eyes while Dondolan tapped impatient fingers.

"The spell went on for hours," the small man continued, "names shouted into the darkness that hurt my ears. At one point I fled, terrified by the shadows that filled the room and danced all around me. When I came back, it was because I heard my master's hoarse cry of triumph.

"He stood in the center of his mystical diagram, holding up something I could barely see, something that gleamed red and black . . ."

"Something cannot gleam black," Dondolan said—a trifle querulously, Bannity thought. "It makes no sense."

"Little of what had happened that night made sense, but I will not change my tale. It gleamed red and black. Elizar held it over his head, crying out with a ragged voice, 'My greatest wish made real . . . !'—and then the roof collapsed."

"Collapsed?" said Bannity. "How? I thought you were in some mountain cavern."

"We were," Feliks agreed. "I still am not certain how it happened—it was like being chewed in a giant's mouth, chewed and chewed, then spit out. When I woke up, we both lay on the slope beneath the entrance to the lair, which was choked with fallen rock. Elizar was as you see him now, crushed and silent, his head all bloody, poor fellow. The Amulet was gone. Everything was gone. I helped him up, and we stumbled and crawled down the hill to a cotsman's deserted shack—the owner had fled when the mountain began to shake. I shaved my master's head and doctored his wounds. We ate what supplies the cotsman had laid in, but when we ran out, we had no choice but to become wandering beggars." The small, wrinkled man spread his hands. "*I can do no magic, you see.*"

"Was the boy in the village, the one Elizar sent to Eader's Church, the first to be . . . touched?"

Feliks shook his head. "My master took a few people's hands, mostly folk who gave generously to our begging bowl, and sometimes things happened. None were harmed, all profited," he added, a little defensively.

"And you," Dondolan demanded. "You must have touched his hands many times since this occurred. What of you?"

"What could happen? I already have my heart's desire. All I have ever wanted was to serve him. From the first moment I saw him outside the Academy, I knew that he was my destiny, for good or bad."

Dondolan sighed. "For bad, certainly, at least until now. You are not a true villain, Feliks, but you have served an evil man."

"All great men are thought evil by some."

"Not all great men graft the heads of wild boars onto the shoulders of peasant farmers," Dondolan pointed out. "Not all great men wear the skins of other wizards for a cloak."

"He killed only those who turned against him," said Feliks stubbornly. "Only those who would have killed him."

Dondolan stared at him for a moment. "It matters little now," he said at last. "As I said, Kettil will have heard by now and guessed who is here. The archmage will come, and things will change."

"Then we must go," said Feliks, rising to his feet with a weary grunt. "We will move on. There are still places we can live in quiet peace, if I can only help my poor master to keep his hands to himself."

"I dare not try to stop you," Dondolan said. "I fear to wake your master if he really sleeps inside that battered skull—I admit I was never his match. But even if you flee, you will not outrun Kettil's power."

It does not matter. What will be, will be, Bannity thought to himself, but a little of his newfound peace had gone with Eli's unmasking. *Whether Elizar is a man transformed or a villain disguised, surely what happens next will be as God wills too. For who can doubt His hand when He has shown us so many miracles here?*

BUT Eli would not leave the wood, despite Feliks's urging. The mute man was as resistant as a boulder set deep in mud: none of his servant's pleas or arguments touched him—in fact, he showed no sign of even hearing them.

Dondolan and Bannity, armed with the knowledge of the miracle worker's true identity, convinced the suddenly terrified village elders that for a while at least, the crowds should be kept away. With a contingent of soldiers from the nearest shirepost, hired with a fraction of the profits from the long miracle-season, they cleared the forest of all the suppliants, forcing them out into the town and surrounding fields, where local sellers of charms and potions gleefully provided them with substitute satisfaction, or at least the promise of it.

Even as the last of the camps were emptied, some of the latest arrivals from beyond the village brought news that Kettil Hawkface himself was on the way. Some had seen nothing more than a great storm swirling around Thundering Crag while the sky elsewhere was blue and bright, but others claimed to have seen the archmage himself speeding down the mountain on a huge white horse, shining as he came like a bolt of lightning. In any case, those who had been turned away from Squire's Wood now had something else to anticipate, and the great road that passed by the nameless village was soon lined with those waiting to see the most famous, most celebrated wizard of all.

Father Bannity could not help wondering whether Elizar sensed anything of his great rival's coming, and so he walked into Squire's Wood and across the trampled site of the camp, empty now but for a couple of hired soldiers standing guard.

Inside the tent wrinkled little Feliks looked up from eating a bowl of stew and waved to Bannity as if they were old friends; but Elizar was as empty-faced as ever, and seemed not to notice that the crowds of pilgrims were gone, that he and Feliks were alone. He sat staring at the ground, his big hands opening and closing so slowly that Father Bannity could have counted a score of his own suddenly intrusive heartbeats between fist and spread fingers. The man's naked face and shaved scalp made the head atop the black robe seem almost like an egg, out of which anything might hatch.

Why did I come here? he asked himself. *To taunt the blackest magician of the age?* But he felt he had to ask.

"Are you truly gone from in there, Elizar?" The priest's voice trembled, and he prayed to God for strength. He now realized, in a way he had not before, that before him sat a man who was of such power that he had destroyed whole cities the way an ordinary man might kick down an anthill. But Bannity had to ask. "Are you truly and completely empty, or is there a spark of you left in that husk, listening?" He had a sudden thought. "Did you bring this on yourself, with your magical amulet? When the time came for your heart's desire to be granted, did God hear a small, hidden part of you that was weary of death and torment and dark hatreds, that wanted to perform the Lord's work for your fellow men instead of bringing them blood and fire and terror?"

Eli did not look up or change expression, and at last Father Bannity went out. Feliks watched him go with a puzzled expression, then returned to his meal.

HE came down the main road with crowds cheering behind him as though he were a conquering hero—which, after all, he was. Bannity watched the people shouting and calling Kettil's name as the wizard rode toward the village on his huge white horse, the same people who only days before had been crouched in the dirt outside Eli's tent, begging to be let in, and the priest wondered at God's mysterious ways.

Kettil Hawkface was younger than Bannity would have guessed, or else had spelled himself to appear so. He seemed a man in the middle of life, his golden hair only touched with gray, his bony, handsome face still firm in every line. His eyes were the most impressive thing about him: even from a distance they glittered an icy blue, and up close it was difficult to look at him directly, such was the chilly power of his gaze.

Bannity and Dondolan met the archmage at the edge of the wood. Kettil nodded at his fellow wizard but hardly seemed to see the priest at all, even after Dondolan introduced him.

"He is in there . . ." Dondolan began, but Kettil raised his hand, and the lesser mage fell silent.

"I know where he is." He had a voice to match his eyes, frosty and authoritative. "And I know what he is. I have battled his evil for half my long life. I do not need to be told where to find him—I smell him as a hound smells his quarry."

Strange, then, that you did not find him before, thought Bannity, then regretted his own small-minded carping. "But he is not the monster you knew, Archmage . . ."

Kettil looked at him then, but only a moment, then turned away. "Such creatures do not change," he said to Dondolan.

Bannity tried again. "He has done much good . . . !"

Kettil smirked. "Has he revived all those he killed? Rebuilt the cities he burned? Do not speak to me of things you do not understand, priest." He slid down off his massive white horse. "I will go, and we will see what devilry awaits."

Bannity had to admit the archmage was as impressive as legend had promised. He strode into the forest with no weapon but his staff of gnarled birch, his long hair blowing, his sky-blue robes billowing as though he still stood on the heights of Thundering Crag. Bannity looked at Dondolan, whose face bore a carefully composed expression that betrayed nothing of what he was thinking, then they both followed the archmage Kettil into Squire's Wood.

To Bannity's astonishment, Eli himself stood in the doorway of the tent, looking out across the great clearing.

"Ho, Devourer!" Kettil's voice echoed, loud as a hunting horn, but Eli only looked at him incuriously, his large hands dangling from his sleeves like roosting bats. "I have found you again at last!"

The hairless man blinked, turned, and went back into the tent. Kettil strode after him, crossing the clearing in a few long paces. Bannity started to follow, but Dondolan grabbed his arm and held him back.

"This is beyond me and beyond you, too."

"Nothing is beyond God!" Bannity cried, but Dondolan the Clear-Eyed

135

looked doubtful. A few moments later little Feliks came stumbling out of the tent, flapping his hands as if surrounded by angry bees.

"They stand face-to-face!" he squawked, then tripped and fell, rolling until he stopped at Bannity's feet. The priest helped him up, but did not take his eyes off the tent. "They do not speak, but stare at each other. The air is so thick!"

"It seems . . ." Dondolan began, but never finished, for at that instant the entire clearing—in fact, all the woods and the sky above—seemed to suck in a great breath. A sudden, agonizing pain in Bannity's ears dropped him to his knees, then everything suddenly seemed to flow sideways—light, color, heat, air, everything rushing out across the face of the earth in all directions, pushing the priest flat against the ground and rolling him over several times.

When the monstrous wind died, Bannity lay for a long, stunned instant, marveling at the infinite skills of God, who could create the entire universe and now, just as clearly, was going to dismantle it again. Then a great belch of flame and a roar of rushing air made him roll over onto his knees and, against all good sense, struggle to sit up so he could see what was happening.

The tent was engulfed in flame, the trees all around singed a leafless black. As Father Bannity stared, two figures staggered out of the inferno as though solidifying out of smoke, one like a pillar of cold blue light, with flame dancing in his pale hair and beard, the other a growing, rising shadow of swirling black.

"I knew you but pretended, demon!" shouted Kettil Hawkface, waving his hands in the air, flashes of light crackling up from his fingertips. "Devourer! I know your treachery of old!"

The shadow, which had begun to fold down over the archmage like a burning blanket, instead billowed up and away, hovering in the air just above Kettil's head. A face could be seen in its roiling, cloudy midst, and Bannity could not help marveling even in his bewildered horror how it looked both like and unlike the silent Eli.

"I will make sure your dying lasts for centuries, Hawkface!" shrieked the dark shape in a voice that seemed to echo all the way to the distant hills, then it rose up into the air, flapping like an enormous bat made of smoke and sparks, and flew away into the south.

"Master!" screamed Feliks, and stumbled off through the woods, following the fast-diminishing blot of fiery blackness until he, too, disappeared from sight.

Kettil Hawkface, his pale robes smeared with ash, his whiskers and hair singed at the edges, strode away in the other direction, walking back toward the village with the purposeful stride of someone who has completed a dangerous and thankless job and does not bother to wait for the approbation he surely deserves.

As he emerged at the forest's edge, he stood before the hundreds of onlookers gathered there and raised his hands. "Elizar the Devourer's evil has been discovered and ended, and he has flown in defeat back to the benighted south," the archmage cried. "You people of the Middle Lands may rest safely again, knowing that the Devourer's foul plan has been thwarted."

The crowd cheered, but many were confused about what had happened, and the reception of his news was not as wholehearted as Kettil had perhaps expected. He did not wait to speak again to his colleague Dondolan but climbed onto his white horse and galloped away north toward Thundering Crag, followed by a crowd of children crying out after him for pennies and miracles.

Bannity and Dondolan watched in silence as the ramrod-straight figure grew smaller and then eventually disappeared. The crowds did not immediately disperse, but many seemed to realize there would be little reason to collect here anymore, and the cries of the food sellers, charm hawkers, and roving apothecaries became muted and mournful.

"So all is resolved for good," Father Bannity said, half to himself. "Elizar's evil was discovered and thwarted."

"Perhaps," said Dondolan. "But a part of me cannot help wondering whose heart's desire was granted here today."

"What do you mean? Do you think . . . they clasped hands?"

Dondolan sighed. "Do not misunderstand me. It is entirely possible that the world has been spared a great evil here today—Elizar was always full of plots, many of them astoundingly subtle. But if they *did* touch hands, I think it is safe to say that only one of them was granted his heart's desire."

"I don't understand."

"Elizar may not have seemed entirely happy as Eli the dumb miracle worker," Dondolan said, "but he did seem peaceful. Now, though, he is the Devourer again, and Kettil once more has an enemy worthy of his own great pride and power."

Bannity was silent for a long time, watching the sky darken as the sun settled behind Squire's Wood. "But surely God would not let Elizar's evil back into the world simply because his enemy missed it—God must have a better plan for mankind than that!"

"Perhaps," said Dondolan the Clear-Eyed. "Perhaps. We will think on it together after we return to the church and you find the brandy you keep hidden for such occasions."

Father Bannity nodded and took a few steps, then turned. "How did you know about the brandy?"

The priest thought Dondolan's smile seemed a trifle sour. "I am a wizard, remember? We know almost everything."

Naming Day

Patricia A. McKillip

Patricia A. McKillip won the very first World Fantasy Award in 1975 with her novel The Forgotten Beasts of Eld, *and has been one of the most distinguished authors in modern fantasy ever since. Her many books include* The Riddle-Master of Hed, Heir of Sea and Fire, Harpist in the Wind, The Book of Atrix Wolfe, The Changeling Sea, The Sorceress and the Cygnet, The Cygnet and the Firebird, Fool's Run, The House on Parchment Street, Moon-Flash, The Moon and the Face, The Throme of the Erril of Sherrill, Song for the Basilisk, Winter Rose, The Tower at Stony Wood, The Night Gift, Riddle of Stars, In the Forests of Serre, Alphabet of Thorn, *and* Od Magic. *She won another World Fantasy Award in 2003 for* Ombria in Shadow. *Her two most recent books are a collection of her short fiction,* Harrowing the Dragon, *and a novel,* Solstice Wood. *Born in Salem, Oregon, she now lives in North Bend, Oregon.*

In the gentle and compassionate story that follows, she shows us that if names have Power—and they do—then you'd better make sure which one fits before you take it.

A VERIL stared dreamily into her oatmeal, contemplating herself. In two days it would be Naming Day at the Oglesby School of Thaumaturgy, the midpoint of the three-year course of study. Those students who had gotten through the first year and a half with satisfactory grades in such classes as Prestidigitation, Legendary Creatures, Latin, Magical Alphabets, The Uses and Misuses of Elements, and The History of Sorcery were permitted to choose the secret names they would need to continue their studies. Averil had achieved the highest marks in every class, and she was eager to investigate more widely, more profoundly, the mysterious and wizardly arts of Thaumaturgy. But under what name? She couldn't decide. What would best express her gifts, her potential, the wellsprings of her magic? More importantly, what would she be happy calling this secret self for the rest of her life?

Think of a favorite tree, Miss Braeburn, her counselor, had suggested. An animal, a bird. You might name yourself after one of those. Or one of the four elements of antiquity. Some aspect of fire, perhaps. Water.

Averil stretched her long, graceful spine, thought of her pale hair and coloring. Swan? she mused. Or something with wind in it? I'm more air than fire. Certainly not earth. Water?

"Mater," she began; she had to start practicing her Latin, in which half the ancient thaumaturges had written their spells. "What do you think about when you think about me?"

Her mother, turning bacon at the stove, flung her a haggard, incredulous glance. She was pregnant again, at her age, and prone to throwing up at odd times. An unfortunate situation, Averil thought privately, since they had moved from a house in the suburbs to a much smaller apartment in the city for Averil's sake, to be as close as possible to Oglesby. Where, she wondered, were her impractical parents planning to put a baby? In the laundry basket? In the walk-in closet with Felix, where it was likely to be shoved under his bed along with his toys and shoes? Her brother chose that moment to draw attention from her compelling question by banging his small fist on the tines of a fork to cause the spoon lying across the handle to go spinning into the air.

"Felix!" their mother cried. "Stop that."

"Bacon, bacon, I want bacon!" Felix shouted. The spoon bounced on his head, then clattered onto the floor. He squinted his eyes, opened his mouth wide. Averil got up hastily before he began to howl.

"Averil—wait. Stop."

"Mom, gotta go; I'll be late."

"I need you to come home right after your classes today." A banshee shriek came out of Felix; their mother raised her voice. "I want you to watch Felix."

Averil's violet eyes skewed in horror toward her squalling baby brother, whose tonsils were visible. He had just turned four, a skinny, noisy, mindless bundle of mischief and energy whom Averil seriously doubted was quite right in the head.

"Sorry, Mom." She grabbed her book bag hastily. After all, her mother had nothing else to do. "I have group study after school."

"Averil—"

"Mom, it's important! I'm good at my studies—one of the best in a decade, Miss Braeburn says. She thinks I can get a full scholarship to the University of Ancient Arts if I keep up my grades. That's why we moved here, isn't it? Anyway, my friends are waiting for me." Something in her mother's expression, not unlike the mingling of admiration and despair that Averil's presence caused in less gifted students, made her round the table quickly, trying not to clout Felix with her book bag, and breathe a kiss on her mother's cheek. "Ask me again after Naming Day. I might have time then."

She discussed the situation with her friends Deirdre, Tamara, and Nicholaus, as they walked to school.

"My mother should understand. After all, she almost graduated from Oglesby herself. She knows how hard we have to work."

"She did?" Nicholaus queried her with an inquisitive flash of rimless spectacles. "Why didn't she graduate? Did she fail her classes?"

Averil shrugged. "She told me she left to get married."

"Quaint."

"Well, she couldn't stay in school with me coming and all the students' practice spells flying around. I might have come out as a wombat or something."

Deirdre chuckled and made a minute adjustment to the butterfly pin in her wild red hair. "Baby brothers are the worst, aren't they? Mine are such a torment. They put slugs in my shoes; they color in my books; they're always whining, and they smell like boiled broccoli."

Tamara, who was taller than all of them and moved like a dancer, shook her sleek black hair out of her face, smiling. "I like my baby brother, but then he's still a baby. They're so sweet before they grow their teeth and start having opinions."

Averil murmured absently, her eyes on the boy with the white-gold hair waiting for her at the school gates. She drew a deep, full breath; the air seemed to kindle and glow through her. "There's Griffith," she said, and stepped forward into her enchanted world, full of friends, and challenges within the craggy, dark walls of the school, and Griffith, with his high cheekbones and broad shoulders, watching her come.

Someone else watched her, too: a motionless, silent figure on the grass within the wrought-iron fence. An intensity seemed to pour out of him like a spell, drawing at her until, surprised, she took her eyes off Griffith to see who the stranger was.

But it wasn't a stranger, only Fitch, who blinked at the touch of her eyes and drew back into himself like a turtle. She waved anyway, laughing a little, her attention already elsewhere.

In her classes, Averil got a perfect score conjugating Latin verbs, correctly pronounced a rune that made Dugan Lawler believe he was a parrot, and, with Griffith, was voted best in class for their history project, which traced the legendary land on which Oglesby stood back through time to the powerful forest of oak trees under which early students were taught their primitive magic. She and Griffith pretended to be teacher and student; they actually reproduced some of the ancient spells, one of which set fire to Mr. Addison's oak cane and turned on the overhead sprinklers. But Mr. Addison, after mending his cane and drying the puddles with some well-chosen words, complimented them on their imaginative interpretation of ancient history.

After school, she and Griffith, Nicholaus, Tamara, and Deirdre went to Griffith's house to study. The place was huge, quiet, and tidy, full of leather-bound books and potted plants everywhere. Griffith had no siblings; his parents were both scholars and understood the importance of study. His mother left them alone in the dining room with a tray of iced herbal tea and brownies; they piled their books on the broad mahogany table and got to work.

Later, when they had finished homework and quizzed each other for tests, talk drifted to the all-important Naming Day.

"I can't decide." Averil sighed, sliding limply forward in her chair and enjoying the reflection of her long ivory hair on the dark, polished wood. "Has anyone chosen a name, yet?"

Tamara had, and Nicholaus. Deirdre had narrowed it down to two, and Griffith said he had had a secret name since he was seven. So they could all give their attention to Averil.

"I thought something to do with air?" she began tentatively. "Wind?"

"Windflower," Griffith said promptly, making her blush.

"Windhover," Tamara offered. Averil looked blank; she added, "It's a falcon."

"I don't think I'm a falcon. More like a—well, something white."

"Snow goose?" Deirdre suggested practically. "Nobody would ever guess that."

"Swan, of course," Nicholaus said. "But that'd be too obvious. How about egret? Or I think there's a snowy owl—"

Averil straightened. "Those aren't really names, are they? Not something really personal that defines me."

"What about a jewel?" Tamara said. "A diamond?"

"Pearl," Griffith said softly, smiling a little, making Averil smile back.

"Something," she agreed, "more like that."

It was all so interesting, trying to find the perfect name for Averil, that nobody remembered the time. Griffith's mother reminded them; they broke up hastily, packing away books and pens, winding long silk scarves around their throats, prognosticating cold suppers and peeved parents.

"Stay," Griffith said to Averil, making a spell with his caramel eyes so that Averil's feet stuck to the threshold.

"Well—"

"Stay for supper. My parents are going out. I'll cook something."

"I should call—"

"Call your mother. Tell her we're working on a project."

"But we're not," Averil objected; true wizards did not need to lie.

"We are," he said, with his bewitching smile. "Your name."

Averil got home later than even she considered marginal for excusable behavior. Fortunately, her father was already being taken to task for his own lateness, and Averil only got added to the general list of complaints. Still enchanted, she barely listened.

"You don't realize—" her mother said, and, "No consideration—"

"Sorry, dear," her father said soothingly. "I should have called, but I kept thinking we'd get the work finished earlier."

"Stone-cold dinner—"

"Sorry, Mom," Averil echoed dutifully.

"If I don't get a moment to myself, I'm going to —"

"After Naming Day, I promise."

"Now, dear, he's barely four. He'll settle down soon enough. Take him to the park or something."

Her mother made a noise like cloth ripping, the beginning of tears. Her father opened his arms. Averil let her book bag fall to the floor and drifted away, thinking of Griffith's farewell kiss.

She escaped out the door without breakfast the next morning after allowing her mother, who was on the phone pleading with a babysitting service, a brief glimpse of her face. At the table, Felix was upending a cereal box over his bowl.

"Bye, Mom."

"Averil—"

"See you, but don't know when. There might be a celebration later. It's Naming Day."

"Av—Felix!"

Averil closed the door to the sound of a gentle rain of Fruitie Flakes all over the floor.

She was halfway down the block, already searching the flowing current of students for Griffith's white-gold hair, when she remembered her book bag. It was still on the living-room floor where she had dropped it; escaping the morning drama in the kitchen had taken up all her attention. She turned back quickly, trying to make herself invisible so that her mother wouldn't start in again at the sight of her. I am wind, she told herself, pulling open the apartment building door. I am . . . spindrift.

Spindrift! There was a name, she realized triumphantly, running up the two flights of stairs rather than wait for the elevator. White as swans' feathers, a braid of wind and wave and foam, always graceful, never predictable . . . She flung the door open, leaving it wide for a hasty escape, and as she rushed in, something shot past her so fast it left only a vague impression of gnarly limbs and light in her eyes before it vanished out the door.

"My wand!"

The screech hit Averil like a spell; she skidded to a stop. This wasn't her apartment, she saw, appalled. She had barged through the wrong door. And there was this—this huge, ancient and incredibly ugly thaumaturge-thing, a witch or crazed wizard, seething at her from behind a cauldron bubbling over a firebed on her living-room floor.

"You let my greyling out!"

"I'm sorry," Averil gasped. Plants crawling up the walls, across the ceiling, whispered with their enormous leaves and seemed to quiver with horror.

"Well, don't just stand there like a gape-jawed booby, get it back!"

Averil closed her mouth, tried to retrieve some dignity. "I'm sorry," she repeated. Her voice wobbled in spite of herself. "I have to get to school. I just came back for my book bag, and I must have gone up an extra floor." She took a step, edging back toward the door. "I'll just—your greyling is probably downstairs; I'll just go see. I won't let it get out the front door. I promise."

Up the stairwell behind her came the distinct rattle of a heavy door fitting its locks and hinges and frame back into place as it closed. The old witch seemed to fill like a balloon behind her cauldron. Her tattered white hair stiffened; her eyes, like thumbprints of tar in her wrinkled skin, slewed and glinted.

"You get my greyling. You get my wand."

"I haven't time!"

"You let them out. You bring them back."

"I have classes! It's my Naming Day!" Even a senile old bag like that must have anticipated her own Naming Day once. If things had names that long ago. "You must remember how important that is."

"You. Get. My. Wand."

"All right, okay," Averil gabbled; anything to get out the door.

The witch's murky eyes narrowed into slits. "Until you bring me back my wand and my greyling, you will be invisible. No one will see you. No one will hear your voice. Until you bring me my greyling and my wand, even your own name will be useless to you."

"I don't have time." Averil's voice had gone somewhere; she could barely whisper. "I have to get to school."

"Then you'd better start looking."

"You can't do that!" Her voice was back suddenly, high and shrill, like a whistling teakettle. "I'm at the top of my class! My teachers will come looking for me! Griffith will rescue me!"

"Go!"

She couldn't tell if she moved, or if the word itself blew her out the door; it slammed behind her, echoing the witch's voice. She stood in the hall a moment, trembling and thoughtless. Then she took a sharp breath—"The greyling!"—and precipitated herself down the stairs two at a time, on the off chance that the witch's familiar still lurked in the hallway below.

Of course it was nowhere in sight.

Averil plunged out the door, trying wildly to look in every direction at once. What exactly was a greyling? She racked her brains; nothing leaped to mind from her Legendary Creatures class. Did it like water? High tree limbs? Caves? Could it speak? She hadn't a clue. A jumble of pallid, root-like limbs and a sort of greeny yellow light were all she remembered. The one must be the greyling, the other the pilfered wand. She hoped desperately that the greyling wouldn't have the power to use it.

A familiar figure crossed the street toward the school. "Tamara!" Averil shouted with relief. Tamara's long stride didn't falter. She called out to someone herself; her voice seemed small, distorted, like words heard from underwater. Ahead of her, a dark head turned; spectacles flashed. "Nicholaus!" Averil cried, hurrying toward them. "Tamara!"

Neither of them turned. They greeted one another, and then Deirdre caught up with them, red hair flying. They chattered excitedly, finally turning to survey the street where surely they would see, they must see Averil running toward them, yelling and waving her arms.

Their faces grew puzzled. A bell tolled once, reverberations overlapping with exaggerated slowness. It was the warning bell; those outside the gates at First Bell would be locked out. The three moved again, quickly. In the distance, Averil could see Griffith, just within the gates, waiting for them, for her.

However fast she followed, they were always faster. As though, she thought, breathlessly sprinting, they were always in the next moment, a slightly different beat in time; she could never quite catch up. She stopped finally with a despairing cry as her friends passed through the gates; they seemed farther away than ever. They spoke to Griffith; he shrugged a little, then pointed toward a high window, where their first class would begin. Maybe Averil's there, his gesture said. First Bell tolled three times. The gates began to close. As the last students jostled inside, Averil noticed one face still peering through the bars, searching the streets. Fitch, she recognized glumly. And then even he turned away, went up the broad stone steps into the school.

Behind her, something crashed. She jumped, then turned in time to see the greyling balanced on the side of the garbage can it had overturned. Amid the litter, a cat puffed itself up twice its size and hissed furiously. The greyling opened its mouth and hissed back. Averil finally saw it clearly: a grotesque imp with big ears and a body so narrow it seemed all skinny limbs and head, like a starfish. It held a stick with a dandelion of light at one end. A cartoon wand, Averil thought disgustedly. More for the goopy Tinkerbell fairy than for an evil-tempered, snag-toothed old hag who had stopped Averil's world.

The greyling leaped, clearing the spilled garbage and the cat. Averil moved then, faster than she had ever moved in her life.

The greyling rolled a huge, silvery eye at her as she gained on it, seeming to realize finally that something was after it. It increased its pace, blowing down the sidewalks and alleyways like a tumbleweed. Averil followed grimly. Nobody else saw it. Other people walked in a tranquil world where bus brakes and car horns made noises in miniature, and the shrieks of kids in the school playground sounded like the distant chirping of well-behaved birds.

Averil pursued the greyling across the park. It skittered up a tree and made faces at her until she drove it out with some well-placed pinecones. It led her up one side of the jungle gym and down the other, then disappeared completely. She found it in the rose garden, with roses stuffed in both ears and its mouth, trying to disguise itself as a bush. It waved the wand at her, shaking a sprinkle of light between them that Averil ran through before she could stop. But nothing happened. She heard several deep, familiar booms, then; the sounds echoed and rippled through the air with viscous slowness, melting into Averil's heart, which grew iron with despair. Second Bell. The Naming Hour itself. And where was she? Chasing an imp through a world where nobody who knew her name could even see her.

A thought struck her. She missed a step, stumbling a little, so that the greyling leaped ahead. It veered into a small forest of giant ferns and vanished.

You're a student of magical arts, the thought said. Do some magic.

She slowed, panting. Eyes narrowed, she searched the stand of ferns for a single quivering leaf, the slightest movement among the shadows and shafts of mellow light. Nothing. She listened, tuning her ears the way she had been taught, to hear the patter of a millipede's feet across a leaf, the bump of a beetle's back against a clod of dirt. She heard the faintest of breaths. Or was it a butterfly's wings, opening and closing in the light?

She drew the rich, dusty light into her eyes and into her mind, where she focused and shaped it into a brilliant, sharply pointed letter of an ancient, magical alphabet, and let it loose in a sudden shout, hoping she was pronouncing it correctly.

The fern grove lit up as though someone had set off fireworks in it. Within the glittering, spinning wheels and sprays of light, the greyling exploded from behind a trunk and scrambled to the very top of a fern tree. It dangled there precariously, wailing at her, its eyes as huge as saucers.

She yelled back at it, "Ha!" and ran to get the wand.

She found it easily as her own fires died: the only glowing thing left on the ground. She studied it puzzledly, carefully touched the puff of light. It didn't burn her, or change in any way; she didn't even feel it. She smelled something, though, that seemed peculiar in the middle of a fern grove.

Vanilla?

She looked up in time to see the greyling gather its spidery limbs and

147

rocket off the fern head in a desperate leap that sent it smack into someone who had emerged out of nowhere to stare up at it. They both tumbled to the ground. The greyling wriggled to its feet, but not quickly enough. A hand shot out to grab its skinny ankle; a voice shouted breathlessly, "Gotcha!"

Averil blinked. The newcomer transferred his grip to the greyling's wrist as he got up off the ground. He smiled crookedly at Averil, who finally found her voice.

"Fitch!"

"Hey."

"What are you—why on earth did you—" The color was pushing so brightly into his face it seemed to tinge the air around him, she saw with fascination; he would have glowed in the dark. Only his fingers, wound around the hissing, whimpering, struggling greyling, hadn't forgotten what he was doing there. Averil's brows leaped up as high as they could go; so did her voice.

"What did you do? Did you follow me?"

"Well." He swallowed with a visible effort. "I could see you, but I couldn't reach you until you made that magic. Then that weird spell forcing the jog in time pushed our moments back together, at least long enough so that—so—"

"Here you are."

"Yeah."

"On your Naming Day."

"Well," he said again, his face growing impossibly redder. "You were in trouble. I don't think real wizards get to choose a convenient time and place to do what they think they have to."

Averil studied him speechlessly. He was taller than she expected; he always seemed to shrink into himself when she was around. His brown, floppy hair did a good job of hiding his face; what she could see of it looked interesting enough. Between his hair and woodsy skin, she'd just assumed his eyes were dark, too. But he'd scarcely let her meet his eyes before, and now she saw the glints of blue within his hair.

Her voice leaped up a few notches again. "You saw me!" He gave a brief nod, dodging the kick the greyling aimed at his shin. "Nobody else could see me! That was part of the spell."

"That's what I thought, when I saw you calling your friends and they didn't notice you."

"Then how could you see me?"

His mouth curled in a little, slantwise smile. "It's one of the things I happen to be good at. Recognizing magic when it's around. Also..." He stuck there, picking at words, ignoring the greyling jumping up and down on his toes. "You might have noticed. I watch you."

"Lots of people do," Averil said hastily, afraid that if he blushed any harder, he might hurt himself.

His eyes came back to her. "You know what I'm saying. I've always wanted to talk to you. But I never thought you'd be interested."

"So you snuck out of school on Naming Day just to talk to me while I was alone for once?"

His smile flashed out at that, changing his entire face, she saw with surprise; it looked open, now, and unafraid. "Right. I thought we might have a conversation while you were chasing this little goblin around garbage cans and up trees."

"Then why didn't you just tell one of the teachers?" she demanded bewilderedly. "You wouldn't have missed your Naming."

"I know my name," he said simply. "I don't need to write it in ancient letters on a piece of tree bark and burn it in an oak fire. That's just a ritual."

Averil opened her mouth; nothing came out. The greyling showed teeth suddenly, aiming for Fitch's fingers. She rapped it sharply on its head with the witch's wand. "I'd better take this thing back before it gets away from me again," she said, as the yellow-green fairy light shaken off the wand dazzled and twinkled in the air around them.

"Where does it belong?"

"To a gnarly old warthog of a witch who put a spell on me when I accidentally let her greyling out."

Fitch grunted, watched the sparkles sail past his nose. "Funny light. Doesn't seem to do much, does it?"

"No. And it smells odd. Like—"

"Vanilla."

Averil shook her head. "Bizarre . . ."

"Do you want me to help you take it back?"

She considered that, tempted, then shook her head again; no sense in introducing the witch to more opportunities for mischief. "No. It's my problem . . . But now you won't be able to get back into the school."

She saw his slanted smile again. "I have my ways."

"Really?"

"Doesn't everyone?"

"No," she said, amazed. "I always follow all the rules. At least at school."

"Well, of course, there's something to be said for that." He paused; she waited. "I just said it."

"You made a joke," she exclaimed. "I didn't even know you could smile." She took the greyling's skinny wrist out of his hold, wondering suddenly what else went on in that obscure realm under Fitch's untidy hair. "I always get perfect grades. How can you know things I don't?"

He shrugged. "I don't know. You're brilliant. Everyone notices what you do. So you have to watch yourself. I get to do things nobody notices."

She mulled that over, while the greyling tried to run circles around her. "Maybe we could talk?" she suggested. "Sometime soon?"

He blushed again, but not so much. "I'd like that."

"I think I would, too." The greyling nearly spun her off her feet, then tangled itself around the foot she stuck in its path. "I'd better finish what I started with the witch," she said grimly, hauling the greyling up. "Thanks for helping me. That was really nice of you."

"You're sure—" Fitch said doubtfully, walking backward away from her.

"I'd like to think all my studying is worth something."

"Okay, then. Good luck with the witch."

"Thanks," she said between her teeth, and dragged the furious greyling in the opposite direction.

The greyling finally stopped struggling when the door to the apartment building closed behind them. It quietly trudged upstairs beside Averil, only muttering a little now and then, its ribbony arm dangling limply in her grasp. She scarcely heard it; she was trying to figure out how Fitch was getting back into the school without being caught. Did he already know how to turn invisible? What other things might he have learned on his own, while she was only learning what was required? Would breaking rules make him a better wizard? Better than, say, Griffith, who would surely have skipped his Naming Day to come and help her, if he had been able to see her. Or would he? More likely, he would have done the practical thing and simply told one of their teachers that she seemed to be in trouble. Try as she might, she couldn't imagine Griffith missing his Naming to sneak out of school and help her catch some witch's demented familiar.

She was thinking so intently that she had opened the door of her own apartment out of habit. Her mother, sitting on the couch and reading, lifted her head to smile at Averil, who remembered, horrified, what she was holding.

"Hi, Mom," she said hastily, backing out before she had to explain the greyling. "Oops. I'll just be a moment—"

"Thanks, Averil." Her mother sighed. "That's the most peaceful morning I've had in years."

The greyling broke free of Averil, ran to the couch, and climbed up beside their mother. "I'm tired," Felix groaned, falling sideways onto her lap. "Really, really, really—"

"Oh, that's wonderful, sweetie."

Averil, frozen in the doorway, remembered finally how to breathe. Her eyes felt gritty, as though fairy dust had blown into them. With great effort, she swiveled them toward the witch's wand in her hand.

Wooden mixing spoon.

"Mom—" Her voice croaked like a frog; she still couldn't move. "How did you—how could you—"

"Well, you saw what I was turning into. Nobody was listening to me."

"But how—"

"I learned a few things at the school before I left to have you." She stroked Felix's hair gently; he was already asleep. "Peace," she breathed contentedly.

"Mom. It was my Naming Day."

Her mother just looked at her. Averil saw the witch in her eyes, then, shadowy, shrewd, filled with remnants of magic. "And did you finally choose a name?"

Averil looked back at the Averil who had been so blithely trying on lovely names and discarding them just that morning. She moved finally, closing the door behind her. She dropped down on the couch next to Felix.

"No," she admitted, twining the spoon handle through her hair. "And now, nothing seems to fit me."

Her mother said after a moment, "I have a name that I haven't used since I left Oglesby, until today. You can have it, if you want."

"Really?" Averil studied her mother, suddenly curious. "What is it?"

Her mother leaned over Felix, whispered it into Averil's ear. The name seemed to flow through her like air and light. Her eyes grew wide; visions and enchantments swirled in her head. "Mom, that's brilliant," she exclaimed, straightening with a bounce. "That's amazing!" Felix stirred; they both patted him until he quieted again. "How did you think of it?" Averil whispered.

"It was just there, when I looked for it. Do you want it?"

"Are you sure? You really want me to have it?"

Her mother smiled wryly. "I really don't want to be tempted to use magic on my children again. Anyway, ever since you became interested in the wizardly arts, I dreamed of giving it to you. Of it meaning all the wonderful magic you could do." She paused, shifted a strand of Averil's shining hair back from her face. "Lately, I haven't been sure that you'd want it."

"I want it," Averil said softly. "I want it more than any other name. I never would have thought of it, but it's perfect. It feels like me."

"Good." Her mother rose then, took the spoon from her. "I'm glad you brought this back; it's my favorite mixing spoon."

"You didn't give me much choice." Averil watched her walk into the kitchen to drop the spoon into the utensils jar. "You make a pretty fierce witch."

"Thanks, sweetie. Are you hungry? Do you want a sandwich before you go back to school?"

"You know they won't let me in after First Bell."

"That's what they say," her mother said with a chuckle. "But once you find your way in, they always let you stay."

Averil stared at her. She glimpsed something then, in the corner of her mind's eye; it grew clearer as she turned her thoughts to contemplate it. Her mother, giving up all the knowledge she had acquired at Oglesby, all that potential, just to go and have Averil and take care of her. And now that incredible name . . .

She drew a sudden breath, whispered, "I didn't miss it."

Her mother, who had stuck her head in the refrigerator and was searching through jars, said, "What?"

"My Naming. You just named me."

Her mother turned, embracing mayonnaise, mustard, pickles, cold cuts and a head of lettuce. "What, sweetie? I didn't hear you."

"Never mind," Averil said, and summoned all her powers to speak words of most arduous and dire magic. "I'll-watch-Felix-for-the-rest-of-the-day-if-you-want-to-go-out."

Her mother heard that just fine.

Winter's Wife

Elizabeth Hand

One of the most respected writers of her generation, Elizabeth Hand won both the Nebula Award and the World Fantasy Award for her story "Last Summer at Mars Hill," and has been a finalist for the World Fantasy Award on a number of other occasions as well. Her books include the novels Winterlong, Aestival Tide, Icarus Descending, Image of Support, Waking the Moon, Glimmering, *and* Black Light. *She's also written a number of* Star Wars *novels, including* Maze of Deception, Hunted, A New Threat, *and* Pursuit, *and movie novelizations such as* Twelve Monkeys, Anna and the King, Catwoman, *and* The Affair of the Necklace. *Her acclaimed short fiction, which has appeared in most of the major markets in science fiction, fantasy, and horror, has been collected in* Last Summer at Mars Hill, Bibliomancy, *and* Saffron & Brimstone. *Her most recent book is the novel* Mortal Love. *Coming up is a new novel,* Generation Loss. *She lives with her family in Lincolnville, Maine.*

In the—appropriately enough—chilling story that follows, she shows us what happens when all the money and influence and bright shiny gadgets of the modern world come into conflict with ancient magic. Magic old and slow and cold, and as immovable as rock.

WINTER'S real name was Roderick Gale Winter. But everyone in Paswegas County, not just me and people who knew him personally, called him Winter. He lived in an old school bus down the road from my house, and my mother always tells how when she first moved here he scared the crap out of her. It wasn't even him that scared her, she hadn't even met him yet; just the fact that there was this creepy-looking old school bus stuck in the middle of the woods, with smoke coming out of a chimney and these huge piles of split logs around and trucks and cranes and heavy equipment, and in the summer all kinds of chain saws and stuff, and in the fall deer and dead coyotes hanging from this big pole that my mother said looked like a gallows, and blood on the snow, and once a gigantic dead pig's head with tusks, which my mother said was scarier even than the coyotes. Which, when you think of it, does sound pretty bad, so you can't blame her for being freaked out. It's funny now because she and Winter are best friends, though that doesn't mean so much as it does other places, like Chicago, where my mother moved here from, because I think everyone in Shaker Harbor thinks Winter is their friend.

The school bus, when you get inside it, is sweet.

Winter's family has been in Shaker Harbor for six generations, and even before that they lived somewhere else in Maine.

"I have Passamaquoddy blood," Winter says. "If I moved somewhere else, I'd melt."

He didn't look like a Native American, though, and my mother said if he did have Indian blood it had probably been diluted by now. Winter was really tall and skinny, not sick skinny but bony and muscular, stooped from having to duck through the door of the school bus all those years. He always wore a gimme cap that said WINTER TREE SERVICE, and I can remember how shocked I was once when I saw him at Town Meeting without his hat, and he had almost no hair. He'd hunt and butcher his own deer, but he wouldn't eat it—he said he'd grown up dirt-poor in a cabin that didn't even have a wooden floor, just pounded earth, and his family would eat anything they could hunt, including snake and skunk and snapping turtle. So he'd give all his venison away, and when people hired him to butcher their livestock and gave him meat, he'd give that away, too.

That was how my mother met him, that first winter fifteen years ago when she was living here alone, pregnant with me. There was a big storm going on, and she looked out the window and saw this tall guy stomping through the snow carrying a big paper bag.

"You a vegetarian?" he said, when she opened the door. "Everyone says there's a lady from away living here who's going to have a baby and she's a vegetarian. But you don't look like one to me."

My mother said no, she wasn't a vegetarian, she was a registered certified massage therapist.

"Whatever the hell that is," said Winter. "You going to let me in? Jesus Q. Murphy, is that your woodstove?"

See, my mother had gotten pregnant by a sperm donor. She had it all planned out, how she was going to move way up north and have a baby and raise it—him, me—by herself and live off the land and be a massage therapist and hang crystals in the windows and there would be this good energy and everything was going to be perfect. And it would have been, if she had moved to, like, Huntington Beach or even Boston, someplace like that, where it would be warmer and there would be good skate parks, instead of a place where you have to drive two hours to a skate park and it snows from November till the end of May. And in the spring you can't even skate on the roads here because they're all dirt roads and so full of potholes you could live in one. But the snowboarding is good, especially since Winter let us put a jump right behind his place.

But this part is all before any snowboarding, because it was all before me, though not much before. My mother was living in this tiny two-room camp with no indoor plumbing and no running water, with an ancient woodstove, what they call a parlor stove, which looked nice but didn't put out any heat and caused a chimney fire. Which was how Winter heard about her, because the volunteer fire department came and afterwards all anyone was talking about at the Shaker Harbor Variety Store was how this crazy lady from away had bought Martin Weed's old run-down camp and now she was going to have a baby and freeze to death or burn the camp down—probably both—which probably would have been okay with them except no one liked to think about the baby getting frozen or burned up.

So Winter came by and gave my mother the venison and looked at her woodpile and told her she was burning green wood, which builds up creosote, which was why she had the chimney fire, and he asked her who sold her the wood, so she told him. And the next day the guy who sold her the wood came by and dumped off three cords of seasoned wood and drove off without saying a word, and the day after that two other guys came by with a brand-new woodstove, which was ugly but very efficient and had a sheath around it so a baby wouldn't get burned if he touched it. And the day after *that,* Winter came by to make sure the stove was hooked up right, and he went to all the cabin's windows with sheets of plastic and a hair dryer and covered them so the cold wouldn't get in, and then he showed my mother where there was a spring in the woods that she could go to and fill water jugs rather than buy them at the grocery door. He also gave her a chamber pot so she wouldn't have to use the outhouse, and told her he knew of someone who had a composting toilet they'd sell to her cheap.

All of which might make you think that when I say "Winter's wife" I'm referring to my mom. But I'm not. Winter's wife is someone else.

Still, when I was growing up, Winter was always at our house. And I was at his place, when I got older. Winter chops down trees, what they call wood lot management—he cuts trees for people, but in a good way, so the forest can grow back and be healthy. Then he'd split the wood so the people could burn it for firewood. He had a portable sawmill—one of the scary things Mom had seen in his yard—and he also mills wood so people can build houses with the lumber. He's an auctioneer, and he can play the banjo and one of those washboard things like you see in old movies. He showed me how to jump-start a car with just a wire coat hanger, also how to carve wood and build a tree house and frame a window. When my mother had our little addition put on with a bathroom in it, Winter did a lot of the carpentry, and he taught me how to do that, too.

He's also a dowser, a water witch. That's someone who can tell where water is underground, just by walking around in the woods holding a stick in front of him. You'd think this was more of that crazy woo-woo stuff my mother is into, which is what I thought whenever I heard about it.

But then one day me and my friend Cody went out to watch Winter do it. We were hanging out around Winter's place, clearing brush. He let us use the hill behind the school bus for snowboarding, and that's where we'd built that sweet jump, and Winter had saved a bunch of scrap wood so that when spring came we could build a half-pipe for skating too.

But now it was spring, and since we didn't have any money really to pay Winter for it, he put us to work clearing brush. Cody is my age, almost fourteen. So we're hacking at this brush and swatting blackflies, and I could tell that at any minute Cody was going to say he had to go do homework, which was a lie because we didn't have any, when Winter shows up in his pickup, leans out the window, and yells at us.

"You guys wanna quit goofing off and come watch someone do some real work?"

So then me and Cody had an argument about who was going to ride shotgun with Winter, and then we had another argument about who was going to ride in the truck bed, which is actually more fun. And then we took so long arguing that Winter yelled at us and made us both ride in the back.

So we got to the place where Winter was going to work. This field that had been a dairy farm, but the farm wasn't doing too good and the guy who owned it had to sell it off. Ms. Whitton, a high school teacher, was going to put a little modular house on it. There'd been a bad drought a few years earlier, and a lot of wells ran dry. Ms. Whitton didn't have a lot of money to spend on digging around for a well, so she hired Winter to find the right spot.

"Justin!" Winter yelled at me as he hopped out of the truck. "Grab me that hacksaw there—"

I gave him the saw, then me and Cody went and goofed around some more while Winter walked around the edge of the field, poking at brush and scrawny trees. After a few minutes he took the hacksaw to a spindly sapling.

"Got it!" Winter yelled, and stumbled back into the field. "If we're going to find water here, we better find a willow first."

It was early spring, and there really weren't any leaves out yet, so what he had was more like a pussy willow, with furry gray buds and green showing where he'd sawn the branch off. Winter stripped the buds from it until he had a forked stick. He held the two ends like he was holding handlebars and began to walk around the field.

It was weird. Cause at first, me and Cody were laughing—we didn't mean to, we couldn't help it. It just looked funny, Winter walking back and forth with his arms out holding that stick. He kind of looked like Frankenstein. Even Ms. Whitton was smiling.

But then it was like everything got very still. Not quiet—you could hear the wind blowing in the trees, and hear birds in the woods, and someone running a chain saw far off—but still, like all of a sudden you were in a movie and you knew something was about to happen. The sun was warm, I could smell dirt and cow manure and meadowsweet. Cody started slapping blackflies and swearing. I felt dizzy, not bad dizzy, but like you do when the school bus drives fast over a high bump and you go up on your seat. A few feet away Winter continued walking in a very straight line, the willow stick held out right in front of him.

And all of a sudden the stick began to bend. I don't mean that Winter's arms bent down holding it: I mean the stick itself, the point that stuck straight out, bent down like it was made of rubber and someone had grabbed it and yanked it towards the ground. Only it wasn't made of rubber, it was stiff wood, and there was no one there—but it still bent, pointing at a mossy spot between clumps of dirt.

"Holy crap," I said.

Cody shut up and looked. So did Ms. Whitton.

"Oh my God," she said.

Winter stopped, angling the stick back and forth like he was fighting with it. Then it lunged down, and he yelled, "Whoa!" and opened his hands and dropped it. Me and Cody ran over.

"This is it," said Winter. He pulled a spool of pink surveyor's tape from his pocket and broke off a length. I stared warily at the willow stick, half-expecting it to wiggle up like a snake, but it didn't move. After a moment I picked it up.

"How'd you do that?" demanded Cody.

"I didn't do it," said Winter evenly. He took the stick from my hand, snapped off the forked part, and tossed it; tied the surveyor's tape to what remained and stuck it in the ground. "Wood does that. Wood talks to you, if you listen."

"No lie," I said. "Can you show me how to do that sometime?"

"Sure," said Winter. "Can't today, got a towing job. But someday."

He and Ms. Whitton started talking about money and who had the best rates for drilling. The next time my mom drove past that field, the drill rig was there hammering at the ground right where Winter's stick had pointed, and the next time I ran into Ms. Whitton in the hall at school she told me the well was already dug and all geared up to pump a hundred gallons a minute, once she got her foundation dug and her house moved in.

Not long after that, Winter announced he was going to Reykjavik.

It was after school one day, and Winter had dropped by to shoot the breeze.

"What's Reykjavik?" I asked.

"It's in Iceland," said my mother. She cracked the window open and sat at the kitchen table opposite Winter and me. "Why on earth are you going to Reykjavik?"

"To pick up my wife," said Winter.

"Your wife?" My eyes widened. "You're married?"

"Nope. That's why I'm going to Iceland to pick her up. I met her online, and we're going to get married."

My mother looked shocked. "In *Iceland*?"

Winter shrugged. "Hey, with a name like mine, where else you gonna find a wife?"

So he went to Iceland. I thought he'd be gone for a month, at least, but a week later the phone rang and my mom answered and it was Winter, saying he was back safe and yes, he'd brought his wife with him.

"That's incredible," said Mom. She put the phone down and shook her head. "He was there for four days, got married, and now they're back. I can't believe it."

A few days later they dropped by so Winter could introduce us to her. It was getting near the end of the school year, and me and Cody were outside throwing stuff at my tree house, using the open window as a target. Sticks, a Frisbee, a broken yo-yo. Stuff like that.

"Why are you trying to break the house?" a woman asked.

I turned. Winter stood there grinning, hands in the pockets of his jeans, his gimme cap pushed back so the bill pointed almost straight up. Beside him stood a woman who barely came up to his shoulder. She was so slight that for a second I thought she was another kid, maybe one of the girls from school who'd ridden her bike over or hopped a ride in Winter's truck. But she didn't have a kid's body, and she sure didn't have a kid's eyes.

"Justin." Winter squared his shoulders and his voice took on a mock-formal tone. "I'd like you to meet my wife. Vala, this is Justin."

"Justin." The way she said my name made my neck prickle. It was like she was turning the word around in her mouth; like she was tasting it. "*Gleour mig ao kynnast per*. That's Icelandic for 'I am glad to meet you.' "

She didn't really have an accent, although her voice sounded more English than American. And she definitely didn't look like anyone I'd ever seen in Maine, even though she was dressed pretty normal. Black jeans, a black T-shirt. Some kind of weird-looking bright blue shoes with thick rubber soles, which I guess is what people wear in Iceland; also a bright blue windbreaker. She had long, straight black hair done in two ponytails—one reason she looked like a kid—kind of slanted eyes and a small mouth and the palest skin I've ever seen.

It was the eyes that really creeped me out. They were long and narrow and very very dark, so dark you couldn't even see the pupil. And they weren't brown but blue, so deep a blue they were almost black. I'd never seen eyes that color before, and I didn't really like seeing them now. They were cold—not mean or angry, just somehow *cold*; or maybe it was that they made *me* feel cold, looking at them.

And even though she looked young, because she was skinny and her hair didn't have any gray in it and her face wasn't wrinkled, it was like she was somehow pretending to be young. Like when someone pretends to like kids, and you know they don't, really. Though I didn't get the feeling Vala didn't like kids. She seemed more puzzled, like maybe we looked as strange to her as she did to me.

"You haven't told me why you are trying to break the house," she said.

I shrugged. "Uh, we're not. We're just trying to get things through that window."

Cody glanced at Vala, then began searching for more rocks to throw.

Vala stared at him coolly. "Your friend is very rude."

She looked him up and down, then walked over to the tree house. It was built in the crotch of a big old maple tree, and it was so solid you could live in it, if you wanted to, only it didn't have a roof.

"What tree is this?" she asked, and looked at Winter.

"Red maple," he said.

"Red maple," she murmured. She ran her hand along the trunk, stroking it, like it was a cat. "Red maple . . ."

She turned and stared at me. "You made this house? By yourself?"

"No." She waited, like it was rude of me not to say more. So I walked over to her and stood awkwardly, staring up at the bottom of the tree house. "Winter helped me. I mean, your husband—Mr. Winter."

"Mr. Winter." Unexpectedly she began to laugh. A funny laugh, like a little kid's, and after a moment I laughed too. "So I am Mrs. Winter? But who should be Winter's proper wife—Spring, maybe?"

She made a face when she said this, like she knew how dumb it sounded; then reached to take my hand. She drew me closer to her, until we both stood beside the tree. I felt embarrassed—maybe this was how they did things in Iceland, but not here in Maine—but I was flattered, too. Because the way she looked at me, sideways from the corner of her eyes, and the way she smiled, not like I was a kid but another grown-up . . . it was like she knew a secret, and she acted like I knew it, too.

Which of course I didn't. But it was kind of cool that she thought so. She let go of my hand and rested hers against the tree again, rubbing a patch of lichen.

"There are no trees in Iceland," she said. "Did you know that? No trees. Long long ago they cut them all down to build houses or ships, or to burn. And so we have no trees, only rocks and little bushes that come to here—"

She indicated her knee, then tapped the tree trunk. "And like this—lichen, and moss. We have a joke, do you know it?"

She took a breath, then said, "What do you do if you get lost in a forest in Iceland?"

I shook my head. "I dunno."

"Stand up."

It took me a moment to figure that out. Then I laughed, and Vala smiled at me. Again she looked like she was waiting for me to say something. I wanted to be polite, but all I could think was how weird it must be, to come from a place where there were no trees to a place like Maine, where there's trees everywhere.

So I said, "Uh, do you miss your family?"

She gave me a funny look. "My family? They are happy to live with the rocks back in Iceland. I am tired of rocks."

A shadow fell across her face. She glanced up as Winter put his hands on her shoulders. "Your mother home, Justin?" he asked. "We're on our way into town, just wanted to say a quick hello and introduce the new wife—"

I nodded and pointed back to the house. As Winter turned to go, Vala gave me another sharp look.

"He tells me many good things about you. You and he are what we would call *feogar*—like a father and his son, Winter says. So I will be your godmother."

She pointed a finger at me, then slowly drew it to my face until she touched my chin. I gasped: her touch was so cold it burned.

"There," she murmured. "Now I will always know you."

And she followed Winter inside. When they were gone, Cody came up beside me.

"Was that freaky or what?" he said. He stared at the house. "She looks like that weird singer, Boink."

"You mean Bjork, you idiot."

"Whatever. Where is Iceland, anyway?"

"I have no clue."

"Me neither." Cody pointed at my chin. "Hey, you're bleeding, dude."

I frowned, then gingerly touched the spot where Vala had pressed her finger. It wasn't bleeding; but when I looked at it later that night I saw a red spot, shaped like a fingerprint. Not a scab or blister or scar but a spot like a birthmark, deep red like blood. Over the next few days it faded, and finally disappeared; but I can still feel it there sometimes even now, a sort of dull ache that gets worse when it's cold outside, or snowing.

✳

THAT same month, Thomas Tierney returned to Paswegas County. He was probably the most famous person in this whole state, after Stephen King, but everyone up here loves Stephen King and I never heard anyone say anything good about Thomas Tierney except after he disappeared; and then the only thing people said was good riddance to bad rubbish. Even my mom, who gets mad if you say something bad about anyone, even if they hit you first, never liked Thomas Tierney.

"He's one of those people who thinks they can buy anything. And if he can't buy it, he ruins it for everyone else."

Though the truth was there wasn't much that he wasn't able to buy, especially in Paswegas. People here don't have a lot of money. They had more after Tierney's telemarketing company moved into the state and put up its telephone centers everywhere, even one not too far from Shaker Harbor, which is pretty much the end of nowhere. Then people who used to work as fishermen or farmers or teachers or nurses, but who couldn't make a living at it anymore, started working for International Corporate Enterprises. ICE didn't pay a lot, but I guess it paid okay, if you didn't mind sitting in a tiny cubicle and calling strangers on the phone when they were in the middle of dinner and annoying them so they swore at you or just hung up.

Once when she heard me and Cody ranking on people who worked at ICE, my mom took us aside and told us we had to be careful what we said, because even if we hated the company, it gave people jobs, and that was nothing to sneeze at. Of course a lot of those people who worked for ICE ended up not being able to afford to live here anymore, because Tierney gave all his friends from away the expensive jobs; and then they bought land here, which used to be cheap, and built these big fancy houses. So now normal people can't afford to live here, unless they were lucky enough to already own a house or land, like my mom and Winter.

But then Tierney got caught doing something bad, sneaking money from his company or something, and ICE got bought by a bigger company, and they shut down all their operations in Maine, and all the people who worked there got thrown out of work and a lot of them who did own their own houses or land got them taken away because they couldn't afford to pay their bills anymore. Then people *really* hated Thomas Tierney; but it didn't do any good, because he never even got in trouble for what he did. I mean he didn't go to jail or anything, and he didn't lose his money or his house down in Kennebunkport or his yacht or his private airplane.

As a matter of fact, the opposite happened: he bought the land next to Winter's. Winter dropped by the day he found out about it.

"That sumbitch bought old Lonnie Packard's farm!" he yelled.

Me and Cody looked at each other and sort of smirked, but we didn't say anything. I could tell Cody wanted to laugh, like I did—who the hell actually says "sumbitch?"—but at the same time it was scary, because we'd never seen Winter get mad before.

"I can't blame Lonnie," Winter went on, shifting from one foot to the other and tugging at his cap. "He had to sell his lobster boat last year 'cause he couldn't pay his taxes, and then he had that accident and couldn't pay the hospital. And it's a salt farm right there on the ocean, so he never got much out of it except the view."

Cody asked, "Why didn't he sell it to you?"

Winter whacked his palm against the wall. "That's what I said! I told Lonnie long time ago, ever he wanted to sell that land, I'd take it. But yesterday he told me, 'Winter, your pockets just ain't that deep.' I said, 'Well, Lonnie, how deep is deep?' And he pointed out there at the Atlantic Ocean, and said, 'You see that? You go out to the Grand Banks and find the deepest part, and I'm telling you it ain't deep as Thomas Tierney's pockets.'"

So that was that. Tell you the truth, I didn't give much thought to it. Where we snowboarded in the woods was safely on Winter's property, I knew that; besides which, it was late spring now, and me and Cody were busy working on that half-pipe behind Winter's house and, once it was done, skating on it.

Sometimes Winter's wife would come out and watch us. Winter had made her a bench from a hunk of oak, laid slats across it, and carved her name on the seat, VALA, with carved leaves and vines coming out of the letters. The bench was set up on a little rise, so that you could look out across the tops of the trees and just catch a glimpse of the ocean, silver-blue above the green. Vala was so tiny she looked like another kid sitting there, watching us and laughing when we fell, though never in a mean way. Her laugh was like her eyes: there was a kind of coldness to it, but it wasn't nasty, more like she had never seen anyone fall before and every time it happened (which was a lot) it was a surprise to her. Even though it was warmer now, she always wore that same blue windbreaker, and over it a sweatshirt that I recognized as one of Winter's, so big it was like a saggy dress. It could get wicked hot out there at the edge of the woods, but I never saw her take that sweatshirt off.

"Aren't you hot?" I asked her once. She'd brought some water for us and some cookies she'd made, gingersnaps that were thin and brittle as ice and so spicy they made your eyes sting.

"Hot?" She shook her head. "I never get warm. Except with Winter." She smiled then, one of her spooky smiles that always made me nervous. "I tell him it's the only time winter is ever warm, when he is lying beside me."

I felt my face turn red. On my chin, the spot where she had touched me throbbed as though someone had shoved a burning cigarette against my skin. Vala's smile grew wider, her eyes too. She began to laugh.

"You're still a boy." For a moment she sounded almost like my mother. "Good boys, you and your friend. You will grow up to be good men. Not like this man Tierney, who thinks he can own the sea by buying salt. There is nothing more dangerous than a man who thinks he has power." She lifted her head to gaze into the trees, then turned to stare at me. "Except for one thing."

But she didn't say what that was.

I had always heard a lot about Thomas Tierney, and even though I had never seen him, there were signs of him everywhere around Shaker Harbor. The addition to the library; the addition to the school; the big old disused mill—renamed the ICE Mill—that he bought and filled with a thousand tiny cubicles, each with its own computer and its own telephone. The ICE Mill employed so many people that some of them drove two hours each way to work—there weren't enough people around Shaker Harbor to fill it.

But now it was empty, with big FOR SALE signs on it. Winter said it would stay empty, too, because no one in Paswegas County could afford to buy it.

"And no one outside of Paswegas County would *want* to buy it," he added. "Watch that doesn't drip—"

I was helping Winter varnish a crib he'd made, of wood milled from an elm tree that had died of the blight. He wouldn't say who it was for, even when I asked him outright, but I assumed it was a present for Vala. She didn't look pregnant, and I was still a little fuzzy about the precise details of what exactly might make her pregnant, in spite of some stuff me and Cody checked out online one night. But there didn't seem much point in making a trip to Iceland to get a wife if you weren't going to have kids. That's what Cody's dad said, anyway, and he should know since Cody has five brothers and twin sisters.

"I think they should make the mill into an indoor skate park," I said, touching up part of the crib I'd missed. "That would be sweet."

We were working outside, so I wouldn't inhale varnish fumes, in the shadow of a tower of split logs that Winter sold as firewood. I had to be careful that sawdust didn't get onto the newly varnished crib, or bugs.

Winter laughed. "Not much money in skate parks."

"I'd pay."

"That's my point." Winter shoved his cap back from his forehead. "Ready to break for lunch?"

Usually Winter made us sandwiches, Swiss cheese and tomato and horseradish sauce. Sometimes Vala would make us lunch, and then I'd lie and say I wasn't hungry or had already eaten, since the sandwiches she made mostly had fish in them—not tuna fish, either—and were on these tiny little pieces of bread that tasted like cardboard.

But today Winter said we'd go into town and get something from Shelley's Place, the hot dog stand down by the harbor. It was warm out, mid-August; school would start soon. I'd spent the summer hanging out with Cody and some of our friends, until the last few weeks, when Cody had gone off to Bible camp.

That's when Winter put me to work. Because along with the crib, Winter had started building a house—a real house, not an addition to the school bus. I helped him clear away brush, then helped build the forms for the foundation to be poured into. Once the concrete cured, we began framing the structure. Sometimes Vala helped, until Winter yelled at her to stop, anyway. Then she'd go off to tend the little garden she'd planted at the edge of the woods.

Now I didn't know where Vala was. So I put aside the can of varnish and hopped into Winter's pickup, and we drove into town. Most of the summer people had already left, but there were still a few sailboats in the harbor, including one gigantic yacht, the *Ice Queen*, a three-masted schooner that belonged to Thomas Tierney. According to Winter she had a crew of ten, not just a captain and mate and deckhands but a cook and housekeeper, all for Tierney; as well as a red-and-white-striped mainsail, not that you'd ever have any trouble telling her apart from any of the other boats around here.

When he saw the *Ice Queen*, Winter scowled. But there was no other sign of Tierney, not that I could see. A few summer holdovers stood in line in front of Shelley's little food stand, trying to act like they fit in with the locals, even though the only other people were contractors working on job sites.

And Lonnie Packard. He was at the very front of the line, paying for a hot dog with onions and sauerkraut wrapped in a paper towel. It was the first time I'd seen Lonnie since I'd heard about him selling his farm to Thomas Tierney, and from the look on Winter's face, it was the first time he'd seen him, too. His mouth was twisted like he wasn't sure if he was going to smile or spit something out, but then Lonnie turned and nodded at him.

"Winter," he said. He pronounced it "Wintah" in this exaggerated way he had, like he was making fun of his own strong accent. "How's it hanging?"

Winter poked at the bill of his cap and gave his head a small shake. "Not bad." He looked at Lonnie's hot dog, then flashed me a sideways grin. "Now *that* looks like lunch. Right, Justin?"

So that's how I knew Winter wasn't going to stay pissed about Lonnie selling his farm, which was kind of a relief.

But Lonnie didn't look relieved. He looked uncomfortable, although Lonnie usually looked uncomfortable. He was a big rough-faced guy, not as tall as Winter but definitely plus-sized, with a bushy brown beard and baggy jeans tucked into high rubber fisherman's boots, which kind of surprised me since I knew he'd had to sell his boat. Then I remembered all the money he must have gotten from Thomas Tierney; enough to buy another boat, probably. Enough to buy anything he wanted.

"Gotta run," said Lonnie. "Got you an assistant there, eh, Winter?"

"Justin does good work," said Winter, and moved up to the window to place our order. For a moment Lonnie stared at him like he was going to say something else, but Winter was already talking to Shelley.

Instead, Lonnie glanced at me again. It was a funny look, not like he was going to speak to me, more like he was trying to figure something out. Lonnie's not stupid, either. He puts on that heavy accent and acts like he's never been south of Bangor, but my mother said he actually has a law degree and fishes just because he likes it better than being a lawyer, which I think I would, too. I waited to see if he was going to talk to me, but instead he turned and walked quickly to where a brand-new SUV was parked in one of the spots reserved for fishermen, got inside, and drove off. I watched him go, then angled up beside Winter to get my food.

Shelley gave me a quick smile and went back to talking to Winter. "See you're putting a house up by your place," she said, and handed him a paper towel with two hot dogs on it, a container of fried clams for Winter, and two bottles of Moxie. Winter nodded but didn't say anything, just passed her some money.

"Regular housing boom going on down there," Shelley added, then looked past us to the next customer. "Can I help you?"

We drove back to Winter's place and ate, sitting outside on a couple of lawn chairs and listening to woodpeckers in the pine grove. The air smelled nice, like sawdust and varnish and fried clams. When I was almost done, Vala stepped out of the school bus and walked over to me.

"*Ertu búinn?*" she said teasingly. "Are you finished? And you didn't save any for me?"

I looked uncertainly at Winter, still chewing.

"Mmm-mm," he said, flapping his hand at me. "None for her! Nothing unhealthy!"

"Hmph." Vala tossed her head, black ponytails flying. "Like I'd eat that—it's nothing but grease."

She watched disapprovingly as the last fried clam disappeared into Winter's mouth, then looked at me. "Come here, Justin. I want to show you something."

"Hey!" Winter called in mock alarm as Vala beckoned me towards the edge of the woods. "He's on the clock!"

"Now he's off," retorted Vala, and stuck her tongue out. "Come on."

Vala was strange. Sometimes she acted like my mother, grumpy about me forgetting to take my shoes off when I went into the school bus, or if me and Cody made too much noise. Other times, like now, she acted more like a girl my own age, teasing and unpredictable.

The way she looked changed, too. I don't mean her clothes—she pretty much wore the same thing all the time—but the way that sometimes she would look old, like my mom does, and other times she'd look the same age as me and my friends. Which creeped me out, especially if it was one of those times when she was acting young, too.

Fortunately, just then she was acting young but looking older, like someone who would be married to Winter. For one thing, she was wearing his clothes, a pair of jeans way too big for her and cuffed up so much you couldn't even see her shoes, and that baggy sweatshirt, despite it being so hot.

"I said *come*," she repeated, and whacked me on the shoulder.

I stood hastily and followed her, wondering if everyone in Iceland was like this, or if it was just Vala.

Under the trees everything was green and gold and warm; not hot like out in the full sun, but not cool, either. It made me sweat, and my sweat and the dim light made the mosquitoes come out, lots of them, though they never seemed to bother Vala, and after a few minutes I ignored them and (mostly) forgot about them. The ground was soft and smelled like worms, a good smell that made me think of fishing, and now and then we'd go by a kind of tree that smelled so good I'd stop for a second, a tree that Winter calls Balm of Gilead, because its buds smell like incense.

Winter owned a lot of land, more than a hundred acres. Some of it he cut for firewood or lumber, but not this part. This part he left wild, because it joined up with Lonnie's land—Thomas Tierney's land, now—and because it was old-growth forest. People think that all the woods in Maine are wild and old, but most of it isn't much older than what you'd find someplace like New Jersey—the trees were cut hundreds or maybe a thousand years ago by the Passamaquoddy or other Indians, and when those trees grew back they were cut by Vikings, and when those trees grew back they were cut by the English and the French and everyone else, all the way up till now.

So there's actually not a lot of true virgin forest, even if the trees look ancient, like what you see in a movie when they want you to think it's someplace totally wild, when it's really, like, trees that are maybe forty or fifty years old. Baby trees.

But these trees weren't like that. These were old trees—wolf trees, some of them, the kind of trees that Winter usually cuts down. A wolf tree is a big crooked tree with a huge canopy that hogs all the light and soil and crowds out the other trees. Wolf trees are junk trees, because they're crooked and spread out so much they're not much good for lumber, and they overwhelm other, smaller trees and keep them from growing up tall and straight so they can be harvested.

When I was little I'd go with Winter into the woods to watch him work, and I was always afraid of the wolf trees. Not because there was anything scary about them—they looked like ordinary trees, only big.

But I thought wolves lived in them. When I said that to Winter once, he laughed.

"I thought that too, when I was your age." He was oiling his chain saw, getting ready to limb a wolf tree, a red oak. Red oaks smell terrible when you cut them, the raw wood stinks—they smell like dog crap. "Want to know the real reason they call them that?"

I nodded, breathing through my mouth.

"It's because a thousand years ago, in England and around there, they'd hang outlaws from a tree like this. Wolf's-head trees, they called them, because the outlaws were like wolves, preying on weaker people."

Where the wolf trees grew here, they had shaded out most other trees. Now and then I saw an old apple tree overgrown with wild grape vines, remnants of Lonnie's family farm. Because even though this was old growth forest, birds and animals don't know that. They eat fruit from the farm then poop out the seeds—that's how you get apple trees and stuff like that in the middle of the woods.

I was getting hot and tired of walking. Vala hadn't said anything since we started, hadn't even looked back at me, and I wondered if she'd forgotten I was even there. My mother said pregnancy makes women spacey, more than usual even. I was trying to think of an excuse to turn back, when she stopped.

"Here," she said.

We'd reached a hollow on the hillside above the farm. I could just make out the farmhouse and barn and outbuildings, some apple trees and the overgrown field that led down to the ocean. There was no real beach there, just lots of big granite rocks, also a long metal dock that I didn't remember having seen before.

It was still a pretty spot, tucked into the woods. A few yards from the farmhouse, more trees marched down to a cliff above the rocky beach. Small trees, all twisted from the wind: except for three huge white pines, each a hundred feet tall.

Winter called these the King's Pines, and they were gigantic.

"These trees are ancient," he'd told me, pointing up at one. "See anything up there?"

I squinted. I knew bald eagles nested near the ocean, but I didn't see anything that looked like a nest. I shook my head.

Winter put his hand on my shoulder and twisted me till I was staring almost straight up. "There, on the trunk—see where the bark's been notched?"

I saw it then, three marks of an axe in the shape of an arrow.

"That's the King's Mark," said Winter. "Probably dating back to about 1690. That means these were the King's Trees, to be used for masts in the King's naval fleet. Over three hundred years ago, this was a big tree. And it was probably at least three hundred years old then."

Now, with Vala, I could see the King's Pines jutting out above the other trees, like the masts of a schooner rising from a green sea. I figured that's what Vala was going to show me, and so I got ready to be polite and act like I already didn't know about them.

Instead she touched my arm and pointed just a few feet away, towards a clearing where trees had grown around part of the pasture.

"Whoa," I whispered.

In the middle of the clearing was a bush. A big bush, a quince, its long thin branches covered with green leaves and small red flowers—brilliant red, the color of Valentines, and so bright after the dim woods that I had to blink.

And then, after blinking, I thought something had gone wrong with my eyes; because the bush seemed to be *moving*. Not moving in the wind—there wasn't any wind—but moving like it was breaking apart then coming back together again, the leaves lifting away from the branches and flickering into the air, going from dark green to shining green like metallic paint, and here and there a flash of red like a flower had spun off, too.

But what was even more bizarre was that the bush made a noise. It was *buzzing*, not like bees but like a chain saw or weed whacker, a high-pitched sound that got louder, then softer, then louder again. I rubbed my eyes and squinted into the overgrown field, thinking maybe Thomas Tierney had hired someone to clean up, and that's what I was hearing.

There was no one there, just tall grass and apple trees and rocks, and beyond that the cliff and open sea.

"Do you see what they are?"

Vala's voice was so close to my ear that I jumped, then felt my skin prickle with goose bumps at her breath, cold as though a freezer door had opened. I shook my head and she touched my sleeve, her hand cold through the cloth, and led me into the clearing, until the bush rose above us like a red cloud.

"See?" she murmured.

The bush was full of hummingbirds—hundreds of them, darting in and out as though the bush were a city, and the spaces between the leaves streets and alleys. Some hovered above the flowers to feed, though most flew almost too fast to see. Some sat on the branches, perfectly still, and that was the weirdest thing of all, like seeing a raindrop hanging in the air.

But they didn't stay still; just perched long enough that I could get a look at one, its green green wings and the spot of red on its throat, so deep a red it was like someone had crushed its tiny body by holding it too hard. I thought maybe I could hold it, too, or touch it, anyway.

So I tried. I stood with my palm open and held my breath and didn't move. Hummingbirds whizzed around like I was part of the quince, but they didn't land on me.

I glanced at Vala. She was doing the same thing I was, this amazed smile on her face, holding both arms out in front of her so she reminded me of Winter when he was dowsing. The hummingbirds buzzed around her, too, but didn't stop. Maybe if one of us had been wearing red. Humming-birds like red.

Vala wasn't wearing red, just Winter's grubby old gray sweatshirt and jeans. But she looked strange standing there, eerie even, and for a second I had this weird feeling that I wasn't seeing Vala at all, that she had disap-peared, and I was standing next to a big gray rock.

The feeling was so strong that it creeped me out. I opened my mouth, I was going to suggest that we head back to Winter's house, when a hum-mingbird flickered right in front of Vala's face. Right in front of Vala's *eye*.

"Hey!" I yelled; and at the same instant Vala shouted, a deep grunting noise that had a word in it, but not an English word. Her hand flashed in front of her face, there was a greenish blur, and the bird was gone.

"Are you okay?" I said. I thought the hummingbird's sharp beak had stabbed her eye. "Did it—?"

Vala brought her hands to her face and gasped, blinking quickly. "I'm sorry! It frightened me—so close, I was surprised—"

Her hands dropped. She gazed at the ground by her feet. "Oh no."

Near the toe of one rubber shoe, the hummingbird lay motionless, like a tiny bright green leaf.

"Oh, I am sorry, Justin!" cried Vala. "I only wanted you to see the tree with all the birds. But it scared me—"

I crouched to look at the dead hummingbird. Vala gazed back into the woods.

"We should go," she said. She sounded unhappy, even nervous. "Win-ter will think we got lost and get mad at me for taking you away. You need to work," she added, and gave me a tight smile. "Come on."

She walked away. I stayed where I was. After a moment I picked up a stick and tentatively prodded at the dead bird. It didn't move.

It was on its back, and it looked sadder that way. I wanted to turn it over. I poked it again, harder.

It still didn't budge.

Cody doesn't mind touching dead things. I do. But the hummingbird was so small, only as long as my finger. And it was beautiful, with its black beak and the red spot at its throat and those tiny feathers, more like scales. So I picked it up.

"Holy crap," I whispered.

It was heavy. Not heavy like maybe a bigger bird would have been, a sparrow or chickadee, but *heavy*, like a rock. Not even a rock—it reminded me of one of those weights you see hanging from an old clock, those metal things shaped like pinecones or acorns, but when you touch them they feel heavy as a bowling ball, only much smaller.

The hummingbird was like that—so little I could cradle it in my cupped palm, and already cold. I guessed that rigor mortis had set in, the way it does when you hang a deer. Very gently I touched the bird's wing. I even tried to wiggle it, but the wing didn't move.

So I turned the bird in my cupped palm onto its stomach. Its tiny legs were folded up like a fly's, its eyes dull. Its body didn't feel soft, like feathers. It felt hard, solid as granite; and cold.

But it looked exactly like a live hummingbird, emerald green where the sun hit it, beak slightly curved; a band of white under the red throat. I ran my finger along its beak, then swore.

"What the frig?"

A bright red bead welled up where the dead bird's beak had punctured my skin, sharp as a nail.

I sucked my finger, quickly looked to make sure Vala hadn't seen me. I could just make her out in the distance, moving through the trees. I felt in my pocket till I found a wadded-up Kleenex, wrapped the hummingbird in it, and very carefully put it into my pocket. Then I hurried after Vala.

We walked back in silence. Only when the skeletal frame of the new house showed brightly through the trees did Vala turn to me.

"You saw the bird?" she asked.

I looked at her uneasily. I was afraid to lie, but even more afraid of what she might do if she knew what was in my pocket.

Before I could reply, she reached to touch the spot on my chin. I felt a flash of aching cold as she stared at me, her dark eyes somber but not unkind.

"I did not mean to hurt it," she said quietly. "I have never seen a bird like that one, not so close. I was scared. Not scared—startled. My reaction was too fast," she went on, and her voice was sad. Then she smiled and glanced down at my jeans pocket.

"You took it," she said.

I turned away, and Vala laughed. In front of the house, Winter looked up from a pile of two-by-sixes.

"Get your butt over here, Justin!" he yelled. "Woman, don't you go distracting him!"

Vala stuck her tongue out again, then turned back to me. "He knows," she said matter of factly. "But maybe you don't tell your friend? Or your mother."

And she walked over to kiss Winter's sunburned cheek.

I muttered, "Yeah, sure," then crossed to where I'd left the varnish. Vala stood beside her husband and sighed as she stared at the cloudless sky and the green canopy of trees stretching down to the bay. A few boats under sail moved slowly across the blue water. One was a three-masted schooner with a red-striped mainsail: Thomas Tierney's yacht.

"So, Vala," said Winter. He winked at his wife. "You tell Justin your news yet?"

She smiled. "Not yet." She pulled up the sweatshirt so I could see her stomach sticking out. "Here—"

She beckoned me over, took my hand, and placed it on her stomach. Despite the heat, her hand was icy cold. So was her stomach; but I felt a sudden heat beneath my palm, and then a series of small thumps from inside her belly. I looked at her in surprise.

"It's the baby!"

"*Eg veit,*" she said, and laughed. "I know."

"Now don't go scaring him off, talking about babies," said Winter. He put his arm around his wife. "I need him to help me finish this damn house before it snows."

I went back to varnishing. The truth is, I was glad to have something to do, so I wouldn't think about what had happened. When I got home that evening I put the hummingbird in a drawer, wrapped in an old T-shirt. For a while I'd look at it every night, after my mother came in to give me a kiss; but after a week or so I almost forgot it was there.

173

A few days later Cody got back from Bible camp. It was September now. Labor Day had come and gone, and most of the summer people. School started up. Me and Cody were in eighth grade; we were pretty sick of being with the same people since kindergarten, but it was okay. Some days we skated over at Winter's place after school. It was getting crowded there, with the piles of split firewood and all the stacks of lumber for the new house, and sometimes Winter yelled at us for getting in the way.

But mostly everything was like it usually was, except that Vala was getting more pregnant and everyone was starting to think about winter coming down.

You might not believe that people really worry about snow all the time, but here they do. My mother had already gotten her firewood from Winter back in August, and so had most of his other regular customers. Day by day, the big stacks of split wood dwindled, as Winter hauled them off for delivery.

And day by day the new house got bigger, so that soon it looked less like a kid's drawing of a stick house and more like a fairy-tale cottage come to life, with a steep roof and lots of windows, some of them square and some of them round, like portholes, and scallop-shaped shingles stained the color of cranberries. I helped with that part, and inside, too, which was great.

Because inside—inside was amazing. Winter did incredible things with wood, everyone knew that. But until then, I had only seen the things he made for money, like furniture, or things he made to be useful, like the cabinets he'd done for my mother.

Now I saw what Winter had done for himself and Vala. And if the outside of the little house looked like a fairy tale, the inside looked like something from a dream.

Winter usually carved from pine, which is a very soft wood. But he'd used oak for the beams, and covered them with faces—wind-faces with their mouths open to blow, foxes and wolves grinning from the corners, dragons and people I didn't recognize but who Vala said were spirits from Iceland.

"*Huldufolk*," she said when I asked about them. "The hidden people."

But they weren't hidden here. They were carved on the main beam that went across the living room ceiling, and on the oak posts in each corner, peeking out from carved leaves and vines and branches that made the posts look almost like real trees. There were *huldufolk* carved into the cupboards, and on benches and cabinets and bookshelves, and even on the headboard that Winter had made from a single slab of chestnut, so highly polished with beeswax that the entire bedroom smelled like honey.

So even though the house looked small from the outside, when you got inside you could get lost, wandering around and looking at all the wonderful carved things. Not just carved so the wood resembled something new, but so that you could see what was *inside* the wood, knots and whorls turned to eyes and mouths, the grain sanded and stained till it felt soft, the way skin might feel if it grew strong enough to support walls and ceilings and joists, while still managing to remain, somehow, skin, and alive.

It was the most amazing house I've ever seen. And maybe the most amazing thing wasn't that it made me want to live in it, but that after spending hours working on it, I began to feel that the house lived in *me*, the way the baby lived inside Vala.

Only, of course, I could never tell anyone that, especially Cody. He would think I'd gone nuts from inhaling varnish fumes—even though I wore a dust mask, like Vala wore a fancy ventilating mask that made her look like Darth Vader.

She was working inside, too, building a stone fireplace. She found rocks in the woods and brought them up in a wheelbarrow. Big rocks, too, I was amazed she could lift them.

"Don't tell Winter," she whispered to me when I found her once, hefting a huge chunk of granite from the edge of the woods. "He'll just worry, and yell at me. And then *I* will yell at *you*," she added, and narrowed her spooky blue-black eyes.

Once the rocks were all piled inside she took forever, deciding which one would go where in the fireplace. When I made a joke about it she frowned.

"You do not want to make rocks angry, Justin." She wasn't kidding, either. She looked pissed off. "Because rocks have a very, very long memory."

It was early morning, just after seven on a Saturday. My mom had dropped me off at Winter's place on her way to see a client. It was a beautiful day, Indian summer, the leaves just starting to turn. I could see two sailboats on the water, heading south for the winter. I would rather have been skating with Cody, but Winter was anxious to get the inside of his house finished before it got too cold, so I said I'd come over and help trim up some windows.

Winter was outside. Vala, after yelling at me about the rocks, had gone up to the bedroom to get something. I yawned, wishing I'd brought my iPod, when upstairs Vala screamed.

I froze. It was a terrifying sound, not high-pitched like a woman's voice but deep and booming. And it went on and on, without her taking a breath. I started for the steps as Winter raced in. He knocked me aside and took the stairs two at a time.

"*Vala!*"

I ran upstairs after him, through the empty hall and into the bedroom. Vala stood in front of the window, clutching her face as she gazed outside. Winter grabbed her shoulders.

"Is it the baby?" he cried. He tried to pull her towards him, but she shook her head, then pushed him away so violently that he crashed against the wall.

"What is it?" I ran to the window. Vala fell silent as I looked out across the yellowing canopy of leaves.

"Oh no." I stared in disbelief at the cliff above the Bay. "The King's Pines—"

I rubbed my eyes, hardly aware of Winter pushing me aside so he could stare out.

"*No!*" he roared.

One of the three great trees was gone—the biggest one, the one that stood nearest to the cliff edge. A blue gap showed where it had been, a chunk of sky that made me feel sick and dizzy. It was like lifting my own hand to find a finger missing. My chin throbbed and I turned so the others wouldn't see me crying.

Winter pounded the windowsill. His face was dead white, his eyes so red they looked like they'd been smeared with paint. That frightened me more than anything, until I looked up and saw Vala.

She had backed against the wall—an unfinished wall, just gray Sheetrock, blotched where the seams had been coated with putty. Her face had paled, too; but it wasn't white.

It was gray. Not a living gray, like hair or fur, but a dull, mottled color, the gray of dead bark or granite.

And not just her face but her hands and arms: everything I could see of her that had been skin, now seemed cold and dead as the heap of fireplace rocks downstairs. Her clothes drooped as though tossed on a boulder, her hair stiffened like strands of reindeer moss. Even her eyes dulled to black smears, save for a pinpoint of light in each, as though a drop of water had been caught in the hollow of a stone.

"Vala." Winter came up beside me. His voice shook, but it was low and calm, as though he were trying to keep a frightened dog from bolting. "Vala, it's all right—"

He reached to stroke the slab of gray stone wedged against the wall, reindeer moss tangling between his fingers, then let his hand drop to move across a rounded outcropping.

"Think of the baby," he whispered. "Think of the girl . . ."

The threads of reindeer moss trembled, the twin droplets welled and spilled from granite to the floor; and it was Vala there and not a stone at all, Vala falling into her husband's arms and weeping uncontrollably.

"It's *not* all right—it's *not* all right—"

He held her, stroking her head as I finally got the nerve up to speak.

"Was it—was it a storm?"

"A storm?" Abruptly Winter pulled away from Vala. His face darkened to the color of mahogany. "No, it's not a storm—"

He reached for the window and yanked it open. From the direction of the cliff came the familiar drone of a chain saw.

"It's Tierney!" shouted Winter. He turned and raced into the hall. Vala ran after him, and I ran after her.

"No—you stay here!" Winter stopped at the top of the stairs. "Justin, you wait right here with her—"

"No," I said. I glanced nervously at Vala, but to my surprise she nodded.

"No," she said. "I'm going, and Justin, too."

Winter sucked his breath through his teeth.

"Suit yourself," he said curtly. "But I'm not waiting for you. And listen—you stay with her, Justin, you understand me?"

"I will," I said, but he was already gone.

Vala and I looked at each other. Her eyes were paler than I remembered, the same dull gray as the Sheetrock; but as I stared at her they grew darker, as though someone had dropped blue ink into a glass of water.

"Come," she said. She touched my shoulder, then headed out the door after her husband. I followed.

All I wanted to do was run and catch up with Winter. I could have, too—over the summer I'd gotten taller, and I was now a few inches bigger than Vala.

But I remembered the way Winter had said *You stay with her, Justin, you understand me?* And the way he'd looked, as though I were a stranger, and he'd knock me over, or worse, if I disobeyed him. It scared me and made me feel sick, almost as sick as seeing the King's Pine chopped down; but I had no time to think about that now. I could still hear the chain saw buzzing from down the hill, a terrible sound, like when you hear a truck brake but you know it's not going to stop in time. I walked as fast as I dared, Vala just a few steps behind me. When I heard her breathing hard I'd stop and try to keep sight of Winter far ahead of us.

But after a few minutes I gave up on that. He was out of sight, and I could only hope he'd get down to the cliff and stop whoever was doing the cutting, before another tree fell.

"Listen," said Vala, and grabbed my sleeve. I thought the chain saw was still running, but then I realized it was just an echo. Because the air grew silent, and Vala had somehow sensed it before I did. I looked at her and she stared back at me, her eyes huge and round and sky-blue, a color I'd never seen them.

"There is still time," she whispered. She made a strange deep noise in the back of her throat, a growl but not an animal growl; more like the sound of thunder, or rocks falling. "Hurry—"

We crashed through the woods, no longer bothering to stay on the path. We passed the quince bush shimmering through its green haze of feeding hummingbirds. Vala didn't pause, but I slowed down to look back, then stopped.

A vehicle was parked by the farmhouse, the same new SUV I'd seen that day down at Shelley's hot dog stand: Lonnie Packard's truck. As I stared, a burly figure came hurrying through the field, the familiar orange silhouette of a chain saw tucked under his arm. He jumped into the SUV, gunned the engine, and drove off.

I swore under my breath.

"Justin!" Vala's anxious voice came from somewhere in the woods. "Come on!"

I found her at the head of the trail near the cliff. Through a broken wall of scrawny, wind-twisted trees I could just make out the two remaining pines, and the bright yellow gash that was the stump of the one that had fallen. The sharp scent of pine resin and sawdust hung in the air, and the smell of exhaust fumes from the chain saw.

But there was no other sign of Lonnie, obviously, or of anyone else.

"Look," said Vala in a hoarse whisper. She clutched me and pulled me towards her, her touch so cold it was like I'd been shot up with Novocain. My entire arm went numb. "There! The boat—"

She pointed down to the boulder-strewn beach where the dock thrust into the bay. At the end of the dock bobbed a small motorboat, a Boston Whaler. Farther out, the hulking form of the *Ice Queen* rose above the gray water, sails furled.

She was at anchor. Several small forms moved across the deck. I squinted, trying to see if I recognized any of them. A frigid spasm shot through my ribs as Vala nudged me, indicating the rocks below.

"Is that him?" she hissed. "This man Tierney?"

I saw Winter loping across the beach towards the dock, jumping from one boulder to the next. On the shore, right next to the end of the dock, stood two men. One was tall, wearing an orange life vest and a blaze orange watch cap and high rubber boots. The other was shorter, white-haired, slightly heavyset, wearing sunglasses and a red-and-white windbreaker, striped like the *Ice Queen*'s sails.

"That's him," I said.

Vala fixed her intense sky-blue gaze on me. "You're sure?"

"Yeah. I've seen his picture in the newspaper. And online."

She stood at the top of the trail and stared down. An angry voice rose from the rocks—Winter's—then another voice joined in, calmer, and a third, calm at first, then laughing. I heard Winter curse, words I couldn't believe he knew. The third man, Tierney, laughed even harder.

I glanced at Vala, still staring at what was below us. One of her hands grasped the branch of a birch tree beside the path. She seemed to be thinking; almost she might have been daydreaming, she looked so peaceful, like somehow she'd forgotten where she was and what was happening. Finally, she shook her head. Without looking back at me, she snapped the branch from the tree, dropped it, and started down the trail towards the beach.

I started after her, then hesitated.

The branch lay across the narrow path at my feet. Where Vala had touched them, the leaves had shriveled and faded, from yellow-green to the dull gray of lichen, and the white birch bark had blackened into tight, charred-looking curls.

I tried to lift the branch. It was too heavy to move.

"It's *my* land now." Thomas Tierney's voice echoed from the cliff face. "So I suggest you get the hell off it!"

I looked down to see Vala's small form at the bottom of the trail, hopping lightly from one boulder to the next as she headed for the dock. I scrambled down the path after her.

But I couldn't go as fast. For some reason, maybe because first Winter, then Vala had raced down before me, rocks had tumbled across the narrow trail. Not big rocks, but enough of them that I had to pick my way carefully to keep from falling.

Not only that: in spots a white slick of frost covered the ground, so that my feet slipped, and once I almost fell and cracked my head. I stopped for a minute, panting. As I caught my breath, I looked away from the beach, to where the cliff plunged into a deep crevice in the granite.

There, caught in the gigantic crack so that it looked as though it had grown up from the rocks, was the fallen pine. It tilted over the water, black in the shadow of the cliff, its great branches still green and strong-looking, the smell of pine sap overpowering the smell of the sea. In its uppermost branches something moved, then lifted from the tree and flew out above the bay—a bald eagle, still mottled brown and black with its young plumage.

I couldn't help it. I began to cry. Because no matter how strong and alive the tree looked, I knew it was dead. Nothing would bring it back again. It had been green when no one lived here but the Passamaquoddy, it had seen sailors come from far across the sea, and tourists in boats from Paswegas Harbor, and maybe it had even seen the *Ice Queen* earlier that morning with her red-and-white-striped mainsail and Thomas Tierney on the deck, watching as Lonnie Packard took a chain saw to its great trunk, and the tree finally fell, a crash that I hadn't heard.

But Vala had.

You stay with her, Justin, you understand me?

I took a deep breath and wiped my eyes, checked to make sure I could still see Vala on the rocks below, then continued my climb down. When I finally reached the bottom, I still had to be careful—there were tidal pools everywhere between the granite boulders, some of them skimmed with ice and all of them greasy with kelp and sea lettuce. I hurried as fast as I could towards the dock.

"You don't own those trees." Winter's voice rang out so loudly that my ears hurt. "Those are the King's Pines—no man owns them."

"Well, I own this land," retorted Tierney. "And if that doesn't make me the goddamn king, I don't know what does."

I clambered over the last stretch of rocks and ran up alongside Vala. Winter stood a few yards away from us, towering above Thomas Tierney. The other man stood uneasily at the edge of the dock. I recognized him— Al Alford, who used to work as first mate on one of the daysailers in Paswegas Harbor. Now, I guessed, he worked for Tierney.

"King?" Vala repeated. *"Hann er klikkapor."* She looked at me from the corner of her eyes. "He's nuts."

Maybe it was her saying that, or maybe it was me being pissed at myself for crying. But I took a step out towards Tierney and shouted at him.

"It's against the law to cut those trees! It's against the law to do any cutting here without a permit!"

Tierney turned to stare at me. For the first time he looked taken aback, maybe even embarrassed or ashamed. Not by what he'd done, I knew that; but because someone else—a kid—knew he'd done it.

"Who's this?" His voice took on that fake-nice tone adults use when they're caught doing something, like smoking or drinking or fighting with their wives. "This your son, Winter?"

"No," I said.

"Yes," said Vala, and under her breath said the word she'd used when I first met her: *feogar.*

But Winter didn't say anything, and Tierney had already turned away.

"Against the law?" He pulled at the front of his red-and-white wind-breaker, then shrugged. "I'll pay the fine. No one goes to jail for cutting down trees."

Tierney smiled then, as though he was thinking of a joke no one else would ever get, and added, "Not me, anyway."

He looked at Al Alford and nodded. Al quickly turned and walked— ran, practically—to where the Boston Whaler rocked against the metal railing at the end of the dock. Tierney followed him, but slowly, pausing once to stare back up the hillside—not at the King's Pines but at the farm-house, its windows glinting in the sun where they faced the cliff. Then he walked to where Alford waited by the little motorboat, his hand out to help Tierney climb inside.

I looked at Winter. His face had gone slack, except for his mouth: he looked as though he were biting down on something hard.

"He's going to cut the other ones, too," he said. He didn't sound disbelieving or sad or even angry; more like he was saying something everyone knew was true, like *It'll snow soon* or *Tomorrow's Sunday.* "He'll pay the twenty-thousand-dollar fine, just like he did down in Kennebunkport. He'll wait and do it in the middle of the night when I'm not here. And the trees will be gone."

"No, he will not," said Vala. Her voice was nearly as calm as Winter's. There was a subdued roar as the motorboat's engine turned over, and the Boston Whaler shot away from the dock, towards the *Ice Queen.*

"No," Vala said again, and she stooped and picked up a rock. A small gray rock, just big enough to fit inside her fist, one side of it encrusted with barnacles. She straightened and stared at the ocean, her eyes no longer sky-blue but the pure deep gray of a stone that's been worn smooth by the sea, with no pupil in them; and shining like water in the sun.

"*Skammastu peî, Thomas Tierney. Farthu til fjandanns!*" she cried, and threw the rock towards the water. "*Farthu! Låttu peog hverfa!*"

I watched it fly through the air, then fall, hitting the beach a long way from the waterline with a small thud. I started to look at Vala, and stopped.

From the water came a grinding sound, a deafening noise like thunder; only this was louder than a thunderclap and didn't last so long, just a fraction of a second. I turned and shaded my eyes, staring out to where the Boston Whaler arrowed towards Tierney's yacht. A sudden gust of wind stung my eyes with spray; I blinked, then blinked again in amazement.

A few feet from the motorboat a black spike of stone shadowed the water. Not a big rock—it might have been a dolphin's fin, or a shark's, but it wasn't moving.

And it hadn't been there just seconds before. It had never been there, I knew that. I heard a muffled shout, then the frantic whine of the motorboat's engine being revved too fast—and too late.

With a sickening crunch, the Boston Whaler ran onto the rock. Winter yelled in dismay as Alford's orange-clad figure was thrown into the water. For a second Thomas Tierney remained upright, his arms flailing as he tried to grab at Alford. Then, as though a trapdoor had opened beneath him, he dropped through the bottom of the boat and disappeared.

Winter raced towards the water. I ran after him.

"Stay with Vala!" Winter grabbed my arm. Alford's orange life vest gleamed from on top of the rock where he clung. On board the *Ice Queen*, someone yelled through a megaphone, and I could see another craft, a little inflated Zodiac, drop into the gray water. Winter shook me fiercely. "Justin! I said, *stay with her—*"

He looked back towards the beach. So did I.

Vala was nowhere to be seen. Winter dropped my arm, but before he could say anything there was a motion among the rocks.

And there was Vala, coming into sight like gathering fog. Even from this distance I could see how her eyes glittered, blue-black like a winter sky; and I could tell she was smiling.

THE crew of the *Ice Queen* rescued Alford quickly, long before the Coast Guard arrived. Winter and I stayed on the beach for several hours, while the search and rescue crews arrived and the Navy Falcons flew by overhead, in case Tierney came swimming to shore, or in case his body washed up.

But it never did. That spar of rock had ripped a huge hole in the Boston Whaler, a bigger hole even than you'd think; but no one blamed Alford. All you had to do was take a look at the charts and see that there had never been a rock there, ever. Though it's there now, I can tell you that. I see it every day when I look out from the windows at Winter's house.

I never asked Vala about what happened. Winter had a grim expression when we finally went back to his place late that afternoon. Thomas Tierney was a multimillionaire, remember, and even I knew there would be an investigation and interviews and TV people.

But everyone on board the *Ice Queen* had witnessed what happened, and so had Al Alford; and while they'd all seen Winter arguing with Tierney, there'd been no exchange of blows, not even any pushing, and no threats on Winter's part—Alford testified to that. The King's Pine was gone, but two remained; and a bunch of people from the Audubon Society and the Sierra Club and places like that immediately filed a lawsuit against Tierney's estate, to have all the property on the old Packard Farm turned into a nature preserve.

Which I thought was good, but it still won't bring the other tree back.

One day after school, a few weeks after the boat sank, I was helping to put the finishing touches on Winter's house. Just about everything was done, except for the fireplace—there were still piles of rocks everywhere and plastic buckets full of mortar and flat stones for the hearth.

"Justin." Vala appeared behind me so suddenly I jumped. "Will you come with me, please?"

I stood and nodded. She looked really pregnant now, and serious.

But happy, too. In the next room we could hear Winter working with a sander. Vala looked at me and smiled, put a finger to her lips then touched her finger to my chin. This time, it didn't ache with cold.

"Come," she said.

Outside it was cold and gray, the middle of October, but already most of the trees were bare, their leaves torn away by a storm a few nights earlier. We headed for the woods behind the house, past the quince bush, its branches stripped of leaves and all the hummingbirds long gone to warmer places. Vala wore her same bright blue rubber shoes and Winter's rolled-up jeans.

But even his big sweatshirt was too small now to cover her belly, so my mother had knit her a nice big sweater and given her a warm plaid coat that made Vala look even more like a kid, except for her eyes and that way she would look at me sometimes and smile, as though we both knew a secret. I followed her to where the path snaked down to the beach and tried not to glance over at the base of the cliff. The King's Pine had finally fallen and wedged between the crack in the huge rocks there, so that now seaweed was tangled in its dead branches, and all the rocks were covered with yellow pine needles.

"Winter has to go into town for a few hours," Vala said, as though answering a question. "I need you to help me with something."

We reached the bottom of the path and picked our way across the rocks until we reached the edge of the shore. A few gulls flew overhead, screaming, and the wind blew hard against my face and bare hands. I'd followed Vala outside without my coat. When I looked down, I saw that my fingers were bright red. But I didn't feel cold at all.

"Here," murmured Vala.

She walked, slowly, to where a gray rock protruded from the gravel beach. It was roughly the shape and size of an arm

Then I drew up beside Vala and saw that it really *was* an arm—part of one, anyway, made of smooth gray stone, like marble only darker, but with no hand and broken just above the elbow. Vala stood and looked at it, her lips pursed; then stooped to pick it up.

"Will you carry this, please?" she said.

I didn't say anything, just held out my arms, as though she were going to fill them with firewood. When she set the stone down I flinched—not because it was heavy, though it was, but because it looked exactly like a real arm. I could even see where the veins had been, in the crook of the elbow, and the wrinkled skin where the arm had bent.

"Justin," Vala said. I looked up to see her blue-black eyes fixed on me. "Come on. It will get dark soon."

I followed her as she walked slowly along the beach, like someone looking for sea glass or sand dollars. Every few feet she would stop and pick something up—a hand, a foot, a long piece of stone that was most of a leg—then turn and set it carefully into my arms. When I couldn't carry any more, she picked up one last small rock—a clenched fist—and made her way slowly back to the trail.

We made several more trips that day, and for several days after that. Each time, we would return to the house and Vala would fit the stones into the unfinished fireplace, covering them with other rocks so that no one could see them. Or if you did see one, you'd think maybe it was just part of a broken statue, or a rock that happened to *look* like a foot, or a shoulder blade, or the cracked round back of a head.

I couldn't bring myself to ask Vala about it. But I remembered how the Boston Whaler had looked when the Coast Guard dragged it onshore, with a small ragged gash in its bow, and a much, much bigger hole in the bottom, as though something huge and heavy had crashed through it. Like a meteor, maybe. Or a really big rock, or like if someone had dropped a granite statue of a man into the boat.

Not that anyone had seen that happen. I told myself that maybe it really was a statue—maybe a statue had fallen off a ship or been pushed off a cliff or something.

But then one day we went down to the beach, the last day actually, and Vala made me wade into the shallow water. She pointed at something just below the surface, something round and white, like a deflated soccer ball.

Only it wasn't a soccer ball. It was Thomas Tierney's head: the front of it, anyway, the one part Vala hadn't already found and built into the fireplace.

His face.

I pulled it from the water and stared at it. A green scum of algae covered his eyes, which were wide and staring. His mouth was open so you could see where his tongue had been before it broke off, leaving a jagged edge in the hole of his screaming mouth.

"*Loksins,*" said Vala. She took it from me easily, even though it was so heavy I could barely hold it. "At last . . ."

She turned and walked back up to the house.

THAT was three months ago. Winter's house is finished now, and Winter lives in it, along with Winter's wife.

And their baby. The fireplace is done, and you can hardly see where there is a round broken stone at the very top, which if you squint and look at it in just the right light, like at night when only the fire is going, looks kind of like a face. Winter is happier than I've ever seen him, and my mom and I go over a lot, to visit him and Vala and the baby, who is just a few weeks old now and so cute you wouldn't believe it, and tiny, so tiny I was afraid to hold her at first but Vala says not to worry—I may be like her big brother now, but someday, when the baby grows up, she will be the one to always watch out for me. They named her Gerda, which means Protector; and for a baby she is incredibly strong.

A Diorama of the Infernal Regions, or The Devil's Ninth Question

ANDY DUNCAN

Here's as vivid an adventure as you're ever likely to meet, funny, folksy, scary, and wise, about a girl who runs from magic of one sort only to run headlong into sinister magic of another kind, make friends with ghosts, live in a house of mystery, and compete with the Devil Himself . . .

Andy Duncan made his first sale, to Asimov's Science Fiction, in 1995, and quickly made others, to Starlight, Sci Fiction, Dying For It, Realms of Fantasy, and Weird Tales, as well as several more sales to Asimov's. By the beginning of the new century, he was widely recognized as one of the most individual, quirky, and flavorful new voices on the scene today. In 2001 he won two World Fantasy Awards, one for his story "The Pottawatomie Giant," and one for his landmark first collection, Beluthahatchie and Other Stories; in 2002 his story "The Chief Designer" won a Theodore Sturgeon Memorial Award. His most recent books are a fiction anthology coedited with F. Brett Cox, Crossroads: Tales of the Southern Literary Fantastic; and a non-fiction book, Alabama Curiosities. A graduate of the Clarion West writers' workshop in Seattle, he was raised in Batesburg, South Carolina, and now lives in Frostburg, Maryland, with his wife, Sydney, where he edits Overdrive magazine, "The Voice of the American Trucker."

MY name is Pearleen Sunday, though I was always called Pearl, and this is the story of how I met the widow of Flatland House and her 473 dead friends and sang a duet with the Devil's son-in-law and earned a wizard's anger by setting that wizard free.

At the time I did these things, I was neither child nor woman, neither hay nor grass. I was like a cat with the door disease. She scratches to be let in or scratches to be let out, but when you open the door she only stands halfway and cocks her head and thinks deep cat thoughts till you could drown her. Had I been on either side of the door that summer, things might have turned out differently, but I could not decide, and so the door stood open to cold winds and marvels.

I grew up in Chattanooga in Professor Van Der Ast's Mammoth Cosmopolitan Musée and Pavilion of Science and Art. Musée is the French word for museum, and cosmopolitan means citified, and Professor Van Der Ast was born Hasil Bowersox in Rising Fawn, Georgia. Whether his were the quality Bowersoxes, who pronounce "Bower" to rhyme with "lower," or the common Bowersoxes, who pronounce "Bower" to rhyme with "scour," I cannot say, for Professor Van Der Ast never answered to either. The rest of the name of Professor Van Der Ast's Mammoth Cosmopolitan Musée and Pavilion of Science and Art is self-explanatory, although the nature of science and art is subject to debate, and it was not a pavilion but a three-story brickfront, and I would not call it mammoth either, though it did hold a right smart of things.

You would not find the museum if you looked today. It sat in the shadow of the downtown end of the new Walnut Street Bridge across the Tennessee River. Years before, General Sherman had built a bridge there that did not last any time before God washed it away, but He seemed to be tolerating the new one for now.

I was told my parents left me in a hatbox in the alley between the museum and the tobacco warehouse. Two Fiji cannibals on their smoke break took pity and took me inside to the Professor, who made me a paying attraction before I was two years of age. The sign, I was told, read TRANSPARENT HUMAN HEAD! ALL LIVE AND ON THE INSIDE! What was inside was me, sucking a sugar tit with a bright lamp behind my head so my little brain and blood vessels could be seen. Every word on the sign was true.

A young girl like myself with no mother, father, or schooling could do worse in those days than work in an educational museum, which offered many career opportunities even for girls with no tattoos or beards and all their limbs. Jobs for girls at Professor Van Der Ast's included Neptuna the Living Mermaid, who combed her hair and switched her tail in a pool all day, and the Invisible Girl, who hid behind a sheet and spoke fortunes into a trumpet, and Zalumma Agra the Circassian Princess, Purest Example of the White Race, who when snatched from the slave traders of Constantinople had left behind most of her clothes, though not enough to shut us down. Our Purest Example of the White Race in summer 1895 was my friend Sally Ann Rummage of Mobile, Alabama, whose mother had been a slave, though not in Constantinople. Sally Ann was ashamed of the museum and wrote her parents that she had become a teacher, which I suppose she had.

I had none of those jobs that summer because I was in that in-between age, and the Circassian Princess in particular was no in-between sort of job. No, I was so out of sorts with myself and the world that Professor Van Der Ast cast me entirely from the sight of the paying public, behind our Diorama of the Infernal Regions.

Now a diorama in those days was only a painting, but a painting so immense that no one ever would see it all at once. It was painted on a long strip of canvas ten feet high, and to see it, you rolled it out of a great spool, like a bolt of cloth in a dressmaker's shop for giants, and as it rolled out of the first spool it rolled back up in a second spool about twenty feet away. In between the spools the customers stood shoulder to shoulder and admired the sights that trundled past.

The spools were turned by an engine, but someone in the back had to keep the engine running and make sure the canvas threaded smooth, without snagging and tearing—for your town may have had a fine new Hell, but Chattanooga's was as ragged and patched as a family Bible. That someone in the back was me. I also had to work the effects. As the diorama moved past, and as Professor Van Der Ast stood on the public side and narrated the spiel, I opened and closed a bank of lanterns that beamed light through parts of the canvas—to make the flames of Hell flicker, and bats wheel through the air, and imps and satyrs wink in and out of existence like my evil thoughts as I sweated and strained like a fireman in a furnace room. Every day in the spotty mirror over my washstand upstairs, I rubbed my arms and shoulders and wondered what man would ever want a woman with muscles, and what man she might want in return.

Ours was the only diorama I ever saw, but Professor Van Der Ast said that one famous diorama in New York City was a view of the riverbank along the entire length of the Mississippi, from Minnesota to New Orleans. Park Avenue swells in boater hats could lounge in air-cooled comfort and watch it all slide past: eagle-haunted bluffs, woodlands a-creep with Indians, spindly piers that stopped at the overalled butts of barefoot younguns, brawling river towns that bled filth for miles downstream. Professor Van Der Ast himself had been no farther north than Cleveland, Tennessee, but he described New York's Mississippi just as well as he described Chattanooga's Infernal Regions. You felt like you were there.

"Observe, my friends, from your safe vantage point this side of the veil, the ghastly wonders of the Infernal as they pass before you. I say, *as they pass before you*!" (The machinery was old and froze up sometimes.) "First on this ancient scroll, bequeathed us by the Chaldean martyrs, witness the sulfurous vapors of Lake Avernus, over which no sane bird will fly. Here is Briareus with his hundred arms, laboring to drag a chain the width of a stout man's waist, and at the end of that mighty leash snaps the hound Cerberus, with his fifty heads, each of his fifty necks a-coil with snakes. Here is the stern ferryman who turns away all wretches who die without Christian burial. Next are the weeping lovers wringing their hands in groves of myrtle, never to be reunited with their soul mates. Madame, my handkerchief. Your pity does you honor. Next is the whip of scorpions that flays those who believed their sins concealed in life. Here is the nine-acre giant Tityus, chained at the bottom of the abyssal gulf. Here are sufferers chin deep in water they are doomed never to drink, while others are doomed to bail the water with sieves."

A weeping schoolmarm might ask: "But what about the realms of the blessed? the Elysian fields? the laurel groves?"

"For such consolations, madam, one must consult canvases other than mine. And here we have the writhing Pandaemonium of pleasure, where all noble and spiritual aims are forgotten in the base fog of sensation and lust. Next is the great—"

"Hey, buddy, could we have a little more light on that there Pandaemonium of pleasure?"

"This is the family show, friend, come back at ten. Here is the great winepress in which hundreds of the damned are crushed together until they burst. Here are the filthy, verminous infants of ingratitude, which spit venom even as they are hoisted with tongs over the fire. Note, ladies and gentlemen, that throughout this dreadful panorama, the plants in view are all thorny and rank, the creatures all fanged and poisonous, the very stones misshapen and worthless, the men and women all sick, feeble, wracked, and forgotten, their only music Hell's Unutterable Lament! Where all suffer horrid torments not for one minute, not for one day, not for one age, not for two ages, not for a hundred ages, not for ten thousand millions of ages, but forever and ever without end, and never to be delivered! Mind your step at the door, next show two thirty, gratuities welcome."

That was Professor Van Der Ast's side of the canvas, the public side. I told no one what I saw on my side: the patches and the stains, the backward paintings, the different tricks played by the light. I could see pictures, too, but only half-glimpsed, like those in clouds and treetops in leafy summertime. The pictures on my side were not horrible. I saw a man wrestling a lightning rod in a storm; and a great river catfish that sang to the crew in the gondola of a low-flying balloon; and a bespectacled woman pushing a single wheel down the road; and a ballroom full of dancing ghosts; and a man with a hand of iron who beckoned me with hinged fingers; and a farmer who waved good-bye to his happy family on the porch before vanishing, then, reappearing, waved hello to them again; and an angry face looking out of a boot; and a giant woman with a mustache throwing a man over the side of a riverboat; and a smiling man going over Niagara Falls in a barrel while around him bobbed a hundred hoodoo bottles, each with a rolled-up message for Marie Laveaux; and a hound dog with a pistol who was robbing a train; and a one-eyed man who lived in a gator hole; and a beggar presenting a peepshow to the Queen of Sheba; and a gorilla in a boater hat sitting in a deck chair watching a diorama of the Mississippi scroll past; and a thousand other wonders to behold. My Infernal Regions were a lot more interesting than Professor Van Der Ast's, and sometimes they lighted up and moved without my having to do a thing.

My only other knowledge of magic at the time was thanks to Wendell Farethewell, the Wizard of the Blue Ridge, a magician from Yandro Mountain, North Carolina, who performed at Professor Van Der Ast's for three weeks each summer. I never had the chance to see his act because, as the Professor liked to remind us, we were being paid to entertain and not to be entertained, but I was told that at the climax he caught in his teeth a bullet fired through a crystal pitcher of lemonade, and I believe it was so because sometimes when a pinhead was not available, the Professor asked me to go onstage after the show and mop up the lemonade and pick up the sharp splinters of glass.

The tricks I saw the wizard Farethewell perform were done after hours, when all the residents of the museum went to the basement for drinks and cold-meat sandwiches and more drinks. I squirmed my way into the front of the crowd around a wobbly table made of splinters and watched as he pulled the Queen of Hearts out of the air and walked coins across his knuckles and floated dollar bills. "Just like the government," he always said when he floated a dollar bill, and we always laughed. He showed us fifty-seven ways to shuffle a deck of cards and seventeen of the ways to draw an ace off the top whenever one was needed, even five times in a row. "Do this in a gambling hall," he said, "and you'll get yourself shot. Do it among you good people, and it's just a pleasant diversion, something to make Little Britches smile."

That was what Farethewell called me, Little Britches. He was the only one who called me that. Big Fred, who played our What-Is-It?, tried it once, and I busted his nose.

If the night wore on and Farethewell drank too much, he got moody and talked about the war, and about his friend, an older man he never named. "The 26th North Carolina mustered up in Raleigh, and I couldn't sleep that first night, without no mountains around to hold me, so I mashed my face into my bedroll and cried. I ain't ashamed of it, neither. The others laughed or told me to hush, but this man, he said, 'Boy, you want to see a trick?' Now, what boy don't want to see a trick? And after he's seen it, what boy don't want to know how it's done?" As he talked he stared into space, but his hands kept doing tricks, as if they were independent of the rest of him. "At New Bern he taught me the back palm, the finger palm, the thumb palm; at the Wilderness the Hindu Shuffle and the Stodart Egg; at Spotsylvania the Biseaute flourish, the Miser's Dream, the Torn and Restored. I learned the Scotch and Soda and the Gin and Tonic before I drank either one; and all through the war, every day, I worked on the Three Major Vanishes: take, put, and pinch." As he said that, three coins disappeared from his hand, one by one. "So that was our war. It kept my mind off things, and maybe kept his mind off things, too. He had the tuberculosis pretty bad, toward the end. The last thing he taught me was the bullet catch, in the stockade at Appomattox, just before he died. I got one of his boots. The rest, they burned. When they turned out his pockets, it was just coins and cards and flash paper. It didn't look like magic no more. It just looked . . . It looked like trash. The magic went when he went, except the little he left to me."

Someone asked, "What'd you learn at Gettysburg?" and Farethewell replied:

"What I learned at Gettysburg, I will teach no man. But one day, living or dead, I will hold the Devil to account for what I learned."

Then he began doing tricks with a knife, and I went upstairs to bed.

My in-between summer came to an end after the last viewing of a Saturday night. As I cranked the diorama back into place, I heard the Professor talking to someone, a customer? Then the other voice got louder: "You ain't nothing but an old woman. She'll do just fine, you watch."

I could hear no more over the winding spool, and I did not want to stop it for fear of being caught eavesdropping. Then the Professor and the wizard Farethewell were behind the diorama with me.

"Shut off that engine, Little Britches. You can do that later. Right now, you got to help me." He had something in his hand, a tangle that glittered in the lamplight. He thrust it at me. "Go on, take it. Showtime was five minutes ago."

"What are you talking about?" It was a little sparkly dress with feathers, and a hat, and slippers with heels. I looked at Farethewell, who was drinking from a flask, and at the Professor, who was stroking his silver beard.

"Pearl, please mind Mr. Farethewell, that's a good girl. Just run along and put that on, and meet us in the theater, backstage." I held the costume up to the light: what there was of the light, and what there was of the costume. "Sukie can't help Mr. Farethewell with the ten o'clock show. She's sick."

"Dead drunk, you mean," Farethewell roared, and lifted his flask. The Professor snatched it away. Something spattered my cheek and burned.

"Get as drunk as you like at eleven," the Professor said. "Pearl, it'll be easy. All you have to do is wave to the crowd, climb into the box, and lie there. Mr. Farethewell will do the rest."

"The blades won't come nowhere near you, Little Britches. The box is rigged, and besides, you ain't no bigger'n nothing. You won't even have to twist."

"But," I said.

"Pearl," said the Professor, like there were fifteen R's in my name. So I ran upstairs.

"What's wrong with you?" Sally Ann cried when I burst in.

I told her while she helped me out of my coveralls and my blue denims and into the turkey suit. "What in the world are they thinking?" Sally Ann said. "Hold still, Pearl, if I don't cinch this, you'll walk plumb out of it."

"My legs are cold!" I yelled.

The hat was nothing I would have called a hat. In a rainstorm it would have been no cover at all. I finally snuggled it down over my hair and got the ostrich plume out of my face. Sally Ann was looking at me funny.

"Oh, my," she said.

"What?"

"Nothing. Come on, let's go. I want to see this. Clothes do make a difference, don't they?"

"Not to me," I said, and would have fallen down the stairs if she hadn't grabbed me. "Who can walk in any such shoes as this?"

There's no dark like the dark backstage in a theater, but Sally Ann managed to guide me through all the ropes and sandbags without disaster. I carried the shoes. Just inside the backdrop curtain, the Professor made a hurry-up motion. I hopped one-legged to get the shoes back on and peered through the slit in the curtain, but was blinded by the lamps shining onto the stage.

Farethewell was yelling to make himself heard over what sounded like a theater full of drunken men. "And now, my lovely assistant will demonstrate that no cutlass ever forged can cut her, that she can dodge the blade of any cavalryman, whether he be a veteran of the Grand Army of the Republic—"

The crowd booed and hissed.

"—or whether he fought for Tennessee under the great Nathan Bedford Forrest!"

The crowd whooped and stomped its approval.

"Here she is," muttered the Professor, as he held the curtain open.

I blinked in the light, still blinded. Farethewell's big callused hand grabbed mine and led me forward. "Ladies and gentlemen, I give you Aphrodite, the Pearl of the Cumberland!"

I stood frozen.

The crowd continued to roar.

Lying on a table in front of us was a long box like a coffin, open at the top. A pile of swords lay beside it.

"Lie down in the box, honey," Farethewell murmured. He wore a long blue robe and a pointed hat, and his face was slick with sweat.

I walked to the box like a puppet and looked down at the dirty pillow, the tatty blanket inside.

"And if you don't believe me when I tell you how amazingly nimble Aphrodite is, why when I am done shoving cutlasses into the box, those of you willing to pay an additional fifty cents can line up here, on the stage, and look down into the box and see for yourself that this young woman has suffered no injury whatsoever, save perhaps to her costume."

The crowd screamed with laughter. Blinking back tears, I leaned over the box, stepped out of the shoes: first left, then right. I looked up and into the face of a fat man in the front row. He winked.

In my head I heard the Professor say: "This is the family show, friend, come back at ten."

I turned and ran.

The noise of the crowd pushed me through the curtains, past Sally Ann and the Professor. In the sudden darkness I tripped over a sandbag, fell and skinned my knees, then stood and flailed my way to the door and into the corridor beyond.

"Pearl! Come back!"

My cheeks burned with shame and anger at myself and the crowd and Farethewell and the Professor and Sally Ann and those stupid, stupid shoes; I vowed as I ran barefoot like a monkey through the back corridors that I would never wear their like again. I ran as fast as I could—not upstairs, not to the room I slept in, but to the one place in the museum I felt was mine.

I slammed the door behind me and stood, panting, behind the Diorama of the Infernal Regions.

Someone, probably the Professor, had done part of my job for me, and shut down all the lamps. It was the job I liked least, snuffing the lights one by one like candles on a cake. But the Professor had not finished rolling up the canvas. It was backstage dark, but up there on the canvas, at eye level, was a little patch of light, flickering.

I'm sure that when I went missing, my friends thought I had run away, but they were wrong. I was running *away* from nothing. I was running *to* something, though I did not know what it was. Running to *what* is the rest of my story—is all my story, I reckon.

I walked right up to the flickering spot on my side of the canvas. The tip of my nose was an inch from the paint. When I breathed in, I smelled sawdust and walnuts. When I breathed out, the bright patch brightened just a little. If you blow gently on a flame, it does not go out, but flares up; that's how the canvas was. I almost could see a room through the canvas, a paneled room. Behind me, a woman's voice called my name, but in front of me, I almost heard music, organ music.

I closed my eyes and focused not on the canvas, but on the room beyond.

I stepped forward.

Have you ever stepped through a cobweb? That's how I stepped out of Professor Van Der Ast's Mammoth Cosmopolitan Musée and Pavilion of Science and Art and into a place without a ticket booth, into my own canvas, my own Infernal Regions.

NOT a funeral, a ball. The organist was playing a waltz.

I opened my eyes.

I was in a ballroom full of ghosts.

I reached behind to feel the canvas, to feel anything familiar and certain. Instead I felt a cold hard surface: a magnificent stained-glass window that ran the length of the wall, depicting mermaids and magicians and a girl at the lever of an infernal engine. Window and room spun around me. My knees buckled, and I sank onto a beautifully inlaid wooden floor.

The room wasn't spinning, but the dancers were. Fifty couples whirled through the room, the silver chandeliers and mahogany paneling and gold-leaf wallpaper visible through their transparent bodies. I never had seen such a beautiful room. The dancers were old and young, richly and poorly dressed, white and black and Indian. Some wore wigs and knee breeches, others buckskins and fur caps, others evening gowns or tailcoats. They didn't look like show people. All moved faster than their actual steps. No feet quite touched the floor. The dancers were waltzing in the air.

Against the far wall was a pump organ, and sitting at the bench with her back to me was a tiny gray-haired lady, shoulders swaying with the force of her fingers on the keys, her feet on the pedals. I tried to see the sheet music through her but could not. She was no ghost; she was substantial. I looked at my hand and saw through it the interlocking diamond pattern of the floor. That's when I screamed.

The music stopped.

The dancing stopped.

The old lady spun on her bench and stared at me.

Everyone stared at me.

Then the dancers gasped and stepped—no, floated—backward in the air, away from me. There was movement beside me. I looked up to see a skinny girl in a feathered costume step out of the stained-glass window. I screamed again, and she jumped and screamed, too.

She was me, and she also was becoming transparent.

"Five minutes break, please, everyone," trilled a little-old-lady voice. "When we return, we'll do the Virginia Reel."

The second Pearl had slumped onto the floor beside me. A third Pearl stepped out of the stained glass just as the old lady reached us. She wore an elaborate black mourning-dress, with the veil thrown back to reveal chubby, ruddy cheeks and big gray eyes. "There, there," she said. "This won't do at all. The first rule of psychic transport is to maintain integrity, to hold oneself together." A fourth Pearl stepped from the glass as the old lady seized my hand and the second Pearl's hand and brought them together, palm to palm. It was like pressing my hand into butter; my hand began to sink into hers, and hers into mine. We both screamed and tried to pull back, but the old lady held our wrists in a grip like iron.

"Best to close your eyes, dear," the old lady said.

My eyes immediately shut tight not of my own doing but as if some unseen hand had yanked them down like window shades. The old lady's grip tightened, and I feared my wrist would break. My whole body got warmer, from the wrist onward, and I began to feel better—not just calmer, but somehow fuller, more complete.

Finally, the old lady released my wrist, and said, "You can open your eyes now, dear."

I did, and it was my own doing this time. I stared at my hands, with their lines and calluses and gnawed-to-the-quick nails, and they were so familiar and so *solid* that I started to cry.

The ballroom was empty but for me—*one* of me—and the old lady kneeling beside me, and a single ghost bobbing just behind her, a little ferret-faced mustached man in a bowler hat and a checked waistcoat that might have been colorful once, but now was gray checked with gray.

"Beautifully done," said the floater. "You have the hands of a surgeon."

"The hands are the least of it, Mr. Dellafave, but you are too kind. Goodness, child, you gave me a fright. Six of you stranded in the glass. Good thing I was here to set things right. But I forget my manners. My name is Sarah Pardee Winchester, widow of the late William Wirt Winchester, and this is my friend Mr. Dellafave." She eyed my costume, reached over, and tugged on my ostrich plume. "Too young to be a showgirl," she said, "almost."

I shuddered and wiped my nose with the back of my wonderful old-friend hand and asked: "Am I . . . Are you . . . Please, is this Heaven or Hell?"

The old lady and the bowler-hatted man both laughed. His laugh sounded like steam escaping, but hers was throaty and loud, like a much younger, much larger woman.

"Opinions differ," the old lady said. "We think of it simply as California."

SHE called the place Llanada Villa, which she said was Spanish for "Flatland House." I had never lived in a house before the widow took me in, so you might call Flatland House my introduction to the whole principle of houses. And what an introduction it was! No house I've seen since has been a patch on it.

There was the size, to start with. The house covered six acres. Counting the rooms that had been walled off and made unreachable except by ghosts, but not counting the rooms that had been demolished or merged into larger spaces, the house had 150 rooms, mostly bedrooms, give or take a dozen. "I've slept in only seventy or eighty of them myself," the widow told me, "but that's enough to get the general idea."

Still the place was not finished. Workmen were always in the process of adding rooms, balconies, porches, turrets, whole wings; or in the process of dismantling or renovating what they had built just the month before. The construction had moved far away from the front of the house, where the widow mostly lived, but the distant sounds of saws and hammers and the men's voices calling to one another—"Steady! Steady! Move it just a hair to the right, please, Bill"—could be heard day and night. They worked in shifts around the clock. Once a week the foremen took off their hats and gathered in the carriage entrance for payday. The widow towed from the house a child's wagon full of heavy sacks, each full of enough gold pieces to pay each foreman's workers the equivalent of three dollars a day. The foremen were all beefy men, but even they strained to heft the bags and tote them away. They never complained, though.

"Aren't you afraid?" I asked the widow, that first payday.

"Of what, dear?"

"Of one of those men breaking into the house, and robbing you."

"Oh, Pearl, you are a caution! You don't need to worry about robbers, oh, no. Not in *this* house."

I suppose intruders would have quickly gotten lost, for many parts of the house simply did not make sense. Staircases led to ceilings and stopped. Doorways opened onto brick walls, or onto nothing, not even a balcony, just the outside air. Secret passageways no taller than the widow criss-crossed the house, so that she could pop in and out of sight without warning, as if she herself were a ghost. The widow told me the front door had never been opened, never even unlocked, since its hinges were hung.

I found the outside of the house even more confusing. If I walked around any corner, I found arched windows, recessed balconies, turrets and witch's caps and cupolas with red tile roofs, and miles of gingerbread trim. If I walked around the next corner, I found the same thing, only more of it. Many houses, I'm told, have only four corners to walk around, but Flatland House had dozens. Looking away from the house was no help, because no matter what direction I looked, I saw the same high cypress hedge, and beyond that, rolling hills of apricot, plum, and walnut trees stretching to the horizon. I never made it all the way around the place, but would give up and go back inside, and where I went inside always seemed to be the breakfast room, with the widow knitting in the wicker chair just where I left her. She always asked, "Did you have a good trip, dear?"

In all those 150 rooms was not a single mirror. Which suited me just fine.

I did get lonely sometimes. Most of the ghosts had little to say—to the living, anyway—beyond "Lovely day, isn't it?" The few indoor servants seemed afraid of me, and none stayed in the house past sundown. The workmen I was forbidden to speak to at all.

"Do you never have any visitors," I asked the widow, "other than the workmen, and the ghosts, and the servants, and me?"

"Goodness, that's enough, wouldn't you say? I know there are 473 ghosts, not counting the cats, and Lord only knows how many workmen coming and going. And don't ever think of yourself as a visitor, Pearl dear. Consider this your home, for as long as you wish to stay."

The only ghost willing to spend time with me, other than the cats, was Mr. Dellafave. Three weeks into my stay at Flatland House, during a stroll around the monkey-puzzle tree, I asked him:

"Mr. Dellafave, what did you do before . . ."

His face had the look of someone expecting his feelings to be hurt but game not to let on.

". . . before you came here?" I finished.

"Ah," he said, smiling. "I worked for a bank, in Sacramento. I was a figure man. I added, mostly, and subtracted twice a week, and, on red-letter days, multiplied. Long division was wholly out of my jurisdiction, that was another floor altogether—but make no mistake, I could have done it. I was ready to serve. Had the third floor been swept away by fire or flood, the long division would have proceeded without interruption, for I'd had the training. But the crisis, like most crises, never came. I arrived at the bank every morning at eight. I went across the street to the saloon every day at noon for two eggs and a pickle and a sarsaparilla and the afternoon papers. I left the bank every day at five, and got back to the boardinghouse for supper at six. Oh, I was a clockwork, I was. 'You can set your watch by Dellafave,' that's what they said at the bank and the saloon and the boardinghouse and, well, those are the only places they said it, really, be-cause those are the only places where anyone took any notice of me at all. Certainly that streetcar driver did not. He would have rung his bell if he had; it's in their manual. That was a sloppy business all around, frankly, a harsh thing to say, but there it is. I know the time had to have been 12:47 precisely, because I walked out of the saloon at 12:46, and the streetcar was not due to pass until 12:49. I was on schedule, but the streetcar was not. I looked up, and there it was, and I flung up my arms—as if that would have helped, flinging up my arms. When I lowered them, I was standing in what I now know as Mrs. Winchester's potting shed. I was never an especially spiritual man, Pearl dear, but I considered myself fairly well versed on all the major theories of the afterlife . . . none of which quite prepared me for Mrs. Winchester's potting shed. I didn't even bring my newspaper."

"But why—"

He held up a hand, like a serene police officer at an intersection. "I have no idea, Pearl, why I came here. None of us does. And I don't mean to imply that we're unhappy, for it is a pleasant place, and Mrs. Winchester is quite good to us, but our leaving here seems rather out of the question. If I were to pass through that cypress hedge over there, I would find myself en-tering the grounds through the hedge on the other side. It's the same front to back, or even up and down."

"I guess Mrs. Winchester is the magnet, and you and the others are . . ."

"The filings, yes. The tacks pulled from the carpet. I stand in the tower sometimes—if you can call it standing—and I look over all these rooftops and chimneys, all connected to the same house, and I'm forced to admit that this is more room than I allowed myself in life. If the boardinghouse were the front door of Llanada Villa, the bank would be at the carriage entrance, and the saloon would be at the third sunporch, the one that's been walled in and gets no sun. Which is such a small fraction of the house, really. And yet the whole house feels such a small part of the Earth, and I find myself wishing that I had ventured a bit farther, when I could."

We walked together in silence—well, I walked, anyway—while I reflected that the owner of the house seemed quite unable to leave it herself. And what about me? Could I leave Flatland House, and were I to leave it, where would I go? Professor Van Der Ast's seemed much farther away than a single continent.

"You'd best get inside, Pearl. The breeze from the bay is quite damp today."

I moved my face toward Mr. Dellafave's cheek, and when he began to blur, I figured I was close enough, and kissed the air.

"Shucks," he said, and dissipated entirely.

I felt no bay breeze, but as I ran back to the house I clutched my shawl more tightly anyway.

THE next day, the earthquake struck.

The chandeliers swayed. The organ sighed and moaned. The crystal chittered in the cabinets. One nail worked its way free and rolled across the thrumming floorboards. A rumble welled up, not from below the house, but from above and around the house, as if the sound were pressing in from all sides. The ghosts were in a mad whirl, coursing through the house like a current of smoke overhead, blended and featureless but for the occasional startled face. I lurched along the walls, trying to keep my balance as I sought the exit nearest me, the front door. Once I fell and yelped as my palms touched the hot parquet.

Plaster sifted into my eyes as I stumbled through the entrance hall. I knew my mistake when I saw that massive front door, surely locked, the key long since thrown away or hidden in a far scullery drawer of this lunatic house. If the entire edifice were to shake down and crush me, this slab of swirling dark oak would be the last thing standing, a memorial to Pearl.

The grandfather clock toppled and fell just behind me, with the crash of a hundred heavy bells. I flung myself at the door and wrenched the knob. It turned easily, as if oiled every day, and I pulled the door open with no trouble at all. Suddenly all was silent and still. A robin sang in the crepe myrtle as the door opened on a lovely spring day. A tall black man in a charcoal tailcoat stood on the porch, top hat in hand, and smiled down at me.

"Good morning," he said. "I was beginning to fear that no one was at home. I hope my knock didn't bring you too dreadfully far. I know this house is harder to cross than the Oklahoma Territory."

"Your knock?" I was too flabbergasted to be polite. "All that was your knock?"

He laughed as he stepped inside, so softly that it was just an open-mouthed smile and a hint of a cough. "That? Oh, my, no. That was just my reputation preceding me. Tell me, pray, might the mistress of the house be at home?"

"Where else would I be, Wheatstraw?" asked the widow, suddenly at my elbow and every hair in place.

"Hello, Winchester," the visitor said.

They looked at each other without moving or speaking. I heard behind me a heaving sound and a muffled clang. I turned just as the grandfather clock resettled itself in the corner.

Then the widow and the visitor laughed and embraced. She kicked up one foot behind. Her head did not reach his chin.

"Pearl," the widow said, "this is Mr. Petey Wheatstraw."

"Pet-ER," he corrected, with a little bow.

"Mr. Wheatstraw," the widow continued, "is a rogue. My goodness," she added, as if something had just occurred to her. "How did you get in?"

We all looked at the front door. It was closed again, its bolts thrown, its hinges caked with rust. No force short of dynamite could have opened it.

The man Wheatstraw nodded toward me.

"Well, I'll be," the widow said. "She makes as free with my house as a termite, this one does. Well, you haven't come to see me, anyway, you old good-for-nothing," she said, swatting him as she bustled past. "It's a half hour early, but you might as well join us for tea."

Wheatstraw offered me an arm and winked. This was far too fresh for my taste, but I was too shaken by the not-quite-earthquake to care. As I took hold of his arm (oak-strong beneath the finery), I felt my muscles complain, as if I had done hard work. I looked over my shoulder at the seized-up door as Wheatstraw swept me down the hallway.

"I heard you were here," Wheatstraw said.

"How?"

"Oh, you're a loud one, Miss Big Feet, clomp clomp clomp." He winked again. "Or is that just your reputation I heard?"

Something was wrong with the corridor, something I couldn't quite put my finger on. Then I realized that it was empty. Everything in the house was back to normal—paintings returned to their nails, plaster returned to the walls—except the ghosts, which were nowhere to be seen. I was so used to them flitting past me and over me and through me, even gliding through my bedroom wall, then retreating with apologies, like someone who didn't realize the train compartment was occupied, that their presence hardly bothered me at all. Their absence gave me a shiver.

"They'll be back after I'm gone," Wheatstraw said.

I laughed. "You telling me you scared off the haints? I mean, are you saying that Mrs. Winchester's, uh, guests don't like you?"

"I'm sure they have nothing against me personally. How could they? Once you get to know me, I'm really a fine fellow, full of learning and grace and wit, a decent dancer, a welcome partner at whist. I never snort when I laugh or drag my shirtsleeves in the soup. No, it must be my business affiliation. The company I represent. The Old Concern. My father-in-law's firm, actually, and my inheriting is out of the question. But these days we all must work for somebody, mustn't we?"

I thought of Sally Ann the Circassian Princess, and of Farethewell's hand on mine. "True enough," I said.

WHEATSTRAW set down his teacup and saucer with a clatter, and said, "Well, enough chitchat. It's question time."

"Oh, Petey," the widow said. "Must you? We were having such a nice visit. Surely that can wait till later."

"I am in no hurry whatsoever, Winchester, but my father-in-law is another story. You might say that impatience rather defines my father-in-law. It is the cause of his, uh, present career. Pearl, please pay close attention."

I said nothing, having just shoved another chocolate cookie lengthwise into my mouth. I never quite realized that I was always a little hungry at Professor Van Der Ast's, until I came to Flatland House.

Wheatstraw rummaged in the inside pocket of his jacket and produced an atomizer. He opened his mouth and sprayed the back of his throat. "La la la la la," he said. "La la la la laaaaa. Pitch-perfect, as ever. Winchester?" He offered her the atomizer. "Don't, then. Now: Pearl."

He began to sing, in a lovely baritone:

Oh, you must answer my questions nine
Sing ninety-nine and ninety
Or you're not God's, you're one of mine
And you are the weaver's bonny.

"Now, Pearl, when I say, 'one of mine,' please understand that I speak not for myself but for the firm that I represent."

"And when you say 'God,'" I said, speaking carefully, "you speak of the firm that you do *not* represent."

"In a clamshell, yes. Now, if you're quite done interrupting—"

"I didn't interrupt!" I interrupted. "You interrupted yourself."

He slapped the table. "The idea! As if a speaker could interrupt himself. Why, you might as well say that a river could ford itself, or a fence jump itself."

"Or a bore bore himself," the widow said.

"You're not helping," Wheatstraw said.

"And I'm not the weaver's bonny," I said, becoming peevish now, "whatever a weaver's bonny is."

"Well," Wheatstraw said, "a weaver is a maker of cloth, such as aprons are made with, and gags, and a bonny is a beauty, a lovely creature, a precious thing."

"I don't know any weavers," I said, "except my friend Sally Ann taught me to sew a button. And I'm not beautiful, or lovely, or precious."

"Granted, that does seem a stretch at the moment," Wheatstraw said. "But we mustn't always take things so literally. When you say, 'I'm a silly goose,' you don't mean you expect to be plucked and roasted, and when you say, 'I'm fit to be tied,' you aren't asking to be roped and trussed, and when you say, 'Well, I'm damned,' you don't mean . . . ."

His voice trailed off. A chill crept into the room. The sunlight through the bay window dimmed, as if a cloud were passing.

". . . anything, really," Wheatstraw continued, and he smiled as the sun came out. "So, for purposes of this song, *if no other*, who are you?"

I folded my arms and forced my shoulders as far as I could into the padding of the love seat and glared at Wheatstraw, determined to frown down his oh-so-satisfied smile.

"I'm the weaver's bonny," I mumbled.

Am not, I thought.

"Fine and dandy," Wheatstraw said. "Now, where was I? I'll have to go back to Genesis, as Meemaw would say." He cleared his throat.

Oh, you must answer my questions nine
Sing ninety-nine and ninety
Or you're not God's, you're one of mine
And you are the weaver's bonny.

Ninety-nine and ninety *what?*, I wondered, but I kept my mouth shut.

What is whiter than the milk?
Sing ninety-nine and ninety
And what is softer than the silk?
Oh, you are the weaver's bonny
What is higher than a tree?
Sing ninety-nine and ninety
And what is deeper than the sea?
Oh, you are the weaver's bonny
What is louder than a horn?
Sing ninety-nine and ninety
And what is sharper than a thorn?
Oh, you are the weaver's bonny
What's more innocent than a lamb?
Sing ninety-nine and ninety
And what is meaner than womankind?
Oh, you are the weaver's bonny.

It was a short song, but it seemed to last a long time; as I sat there determined to resist, to be defiant and unamused, I realized I wasn't so much listening to it as being surrounded by it, filled by it, submerged in it. I was both sleepy and alert, and the pattern in the parquet floor was full of faces, and the love seat pushed back and kneaded my shoulders, and the laces of my high-topped shoes led into the darkness like tracks in the Lookout

Mountain tunnel. I could not vouch for Wheatstraw being a decent dancer as he claimed (though I suspected *decent* was hardly the word), but the man sure could sing. And somewhere in the second hour of the song (surely, I think now upon telling this, some lines were repeated, or extended, or elaborated upon), Wheatstraw's voice was joined by a woman's, his voice and hers twined together like fine rope. That voice was the widow Winchester's: *And you are the weaver's bonny.*

I sucked air and sat up as if startled from a dream, but felt less alert than a second before. The song was over. The widow pretended to gather up the tea things, and Wheatstraw pretended to study his fingernails.

"That part about womankind is insulting," the widow said.

"I didn't write it," he said. "The *folk* wrote it."

"Menfolk," she said.

"Eight," I said, and only after I said it did I realize why I had said it.

"Hm?" Wheatstraw asked, without looking up.

The widow held a tipped teacup, looking at nothing, as a thread of tea like a spider's descended to the saucer.

"Eight," I repeated. "Milk, silk, two; tree, sea, four; horn, thorn, six; lamb, kind, eight." I sang, rather than spoke, in surprise at my voice: "*Oh, you must answer my questions nine* . . . It ain't questions nine, it's questions eight. What's the ninth question?"

Wheatstraw looked at the widow, and the widow looked at Wheatstraw. "Maybe that's it," Wheatstraw murmured. " 'What's the ninth question,' maybe that's the ninth question."

"No," I said.

"Why no?" Wheatstraw cooed.

"Because," I said. "Because that would be stupid."

Wheatstraw laughed and slapped his thigh with his hat. The widow slammed two plates together.

"Indeed it would be," she snapped. "Petey, take these plates. Take them, I say. Do a lick of work for once in your lazy son-in-law of a life."

"So what's the ninth question?" I asked again.

"That's for you to tell us," Wheatstraw said.

"To tell *you*, you mean," the widow said, driving him from the room beneath a stack of dishes. "Don't drag *me* into this."

"Oh, excuse me, Lady Astor, whose house is it? The girl's a wizard, Sarah, and you can't stow a wizard in the china cupboard like a play-pretty, like one of your ghosts, like Mr. Dellafave in there," he shouted as he passed a china cupboard. Its door trembled, and someone inside squeaked.

"You know the rules," Wheatstraw continued as we all entered the kitchen in a clump. He dumped the dishes into the sink with a crash and whirled to face us. I tried to hide behind the widow, though she was a foot shorter. Wheatstraw pointed at her like he wanted to poke a hole in the air. His gentleman's fingernail was now long and ragged, with something crusted beneath, and his eyes were red as a drunkard's. "Just look at her," he said. "Just stand near her, for pity's sake! She's stoked with magic like a furnace with coal, and the wide world is full of matches. She's in a different world now, and she has got to learn." He turned to me. "Tea party's over, my dear. From now on, it's test after test, and you have your first assignment, your first nine questions."

"Eight," I said.

He threw back his head and roared like a bull. I clapped my hands over my ears and shrieked. Our dresses billowed as if in a strong wind. The cords stood out on Wheatstraw's neck. His hot breath filled the room. Then he closed his mouth, and the roar was gone. "All righty then," he said. "Eight it is. You owe the Old Concern eight answers—and one question." He jammed his hat two-handed onto his head down to his eyebrows, then sprang into the sink. He crouched there, winked, and vanished down the drain with a gurgle. His hat dropped to the porcelain and wobbled in place until it, too, was snatched into the depths. Wheatstraw's voice chuckled through the pipes, and ghosts flowed keening from the faucet.

"Showoff," the widow said. She squeezed my arm. "He's a liar, too. Absolutely terrible at whist."

"When he said I had to answer those questions, was that a lie, too?"

"Ah, no, that part was true enough."

"And the part about me being . . . a wizard?"

The widow smiled. "Truest of all," she said.

"ALL wizards have much the same talents," said the widow, as she washed the unbroken dishes, and I dried them, "just as all carpenters, all painters, all landscapers do. But each wizard also has a specialty, some talent she is especially good at. Some work at the craft for decades before realizing what their specialty is. Some realize what it was only in hindsight, only on their deathbeds, if they ever realize it at all. But other wizards have their talents handed to them, almost from birth, the way we all are granted the earth and the sky.

"I myself was no taller than a turnip when I realized that many of the little friends I played with every day, in the attic and beneath the grape arbor and in the bottom of the garden, were children that others could not see, and I realized, too, that my parents did not like for me to speak of them, to say, 'Oh, Papa, how funny! Little Merry just passed through your waistcoat, as you were stirring your tea.' How cross he became that day."

She wrung dry a dishcloth in her tiny fists. I blew soap bubbles from my palm into the face of a sleeping tabby as it floated past. The bubbles bobbed through the cat, or was it the other way around? The bubbles had been scrubbing dishes with pumice, so the bubbles were reddish in color and seemed more substantial than the wholly transparent cat. Then the bubbles vanished, and the tabby remained.

The widow continued: "And so I began keeping my talent secret, and once you start keeping your talents secret, why, you're well along the path of the wizard."

"My talents are a secret even from me," I said.

"There now, you see how wrong you can be?" said the widow. She popped my shoulder with the dish towel. "You play with dead cats. You converse with all my boarders. You unbind the front door and then bind it again without half-trying. You come here from Tennessee in a single step, as if the world were a map you could fold. My goodness, that's a step even Paul Bunyan couldn't take, and Paul is a big, big man." After a moment's reverie, she shook her head and with a great splash yanked free the plug. "Well, that's done!" she cried over the rush of the emptying sink. "May it all go down Wheatstraw's gullet." She stood on tiptoe and kissed my cheek. Her kiss was quick, dry, and powdery, like the dab of a cotton swab. "Never you fret, child," she said, taking my arm and leading me down the steps into the garden. "You've got talent to burn, as Mr. Winchester would have said. And now that you've begun to focus, well, you'll tumble across a specialty or three very soon, I daresay."

"Mr. Wheatstraw said I'm in a different world now."

The widow snorted. "Different world, indeed! You can't change worlds like garters, my dear. This is the same world you were born into, the same world you are stuck with, all the days of your life. Never forget that. But the older you get, and the more traveling you do, why, the more of this world you inevitably will see—and inevitably be *able* to see, I daresay."

"Because I walked through the diorama, you mean?"

"That was a powerful bit of traveling, indeed it was. Doubtless it broadened your mind a bit. Who knows? A few weeks ago you might have been as ignorant of the spirit world as my carpenters, might have looked right through Mr. Dellafave without even seeing him, much less being able to converse with him. And what a shame that would have been," she said, not sounding quite convinced.

I considered telling her that Mr. Dellafave was in love with her, but decided she knew that already. Instead, I finally dared to ask a question.

"Mrs. Winchester. In all these years since Mr. Winchester died, has he ever, well . . . visited?"

"Ah, that's sweet of you to ask, child," said the widow, with a sniff and a toss of her head. "No, not yet, though early on I looked for him and listened for him, by day and by night. Especially by night. I confess I even hired a medium or two to conduct a séance—for those were all the rage, a few years ago." She waved absently as we passed a headless brakeman, who raised his lantern to her. "A phantom herd of buffalo might have stampeded through the parlor without those frauds noticing. And the mess! We mopped up ectoplasm for days." She leaned against the trunk of an English yew and stared, not unhappily, into the sky. "I finally concluded that Mr. Winchester—like my mama and papa, and my old nurse, and my little dog, Zip, that I had when we were first wed, and my poor child Annie—that I will be reunited with none of them until I'm as insubstantial as that lady in the pond over there."

In silence, we watched the woman as she rose from the water, stood a few moments on the surface, then sank out of sight amid the lily pads, her face unreadable. Her dress was from an earlier time. Where had all her lovers got to, I wondered, and what did she remember of them?

"I'll tell you the puzzle that worries me," the widow Winchester abruptly said, "and it's not Mr. Winchester, and it's not where all the dogs go. What worries me is that in all these years of receiving the dear departed in my home, I have met not one—not one—who was, in life, a wizard."

"SARAH!" the man yelled. "Sarah!"

The widow and I ran to the bay window in the parlor. I knew that voice.

A two-horse wagon had pulled up in front of the house, and a big man in a black suit and black hat was climbing out of it. It was a warm fall day, but his hat and shoulders were dusted with snow, and ice clung to the spokes of the wheels. The wagon was faded blue and covered with painted stars and crescent moons. The side read:

WIZARD OF THE BLUE RIDGE

MAGICIAN OF THE OLD SOUTH

PURVEYOR OF MAGIC AND MIRTH

He removed his hat and called again: "Sarah! I got him! I finally got him!"

It was Mr. Farethewell.

By the time we reached the front door—which the widow opened with a wave of her hand—a horse and rider had galloped up. It was Petey Wheatstraw, dressed like a fox hunter in red coat, white breeches, and high boots.

"Winchester, do something!" he yelled as he dismounted. "Farethewell's gone crazy."

"Crazy, nothing," Farethewell said. "He's trapped like a bug in a jar."

"Who is?" the widow asked.

"Old Scratch himself!" Farethewell replied. "Here's your Devil."

He went to the back of the wagon and began dragging out something heavy, something we couldn't yet see.

The widow looked to Wheatstraw. "Is this true?"

He threw up his hands. "Who knows? No one's seen the Old Man in days."

Farethewell dragged the whatever-it-was a little closer to the end of the wagon, and an old boot thumped to the gravel. I stepped closer, out of the shadow of the porch.

"Well, hello, Little Britches," said Farethewell. "Sarah told me you were here. So you decided to pull some magic after all?" He pulled a flask from his jacket, looked at it, then laughed and flung it across the yard. It landed in the rosebushes with a clank.

"She told you?" I cried. I got behind a pillar. Just the sight of Farethewell made me feel flushed and angry. "You *know* each other?"

"Well, he *is* a wizard," Wheatstraw said.

Farethewell stood there, hands on hips, and looked pleased with himself. The widow peered into the wagon.

"Where is he? Is that his boot?"

Farethewell snatched her up and hugged her and spun her around. "That ain't his boot. That's him! He's in the boot! Come look, Little Britches!"

"Don't you call me that," I yelled, but I stepped off the porch anyway. Farethewell took hold of the boot with both rough hands and walked backward, hunched over, dragging the boot toward the house as if he dragged a big man's corpse. The boot tore a rut in the gravel.

"Couldn't be," Wheatstraw said.

"It is!" Farethewell said.

"Blasphemy," the widow said.

"Bad for business, anyway," Wheatstraw said.

Farethewell let go of the boot and stepped back, gasping, rubbing the small of his back with his hands. "I run him down in the Sierras," he said. "He'd a got away from me, if he had just let go of that chicken. Seven days and seven nights we fought up and down them slopes. The avalanches made all the papers. I've had this boot since Appomattox. It's my teacher's boot, hexed with his magic and with his blood. On our eighth day of wrestling, I got this jammed down over the Devil's head, and just kept on jamming till he was all inside, and now the Devil will pay!"

We all gathered around the boot.

"It's empty," the widow said.

Wheatstraw cackled. "Sure is. Farethewell, you are crazier than a moonstruck rat."

I did not laugh. Peering out through the laces of the boot was a face. The two blue eyes got wider when they saw me. The face moved back a little, so that I could see more of it.

It was Farethewell in the boot.

I looked over my shoulder. Yes, big Farethewell stood behind me, grinning. But the tiny man in the boot was Farethewell also, wearing a robe and pointed hat, as I last had seen him at Professor Van Der Ast's.

The little Farethewell hugged himself as if he were cold and began silently to cry.

"What's the matter, child?" the widow asked. I shrugged off her little spindly hand of comfort. It was like twitching free of a spider.

"What you see in there?" Wheatstraw asked.

"Tell them, Little Britches!"

"Don't take on so, dear. What could you possibly see? This has nothing to do with you."

"Maybe it does," said Farethewell. "Who you see in there, girl? What's this varmint to you?"

"What's his name this time?" Wheatstraw asked. "The Old Man answers to more names than the Sears and Roebuck catalog."

I didn't answer. Little Farethewell was backing up, pressing himself flat against the heel of that old floppy boot. I stepped forward to see him better, and he shook so the whole boot trembled.

"He's scared," I said, more loud and fierce than I meant to sound, for in fact this scared me worse than anything—not that I was faced with a second Farethewell the size of a doll you could win with a ball toss, but that I was more fearsome to him than his larger self was. What kind of booger did he take me for? This scared me but made me mad, too. I snarled and made my fingers into claws like Boola the Panther Boy and lunged.

"Yah!"

Little Farethewell twitched so hard the boot fell over. The sole was so worn you could see through it nearly, and a gummy spot at the toe treasured a cigarette butt and a tangle of hair.

"He's ours," big Farethewell hissed into my ear. "Whatever face he's showing you, girl, whoever he once was to you, he is ours now and no mistake. All the way here, off the slopes and down the river and through the groves, it was all I could do to keep him booted and not kicking the boards out of the wagon, but now you got him broken like a pony. And a girl loves a pony. He's mine and yours together now."

"Don't listen," the widow said.

"Sarah. You forgetting what we got in there? You forgetting Gettysburg, Cold Harbor, Petersburg? The tuberculosis that carried off your William, the marasmus that stole Annie from the cradle? Don't you care what this *thing* has done to the world, what it still could do? Ain't you learned nothing?"

"Some things ain't fit to be learned," the widow said, "and some wizards breathing God's free air are cooped up worse than this creature is. Petey, tell him. You've seen worse than Cold Harbor, worse than any of us."

Wheatstraw did not answer at once. He did not seem to be listening. He was in the act of dusting a metal bench with his handkerchief. He slowly refolded the handkerchief, then flicked off one last spot of dust and sighed and settled himself on the bench, perched on the edge as if delicacy alone could keep his breeches away from the iron. The moment he sat, a transparent cat jumped onto his lap and settled itself. Wheatstraw scratched between its ears as it sank out of sight, purring, until Wheatstraw was scratching only his leg.

"What I see," Wheatstraw finally said, "is that whatever half-dead thing you dragged in, Farethewell, it ain't yours anymore. It's Pearl's."

"Pearl's!" said Farethewell and the widow, together.

"Pearl's," Wheatstraw repeated. "Otherwise, she couldn't see it, could she? So it's hers to do with as she will. And there ain't no need in y'all looking like you just sucked down the same oyster. Folks making up their own minds—why, that's the basic principle of the Old Concern, the foundation of our industry. And besides," he added, as he leaned back and tipped his felt hat over his eyes and crossed his legs at the ankles, "she's done made it up anyhow."

When he said that, I realized that I had.

"No," Farethewell said.

I picked up the boot. It was no heavier for me than a dead foot. The thought made me shiver.

"Wheatstraw," said Farethewell. "What have you done to me, you wretch? I can't move."

"It ain't my doing."

"Nor mine," said the widow.

"Pearl. Listen to me."

I held up the boot and looked at it, eye to eyelet. The trembling shape no longer looked much like Farethewell—more like a bad memory of him, or a bad likeness of him, or just a stain on a canvas that put you in mind of him, if you squinted just right. To whatever it was, I said, "Go home."

Then I swung the boot three times over my head and let it fly.

"*Noooo!*" Farethewell yelled.

The boot sailed over the fence and past the point where it ought to have fallen back to earth and kept on going, a tumbling black dot against the pale sky like a star in reverse, until what I thought was the boot was just a floater darting across my eye. I blinked it away, and the boot was gone.

Mr. Farethewell stared into the sky, his jaw working. A tear slid down his cheek. He began to moan.

"Whoo! Don't reckon we need wait supper on him tonight," Wheatstraw said.

"I knew it," the widow said. She snapped her fingers in Wheatstraw's

213

face. "I knew it the moment she and her fetches stepped out of the ball-room window. Her arrival was foretold by the spirits."

"Foretold by the spirits, my eye," Wheatstraw said. "She's a wizard, not the three-fifty to Los Angeles."

Farethewell's moan became a howl.

I suddenly felt dizzy and sick and my breath was gone, like something had hit me in the gut. I tried to run, without quite knowing why, but Farethewell already had lunged across the distance between us. He seized my shoulders, shook me like a rag, howled into my face.

"I'm sorry!" I cried. "I had to do it. I had to!"

He hit me then, and I fell to the grass, sobbing. I waited for him to hit me again, to kill me. Instead the widow and Wheatstraw were kneeling beside me, stroking my hair and murmuring words I did not understand. Farethewell was walking jerkily across the yard, like a scarecrow would walk. He fell to his knees in the rosebushes and scrabbled in the dirt for his flask, the thorns tearing his face.

I stayed in bed a few days, snug beneath layers of goose down. The widow left the room only to fetch and carry for me. Mr. Dellafave settled into a corner of the ceiling and never left the room at all.

When she felt I was able, the widow showed me the note Mr. Farethewell had left.

> *I never should have hit you, Little Britches, and I am sorry for it, but you never should have got between me and the Devil. Many women and children in Virginia got between the armies and died. Hear me. Farethewell.*

"His fist didn't hurt you," the widow said.

"I know," I said. "Doing what I did with the boot, that's what hurt me. I need to find out what I did and how to do it right. Mrs. Winchester?"

"Yes, child."

"When I am better, I believe I shall take a trip."

"Where, child?"

"All over," I said. "It was Mr. Dellafave's idea, in a way. I need to see some of the other things in the diorama, and I need to meet some other wizards. As many as I can. I have a lot to learn from all of them."

She pulled a handkerchief out of her sleeve and dabbed her eyes. "I can't go with you," she said.

"But I'll always come back," I said. "And you mustn't worry about me. I won't be alone."

✶

I considered walking back through the ballroom window, but I had been there before. I ran my finger over the pebbled face of the stained-glass girl to say good-bye.

When I walked out the front gate of Flatland House, toting an over-stuffed carpetbag, I half expected to find myself walking in at the back, like Mr. Dellafave. But no, there were the orchards, and the lane leading over the hill to San Jose, and Petey Wheatstraw sitting cross-legged on a tall stump like a Hindu fakir.

I waved. He waved and jumped down. He was dressed like a vagabond, in rough cloth breeches and a coarse shirt, and his belongings were tied up in a kerchief on the end of a stick.

"You're a sight," I said.

"In the future," he replied, "they'll call it *slumming*. Which way?"

"That way, to the top of the hill, then sideways."

We set off.

"Also, Mr. Wheatstraw, I have some answers for you."

"Are you prepared to sing them? Anything worth saying is worth singing."

"I am."

"You're so agreeable this morning. It can't last." He sang:

Oh, you must answer my questions nine
Sing ninety-nine and ninety
Or you're not God's, you're one of mine
And you are the weaver's bonny.

I sang back:

Snow is whiter than the milk
Sing ninety-nine and ninety
And down is softer than the silk
And I am the weaver's bonny.

Heaven's higher than a tree
Sing ninety-nine and ninety
And Hell is deeper than the sea
And I am the weaver's bonny
Thunder's louder than a horn
Sing ninety-nine and ninety
And death is sharper than a thorn
And I am the weaver's bonny
A babe's more innocent than a lamb
Sing ninety-nine and ninety
And the Devil is meaner than womankind

—"And MANkind, too," I said, interrupting myself—

And I am the weaver's bonny.

Wheatstraw gave me a half-mocking salute and sang:

You have answered my questions nine
Sing ninety-nine and ninety
And you are God's, you're none of mine
And you are the weaver's bonny.

Then I asked him the ninth question, and he agreed that it was the right question to ask, so right that he did not know the answer, and together we reached the top of the hill and walked sideways, right off the edge of the world.

JUST this year I made it back to Chattanooga. The town was so changed I hardly recognized it, except for the bend in the river and the tracks through the tunnel and Lookout Mountain over everything.

The new bridge is still hanging on, though it's no longer new and carries no proper traffic anymore, just visitors who stroll along it and admire the view and take photographs. Can you call them photographs anymore? They need no plates and no paper, and you hardly have to stand still any time to make one.

At the end of my visit I spent a good hour on the bridge, looking at the river and at the people, and enjoying walking my home city on older, stronger legs and seeing it with better eyes and feeling more myself than I had as a girl—though I'm still not as old-looking as you'd expect, thanks to my travels and the talents I've picked up along the way.

How you'd *expect* me to look at my age, I reckon, is *dead*, but I am not that, not by a long shot.

I wondered how many of these young-old people creeping along with the help of canes, and candy-faced children ripping and roaring past me, and men and women rushing along in short pants, my goodness, their stuck-out elbows going up and down like pistons—how many of them dreamed of the world that I knew. But what had I known myself of the invisible country all around, before I passed into the Infernal Regions?

Up ahead, sitting on one of the benches along the bridge, was a girl who put me in mind of my old Chattanooga friend Sally Ann Rummage, with her red hair and her long neck and her high forehead like a thinker. Probably about sixteen, this girl was, though it's hard to tell; they stay younger so much longer now, thank goodness. She didn't look very happy to be sixteen, or to be anything. A boy was standing over her, with one big foot on the bench like he was planting a flag, and he was pointing his finger in her face like Petey Wheatstraw was known to do, and his other hand was twisting her pretty brown jacket and twisting her shoulder, too, inside it, and she looked cried-out and miserable. He was telling her about herself, or presuming to, and when he glanced my way—no more seeing me than he would a post or a bird or a food wrapper blowing past—I saw that he was Farethewell. He was high-cheeked and eighteen and muscled, where Farethewell was old and jowly, and had a sharp nose unlike Farethewell, and had nothing of Farethewell's shape or face or complexion, but I recognized him just the same. I would recognize Farethewell anywhere.

I stood behind him, looking at her, until she looked up and met my gaze. This is a good trick, and one that even nonwizards can accomplish.

The boy said to me something foul that I will not lower myself to repeat, and I said, "Hush," and he hushed. Of all the talents I've learned since I left Flatland House, that may be the handiest.

The girl frowned, puzzled, her arms crossed tight to hold herself in like a girl I once knew in a California parlor long ago. I smiled at her and put in her head the Devil's ninth question:

Who am I?

And while I was in there, in a thousand places, I strewed an answer like mustard seeds: *I am the weaver's bonny.*

Then I walked on down the bridge. The sun was low, the breeze was sharp, and a mist was forming at the river bend, a mist only I could see. The mist thickened and began to swirl. The surface of the water roiled. In the center of the oncoming cloud, twin smokestacks cleaved the water, then the wheelhouse, then the upper deck. The entire riverboat surfaced, water sluicing down the bulkheads, paddle wheel churning. I could read the boat's bright red markings. It was the *Sultana*, which blew up in 1865 just north of Memphis, at the islands called the Hen and Chickens, with the loss of seventeen hundred men. And my, did she look grand!

At the head of the steps to the riverfront, I looked back—for wizards always look back. Have I not been looking back since I began this story, and have you not been looking back with me, to learn the ways of a wizard? I saw the girl striding away from the boy, head held high. He just stood there, like one of Professor Van Der Ast's blockheads with a railroad spike up his nose. The girl whirled once, to shout something at him. The wind snatched away all but one word: "—ever!" Then she kept on walking. The mustard was beginning to sprout. I laughed as loudly as the widow Winchester, and I ran down the slick steps to the river, as giddy as a girl of ninety-nine and ninety.

Barrens Dance

PETER S. BEAGLE

Peter S. Beagle was born in New York City in 1939. Although not prolific by genre standards, he has published a number of well-received fantasy novels, at least two of which, A Fine and Private Place and The Last Unicorn, were widely influential and are now considered to be classics of the genre. In fact, Beagle may be the most successful writer of lyrical and evocative modern fantasy since Bradbury, and is the winner of many Mythopoeic Fantasy Awards and Locus Awards, as well as having often been a finalist for the World Fantasy Award, and a Hugo Award winner for his story "Two Hearts," a coda to The Last Unicorn. Beagle's other books include the novels The Folk of the Air, The Innkeeper's Song, The Unicorn Sonata, and Tamsin. His short fiction has appeared in places as varied as The Magazine of Fantasy & Science Fiction, The Atlantic Monthly, Seventeen, and The Ladies' Home Journal, and has been collected in The Rhinoceros Who Quoted Nietzsche and Other Odd Acquaintances, The Magician of Karakosk, and The Line Between. He has written the screenplay for several movies, including the animated versions of The Lord of the Rings and The Last Unicorn; the libretto for an opera, The Midnight Angel, based on his story "Come Lady Death;" and a popular autobiographical travel book, I See By My Outfit. Scheduled for release in the next year are three new novels: Summerlong, I'm Afraid You've Got Dragons, and Sweet Lightning, a 1950s baseball fantasy.

In the tense and compelling story that follows, he takes us deep into the wastelands of the Barrens in winter, to witness an intricate pavane of love and lust, obsession and devotion, magic both evil and good, and the kind of loyalty that persists beyond the skin . . .

IT is a curious thing, our companionship, when you think about it. Here we are, once again taking our customary turn together in these green, green hills of your kindly west country—as always, I thank you for keeping an old man company, young as you are—and we talk and ponder and laugh, and tell our stories; and all you truly know of me, as long as you have known me, is that I come from the Northern Barrens. No, think about it, before you answer. Is it not so? Think about it.

Now. If you recall the old saying, *strange as a tale out of the Barrens*? Very good. This is one, and you will have to decide in your own mind how much of it you choose to believe. I believe it all—but then, I have reasons.

This story begins with a wizard named Carcharos. Whatever you may have been told, most wizards are neither good nor bad. They are as they are, and they do as they do; and such words have no more meaning for them than they would to a *sheknath*. Only another wizard has the slightest notion of how a wizard thinks or feels. For myself, I cannot call to mind a single one who could be considered altogether benign—no, not even Kirisinja herself. But by the same token, there is almost no such thing as a purely evil wizard. Almost.

Carcharos. One tends to think of wizards either as bearded and severe, bearded and bumblingly kind, or bearded and dark and vaguely sinister. Carcharos was none of these things. There were broad blond planes to his friendly face, and if his blue eyes were a bit small, they were yet as candid as they could have been. His hair was red-gold in any light, as though the sun were always behind him. When he spoke, there was a deep thrum to his voice, like the singing of a giant cicada. There was no one living in the Barrens who was not afraid of Carcharos.

Yes, there was. One person. But that comes later in the story.

Should Carcharos wander by a farmer's cottage of an evening and ask quite politely—always politely—for the last bit of food in the house, or the last bottle of wine, or even the piglet fattening for Thieves' Day, the entire family would scuttle to do his bidding. That you can envisage, surely—but what would you have thought afterwards, Carcharos gone, had you then seen them all hurry out to peer at the red earth of the threshold and the sad little front garden, to see if the wizard's dusty footprints turned in such a way, fell into such a pattern, as to suggest that he might have been dancing? And if they had . . . oh, if by chance they had, then what would you have thought to see those farmers running, the lot of them, on the instant, as fast and as far as ever they could? Taking nothing—*nothing*—and never returning? I think you might have stared at those tracks for a while, yes?

Carcharos was the only wizard I have ever known, or heard of, whose power expressed itself entirely through dance. Most people imagine wizards as working their will by way of magical gestures, incantations—even song, like Am-Nemil, or Savisu himself, whose speech, from his infancy, was so distorted that he could not make himself understood in any other manner. But dance . . . as far as I have ever determined, there was no one but Carcharos. I could be wrong. I am not nearly as learned in these matters as I may sound. Lanak, the magician of Karakosk, whom I still visit when I can, for his company and his black beer, has always been of the opinion that Carcharos had discovered a means of somehow aligning his body with the universal lines of force, thus tapping that endless power by means of movement alone. Here again, I have no opinion, this way or that, but it could be so.

The Northern Barrens is a patchwork land, its rolling red desolation broken miles apart by scraps of arable land, farmed by solitary family groups who rarely see each other. Yet somehow all stories travel—almost overnight, it often seems—from the stony eastern edge I know best to the endless clay hills traversed only by a few wild wanderers who yet refuse to believe that there is no such thing as a *drast* mine. Even they told of Carcharos when I was yet of that country, and I am sure they still do. Stories linger for a long time in the Barrens.

I have heard at more than one fire, for instance, the tale of Carcharos's annihilation of an entire family and their farm, for no other reason but that he disliked the taste of the well water they had eagerly offered him when he appeared at their door one evening. The story says that he summoned against them creatures such as no one had ever seen before, that the few surviving witnesses prayed never to see again, and never flushed out of their dreams. And there was a man, a lordling's revenue collector, who refused to yield up a splendid black stallion that the wizard fancied. To be fair, Carcharos asked him twice—gently and courteously, by all accounts—before he called down lightning, lightning out of a cloudless sky, that lifted the bailiff into the air, tracing his outline in fire, whirling him this way and that, like a dry leaf crumbling in the wind. What it spilled to the ground, when it finally grew bored with playing with him, was a handful of gray-and-black ashes. No more than that.

I see the usual questions in your eyes: why was Carcharos what he was? What can his dance possibly have been like? Why did a wizard of his stature remain in such a backwater as the Northern Barrens, with so little scope for his desires? To begin with the easiest one, Carcharos was not to be found in the Barrens at all times; indeed, he traveled widely, and there are accounts of appearances as far south as Bitava, and as far to the west as Grannach Harbor and Leishai, on the coast itself. Yet he always, always came back to that stark wild, fled by so many from the day it was made. Sooner or later, he always returned to the Barrens.

Now I believe the reason for this lies in the question of Carcharos's nature. Unlike some wizards, he was not an especially ambitious man: he had no vast vision of dominance, no limitless dreams of world conquest. You might say he was more like an immensely strong and cruel highwayman, riding the great red hills with power swinging at his side, instead of a rapier. What he saw and wanted he took, and most likely had more pleasure in the act than from the thing itself. But exercising his power over that one family, that one poor man, even . . . that suited him just as well as mastering a dozen kingdoms. Quite restrained, in a way, when you think about it.

Although I know nothing of his upbringing or his studies, the fact that he was as unequivocally evil as he was still surprises me more than it shocks me. I have always believed that magic has its own immutable nature, and in some way resists being practiced contrariwise, to this use or that. But Carcharos was Carcharos, and if he was able to defy the very spirit and essence of magic . . . well, he paid dearly enough for it, in the end.

Now, much of what follows is clumsily stitched together from things that are presumed to be general knowledge—which does not mean for a minute that they are even half-true—and a deal of rumored rubbish which yet might mean *something* to a wise listener. But what may make this tale a bit different is that I was there when Carcharos—terrible, heartless Carcharos—fell in love with the wife of the *shukri* trainer.

Not that you would have called it love, I am sure, nor would almost anyone who imagines that he knows what the word means. Since I never have, I can only say that Jassi Belnarak, daughter of generations of *shukri* trainers and wife to another—big young Rijo Belnarak—was pretty enough, and good-hearted with it; but why the wizard Carcharos should have been so instantly besotted with her is more than I can tell you. But so it was.

Coming from the south, you may not know very much about *shukris* and *shukri* folk? Ah . . . Well, the first thing to know is that, no matter how docile and domesticated they may seem, no matter if they sleep in your bed or eat from your hand, *shukris* are *always* wild, wild in their hearts and bones. The second thing is that when they link with human beings—and not all of them do, far from it—it is not merely for life, but for something rather longer and deeper. A *shukri* belongs to no one—never, not ever—but if you should connect with a *shukri*, then you belong to it, simple as that. It is less a thing of the heart—whatever *shukris* are, one would not call them lovable or demonstrative—than of the soul.

People who have doings with *shukris* are usually much like their charges: swift and lean and supple—and fierce, too, until they decide to like you. If they decide otherwise . . . well. As a group, *shukri* trainers are amiable enough, but they have no real interest in anyone not of their fraternity, and they volunteer nothing. They will talk *shukri* as long as you like, happy to brag on this one's intelligence, that one's knack for cartwheels or somersaults; they may even pass on a hint, a nibble of their world's rich folklore—improbable herbal additions to a training diet, favored cures for an animal down with *jandak* poisoning, the proper tone of voice to employ when addressing a female in season. But the link, the *link* . . . no, I doubt they speak of that even to one another.

Rijo Belnarak was unusual for his trade. Not lean, and not swift, but big, as I have said. He moved heavily, though not without grace, and instead of distance and wariness there was a sweetness in him which he thought unmanly and did his best to deny. But the dozen-odd *shukris* whom he raised and tended, and taught to play games and carry messages, to tumble on a tightrope, and to dance along his entire body like a crackle of black fire—his *shukris* knew who he was. Blood-drinking little killers they are, never forget it, but they knew Rijo Belnarak.

So did Jassi Grod, as she was called at seventeen when she wandered from her particular fold in the red hills into the dusty wrinkle we knew, and came to live with Rijo. There was never a choice for her, once she laid eyes on him: not merely because trade calls to family trade, but because of the sympathy between her quick, clever soul and his grave and gentle one. Marriage, when it did happen, was wholly incidental between those two.

It was at a hill fair that Rijo and Jassi first encountered the wizard Carcharos. Few imagine that the Barrens lend themselves to such things as markets, let alone fairs, but in fact there are quite a few; how else should such folk survive but by selling things to one another? Rijo and Jassi and their *shukris* (she had brought him eight from her family—a dowry, if you like) could be found at every one of them, performing on improvised plank stages several times a day, always to larger crowds than any other entertainer, rival trainers included. Part of the attraction lay in their looks, certainly: in the contrast between the big, slow man and the slight, lithe, white-haired woman who moved like a *shukri* herself. (Jassi was born with white hair—the legend that it turned so on her wedding day is not true. I was there.)

And I was there also when Rijo Belnarak looked up during a performance (he was demonstrating how Shas, his very favorite *shukri*, could swing and leap like an acrobat from his earring to Jassi's and back) to meet the blue eyes of Carcharos. The wizard was sitting his horse in the rear of the crowd, more than half-hidden in the shadow of a tree. But Rijo knew that he was watching the two of them, and not any *shukri*, and he knew as well that the one Carcharos was studying most closely was his wife, Jassi. He did *not* know—not then—that Carcharos was a great wizard, but he did not need to. Rijo thought almost as heavily as he moved, but he saw deeper than most.

And what do you suppose that Carcharos saw, or felt, or thought, at that first sight of Jassi Belnarak? I wonder it still, though I doubt greatly, wicked-wise as he was, whether Carcharos ever spent much time finding exact words for his feelings. At that moment he simply wanted her, and he called her to him, that being at once the most direct means of taking possession and announcing it to the world at the same time. As it happened, I was some distance away, but I was looking at him when he abruptly slipped from his saddle, causing an immediate stir in the crowd, as spectators scurried to get clear of him. He looked around him with his friendly blue eyes, and he smiled just a little, and he began to dance.

How am I to picture out Carcharos's dance for you? There was nothing acrobatic or flamboyant about it, not in any way; it was more of a sliding walk, a rhythmic easing to and fro, such as serpents are said to employ to hypnotize their prey. Now and then he wheeled in a sudden circle; now and then he paced swiftly forward or swiftly back; once in a while he cast his arms wide or raised them above his head, or held them straight out before him, at once beckoning and begging. No more than that, never any more than that, to Carcharos's dancing.

Often he clasped his hands behind him; and always he gazed only at the ground as he paced this way and that, looking neither like a wizard nor a dancer, but for all the world like a philosopher enmeshed in some profound question. Nor did he once raise his eyes to glance at the handsome couple performing with their little animals. I remember. I was there.

And Jassi Belnarak . . . Jassi caught Shas in midspring—how wrathfully the *shukri* hissed and chittered at her, outraged at the interruption—handed him to her puzzled husband, stepped down from the muddy, swaying plank stage, and walked into the suddenly silent crowd, which parted before her like water before a ship's bow. She was smiling very slightly, and her dark olive skin seemed lighted from within.

The wizard Carcharos went on dancing, still never looking up as Jassi drew near, not until she stood before him, waiting his will. Back on the stage, Rijo uttered a kind of soft, dazed bellow, dropped Shas and all the other *shukris* sporting on his shoulders and in and out of his pockets to the planks, and charged after his wife. His passage was as earnestly hindered by onlookers as Jassi's had been unchecked, for all were desperate to keep him from the power of the wizard. But he was a strong man in a rage, and he shrugged them aside and lumbered on.

Carcharos was closing his long, graceful hands on the spellbound Jassi Belnarak, to lift her to his saddle, just as Rijo reached them. The big man struck the wizard's hands away from her and raised his own fist for a blow that would have shivered an anvil into splinters—but Carcharos turned toward him, and his feet moved in a different dance: quicker, sharper, the steps like knife thrusts now. Indeed, Rijo doubled over, crumpling in silent, openmouthed agony, just as though he *had* been stabbed. Jassi blinked, shook her head violently, and began to scream enough for the two of them. Spectators were backing away, as a mighty tide sweeps a beach clean, and the wizard Carcharos danced on.

What would have happened—what vengeance he would have danced into being . . . well, I can make just enough of a guess at it to be most grateful for the failings of an old man's imagination. There is, however, nothing wrong with my memory—which is why, all these years later, I yet cherish the look on his face when the *shukri* sprang up at him from the loose open gorget of Jassi's dress and bit him on the nose.

Ah, you laugh now at the image in your mind—the renowned wizard, in the very act of leveling some dreadful curse, staggering backward with a furious little animal clenched to his nose—but you might not have laughed then. No one else did, I can assure you. Beyond a grunt, Carcharos made no sound. He gripped the *shukri* in both hands, squeezing it mercilessly, wringing it like a dishclout. The fearless creature (Shas's mate, Killy, it was) opened its jaws in a hiss of pain, and then bit down again, this time sinking its teeth into the wizard's lower lip. Carcharos tore it free, spitting blood, and hurled it after the retreating crowd, which, by this time, included Rijo Belnarak and his wife. The big man had swept Jassi up in his arms and run for it—with Killy scurrying a jump behind—faster than anyone would ever have thought he could move. His mind may indeed have worked in rather a measured fashion, but his instincts were sound.

Carcharos did not follow. He had his nose, his lip, and his pride to nurse, and—far more vital than any of these—his revenge to consider. To want and to have had been the same thing to him all his life; what made this wanting somehow different was that it had been a very long time since anyone had denied him his desire; and, further, that, for no reason he could put a name to, he was now determined that Jassi Belnarak should desire *him*, that she should come to him of her own choice, utterly uncompelled by magic. Much better than merely destroying her husband, that would be—oh, much, *much* better. He could already taste Rijo's shame and dishonor in his bloody mouth.

Jassi herself was a good while in understanding exactly what had happened to her. When she did finally shake free of Carcharos's summoning, she became at once infuriated and extremely frightened. I think she had more experience of wizards than Rijo; at all events, she knew better than he how close both of them had come to annihilation. From that moment she was resolved to keep her family—*shukris* included—as clear of Carcharos as she could, at whatever cost, even if it meant abandoning a performance, or their home itself, at a moment's warning. She determined that neither she nor Rijo would never, *ever* again raise their eyes to meet those friendly blue eyes, not ever again. And Rijo already knew, though they had not been married very long, what I have known all my life: that Jassi Belnarak is an extremely determined woman.

But resolute and cunning as she was, Carcheros had been cunning for longer than she had been alive; and stubborn courage is most often overmatched against malevolent old wisdom. Wanting what he wanted from her, he knew better than to dog her steps or haunt her hours, as she so feared. Rather, he employed all his sly arts and twisty skills to her benefit, bestowing every sort of blessing upon her—if one may use such a word in connection with such a man—without once showing himself. Being the wizard he was, he danced up for her neither money nor jewels nor clothing, nor with anything else that she could have thrown back in his face. No, his offerings were all of sunshine and starlight—Carcharos was always a weathermaster—of perfect days, and the *shukris* in perfect health, performing for the love and pride of it, and gaping, cheering crowds paying eagerly to see them. It galled him, I am sure of it, to think of Rijo sharing this bounty with her; but he doubtless cheered himself with the thought that, however ignorant of its origin her loutish husband might be, Jassi Belnarak would know. And, of course, he was quite right.

Jassi woke every morning to the sight of legendary creatures grazing in her garden—itself once a ragged, half-dead shambles for lack of care, now as radiant as a stained-glass window with new color every day—and she knew who had sent them. She drew great wonder—how not?—from the vision of an immortal *kailash* spreading its thunderous wings in her apple tree to greet her . . . wonder, but no joy, no more than she felt on the midnight when a blue-gray *liramaja* looked into her eyes and lowered its horn and its impossibly soft muzzle into her hand. No joy in any of this, no matter how much she may have hungered to take joy, because she knew.

Carcharos was bad to his toenails, evil to the roots of his hair, but he was not a fool. It is easy enough to follow his reasoning, even from this distance: if glorious miracles could not draw Jassi Belnarak to him—so be it, he would find something that would. And indeed, after a time, a new design awoke in him. He knew even less about women than most men do, but he did understand that they often have surprising difficulty in rejecting ugliness outright (why else have we all those tales of princesses and frogs?), and piteous vulnerability they dare not refuse. Very well: he would approach Jassi, not as the all-conquering master he so obviously was, but as a beggar, a faltering suppliant, lost and helpless without her love. A wise friend might, perhaps, have counseled him otherwise, but Carcharos had no friends.

So he proceeded to accost Jassi Belnarak regularly, most often in the woods, when she went there in search of blue *dalda* flowers (not the white, so often poisonous), which, brewed into a decoction, do wonders for a *shukri*'s coat and digestion. Clad always in his shabbiest, most outworn garments, his eyes so doggedly downcast that he tended to trip over things, Carcharos would mumble his forlorn need of her, careful never to look directly at her, nor ever to move in any threatening way—any dancing way. It was a rare sight, and a curiously moving one.

Or it would have been moving, if it had been even a little less patently artificial. Of all the human emotions, the one hardest to counterfeit—so I have found, anyway—is humility, and Carcharos had not the smallest acquaintance with it. Jassi Belnarak made every effort, for her life and Rijo's life, to keep from laughing; but on his fifth such visitation, when Carcharos spoke haltingly of his determination to retire into the mountains, if she would not have him, and become a *saleh*, a holy hermit, then it was all suddenly too much for her. All fear and caution collapsed within her, and she laughed.

She always had the most *sharing* sort of laugh, Jassi Belnarak did. There was never any cruelty in it, only delight and invitation.

Ah, and here we are once more, back at my own front door that always sticks so in wet weather. Come in, do, I'll put the kettle on . . . What? Bide, bide a little. We will come to that.

No living person had ever laughed at the wizard Carcharos. For a moment he stared at the young woman before him, now stricken with amusement—not even so much at his hypocrisy, but at his utter gracelessness—and his blue eyes burned brighter and brighter, until they were actually white as ashes with fury. Yet he never lifted a hand nor spoke a word to her, nor did he dance a single terrible step toward her destruction. He simply turned and walked away.

When your life is all taking, what need to learn courtship? Carcharos's passion for Jassi Belnarak deepened and darkened with every sleepless night, but it did not keep him from understanding that neither beneficence nor meek wistfulness would win her honestly. Power would have to do, after all; and I think that for the only time in that bad life, Carcharos may truly have regretted the necessity of forcing his will on another person. The moment can't have lasted long, but I think further that it may have been the closest Carcharos ever came to knowing love.

But what he knew he turned to an ill purpose, as you might imagine. Jassi Belnarak plainly had no more fear of him, not for herself—but for someone who mattered to her more than her own life? If sacrificing herself for her husband's sake were to prove the last thing that Jassi ever did willingly for her new master . . . well, then, so be it, however bitter the taste to Carcharos. Pride had always been his substitute for honor, but his pride was so long gone from him that he could barely recall the feel of it. And so be that, too.

I have known several wizards in my life who would have been capable of doing what Carcharos did to Rijo Belnarak. I have never known another who *would* have done it. Jassi and Rijo had lain down in long, slow love the night before, and Jassi, reluctant to let herself rouse fully in the morning, only came completely awake when she embraced her husband, welcoming the new day, and immediately realized that his soul was gone in the night. A man might take longer, I think—I could be wrong about this—but although Rijo responded to Jassi's caress with a smile and a languorous arching of his back, she knew at once, beyond any question, that she might as well have been petting or grooming a *shukri*. His eyes were peacefully empty, just as a *shukri*'s eyes go when you scratch its stomach; his tenderly ugly face reflected her not at all; there was no trace of *Rijo* in a single hair or scar or fingernail of the familiar generous body lying so close beside her.

I cannot tell you with any sureness that she lay still for a while, still holding the beloved shell of her husband as sweetly as always. But I knew her, and I believe she did. By and by, however, she arose and briskly dressed herself—not in the worn trews and tunic she wore for her daily work with the *shukris*, but in the dark green *hedau*-woven gown that Rijo had ordered all the way from Chun for her last birthday. It was the only such garment she had; with it she put on her best shoes—the silver-scaled ones he teasingly called her "queen's-coming-to-dinner pair"—and her finest shawl, which had belonged to her mother, and was the color of the restless sea off Cape Dylee. Then she kissed Rijo good-bye—he smiled pleasantly at her again—and she went to say farewell to the *shukris*, calling each by name and speaking a few words of affectionate memory to each in turn. And then she walked away from her house, down the stone-flagged path into the woods, where she knew the wizard Carcharos would be waiting for her on his black horse, and she never looked back.

No man was present to hear the words they spoke to one another when they met in a certain clearing, and such . . . creatures . . . as did overhear were hardly of a sort to draw their understanding from language. But it was surely a striking confrontation under the trees, for Carcharos was a handsome man, as I said at the beginning, strongly made and of a commanding presence, while little Jassi Belnarak, with her white hair and her deep, dawn gray gaze, carried herself more royally than any queen. They faced each other in silence for a time, before Jassi said, "Give my man back his soul."

And Carcharos responded, "Give me back mine," and waited calmly for the answer—long in coming, surely, but the only one it could have been.

"When you have restored my husband, I will go away with you."

Carcharos knew everything about Jassi Belnarak—everything, at least, except the part that always escapes those possessed by such wanting—and he certainly knew that she was one who kept her word. Nevertheless, he was never a whit more gracious in victory than in defeat, and he bargained with her, even at such a moment. He said, "Up, then—here, in the saddle before me. Only then will I credit your submission, and loose your husband's soul to him."

And Jassi yielded. I know this.

She came straight to the black horse, never hesitating, and never once looking back at the cherished life she was leaving forever. Had she done so—had she stolen a last glance over her shoulder as she mounted Carcharos's horse—she would have seen her *shukris*, every one of them, gathered at the edge of the clearing. They sat watching, all on their hind legs, bracing themselves with their tails—as *shukris* will do when something catches their curiosity—and their small, jeweled eyes were burning red as wayward stars. The tamest *shukri* is bone-wild, as I've said; and a group of them can be quite frightening, especially when they are completely silent, not hissing or chittering . . .

. . . because of a certain thing *shukris* can do together, when their wills are joined.

There is nothing in this thing of fangs or blood or torn-out throats. Most often it is spoken of as a myth, a legend, a matter of folklore. There cannot be more than three or four people alive who have seen it done.

I am one of them.

I know exactly what happened when Jassi and Rijo Belnarak's *shukris* saw their mistress about to be carried off by the wizard Carcharos. I can see, as I see you now, how they drew close together—so close, in fact, that in the lingering morning mist you might have thought them only one great animal stretching up and crouching to spring. You might even have imagined that one beast actually speaking one fierce word—a word to scrape along all your bones, until your flesh itself rebelled, yearning desperately, desperately, to shake free of them. And so it happened . . .

I know this. I was the *shukri* who spoke that word.

No, no, you can go on sipping your tea. It's wretched stuff, I know—I apologize for it. I have never had the knack of tea. No, I am neither mad nor likely to leap at your throat, I promise you. Once the change is made, it is made—there is no way for me ever to turn back into a *shukri* again. Everything comes at a price, you see.

It was Carcharos's moment of purest triumph, I suppose, to be at last holding her in surrender, his hands on her waist and the smell of her strange white hair in his nostrils. As he had sworn—and *all* wizards are bound to honor their pledges, for good or ill—he spoke the three words that freed Rijo Belnarak's soul to hurry home to his body. A breath later, a blink later, a heartbeat, what perched on his saddlebow had thick white fur, a short straight tail, red eyes, round ears, and a rounded muzzle aglitter with little sharp fangs. Those fangs raked Carcharos's wrist when he clutched frantically at the creature that had been Jassi Belnarak—then the white *shukri* was on the ground and racing for the trees. Her companions closed around her, as though to hide her from his sight, but he shut his eyes and saw her all the same: a tiny scampering brand, blazing through both the darkness of the woods and the shadows of his own soul. Then she was gone from him, and he threw back his head and howled, and trees began to fall.

If you should ever travel the Barrens, you will meet any number of folk who will gladly show you—for a couple of coppers, of course—the place, the wood where all this happened. You could easily find it yourself, though; there's no missing it, even for a stranger. The downed trees have never been replaced by so much as a sprig of new growth; they lie where they crashed to earth, blackened as though fire had swept over them, as is the ground itself. There is no life in that place, no life at all, not for more than a mile around— I once paced it out carefully to the point where one begins at last to see a few rabbits in the thin young brush, and to be grateful for weeds. That whole section of the wood has been gutted, leveled, razed to a void that folk say still echoes with the madness of Carcharos. For he went mad then, never doubt it, or he would never have done what he did when the white *shukri* slashed his wrist and fled away. Oh, never doubt that he went mad.

The footprints will tell you.

In the end, the most frightening thing is not the forest's devastation, not the cold shadows where there are no trees to cast them, not the overwhelming sense that you can actually touch the lifelessness. It is the *footprints*, scored so deeply into that hard, hard ground that not even a flood nor an earthquake will ever wash them away, burn them away. They are as plain as though he had stepped them off yesterday, those tracks left by the wizard Carcharos when he stalked that terrible dance floor long ago. You can see the smudged prints where he wheeled and spun, the furrows where he glided forward or back in one long stride, the triangular marks where he surely rose on the balls of his feet, raising his arms to the sky. And you can clearly follow the movement of the dance, straight as a stormwind, straight toward what would have been the deep core of the wood, before it fell. Follow it, sitting here far away with me—follow now . . .

Up high on one leg—you see him, do you not?—the other lunging out, scornfully kicking the earth away beneath him like a hangman's ladder. But even a wizard's foot must touch ground soon or late, and so does this one, leaving a small four-toed print, with claws. Then comes another, and another after that, and another, all bunched close together at first, as he finds his new equilibrium—then lengthening out into the long, flying bounds of a *shukri* with its prey in sight. He was gray, a darkish gray, with no trace of his red-blond glory. I cannot say why that should have been.

There were other footprints, too, that day. I made them.

Barely visible, I'm sure they were, and doubtless gone soon, not having been danced into the deep flesh of the earth by a wizard so maddeningly cheated of his wicked heart's desire. They would likely have been difficult to read, even for a skilled tracker, since it took me far, far longer than it did Carcharos to learn the trick of balancing on two feet, after a lifetime on four. I hobble somewhat still, no disguising that—you have always been most kind about matching your steps to mine, and gracious enough neither to ask questions nor to take my arm. But this is nothing compared . . . compared to the way I lurched and crawled, tottered and stumbled and crawled again out of that torn, tormented wood—I, who before had only tumbled in air, whose own dance carried me flying between the hands of two humans who were mine, *mine*, as surely and always as all my flying family were mine. For Jassi and Rijo Belnarak, I crawled. And crawl now, here with you.

No, until it happened I had no idea that I would be the one chosen to make the exchange. We—oh, yes, I still say *we*, even now—we never know how the choice happens, or on whom it will fall. What we do know is that it is our choice, always, made together. Made out of . . . love? We have no such word, we *shukris*, but we know that nothing is won without sacrifice. One *shukri* more, one human more—a trade, a balance. So it must be, so the magic runs. *Our* magic.

But if any wizard but Carcharos has ever worked such a shape-shifting upon himself, I know nothing of it. I was looking straight at him when he changed, as my new form closed over me, and I will swear on my deathbed that he never cared for a moment whether the transformation was reversible or not. Not for a moment.

Carcharos was never seen or heard of again—not in the Barrens, anyway, I can vouch for that. Oh, there were rumored sightings, legends—as there still are, to this day—but they have always proved false. In a strange way, I rather miss him, I do. He was an evil man who took pleasure and nourishment from his evil, but he was *ours*, he was of the Barrens, do you understand? There is an old saying that nothing ever came out of the Northern Barrens but weak cattle and weaker ale. Carcharos was an exception. We should not be proud of him, but there you are.

As for Jassi Belnarak . . . well, now, that is possibly another story. Rijo lives still, you know, and still trains and performs with his famous *shukris*, old as he is. He has never remarried; and for all his undoubted sorrow at the disappearance of his wife, for all these years there has always been an . . . an *air* about him, the *sense* of a secret smile, as though he were holding something deep and near that might interest you, if you learned it.

And so, inevitably, the other rumors began to take root and sprout up, and grow. It is said everywhere, by people unborn when this tale took place, that Jassi Belnarak still comes to her husband every month, under the full moon, when she is somehow able—or allowed?—to take her human form for that little time. And it is believed also that the gray *shukri* that is the wizard Carcharos still hunts the white *shukri* through the forest, night and day, never capturing her, nor even drawing close enough to catch sight of her, but never losing her scent, never giving up.

Do I believe the stories myself? No, none of them, certainly not, not at all.

Oh, yes. Oh, yes, with all my heart, and if you cannot understand how I can hold both the dream and the doubt in that same heart . . . well, it is very nearly a human heart, after all. But I wish it so, because I was there, and it should be so. I was there, as surely as one day soon I will not be here—I was *there*, and I saw them, and I knew them, and what I lost I gave freely, and it *should* be so. It should be so.

Stone Man

NANCY KRESS

Here's a walk down the Mean Streets of today's big cities, which can be made even meaner by battling wizards—unless you can get a little help from your friends . . .

Nancy Kress began selling her elegant and incisive stories in the midseventies and has since become a frequent contributor to Asimov's Science Fiction, The Magazine of Fantasy & Science Fiction, OMNI, Sci Fiction, and elsewhere. Her books include the novel version of her Hugo- and Nebula-winning story, "Beggars in Spain," and a sequel, Beggars and Choosers, as well as The Prince of Morning Bells, The Golden Grove, The White Pipes, An Alien Light, Brainrose, Oaths and Miracles, Stinger, Maximum Light, Probability Moon, Probability Sun, Probability Space, Crossfire, and Nothing Human. Her short work has been collected in Trinity and Other Stories, The Aliens of Earth, and Beaker's Dozen. Her most recent book is the novel Crucible. In addition to the awards for "Beggars in Spain," she has also won Nebula Awards for her stories "Out of All Them Bright Stars" and "The Flowers of Aulit Prison."

JARED Stoffel never even saw the car that hit him. He ollied off the concrete steps of the Randolph Street Rec Center down onto the street and was coming down on his skateboard when *wham!* his butt was smacked hard enough to rattle his teeth and Jared went down. A second before the pain registered, he threw up his arms to shield his face. The Birdhouse went flying—he saw it in the air, wheels spinning, a moment before his body hit the street. All at once he was smothered under *a ton of stones he couldn't breathe he was going to die and someone was screaming but it*

was mostly the rocks—God the boulders flying to land on top of him, under him, everywhere . . .

Everything went black.

✱

"YOU with us yet, child?"

"Rocks." It came out "bogs." Jared put his hand to his face. The hand stopped an inch away on his swollen mouth.

"How many fingers am I holding up?"

"Who."

"What day is it?"

"Breeday."

"Just rest a while. You took a nasty fall." The blurry old nurse dressed in some stupid pants with yellow ducks on them stuck a needle in Jared's arm and went away.

When he came to again, everything was clearer. A TV on a shelf high up near the ceiling droned out some news about an earthquake someplace. An old man in a white coat sat in a chair by Jared's bed, reading. Jared tried to sit up, and the man rose and eased him back down. "Just stay quiet a little longer."

"Where am I?"

"Perry Street Medical Center. You got hit by a car while skateboarding, but you have nothing more than two fractured ribs and a lacerated hand. You're a very lucky young man."

"Oh, right. Just lousy with luck." The words came out correctly; his lips weren't nearly as swollen. The tiny room had no windows. How long had he been in here?

"I'm Dr. Kendall and I need some information. What's your name, son?"

"I'm not your son." Jared lay trying to remember this accident. Shawn— he'd been skateboarding with Shawn. Shawn had yelled when Jared got hit. "Shawn?"

"Your name's Shawn? Shawn What?"

"I'm not Shawn, dumb-ass. He's my friend, with me. Where's Shawn?"

The doctor grimaced. "Some friend. He took off running as soon as the ambulance arrived. What were you two doing that he didn't want to get caught? Never mind, I don't want to know. But I do need to know your name."

"Why?"

"To notify your parents, for one thing."

"Forget it. She won't come."

Something moved behind the doctor's eyes. He glanced up at the TV, still showing pictures of an earthquake, then returned to watching Jared closely. Too closely. The guy was maybe fifty, maybe sixty, with white hair, but that didn't mean he couldn't be a—was he even really a doctor? Jared said, "Hey, stop staring like that, sicko."

"Ah," the doctor said sadly. "I see. Damn. But I still need to know your name. For the records we—"

"I don't got any insurance. So you can just let me out of here now." Again Jared tried to sit up.

"Lie down, son. We can't release you yet. Now please tell me your name."

"Jared."

"Jared What?"

"None of your business." If he didn't say any more, maybe they'd throw him out of here. The doc said he wasn't hurt bad. He could crash at Shawn's. If Ma saw him like this, she'd smash the Birdhouse for sure. She—

"Hey! Where's my deck?"

"Your what?"

"My deck! The Bird! My skateboard!"

"Oh. I'm afraid I don't know."

"You mean you just left it in the *street*?" Gone now, for sure. And it had been a huge set of trouble to steal it!

Again that strange expression in Kendall's eyes. He said quietly, "Jared, I will personally replace your skateboard, buy you a brand-new and very good one, if you will answer some questions for me first."

"You? Buy me a new deck? For giving you what?"

"I already told you. All you need do is answer some questions."

"Nobody gives away new decks for free!"

"I will, to you." Kendall's eyes, Jared saw, were light brown, full of some emotion Jared didn't understand. But he wasn't picking up rip-off vibes from the man. Hope surged through him. A new deck . . . maybe an Abec four . . .

He squashed the hope. Hope just got you hurt.

Kendall reached into his pocket and drew out a wad of bills. "How much does a good skateboard cost?"

Jared's eyes hung on the money. He could get a Hawk deck . . . good trucks and wheels . . . "Two hundred dollars." Maybe the old guy didn't know what stuff cost.

Kendall counted ten twenties and held them out in his closed hand. "After you answer three questions."

"Just three? Okay, but better not try anything perv."

"First, your name and address."

"Jared Parsell, 62 Randolph."

Kendall withdrew his hand. "You're lying."

How did the old bastard *know*? "Wait, don't put the money away . . . I'm Jared Stoffel, and I live at 489 Center Street." When he lived anywhere at all. Ma, strung out on crystal most of the time, only noticed when he screwed up, not when he stayed away. She was pretty lame about time.

Kendall said, "When were you born?"

"April 6, 1993."

Closing his eyes, Kendall moved his lips silently, as if figuring something. Finally, he said, as if it mattered, "Full moon."

"Whatever."

"Now the last question: How did all those stones get around you during the hit-and-run?"

"What?"

"When the ambulance arrived, you were lying on, and were covered with, small stones. They appear to have come from a flower bed on the other side of the Recreation Center. How did they get with you?"

A vague memory stirred in Jared's mind. Rocks—he was being smothered with rocks, and someone—him—said "bogs." And Shawn yelled something as Jared fell, something Jared couldn't remember now . . . Jared had thought the rocks were in his mind—something from, like, the pain of the accident. Not real. But maybe . . .

Kendall was watching him sadly. Why sad? This old psycho gave Jared the creeps.

"I don't know anything about any stones."

"You and Shawn weren't playing some game involving the stones? Throwing them at cars or something?"

"Jesus, man, I'm thirteen, not eight!"

"I see," Dr. Kendall said. He handed the two hundred dollars to Jared, who seized it eagerly, even though leaning forward caused pain to stab through his torso. Jared moved his legs toward the end of the bed.

Kendall eased them back. "Not yet, son, I'm afraid." He looked even sadder than before.

"Get your hands off me! I answered your stupid questions!"

"Yes, and the money is yours. But you can't leave yet. Not until you see one other person."

"I don't want to see any more doctors!"

"It's not a doctor. *I'm* a doctor. Larson is a . . . well, you'll see. Larson!"

The door opened and another man entered. This one was young, big, tough-looking, with long hair and a do-rag. He wore a leather jacket and gold necklace, serious gold. A dealer, maybe a gangbanger, maybe even a leader. Or a narc. He stood at the end of Jared's bed, big hands resting lightly on the metal railing, and stared unsmiling. "So is he, Doc?"

"Yes."

"You sure? Never mind, I know you don't make mistakes. But, God . . . *look* at him."

"Look at your dumb-ass self," Jared said, but even to him the words sounded lame. Larson scared him, although he wasn't going to admit that.

"Watch your mouth, kid," Larson snarled. "I don't like this any better than you do. But if you are one of us, then you are. The doc doesn't make mistakes. Damn it to hell anyway!"

"If I'm what? What am I?" Jared said.

"A wizard," Dr. Kendall said. "You're a wizard, Jared. As of now."

LARSON left the explanations to Kendall. With a disgusted look over his shoulder at the hospital bed, Larson stormed out, slamming the door. Jared caught the scandalized look of a passing nurse just before the door shook on its hinges.

"A wizard. Yeah, right," Jared said. "Any minute now I'm gonna turn you into a pigeon. No, wait—you're already a pigeon if you believe that crap."

"I'm afraid it's true," Kendall said. "During your accident you summoned those rocks. The smoothest stones from the flower bed flew through the air and landed on you, under you, around you. You skidded across the pavement on them as if on ball bearings. That broke your fall, maybe saved your life."

"Right. Anything you say."

"You were born under the full moon, also a requirement, although we don't know why. You—"

"And you're a wizard, too, huh?"

"No," Kendall said sadly, "I'm not. I can spot one, is all, and so the Brotherhood uses me."

"Uh-huh. So you can't, like, show me something wizardy right now, and Larson left before he had to. Convenient."

"Nothing 'wizardy' could be done here anyway. Not here, in the presence of metal. Not by any wizard now living." Kendall leaned forward, his hands on his knees. "Magic is very old, Jared, much older than even the most primitive civilization. It governs only the things found in nature, and it cannot operate near to the things that are not. The only reason you could summon those stones at all is because your skateboard went flying, you weren't carrying a cell phone, and you had on pull-on running shorts with no zipper."

"You leave my shorts out of this," Jared said. "How come I never did any magic before, huh? You tell me that?"

"That's easy. Your accident. The ability to do magic, among those who possess it at all, is only released in the presence of pain."

"Pain?"

"Yes, Jared," Kendall said quietly. "Everything in life costs, even magic. The price is pain."

This was the first thing the old man had said that made any sense to Jared. He knew things cost. He knew about pain.

But the rest of it was pure psycho bull. And bull with a reason. He said, "So now you tell me I'm going to one of those wizard schools, huh? Like in that book? Only guess what—it'll really turn out to be just another lockdown, like Juvie."

"There is no such thing as a wizard school. All we have is the Brotherhood, and that all too inadequate to its task."

"Listen, this sucks. I'm outta here, man. What do I gotta sign?"

"You're a minor. A parent must sign your release forms."

"Like that's gonna happen. My mom's strung out most of the time and my dad's long gone. You wait on a parent, I'll be here forever. Where's my clothes?"

"You can't—"

"Watch me. I ain't waiting here for Child Services to stick me in a foster home. And I ain't listening to no more of your bull, neither."

"You can talk better than that when you want to," Kendall said. "I've heard you do so. Here, if you're really going—no, your shoes are in that cupboard over there—take this. It's my home address. You can come see me anytime you want, Jared. For any reason."

"Don't hold your breath." He found the shoes, finished dressing, and walked out of the medical center. He had to lean twice against walls to do it, breathing deeply and fighting his own stomach, but he did it.

"Welcome to the Brotherhood, Jared," Kendall said sadly.

"Forget you," Jared said.

IT was a week before he could make it out of the house. He lay in his bedroom, fighting the pain, distracting himself with the songs on the radio and with the Game Boy he'd stolen three months ago. Ma had sold the Xbox, but he'd hidden the Game Boy and the radio behind the broken dishwasher, and she hadn't found them. He should have gotten painkillers before he left the clinic. The old doc would probably have given him some, but Jared hadn't thought of it. Fortunately, it was one of the times when there was food in the house. Ma's new guy, whom Jared encountered in the kitchen in his underwear, liked to eat well.

After a week the bedclothes, not too clean to begin with, stank, but Jared felt better. He knew he was better because he was bored. The day after that he dressed and went out. He didn't find anybody on the street. Then he remembered that school had started.

He walked to Benjamin Franklin Middle School, scowled at the security guard, and passed through the metal detector. When classes changed, kids flooded into the halls.

"Hey! Shawn!"

Shawn Delancey glanced up from the girl he was talking to, and a strange expression crossed his face. He nodded coolly. Jared hobbled over to him.

"I'm back, man."

"Yeah, I see."

"So what you doing here? In school?"

Shawn didn't answer. He turned back to the girl, without introducing her. Jared felt his face grow hot.

"Hey, you dissing me, Shawn?"

"I'm busy right now. Can't you see that?"

This had never happened before. He and Shawn were *tight*, had always been tight. The girl snickered. Jared limped away.

The prick, the bastard . . .

But he couldn't let it go. He caught Shawn later, leaving school after fourth period, carrying his deck. Jared stepped out from an alley and said, "Shawn. What's wrong, man?"

"Nothing. I gotta go."

Anger and hurt made him desperate. "Dude, it's me! Me!"

Shawn stopped, turning from embarrassment to anger. Maybe, Jared suddenly thought, they were the same thing. "Just leave me alone, Jared, okay? I don't need you and your lame crap!"

His crap. He didn't have any crap except . . . it was weird and stupid, but he couldn't think of anything else. He said quietly, testing, "The stones?"

"I don't know how you did that, but . . . just leave me alone!" Shawn hurried off.

So it had been the stones. And the stones had happened. They really had. Only it had been some kind of freak accident, wind devil or something, not any freaking magic.

"Forget you!" he yelled after Shawn, but Shawn was already on his board, skimming lightly out of Jared's sight.

WITH Kendall's two hundred dollars, Jared bought a new deck, a deluxe Hawk, plus awesome trucks and wheels. He spent every day alone, in another neighborhood, painfully regaining his mobility and skill. After what happened with Shawn, he didn't want to approach his other friends, and anyway he didn't have too many other friends. Mostly it had been him and Shawn.

Ma's boyfriend broke up with her, and Jared didn't want to be home with her much; she was always wailing, or else out scoring. When the boyfriend's food was gone, she barely bought more. Sometimes Jared's stomach growled while he practiced, over and over, ollies and kickflips and fifty-fifty grinds and even a few hardflips. He sped around the neighborhood, a better one than his own, past trees turning from green to red and gold, past little kids on trikes, past bright flowers in beds edged with stones.

All the stones stayed where they were supposed to.

It was hunger and cold that finally made him pull out the card Dr. Kendall had given him at the clinic. Hunger, cold, and maybe loneliness, although he didn't like to admit that. The address was not far away, on Carter Street. Jared skated over, preparing an excuse in his mind.

Kendall's house wasn't much, a small two-story—weren't doctors supposed to make a lot of money? Neat bushes surrounded it, and the porch light shone cheerfully in the October dusk. Jared rang the bell and scowled.

"Hi, Doc, something's wrong with my hand. You must not've fixed it right."

"Come in, Jared," Kendall said. Why did the guy always look so sad to see him? What a crock. But the house was warm and smelled of meat roasting. Jared's mouth filled with sweet water. "Let me see your hand . . . you had slight damage to your left transverse ligament from the stones, but it looks all right now. Would you like to stay to dinner?"

"I already ate," Jared said, scowling more deeply. His stomach growled.

"Then have a second dinner just to keep me company. My housekeeper just left, and she cooks a lot on Mondays so she doesn't have to do much the rest of the week." Kendall led the way to the tiny dining room without giving Jared a chance to answer, so he followed. The room had a big table, real curtains, a china chest filled with dishes. Kendall set a second place.

Roast beef and mashed potatoes and peas and a pudding that tasted of apples. Jared tried not to gobble too hard. When he finished, he glanced out the window. A cold rain fell. That sucked—it was too easy to snap a board in the rain, and, anyway, the wood got all soggy.

Kendall, who had been silent throughout dinner, said, "How about a game of Street Fighter?"

"You play Street Fighter? You? I know it's an old game and everything, but . . . you?"

Kendall had a new Nintendo for the vintage game. He wielded the controllers pretty well for an old guy. Jared beat him, but only barely. As they played, Kendall said casually, "So how's everything going?"

"Like what . . . got you!"

"Like, have you attempted any wizardry?"

"Cut the crap, man."

"All right. How's school?"

He said it in such a fake, prissy tone that Jared had to laugh. Then he didn't. Throwing down the controller in midgame, abruptly he stood. "I gotta go."

242

"School's not going well?"

"Nothing's going well, thanks to you guys," Jared shouted, before he knew he was going to say anything at all. "Shawn won't hang with me and the rest is just crap and—"

"Shawn is avoiding you?" Kendall said. "What about the other kids?"

"None of your business! Now let me outta here!"

"The door is that way," Kendall said calmly. "And you're welcome for dinner," but Jared was already halfway out the front door, yanking up his collar against the rain, furious at . . . something.

Everything.

"Come back whenever you like," Kendall called after him. "I've got Super Smash Brothers, too."

HE went back. The first time back, he planned on breaking in and stealing the Nintendo. But Kendall was there, so he didn't, and they had dinner again, and played the Nintendo, and after that Jared didn't pretend there was still something wrong with his hand. Pretty soon he was there nearly every night. During the day he skated if the weather was sunny, hung out aimlessly at the mall if it wasn't, or watched TV at home if Ma wasn't there. Kendall never mentioned wizard stuff again. The food was always good. After a few weeks, Jared started doing the dishes. Sometimes they played Nintendo; sometimes Jared watched TV while Kendall read. Jared wasn't much of a reader. The house was warm.

At six thirty, they always had to stop and watch the news on TV. If there was an earthquake or a flood or a story about some farming problem, Kendall leaned forward intently, his hands on his knees.

On a cold night in November, when Jared knew the heat was off at home, he stayed the night in the guest room. At four A.M., with Kendall asleep, Jared prowled the house. Not to steal anything, just to look for . . . something.

In a drawer of the dining room china cabinet, under a pile of table-cloths, he found the picture. It was totally weird: a group of seventeen people who didn't look like they belonged together. A heavy, middle-aged woman in brown stretch pants and a pink top. A man in a blue uniform with a square badge like a security guard. Two kids, seven or eight, who looked like twins, in miniature gang clothing. An old woman in some kind of long gown. A black man in a gray suit, holding a briefcase. A guy in one of those lame Hawaiian shirts, grinning like an idiot. An Asian kid holding an armful of books.

And Shawn.

Jared stared at the picture. It really was Shawn. But what was this group? It sure as hell wasn't Shawn's family.

"Would you like some coffee?"

Jared whirled around. Kendall stood in the doorway in some old-guy pajamas. He didn't look mad, just that sad-thing, which was getting really old.

"Who are these guys? Why is Shawn here?"

"I just put the water on, Jared. Come into the kitchen."

Jared stood beside the kitchen table, refusing to sit down, while Kendall puttered with teakettle and instant coffee. "I asked you a question—who are those people? Is that your dumb-ass 'Brotherhood'?"

"You remembered that I mentioned them," Kendall said with pleasure. "I didn't know if you would. You were still on painkillers."

"I'm not stupid, man!"

"I know you're not. And no, that's not the Brotherhood. That's the Other Side."

"Other side of *what*? Make sense!"

Kendall poured hot water into his cup, stirred it, and sat across the table. "Jared, didn't you think it odd that Shawn avoided you after your accident? Instead of thinking it rather cool that you could command rocks?"

" 'Rather cool,' " Jared mocked viciously. " 'Command rocks.' C'mon, give me an answer! What's Shawn doing with those people?"

"He's one of them. And he had no idea you were a wizard, too, until the car hit you. And now he's staying away from you so you won't inadvertently discover what he is. You see, that's our main advantage over the Other Side. We know a lot more about them than they know about us."

" 'Us'? I thought you said you wasn't a wizard!"

"I'm not. But I work with them. Pain releases the power, remember. I'm a doctor. I see a lot of pain. Sometimes it brings us one of our own, sometimes one from the Other Side. My position at the Medical Center is how we've been able to identify so many of them."

"I don't believe any of this crap."

"Fortunately, your believing or not believing does not change the reality." Kendall sipped his coffee. "I wish belief was all it took to make the Other Side disappear."

" 'The Other Side.' Give me a break. And what are they supposed to be doing that's so bad? What you got against Shawn? You think he's going to set off a bomb or something?"

"I already told you, magic doesn't operate in the presence of metal, which bombs require. Magic is considerably older than that. It belongs to the sphere of nature, of grass and wind and animals and plants. And rocks, the oldest of all nature."

"Right. Sure. So Shawn's gonna mess up the world by growing the wrong grass? Get real!"

Abruptly Kendall leaned forward. "*You* get real, Jared. Your ignorance is appalling—what are they teaching you in that school? Yes, the Other Side might 'mess up the world' by growing the wrong grass, if there's profit in it. Money or power profit. Don't you know that there's money to be made from drought, from famine, from hurricanes, from killer bees, from mutated plants? There's always money to be made in disasters. You cause them, then you charge heavily to clean them up, as just one example. You're poised and ready with whatever is needed, because you know exactly when and where the disaster will occur. And no one ever suspects you caused it, because hurricanes and volcanoes and droughts and invasive plant species are all *completely natural*. Plus, no one in the developed countries, where money flows like green water, even believes in magic anyway. Now do you get it?"

"No," Jared shouted. "You telling me Shawn is rich from this magic? Man, he don't even have a decent deck!"

"No, because riches now would draw attention to the Other Side. And it takes a lot of international coordination to pull off a big profit from a major disaster. They've already managed a couple of small ones—did you read in the paper about that unexpected flood, along the Big Thompson River in Colorado? No, of course you didn't, you don't read the papers. But we think that flood was one of theirs. We're still organizing, too. One day Shawn will be very rich, and very powerful, although most of the world will never know how he did it. The FBI will assume drugs and spend futile years trying to prove it."

"So now you can see the future, too!"

"No, of course not, I just—"

"You're just full of crap! You're crazy, man, you know that? The biggest loser ever, and this sucks!" Jared jerked at the locks on the kitchen door, yanked it open, and bolted outside.

"Jared . . . wait . . . don't—"

He was already gone, skimming along the cold sidewalk in the dark.

The man was more than crazy, he was totally gone. Psycho. Loony-bin. Jared was never going back there.

Where else was he going to go?

Jared shivered. Last evening's rain had stopped, but it was really cold out. His hoodie wasn't enough for this weather. He had to move faster, stay warm, get home.

Home. The heatless apartment where Ma and her new boyfriend would be sleeping under all the blankets, including Jared's, or—worse—up fighting, strung out on crystal. And getting home alone, this time of almost morning when only the gangbangers were out on the streets . . .

He stopped under a streetlight. For one terrible minute, he thought he might cry.

Bag that. And bag all the psycho stuff Kendall had been telling him, too. The old man had been kind to him. So what if he was crazy? He wasn't dangerous, and it wasn't like Jared hadn't dealt with worse. He could deal with anything he had to. And Kendall's place was warm, and had food.

Why *had* Shawn reacted so weird to Jared's accident?

He spun his board around and skated back to Kendall's, thinking hard.

The back door to Kendall's house still stood wide open. In the kitchen, the chairs were knocked over, and Kendall's coffee sloshed all over the floor. Blood smeared the table. Jared searched the whole house; Kendall was gone.

He found a flashlight in a kitchen drawer and took it outside. Fresh tire marks slashed across a corner of the soggy lawn. They led down Carter Street—but where after that?

He should call the cops.

Oh, like cops would believe in the kidnapping. If an adult went missing, they wouldn't even start looking for him for a couple of days. And they certainly wouldn't believe Jared, who had a bunch of citations, unpaid, for illegal skating at the Civic Center and the library.

It was only after he thought all this that Jared saw what it meant: that *he* believed Kendall had been kidnapped, and by the so-called "Other Side." The second he realized this, he started shaking. *Cold*, he thought. It was just the cold. Just the cold.

In the dark he skated to one end of the block, peered down it. Nothing. The other end of the block—also nothing.

No one else had been as good to him as Kendall had. Nobody, not ever.

There was no way to know which way the psychos had taken Kendall. No real way. Unless . . .

Jared looked around with his flashlight. The house next door to Kendall had a flower bed edged with stones. Feeling like the biggest lamebrain in the whole crappy world, Jared picked up three of the rocks and thought, *Which way?*

Nothing happened, so he said it out loud: "Which way?"

Nothing happened.

He stepped away from his deck, with its metal trucks, and tried again. Nothing.

His hoodie had a a metal zipper so, shivering, he took it off and laid it on top of the deck, twenty feet away. "Which way, you psycho stones?"

Nothing.

His jeans had a metal zipper and studs. "No way," Jared said aloud, but a second later, shivering, he stripped them off and put them on top of his hoodie. In his underwear, shoes and socks, and T-shirt, he scanned the street. Nobody there—it was four thirty in the morning. He picked up the rocks again. "Which way, you little bastards?"

The rocks grew warm in his hand.

Jared shrieked and dropped them. A sharp pain shot through his wrist, gone in a moment. The stones fell in a straight line toward the north end of Carter Street. Jared stared, disbelieving. He did it again, this time facing south. The rocks got warm, he dropped them, and they swirled around his body to form a line going north. The sharp pain hit his wrist.

He closed his eyes. No way. *This psycho stuff doesn't happen.* All at once he would have given anything, anything in the entire world, to be back skating at the Civic Center with Shawn, ollieing off the steps and trying to do grinds down the rail, trying to land a 540 flip.

Instead, he picked up his clothing and the three rocks, got on his deck, and skated north.

At the next intersection, he again walked away from the board and jeans and hoodie, and said, "Which way?" The rocks pointed east.

Two more turns and he was glad to see the interstate, no turns off it for a long ways. His wrist throbbed from the repeated flashes of pain. Jared put his jeans and hoodie back on. His legs felt like ice—not a good way to skate. But he wasn't going to do any tricks, just straight skating, and the speed would warm him. He skated up the on-ramp, then along the highway, dodging the trucks that blatted angry horns at him, keeping a sharp eye out for cops.

At the first exit, he got off the highway and did the stones thing. They told him to get back on. Jared glanced at the sky, worried; already it was starting to get red in the east. He put on his clothes and skated back onto the highway. His stomach grumbled and he cursed at it, at Kendall, at the world.

At the next exit, the stones told him to follow a deserted stretch of country road. Jared noted its name: County Line Road.

The house wasn't far, fortunately: the third house, set back in the woods. A white van with muddy tires sat in the driveway. The van said MCCLELLAN SECURITY. Jared remembered the man in the blue uniform in the picture.

He crept up to the house. All the curtains were shut and the basement windows painted black, but when he put his ear to the grimy glass, Jared could hear noises in the basement.

A thud. A groan. Then, "Once more, Doctor—all the names, please. Now. This is getting boring."

Silence. Then Kendall screamed.

They were torturing him to get the Brotherhood names! Including Jared's name. "*You see, that's our main advantage over the Other Side. We know a lot more about them than they know about us.*" That's what Kendall had said. But now—

No, not Jared's name. They already had Jared's name, thanks to Shawn. And if Jared had stayed five minutes longer at Kendall's house, they'd have had him down in that basement, too.

He could skate away. Get back on the highway, never go home again, go . . . where?

Kendall screamed again.

A rage filled Jared. He thought he'd been angry before—at Shawn, at his mother, at the cops, at the crap that happened and went on happening and never seemed to stop. But it hadn't been anger like this. This was the mother of angers, the huge one, the serious-hang-time-in-orbit of anger.

Woods bordered the back of the house. Jared thrashed a little way into them, shoved his deck under some bushes, added his jeans and hoodie. Then he stood there, twigs scratching his bare legs and some kind of insects biting at his face, and closed his eyes. He pictured rocks. All kinds of rocks, all sizes, pointy and smooth and rough, smashing through the black-painted basement windows and into the heads of every single bastard down there except Kendall. He pictured the blood and the wounds and the—

Jared screamed. Pain tore through his whole body, dropping him into the bushes. His arms and legs were on fire, he was going to die, he would never skate again—

The pain vanished, leaving him gasping. He staggered to his feet, just in time to see the rocks homing in on the house, flying in from every direction like fighter jets on some video game, but real and solid as Jared himself. All the painted windows smashed, and Jared heard yells and screams from the house. Then silence.

It couldn't have happened.

It did happen.

He struggled out of the bushes and ran to the front door. It was locked, and so was the back door. Finally, he ran to the closest busted window, knocked out the glass still stuck around the edges, and slid into the basement, careful to land on his sneakers amid the shards and splinters of glass.

Two men and a woman lay bleeding on the floor, covered with stones. Kendall was tied to a chair, gaping at him. The old man had a gash on his forehead and serious blood on the arm of his pajamas. Jared picked up the knife somebody had dropped and cut Kendall's ropes. He doubled over, gasping, and Jared was afraid Kendall was having a heart attack or something. But then he straightened and staggered to his feet.

"Jared . . . I'm all . . . right . . ."

"Sure you are. Never better, right? C'mon." Jared helped him up the stairs, but then didn't know what to do next.

Kendall did. He gasped, "Go back downstairs and get a cell phone from anybody who has one. Be careful—they're not dead. Don't kill anybody, Jared—we don't want a murder investigation. Then come back up here and lock the door at the top of the stairs."

Jared did as he was told, a sudden sick feeling in his stomach. It fought with a feeling of unreality—*this can't be happening*—that only got stronger when he again saw all the stones lying around the basement.

He'd done that. Him, Jared Stoffel.

Kendall called somebody on the cell, said, "Code blue. The address is . . ." and looked at Jared. Jared gave it to him. They only had to wait a few minutes before a car screeched up and they went out to meet it. A silver Mercedes S, at least seventy grand. Jared blinked. A pretty black girl jumped out. She had on a school uniform like rich girls wore, green skirt and jacket and a little green tie on a white blouse. Ordinarily Jared hated kids like that, rich snobs, but now was different.

"He did it?" she said, talking to Kendall but staring at Jared, her eyes wide. "How did—"

"I don't know yet," Kendall said.

"How much—"

"I hadn't yet told them anything. But I would have, Denise."

She nodded, grimaced, and tenderly helped Kendall into the car, apparently not caring that he got blood on the leather seat. Jared climbed into the back. Denise must be old enough to drive, he figured, but she didn't look it. Was the Mercedes hers, or her family's, or maybe stolen?

She pulled the car onto the road and accelerated hard. Over her shoulder Denise threw Jared a glance at once respectful and a little scared. He sat up straighter in the backseat. She said, "Stones?"

"Yeah," Jared said.

"We don't have anybody that can do stone."

He liked the tone of her voice. It let him say, "What do you do?"

"Wind. But strictly small-time. You're *gifted*, dude."

"You ain't seen nothing yet. You should see me skate."

In the front seat, one arm cradled carefully in the other, Kendall smiled.

"NO," Larson said. "Absolutely not." He wore his do-rag again and it looked, Jared thought, just as dumb as the first time. Larson himself looked furious.

"I don't think we have a choice," said the older woman in a business suit. Probably she'd been getting dressed for work when they pulled up, just like Denise had been getting ready for school. This house must be the woman's—it looked like something a business lady would have, nice but really boring. Light brown rugs, brown furniture, tan curtains. The lady acted like she was in charge. Trouble was, Larson acted in charge, too. Jared thought they'd square off for a fight, but things didn't work like that around here.

"We do have a choice, Anna," Larson said. That was her name—Anna. "There's a number of cities we could send them to."

Jared said sharply, "Send? You mean me and the doc? Nobody's sending me no place!"

Anna said, "I'm afraid we have to, Jared. The Other Side now knows about both of you. They'll eliminate you if they can, and we might not be able to protect you."

"Oh, right. You can't just put a spell around my house or something? No? I guess you're not real wizards after all!"

A voice behind him said, "I'm afraid it doesn't work that way," and Jared spun around. Denise, back from parking the car someplace. If he'd known she was coming back, he wouldn't have sounded so snotty.

She said to Jared, "I can do wind magic, and Anna can communicate with wild animals, and so on, but only when we're present at the scene, Jared. There's no such thing as a spell that can just be left in place to guard someone. I wish there was."

If anybody else had explained it like that to Jared, he wouldn't have felt so stupid now. Kendall was off in a back room of this house, getting patched up or something. Jared crossed his arms over his chest and scowled. "I can't just leave and, like, move to some other city! I've got Ma and school and crap!"

Larson said brutally, "If you don't go, you're dead. And some of us, the ones you can identify, will be with you."

"But my ma—"

"Will be told that you've been taken away from her by Child Protective Services. She'll believe that."

Jared felt hot blood rush into his face. So Larson knew all about his mother! Furious and embarrassed, he turned to slam out of the room, but Denise blocked the doorway.

Larson said, "We don't need to send him to Tellerton. Send him somewhere else, to a nonactive cell. We don't need a kid this angry in the very center of the Brotherhood."

"I disagree," Anna said.

"No one will be able to control him. He'll endanger everybody there."

"I won't endanger nobody I don't want to!" Jared said.

Anna said, "I think that's true, Larson. And Nick will be with him."

Denise, still standing in the doorway, spoke in a low voice that only Jared could hear. "I know it's hard to be sent away. But Anna's right—you'll have Dr. Kendall with you. And the place you're going . . . I know for a fact that it has an awesome skate park."

"It does?"

"The best."

He blurted, "Will you come there to see me skate?" and instantly hated himself. She was too old for him, she would think he was a little kid, she'd shame him in front of Larson—

"Sure. I think that one way or another, we'll end up working together, anyway. Things are going to get much more serious soon, we'll need every wizard we can get, and we don't have a good stone man. You're really talented."

That was the second time she'd said that. Jared turned back to Anna, ignoring Larson. "Okay. I'll go. Where is this Tellerton?"

"In Virginia."

Jared blinked. "I—"

"Zack will drive you both down there this afternoon. The sooner you get out, the better."

"My stuff! I have—"

"It has to stay here. They'll get you new belongings in Tellerton. Don't worry, Jared, you're one of us now." Anna left. Larson said, "Wait a minute, Anna, I want to talk more with you about the hurricane." He strode after her.

Jared was left alone with Denise. He blinked, scowled, and said, to say something, "What hurricane?"

"It was on the early-morning news," Denise said somberly. "A big hurricane suddenly changed direction and came ashore in Florida, and the hurricane season is supposed to be over. Eight people dead so far. At least one big warehouse was destroyed that we found out had just been bought by the Other Side. Now they'll file all kinds of insurance claims on the stuff inside. Anna, one of our lawyers, just tracked the purchase and the warehouse insurance yesterday, but she hasn't had time to follow through."

Jared tried to understand. Denise was smart; all these people were smart. And wizard stuff seemed to involve nonmagic things like insurance claims, which Jared had never thought about. But one thing was clear to him, the part about eight people dead. So far.

He said, "They'd really do that? Kill, like, innocent people just to make money?"

"They would. They do."

He felt a little dizzy. Too much stuff, too fast. Wizards and magic and moving away and stones . . . He could still feel the rocks warm in his hands, ready to tell him things. Him, Jared Stoffel, who nobody except Shawn ever told anything.

And Shawn . . . the so-called friend he'd trusted like a brother . . .

"Shawn is gonna pay," he said to Denise.

"Yes," Denise said, and *that* was what decided him. No lame bull about not being into revenge, or calming himself down, or being too angry a kid to be useful. Just: *Yes*. She understood him.

All at once, Jared felt like he'd just ollied off a twelve-set and was doing serious hang time in the air.

A wizard. He was a wizard. He didn't want to be, but he was. A stone man. And everything was different now.

Maybe that was a good thing.

He could learn about insurance claims or whatever. He wasn't dumb. He had learned to do a Back-180 down a four-set; he could learn what he needed to. He could.

"Welcome to the Brotherhood, Jared," Denise said softly.

"Thanks," Jared said.

The Manticore Spell

JEFFREY FORD

Even with the most powerful of wizards, what goes around comes around . . .

Although a relatively new writer, Jeffrey Ford has made a big impact fast, winning the World Fantasy Award in 1998 for his first novel, The Physiognomy, *and since going on to win two World Fantasy Awards in 2003, for his story "Creation" and his collection* The Fantasy Writer's Assistant and Other Stories. *He also won a Nebula Award in 2004 for his story "The Empire of Ice Cream." His fiction has appeared in* The Magazine of Fantasy & Science Fiction, Sci Fiction, Lady Churchill's Rosebud Wristlet, Black Gate, Polyphony, Argosy, The Green Man, *and many other markets, and has been collected in the above-mentioned* The Fantasy Writer's Assistant and Other Stories. *Ford's other books include the novels* Vanitas, Memoranda, The Beyond, *and* The Portrait of Mrs. Charbuque. *His most recent books are a chapbook novella,* The Cosmology of the Wider World, *and his first mystery novel,* The Girl in the Glass. *Coming up is a new collection,* The Empire of Ice Cream. *He lives in Medford Lakes, New Jersey.*

THE first reports of the creature, mere sightings, were absurd—a confusion of parts; a loss of words to describe the smile. The color, they said, was a flame, a hot coal, a flower, and each of the witnesses tried to mimic the thing's song but none could. My master, the wizard Watkin, bade me record in word and image everything each one said. We'd been put to it by the king, whose comment was, "Give an ear to their drollery. Make them think you're thinking about it at my command. It's naught but bad air, my old friend." My master nodded and smiled, but after the king had left the room, the wizard turned to me and whispered, "Manticore."

"It's the last one, no doubt," said Watkin. We watched from the balcony in late afternoon when the king's hunters returned from the forest across the wide green lawn to the palace, the blood of the Manticore's victims trailing bright red through the grass. "It's a very old one," he said. "You can tell by the fact that it devours the horses, but the humans often return with a limb or two intact." He cast a spell of protection around the monster, threading the eye of a needle with a hummingbird feather.

"You want it to survive?" I asked.

"To live till it dies naturally," was his answer. "The king's hunters must not kill it."

Beneath the moon and stars at the edge of autumn, we sat with the rest of the court along the ramparts of the castle and listened for the creature's flutelike trill, descending and ascending the scale, moving through the distant darkness of the trees. Its sound set the crystal goblets to vibrating. The ladies played hearts by candlelight, their hair up and powdered. The gentlemen leaned back, smoking their pipes, discussing how they'd fell the beast if the job was theirs.

"Wizard," the king said. "I thought you'd taken measures."

"I did," said Watkin. "It's difficult, though. Magic against magic, and I'm an old man."

A few moments later, the king's engineer appeared at his side. The man carried a mechanical weapon that shot an arrow made of elephant ivory. "The tip is dipped in acid that will eat the creature's flesh," said the engineer. "Aim anywhere above the neck. Keep the gear work within the gun well oiled." His Highness smiled and nodded.

A week later, just prior to dinner, at the daily ritual in which the king assessed the state of his kingdom, it was reported that the creature devoured two horses and a hunter, took the right leg of the engineer's assistant, and so twisted and crumpled the new weapon of the engineer that the poison arrow set to strike the beast turned round and stabbed its inventor in the ear, the lobe of which dripped off his head like a lit candle.

"We fear the thing may lay eggs," said the engineer. "I suggest we burn the forest."

"We're not burning down the forest," said the king. He turned and looked at the wizard. Watkin faked sleep.

I helped the old man out of his chair and accompanied him down the stone steps to the corridor that led to our chambers. Before I let him go, he took me by the collar and whispered, "The spell's weakening, I can feel it in my gums." I nodded, and he brushed me aside, walking the rest of the way to his rooms unassisted. Following behind, I looked over my shoulder almost positive the king was aware that his wizard's art had been turned against him.

I lay down in my small space off the western side of the workroom. I could see the inverted, hairless pink corpse of the hunch monkey swinging from the ceiling in the other room. The wizard had written away to Palgeria for it five years earlier, or so said his records. When it arrived, I could see by his reaction that he could no longer remember what he'd meant to do with it. Two days later, he came to me and said, "See what you can make of this hunch monkey." I had no idea, so I hung the carcass in the workroom.

From the first day of my service to Watkin, he insisted that I tell him my dreams each morning. "Dreams are the manner in which those who mean you harm infiltrate the defenses of your existence," he told me during a thunderstorm. It was mid-August, and we stood, dry, beneath the spreading branches of a hemlock one afternoon as a hard rain fell in curtains around us. That night, in sleep, I followed a woman through a field of purple flowers that eventually sloped down to the edge of a cliff. Below, an enormous mound of black rock heaved as if breathing, and when it expanded I could see through cracks and fissures red and orange light radiating out from within. The dream woman looked over her shoulder and said, "Do you remember the day you came to serve the wizard?"

Then the light was in my eyes and I was surprised to find I was awake. Watkin, holding a lantern up to my face, said, "It's perished. Come quickly." He spun away from the bed, casting me in shadow again. I trembled as I dressed. I'd seen the old man pull, with his teeth, the spirit of a spitting demon from the nostril of one of the ladies of court. Unfathomable. His flowered robe was a brilliant design of peonies in the snow, but I no longer trusted the sun.

I stepped into the workroom as Watkin was clearing things from the huge table at which he mixed his powders and dissected the reptiles whose small brains had a region that, when mashed and dried, quickened his potions. "Fetch your pen and paper," he said. "We will record everything." I did as I was told, then helped him. At one point he tried to lift a large crystal globe of blue powder, and his thin wrists shook with the exertion. I took it from him just as it slipped from his fingers.

Suddenly, everywhere, the scent of roses and cinnamon. The wizard sniffed the air and warned me that its arrival was imminent. Six hunters carried the corpse, draped across three battle stretchers and covered by the frayed tapestry of the War of the Willows, which had hung in the corridor that ran directly from the Treasury to the Pity Fountain. Watkin and I stood back as the dark-bearded men grunted, gritted their teeth, and hoisted the stretchers onto the table. As they filed out of our chambers, my master handed each of them a small packet of powder tied up with a ribbon—an aphrodisiac, I suspected. Before collecting his reward and leaving, the last of the hunters took the edge of the tapestry and, lifting the corner high, walked swiftly around the table, unveiling the Manticore.

I glanced for a mere sliver and instinctually looked away. While my eyes were averted, I heard the old man purr, squeal, chitter. The thick cloud of the creature's scent was a weight on my shoulders, and then I noticed the first buzz of the flies. The wizard slapped my face and forced me to look. His grip on the back of my neck could not be denied.

It was crimson and shades of crimson. And after I noted the color, I saw the teeth and looked at nothing else for a time. Both a wince and a smile. I saw the lion paws, the fur, the breasts, the long beautiful hair. The tail of shining segments led to a smooth, sharp stinger—a green bubble of venom at its tip. "Write this down," said Watkin. I fumbled for my pen. "*Female Manticore*," he said. I wrote at the top of the page.

The wizard took one step that seemed to last for minutes. Then he took another and another, until he was pacing slowly around the table, studying the creature from all sides. In his right hand he held the cane with the wizard's head carved into the head of it. Its tip was not touching the floor. "Draw it," he commanded. I set to the task, but this was a skill I was deficient at. Still, I drew it—the human head and torso, the powerful body of a lion, the tail of the scorpion. It turned out to be my best drawing, but it too was terrible.

"The first time I saw one of these," Watkin said, "I was with my class as a boy. We'd gone on a walk to the lake, and we'd just passed through an orchard and onto a large meadow with yellow flowers. My teacher, a woman named Levu, with a mole beside her lip, pointed into the distance, one hand on my shoulder, and whispered, 'A husband and wife Manticore, look.' I saw them, blurs of crimson, grazing the low-hanging fruit by the edge of the meadow. On our way back to town that evening, we heard their distinctive trill and then were attacked by two of them. They each had three rows of teeth chewing perfectly in sync. I watched them devour the teacher as she frantically confessed to me. While I prayed for her, the monsters recited poems in an exotic tongue and licked the blood from their lips."

I wrote down all of what Watkin said, although I wasn't sure it was to the point. He never looked me in the eye, but moved slowly, slowly, around the thing, lightly prodding it with his cane, squinting with one eye into the darkness of its recesses. "Do you see the face?" he asked me. I told him I did. "But for that fiendish smile, she's beautiful," he said. I tried to see her without the smile, and what I saw in my mind was the smile without her. Suffice to say, her skin was crimson as was her fur, her eyes yellow diamonds. Her long hair had its own mind, deep red-violet whips at her command. And then that smile.

"She lived next to me, with hair as long as this but golden," Watkin said, pointing. "I, a little younger than you, she a little older. Only once we went out together into the desert and climbed down into the dunes. Underground there, in the ruins, we saw the stone-carved face of the hunch monkey. We lay down in front of it together, kissed, and went to sleep. Our parents and neighbors were looking for us. Late in the night while she slept, a wind blew through the pursed lips of the stone face, warning me of *treachery* and *time*. When she woke, she said in sleep she'd visited the ocean and gone fishing with a Manticore. The next time we kissed was at our wedding.

"Draw that," he shouted. I did my best, but didn't know whether to depict the Manticore or the wizard with her at the beach. "One more thing about the smile," he said. "It continually, perpetually grinds with the organic rotary mechanism of a well-lubricated jaw and three sets of teeth— even after death, in the grave, it masticates the pitch black."

"Should I draw that?" I asked.

He'd begun walking. A few moments later, he said, "No."

He laid down his cane on the edge of the table and took one of the paws in both his hands. "Look here at this claw," he said. "How many heads do you think it's taken off?" "Ten," I said. "Ten thousand," he said, dropping the paw and retrieving his cane. "How many will it take off now?" he asked. I didn't answer. "The lion is fur, muscle, tendon, claw, and speed, five important ingredients of the unfathomable. Once a king of Dreesha captured and tamed a brood of Manticore. He led them into battles on long, thousand-link, iron chains. They cut through the forward ranks of the charging Igridots with the artful tenacity His Royal Highness reserves for only the largest pastries."

"Take this down?" I asked.

"To the last dribbling vowel," he said, nodding and slowly moving. His cane finally tapped the floor. "Supposedly," he said, "there's another smaller organ floating within their single-chambered hearts. At the center of this small organ is a smaller ball of gold—the purest gold imaginable. So pure it could be eaten. And if it were, I am told the result is one million beautiful dreams of flying.

"I had an an uncle," said the wizard, "who hunted the creature, bagged one, cut out its ball of gold, and proceeded to eat the entire thing in one bound. After that, my uncle was sane only five times a day. Always, he had his hands up. His tongue was always wagging, his eyes shivering. He walked away from home one night when no one was watching. He wandered into the forest. There were reports for a while of a ragged holy man but then a visitor returned his ring and watch and told us his head had been found. Once it was safely under glass, I performed my first magic on it and had it tell me about its final appointment with a Manticore.

"Take a lock of this hair, boy, when we're done," he said. "When you get old, tie it into a knot and wear it in your vest pocket. It will ward off danger . . . to an extent."

"How fast do they run?" I asked.

"How fast?" he said, and then he stopped walking. A breeze blew through the windows and porticos of the workroom. He turned quickly and looked over his shoulder out the window. Storm clouds, lush hedge, and a humidity of roses and cinnamon. The flies now swarmed. "That fast," he said. "Draw it."

"Notice," he said, "there is no wound. The hunters didn't kill it. It died of old age, and they found it." He stood very silent, his hands behind his back. I wondered if he'd run out of things to say. Then he cleared his throat, and said, "There's a point at which a wince and a smile share the same shape and intensity, almost but not quite the same meaning. It's at that point and that point alone that you can begin to understand the beast's scorpion tail. Sleek, black, poisonous, and needle sharp, it moves like lightning, piercing flesh and bone, depositing a chemical that halts all memory. When stung you want to scream, to run, to aim your crossbow at its magenta heart, but alas . . . you forget."

"I'm drawing it," I said. "Excellent," he said, and ran his free hand over one of the smooth sections of the scorpion tail. "Don't forget to capture the forgetting." He laughed to himself. "The Manticore venom was at one time used to cure certain cases of melancholia. There's very often some incident from the past at the heart of depression. The green poison, measured judiciously, and administered with a long syringe to the corner of the eye, will instantly paralyze memory, negating the cause of sorrow. There was one fellow, I'd heard, who took too much of it and forgot to forget—he remembered everything and could let nothing go. His head filled up with every second of every day, and it finally exploded.

"The poison doesn't kill you, though. It only dazes you with the inability to remember, so those teeth can have their way. There are those few who'd been stung by the beast but not devoured. In every case, they described experiencing the same illusion—an eye-blink journey to an old summer home, with four floors of guest rooms, sunset, mosquitoes. For the duration of the poison's strength, around two days, the victim lives at this retreat . . . in the mind, of course. There are cool breezes as the dark comes on, moths against the screen, the sound of waves far off, and the victim comes to the conclusion that he or she is alone. I suppose to die while in the throes of the poison is to stay alone at that beautiful place by the sea for eternity."

I spoke without thinking. "Every aspect of the beast brings you to eternity—the smile, the purest gold, the sting."

"Write that down," said Watkin. "What else can you say of it?"

"I remember that day I came to serve you," I said, "and on the long stretch through the poplars, my carriage was stopped due to a dead body in the road. As the carriage passed, I peered out to see a bloody mess on the ground. You were one of the people in the crowd."

"You can't understand my invisible connection to these creatures—a certain symbiosis. I feel it in my lower back. Magic becomes a pinhole shrinking into the future," he said.

"Can you bring the monster back to life?" I asked him.

"No," he said. "It doesn't work that way. I have something else in mind." He stepped over to a workbench, left the cane there, and lifted a hatchet. Returning to the body of the creature, he walked slowly around it to the tail. "That was my wife you saw in the road that day. Killed by a Manticore—by this very Manticore."

"I'm sorry," I said. "I'd think you'd have tried harder to kill it."

"Don't try to understand," he said. He lifted the hatchet high above his head and, with one swift chop, severed the stinger from the tail of the creature. "Under the spell of the poison, I will go to the summer house and rescue her from eternity."

"I'll go with you," I said.

"You can't go. You could be stranded in eternity with my wife and me—think of that," said Watkin. "No, there's something else I need you to do for me while I'm under the effects of the venom. You must take the head of the Manticore into the forest and bury it. Their heads turn into the roots of trees, the fruit of which are Manticore pups. You'll carry the last seed." He used the hatchet to sever the creature's head while I dressed for the outdoors.

I'd learned to ride a horse before I went to serve the wizard, but the forest at night frightened me. I couldn't shake the image of Watkin's palm impaled on the tip of the black stinger and his rapidly accruing dullness, gagging, his eyes rolling back behind their lids. I carried the Manticore head in a woolen sack tied to the saddle and trembled at the prospect that perhaps Watkin was wrong and the one sprawled on the worktable, headless and tailless, was not the last. For my protection, he'd given me a spell to use if it became necessary—a fistful of yellow powder and a half dozen words I no longer remembered.

I rode through the dark for a few minutes and had quickly had enough of it. I dismounted and dug a hole at the side of the path, standing my torch upright in it. It made a broad circle of light on the ground. I retrieved the shovel I'd brought and the head. After nearly a half hour of digging, I began to hear a slight murmuring sound coming from somewhere close by me. I thought someone was spying from a darker part of the forest, then I took it for the whirring of a Manticore's tritoothed jaws and was paralyzed by fear. Two minutes later, I realized the voice was coming from inside the sack. When I looked, the smile was facing out. The Manticore's eyes went wide, that chasm of a mouth opened, flashing three-way ivory, and she spoke in a foreign language.

I took her out of the sack, set her head up at the center of the circle of torchlight, brushed back her hair, and listened to the beautiful singsong language. Later, after waking from a kind of trance brought on by the flow of words, I remembered the spell Watkin had given me. Laying the powder out on the upturned palm of my hand, I aimed it carefully and blew it into the creature's face. She coughed. I'd forgotten the words, so said anything that I recalled them sounding like. Then she spoke to me, and I understood her.

"Eternity," she said, then repeated it, methodically, with the precise same intonation again and again and again . . .

I grabbed the shovel and started digging. By the time I had dug a deep enough hole, my nerves were frayed by her repetition, and I couldn't fill the dirt in fast enough. When the head was thoroughly buried, its endless phrase still sounding, muffled, beneath the ground, I tamped the soil down, then found an odd-looking green rock, like a fist, to mark the spot for future reference.

Watkin never returned from the place by the sea. After the venom wore off, his body was lifeless. I then became the wizard. No one seemed to care that I knew nothing about magic. "Make it up till you've got it," said the king. "Then spread it around." I thanked him for his insight but was aware he'd eaten pure gold and now, when not soaring in his dreams, was rarely sane. The years came and went, and I did my best to learn the devices, potions, phenomena that Watkin had bothered to record. I suppose there was something of magic in it, but it wasn't readily recognizable.

I was able to witness Watkin's fate by use of a magic looking glass I'd found in his bedroom and learned to command. It was a tall mirror that stood on the back of his writing desk. In it I could see anywhere in existence with a simple command. I chose the quiet place by the sea, and there before me were the clean-swept pathways, the blossoming wisteria, the gray and splintering fence board. Darkness was coming on. The woman with golden hair sat on the screened porch in a wicker rocker, listening to the floorboards creak. The twilight breeze was cool against sunburn. The day seemed endless. As night came on, she rocked herself to sleep. I ordered the mirror to show me her dream.

She dreamed that she was at the beach. The surf rolled gently up across the sand. There was a Manticore—her crimson resplendent against the clear blue day—fishing at the shoreline with a weighted net. Without fear, the woman with bright hair approached the creature. The Manticore politely asked, with smile upon smile, if the woman would like to help hoist the net. She nodded. The net was flung far out and they waited. Finally there was a tug. The woman with the golden hair and the Manticore both pulled hard to retrieve their catch. Eventually they dragged Watkin ashore, tangled in the webbing, seaweed in his hair. She ran to him and helped him out of the net. They put their arms around each other and kissed.

Now I keep my ears pricked up for descriptions of strange beasts in the heart of the forest. If a horse or a human goes missing, I must get to the bottom of it before I can rest. I try to speak to the hunters every day. Reports of the Creature are vague but growing, and I realize now I have some invisible connection to it, as if its muffled, muted voice is enclosed within a chamber of my heart, relentlessly whispering, "Eternity."

Zinder

TANITH LEE

Here's a strange and lyrical story about an Ugly Duckling who turns out to be very much more than just a swan . . .

Tanith Lee is one of the best-known and most prolific of modern fantasists, with more than a hundred books to her credit, including (among many others) The Birthgrave, Drinking Sapphire Wine, Biting the Sun, Night's Master, The Storm Lord, Sung in Shadow, Volkhavaar, Anackire, Night's Sorceries, The Black Unicorn, Days of Grass, The Blood of Roses, Vivia, Reigning Cats and Dogs, When the Lights Go Out, Elephantasm, The Gods Are Thirsty, Cast a Bright Shadow, Here in Cold Hell, Faces Under Water, White As Snow, Mortal Suns, Death of the Day, *and* Piratica: Being a Daring Tale of a Singular Girl's Adventure Upon the High Seas, *and the collections* Red As Blood, Tamastara, The Gorgon, Dreams of Dark and Light, Nightshades, *and* Forests of the Night. *Her short story "The Gorgon" won her a World Fantasy Award in 1983, and her short story "Elle Est Trois (La Mort)" won her another World Fantasy Award in 1984. Her most recent books are* Metallic Love *and a sequel to* Piratica *called* Piratica II: Return to Parrot Island. *Soon to be published is another new novel,* No Flame But Mine. *She lives in the south of England.*

A clod of earth, hard, ugly, and brown, flew through the air. It went high enough that it caught the sinking rays of the large hot sun, and for a moment it gleamed too, the clod, become a smooth shape of purest gold, spangled with rubies. Then the light left it. It was only a chunk of common earth as it smacked home on the thing it had been thrown at.

The thing, hit on the head, lost its balance at the impact of the blow, and fell.

The young men standing in the village street doubled over, grunting and hooting with laughter.

An old woman, hobbling by with her goat led on a string, mouthed curses at the louts under her breath.

"Cheer up, Granny! It's only Quacker we've knocked down."

"God sees all," said Granny. "You'll fry in Hell."

The young men frowned, slightly scared by the mention of the furious and vengeful God in the village church, whose Eye, apparently, was everywhere. But the old woman had already padded off. She cared nothing for any of them, and certainly not for Quacker. And anyway, Quacker was already hauling himself up on to his short, bloated legs. He hadn't been hurt.

"Look at it!" said the son of the village's overseer. ("It" meant Quacker.) They looked. Though they had seen Quacker often enough before.

Quacker was aged about fifteen or sixteen. Who could be sure? Either way, the age of a man. He was the son of a loose woman despised by everyone, even the men who occasionally liked to get drunk with her. Quacker, however, had never been human. Anyone could see *that*. Even as a baby, it had been revoltingly obvious that he wasn't, and the overseer, and other important men of the village, had been for having him smothered at once— or, since winter was coming on, left on a hill for hungry wolves. For some reason, this wasn't done. No one could really say why not. Though they believed by now, one and all, that it was due to their sentimental kindness and godliness that they had spared the life of this misshapen idiot who, as he grew and began to talk, sounded more like a duck than even the village ducks did.

Quacker's head was round and too big. Thin hair was plastered over it in dark greasy streaks. His eyes, also too big, bulged, pale and cloudy. He had a nose and mouth and teeth. That was all you could say for them. The rest of his body was a sort of fat, almost formless, mass, out of which stuck two short fat arms with hands that were too small, and two trunklike bowed legs with feet that were, like head and eyes, also too big.

He was dressed, more or less, as all the males were in the village, except that he had no knife in his belt for hunting or cutting up food.

He didn't seem upset at being knocked over. He never did seem upset, not even that time early last winter, when two or three witty jokers had thrown him in the duck pond, on which ice was already forming. Quacker, rather than freeze or drown—which was probably what had been wanted—simply bobbed up to the surface, cracked the thinner ice with his horrible head, and somehow lurched to the shore. Here he got out and shambled away.

The young men had grown tired of watching Quacker, so they rambled off to the tavern.

By now the sun was on the very edge of the fields, turning their late-summer richness to the same wonderful gold and scarlet.

In this light, Quacker also took himself up the street, and next over a low wall, into a little crowd of woodland. His mother's hovel lay there, just outside the village.

It was a grim sight, sagging walls and broken roof, the patch of garden, where some might have grown beans and onions, all spiked with rank bristly weeds, and dominated by a dead fruit tree.

Quacker paused a moment at the door, hearing his mother singing in her dull voice a miserable song of lost love. He could hear too the pot of Life-Water clinking in her hand against the cup, once, twice, an interval, and then again, and again.

The sky beyond the dark wood had flushed to deep blood and purple.

"Zinder?" called the mother quaveringly, "is that you?"

"Yes, Mother," said Quacker—or actually Zinder, for *Zinder* was his given name. The noise he made could have been mistaken for quacking, but the woman had got used to it, it seemed, and knew what he said.

So she cursed him. "May the sky fall on you, you filthy beast. Why *is* it you? I hope and hope every day that you'll lose yourself—or break your neck—or a bear will eat you—and you never *will* come back! But there you are again. Hurry and get in then. I expect a visit from the Great Hunter. If he sees *you*, he'll be off—can't stand to look at you, no more than can I! What a life I might have had if it hadn't been for *you*."

The Great Hunter was one of the village's most important men, as his nickname suggested. It was really quite unlikely he would be stopping by, but you never knew.

Quacker entered the hovel and lurched to his hidden place behind the stove.

An old piece of wolfskin hung down here, and logs were piled up. At all hours, thick shadow fell there, beyond the glimmer of the stove, or any sunshine that might show in the doorway or the one window. Once Quacker—Zinder—was inside the "cave" the skin and the logs made, providing he kept completely still and quiet, no one else need ever know he was there at all.

There was nothing to eat. She had forgotten, as she usually did, to place a crust or bit of rind for him on the floor, by the dirty, flea-filled mat that was his bed.

A large yellow candle was available to give light in the main part of the hovel. But not much of that light either ever crept into Zinder's bedroom. He had no means to make light for himself. Nor was there anything in the "cave" to amuse him. He had no possessions, unless you counted the mat.

He seated himself quietly on the ground.

Outside, in the outer world of the hovel, the village, the earth, all after-glow had vanished. Cool blueness came, then violet, then gray, then black. Through a tiny chink in the logs, Zinder could see a blink of silver stars flowering in the sky.

Tonight, Mother didn't light the candle, not even to welcome the hoped-for Great Hunter. She drank and sighed, sighed and drank, and sang her angry sad songs. Until at last she fell asleep, snoring too with an angry sad sound. Zinder lay down then on the mat.

And as he did, he laughed.

THE whole village, apart from the men up the track in the tavern, and the odd wakeful baby, is asleep soon after moonrise.

But this is always when Zinder properly wakes up.

He looks forward to it, though even the days here are quite interesting to him, as he goes roaming about and seeing what needs to be done. The assaults, and the tricks the villagers play on him, let alone their curses, don't upset him. Not even those of his mother. They don't hurt, they run off him like water—off the back of a duck. You can't hurt Zinder.

But night is the best time of all.

First, very gently—and with the skill of much practice, since he has consciously done this from four years of age—Zinder carefully extracts himself from his own outer body.

If anyone could see—no one does or ever has—it would look as if his ghost or *soul* has risen straight up out of his chest. Zinder then stands upright on the Zinder who still lies down, with cloudy eyes shut and mouth curved in a smile. The second Zinder is a man of sixteen. He is tall, strong, and slim of build. His hair, black as night, pours back from his face and cascades like a waterfall over his shoulders to his waist. He has a strong face also, and his eyes are a somber and serious blue. He wears the finest clothes, dusk color and moon-and-night color, like the rest of him.

Stepping off his outer Zinder-shell, he bends down and gives it a friendly caress, brushing the thin hair from its forehead. (At once the bruise the flung clod had made begins to disappear. It was healing fast anyway, he has simply hurried the repair along.) Then Zinder walks out into the room, where his mother lies snoring in her chair with her mouth open.

He smooths her face with one finger, painstakingly removing some of the stress and nastiness, as if he were washing it away with a cloth. She sighs in her sleep and stops snoring, breathing now more easily. Then he taps the empty Life-Water pot with his knuckles. It refills at once with clean water— but this water is magic. Though it tastes of alcohol and brings cheerfulness, it causes no harm to whoever drinks it. After that, Zinder opens the cupboard and stares in at the unfilled space until a small loaf appears, a slab of cheese, and a slice of meat. He closes the cupboard.

Going out of the door, he looks around and sees that the vicious weeds in the garden are beginning secretly to change, as he has commanded them to do. Berries are starting to appear under the spiny leaves. The dead apple tree is also coming back to life.

Just then a wild rabbit runs out of the trees and pauses at the edge of the garden, startled, gazing up at Zinder. Zinder whistles softly. The rabbit bolts right over to him and, with complete confidence, lets him pick it up. He smooths its fur, rather as he had smoothed his mother's face. This time he is giving it protection from the night and the predatory things of the night. The rabbit's fur is dusty gray, smelling of mushrooms and long grass.

After the rabbit bounds away again, Zinder goes up on the roof of the hovel. He doesn't climb up there, of course. He flies. The wings that spring from his back are black like his hair, but have the velvety, barbed feathers of a giant crow. They flap slowly, rhythmically, behind him, as he sits on the roof, shifting, by thought, broken tiles and matted straw, until generally everything is better than it was—though not so much better that anyone will suspect something uncanny has been at work. The very last thing his poor, useless, silly mother needs is to be accused of witchcraft.

She isn't in any fit state now to receive a visit from the Great Hunter, which is a real pity, because from up here, Zinder can clearly see the man going home with his catches and kills, along the path between the fields. Zinder sends him a thought, however, just a mild one . . . Maybe the Hunter would like to call tomorrow? Zinder knows it will cheer his mother up and do neither of them any harm. The only true reason the Hunter ever does visit is because he vaguely scents something magic all over the hovel. Without understanding that he does, the Hunter has come to believe that the *mother* is, in some inexplicable way, magical. And so he thinks that perhaps he loves her, just a bit. Besides, the spelled Life-Water does him good. There's nothing so nice at the tavern, he knows that.

The moon tonight is lovely, round, and ivory white. But it isn't yet time to travel on into the higher sky. This is Zinder's village, and he still has a few things to do here.

First he flies lightly over to the house of the old woman with the goat. When they trudged by this evening, he could see the goat wasn't too well, and the woman depends on the goat for milk, also on its shed hair, which she combs off, spins, and weaves into blankets.

She is asleep indoors. He sends a shaft of healing in through the smoke hole of the stovepipe, to deal with her bad back. The goat meanwhile is standing outside drearily, looking at the moon with its slot-pupiled eyes. Zinder dives down out of the moon, and the goat bleats in alarm, but the next minute Zinder's spell covers the goat like a cool, firm, drenching wave. The slot eyes fix, then the goat begins to feel better than it has for some time. Zinder, studying it watchfully, sees it seem to light up softly inside. That's done then. Fine.

He mends and rearranges the other things he needs to quite swiftly. The fields, checked by him every few nights, are blooming and will give this year an especially lavish harvest. The well needs unblocking—again—but that only takes two seconds. The baby with the cough is better. The woman with rheumatism, and the man with the itch, are recovering and need no further help. (The woodcutter's son, who severed his finger last month, still hasn't realized that it is growing back as good as new. The idea Zinder sent into his mind, which was to pray for such a miracle, will cover the event nicely and make the little priest in the church happy too.)

As Zinder finally drifts away from the village, still flying low, he sees three or four of his clod-slinging tormentors gathered outside the tavern. Unlike the life-giving Life-Water Zinder can supply by magic at home, the stuff in the tavern is both unpleasant and gut-rotting, and also causes aggression. The young men are getting ready for a fight.

They can't see Zinder hovering over their heads, only about ten feet up in the air and in the full blaze of the moonlight. No human ever does see him unless he allows it, but animals do. The wolf and fox, the bear, even the guard dogs of men, are always lifting their heads to watch him go by.

Zinder observes the fight, which is too blundering and clumsy to cause much injury.

But these youths are the ones who attack him the most. Now surely is the time for revenge—what will Zinder, the unknown magician, do?

He laughs, silent, and casts a bolt like lightning at them, which knocks all four over on their backs. None of them is harmed or bruised. They feel, landing, as if they fell on deep feather mattresses. The blow itself has in fact made them feel wonderful, far more effectively than the alcohol. They lie there, looking up at Zinder (whom they can't see) and the moon and the sparkles of the stars. He sends new ideas among them.

"It's a beautiful night," says one. "I could make up a song . . ."

"Too beautiful to fight," says one. "I could woo a girl . . ."

"I wish I hadn't stolen that coin, perhaps I'll pay it back . . ." says one.

"I wish I had a bed as soft as this," says the last.

Zinder flies away and heads up, up into the enormous open dome of the night.

An owl passes below him, white-winged as if floating on two sails, its face like a cat's with two golden eyes.

He flies towards the north, the young man, on his own black wings. A city is there, something the village talks about disbelievingly, as if it can't possibly be real.

Below, fields and forests, hills and gullies pass. Far, far off, a wall of impressive mountains rises, and marches north where Zinder flies, its dim sugary tops moon-outlined. There is a wide, smooth-flowing river, on which the moon paints Zinder's shadow. (For he has one. This second body of his isn't a ghost, but made of flesh, just like the outer body he wears in the village.) A salmon leaps in the river, eager to catch some of the sorcerous shadow in its mouth. Even fish know, apparently, that Zinder is good news.

The city gradually begins to pay out its own light across a long plain, where blond grain grows thick. A road leads cityward, and on the road, even by night, traffic moves—carts and wagons, riders, patrols of city soldiers, and the carriages of the rich.

Then the city seems to stand up from the plain as the mountains had done. It too shows a circle of high walls—high as the mountain wall they seem. They have towers on them like sharp teeth, but the towers are pierced, like the eyes of needles, by fierce threads of light. On the great gateways, torches flare. While inside, where the massive buildings are, everything looks like black paper or lace held up in front of candleflames, because of the thousands of lit doors and windows.

At the very center of the city is a high hill, and here perches the fortress-palace. So much of it is tiled or gilded, and its windows and doors are so large, that it seems to be made entirely of fire.

Zinder flies slow and steady in over the city, over its traffic and its people, its sentry towers, churches, houses and gardens, over a night market roped in a necklace of lamps.

Yet the flight is often interrupted.

Seeing something, or *sensing* it, Zinder now and then swoops down. He breaks the ladder of a murderous-looking robber in an alleyway, catches the man, and drops him in a puddle of very good beer. He picks up a fallen child, heals its grazes. He makes a slow pot boil and one that boils too fast calm down. A man beating a dog he pushes flat, and stands on him, so that the man howls in terror at this unseen weight pinning him to the ground, while the dog runs to safety. He holds the hand of someone who is dying, whispering hope into their ears. The journey across the city, which need only take him a clutch of minutes, lasts two hours and more.

One ultimate special treat he allows himself. An old man is praying in a small church under the palace hill. His fingers are crippled to claws from rheumatism. Shifty as any thief, Zinder slides through a window, grips the hands of the old man in gloves of cool warmth, and heals him sharp as a smack. And this time, Zinder allows his patient to glimpse the hint of the shadow of one black wing. Perfect. Listen to him! The old man believes he has been cured by an angel.

But by now, is Zinder late? Oh, no.

The city, and the palace particularly, are the exact opposite of a village that wakes at sunrise and falls asleep when the sun goes down. The palace gets up regularly at noon and is awake all night long. Night is day. Dawn is sunset.

Soaring, Zinder wings in over the gilded roofs, which have carved on them statues of strange birds and animals. These seem to be able to see him too—a couple of carved stone heads creakily turn to watch him go by.

Then there is a balcony. Zinder glances down.

A princess, with hair white as the barley grain on the plain outside, is leaning her head on her jeweled hand, gazing at the moon. "Will the wizard never return to us?" she asks. "We miss him so."

She uses the word *wizard* which, here, means *wise man*. She hasn't seen him though. He hasn't allowed her to.

Zinder turns away and flies to a huge bright open window, and straight through into a golden hall.

THE scene is spectacular—like a dream, in its own way, except he has often come here or to other such palaces. So Zinder isn't unused to these gleaming glamours. There are vast candlebranches of gold, the hundreds of clean white candles burning in them with such clear flames they are like crystal butterflies. There are silver fretworks over walls hung with red silk, and floors of icy marble.

The King and his nobles feast.

Gigantic trays of beaten gold continually come in, on which balance gigantic roasts dressed with smaller roasts, fruit, and vegetables. Parades come and go of silver jugs of red wine and alabaster jugs of pink wine, and jugs made from transparent quartz, holding white wine so pure that it is *green*. On the tables, draped in white cloths dripping crimson tassels, sit castles built of ice and sugar.

The feasters themselves are dressed in garments so thickly embroidered with colored silk and pearls that they are like armor—the men and women can only move very slowly and stiffly.

What a noise! Music and shouting, small dogs yapping, and, in gold cages, birds that talk and sing.

Unseen, Zinder lands deftly in the middle of the room. He spreads his wings to their widest.

Then he appears.

Worse noise—uproar—knives and metal plates falling with a series of clanks, a jade jug worth millions of coins dropped and shattering.

After which, utter *silence*.

In the silence, Zinder gently speaks.

"Good evening."

He can speak like a king himself. He has always known how. No one ever had to teach him, just as, when in his own village, nobody had to teach him how to quack.

But once he *has* spoken (and mentally reached out to mend the jade jug with a thought), the uproar all-round starts again. Nobles come struggling up in their stiff clothes to clap him on the back or wring his hands, the ladies touch the edges of his crow-velvet wings. The King himself leaves the table and comes over to Zinder. The King and Zinder bow lightly to each other: equals.

"How may I assist you?" Zinder politely asks.

"We need nothing, sir, I assure you. My sick chief cook has recovered, thanks to your powers—and behold the feast! The trees that wouldn't fruit in my cherry orchard have all gone mad, and cherries big as apples are exploding from them!"

The King, so far, has never asked Zinder to do anything he would have to refuse. In other cities, it has quite often been different. Many kings, having seen Zinder's magical powers, promise fortunes to him—as if he couldn't conjure fortunes for himself if he wanted—in return for his help in wars or invasions. Mainly, they want particularly disgusting types of war machines or weapons to be invented for them, mentioning things that breathe unquenchable fire or shake the ground like earthquakes. Such interviews are no fun. Zinder always refuses, won't give an inch. Sometimes then the kings get angry, one or two even order their guards to seize and punish Zinder. The results of this kind of order, though perhaps amusing—men spinning about with their swords turned into fresh loaves of bread, that sort of thing—never end in Zinder's capture. The kings sulk. Only once did Zinder offer any help in a war. He built up the walls of a town so high, and made the gates so strong, that they were impassable. And he formed a dragon that chased the enemy away, but it breathed nonflammable flame, and there were no casualties. Dragon, high walls, and impenetrable gates melted into air once the threat was removed.

Zinder and the King walk about the hall, while everyone else claps and smiles. And Zinder becomes aware that the King is about to ask him for something impossible after all.

"Between ourselves," says the King, "my daughter—" Zinder says nothing.

They reach the semiprivacy of a huge open window. The city lies below, scattered over the night like splinters of broken golden jade.

"Should you consider becoming my son-in-law," says the King, "I could extend, to a remarkable mage like yourself—"

Zinder breaks in quietly. "I'm sorry."

"You've received a better offer?"

"Not at all."

Zinder is far too tactful to tell the King how many offers of royal marriage *have* come his way.

AT that moment, having learned from her maid that the Wizard Zinder is in the dining room, the princess herself rushes—rather slowly, due to her clothes—into the room. Her jewelry flashes on her as if she had run in out of a rain of stars.

Halfway along the hall, she recalls that she is a princess. Then she walks incredibly slowly. Reaching Zinder, she is pale as her pale hair, and then pink as the wine in the alabaster jugs.

"Why were you away so long? Months have dragged by since I—we— saw you."

"I have a lot to do," Zinder says.

He smiles at her kindly, though he is sorry to smile, in a way, because he knows this makes her like him more. Every night he is somewhere, another city, or a town, or a little village like his own. Zinder is genuinely busy by night, polishing up the world, making it, where he can, better. And where he can't, comforting it.

But the princess is in love with him.

He leans to her ear and whispers, "Forget me. I'll send you another to love. He will be handsome, rich, and far more suitable than I."

"But you are handsome," murmurs the princess, dreamily, forgetting everything else. "You are rich in magic."

"The one I'll send to you will be rich in the way of a king. And much more handsome. Trust me."

The spell takes hold. She sighs. Two tears drop out of her eyes, heavy as glass beads, and stain the edge of her dress. But the stain quickly vanishes in the heat of the room.

As for the rest of the people there, they haven't seen any of this. Instead, they saw seventeen swans with silver feathers and turquoise crowns fly in at the windows and circle round, singing of joy and wealth to come.

It is true he will send her a prince. Already, on a journey to the East, Zinder has located just the right man. So into his brain Zinder has blown a powder of thoughts about a blond princess—exactly as he has also blown into *her* blond thoughts the idea of a young leopard of a prince. The swans finish their song. Unicorns enter and conduct a warlike fight that ends in honorable truce. Zinder sits down at the King's right, and eats his first meal of the day or night.

After the unicorns fly off, white geese appear and become a troupe of maidens clothed in golden tissue, who dance. Dance over, they spread goose wings and also fly off into the night. Last, the moon sails to the window to cries and gasps of fear from the feasters in the hall. But the moon is shown to be a round white ship with gossamer sails, and she fires a silver cannon into the room that showers everyone with ribbons and sweets. Then the moon too fades. All this has allowed Zinder to finish his meal. The princess too has cheered up. Zinder magics a blue rose onto her plate. When next he has time to visit this city, she will be happily engaged to the leopard prince.

The huge palace clock, made to look like an ebony turtle, strikes one in the morning, then two, three, four.

Zinder changes half the candleflames into butterflies, which glitter off into the dark.

In the half-light, he leaves the King and his court as suddenly as he came, disappearing before their very eyes, as always, and as they expect him to.

The real moon is down.

But from so high up, Zinder can soon see the tails of the clouds. They are catching a faint early sheen from the hidden waking of the sun.

He must go fast now, homewards.

The mighty city swims far behind, the forests unfurl below, full of leaping deer, wolves slinking like last moonbeams, brown summer ermine that play squeaking along the banks of streams narrow, from up here, as slow-worms.

Quickly, noting a splash of red, Zinder descends to puff out a burning hut with a single breath. A cruel hunter, who greedily always takes more hares than he needs for the pot, Zinder fills with a dream of the hunter's own wife, now herself a hare. (She is grieving over the hunter, also a hare, whom someone has killed in a trap.). A widow sobbing by a grave among the trees, Zinder whispers to consolingly. He puts a handful of money in her pocket and a sprig of something that will grow into a bush of flowers. Their perfume, once she makes them into scent, may well bring her a fortune.

But dawn is impatiently pushing up the heavy lid of the sky.

Here the morning comes, trying to outrace him.

Zinder sprints for the village.

Before the first eyes open there, he must be back inside his village shell.

He makes it with a single heartbeat to spare, sinking down, sinking in. Ready now to face another interesting day as Quacker.

Zinder-Quacker never asks himself why any of this happens, or how he does it. Why he *does* do it is obvious enough. He loves pleasure, and he loves power. And it is sheer pleasure to him, the greatest pleasure of all, to do what he does, shifting the earth a little on her axis. Anyone can make a world suffer and cry. It requires no imagination. Child's play, and no challenge at all. But to fix the broken jugs of despair, unkindness, illness, and ill fortune—this takes a creative mind. The power of it is staggering: to rock life, take it by surprise. Besides, to Zinder, it is endlessly interesting.

Even so, how *can* he do it? What is he, this being, coiled up inside the outer case of Quacker?

He doesn't know. Can't be bothered to try to find out. It was always there in him. Even when he lay in the cradle—that mound of baby the villagers had loathed and wanted to feed to wolves. Yes, even then he would fly out of himself by night, circling in the air, no larger than a moth, invisible, pushing roof tiles together, tickling mice to make them safe. Laughing to himself. At four, when reason came and he began to think in words, then he knew that he did this. That was all. He simply knew. With practice his skill has grown, which isn't unusual surely, where someone is in a truly well-liked job, for which they have a talent.

For now, he sleeps a moment. A moment is all Zinder needs, or Quacker.

And then a coral strand of sunrise, as it normally does, needles through the cave of logs, and fills his shut eyes like two spoons, so they open.

Now, it is Quacker. But Quacker, by day, also knows happiness—and is never afraid. Without considering, just as he never considers the ins and outs of it all when he is Zinder, Quacker grasps that nothing, in the end, can wreck him or deflect him from what he is. For Quacker is Zinder, and Zinder is Quacker. The answer is the riddle, the riddle is the answer.

Even as he sat up, as always, Quacker laughed.

That morning, two of the young men from the village, on their way to the fields with sore heads, one worrying about a coin he stole, and one longing for a feather bed, cornered Quacker at the edge of the woods.

They pushed him over and kicked him.

One heard the snap, he thought, of a bone.

"Let's drive the foul monster out! Bad luck it is! It's better off dead."

Quacker lay on the tree roots, not hurt, for he could feel the broken leg mending totally in seconds.

The brave youths didn't know. They bent down over him, swearing and snarling. Would they kill him? Would it work?

An awful growl rang out.

Had a black bear charged out of the woods?

Jumping back, the attackers saw no bear. It was the Great Hunter, standing there instead with his knives and his bow, and a scowl on his face fit to pare potatoes.

"Get off him, you scum! Or I'll do for the pair of you myself!"

When the two youths had fled, grumbling that the old fool must have gone sweet on Quacker's loose mother, the Hunter himself came over and lifted Quacker to his feet.

"Thank you kindly," said Quacker, with the grace of a king.

For the first time the Great Hunter understood, *heard* Quacker. Embarrassed, astonished, he instinctively almost bowed. "You're welcome," muttered the Great Hunter.

Billy and the Wizard

TERRY BISSON

Just what do you do when you find the Devil rummaging through your garage . . . ?

Terry Bisson is the author of a number of critically acclaimed novels such as Fire on the Mountain, Wyrldmaker, *the popular* Talking Man *(which was a finalist for the World Fantasy Award in 1986),* Voyage to the Red Planet, Pirates of the Universe, The Pickup Artist, *and, in a posthumous collaboration with Walter M. Miller, Jr., a sequel to Miller's* A Canticle for Leibowitz *called* Saint Leibowitz and the Wild Horse Woman. *He is a frequent contributor to such markets as* Sci Fiction, Asimov's Science Fiction, OMNI, Playboy, *and* The Magazine of Fantasy & Science Fiction. *His famous story* "Bears Discover Fire" *won the Hugo Award, the Nebula Award, the Theodore Sturgeon Memorial Award, and the Asimov's Reader's Award in 1991, the only story ever to sweep them all. In 2000, he won another Nebula Award for his story* "macs." *His short work has been assembled in the collections* Bears Discover Fire and Other Stories *and* In the Upper Room and Other Likely Stories. *His most recent books are a chapbook novel,* Dear Abbey, *and two new collections,* Numbers Don't Lie *and* Greetings. *He lives with his family in Oakland, California.*

BILLY had a secret. He liked to play with dolls. One of Billy's dolls could talk. His name was Clyde. Clyde only talked when Billy pulled his string.

One day Billy pulled his string.

"Would you like to meet the Wizard?" Clyde asked.

Billy was surprised. Clyde had never asked a question before. Billy pulled his string again.

"How about it?" Clyde asked. "How many little boys get to meet the Wizard?"

"What's he the Wizard of?" Billy asked. He pulled Clyde's string again.

"He's the Wizard of Everything," Clyde said. "And he's hiding in the garage."

"What's he hiding from?" asked Billy. He pulled Clyde's string again.

"He's the Wizard of Everything," said Clyde. Sometimes Clyde said the same thing over and over. "And he's hiding in the garage."

BILLY looked in the garage. There was nothing in the garage but old magazines.

"I looked in the garage," said Billy. "But I didn't see any Wizard."

He pulled Clyde's string.

"Of course not," said Clyde. "He's hiding. You have to look harder."

Billy looked harder. "I still don't see any Wizard," he said. He pulled Clyde's string.

"Of course not," said Clyde. "He's hiding. You have to look harder."

Billy looked harder. He looked through all the magazines.

Finally, he found one called *Today's Wizard*. He opened it up, and there was the Wizard. He was little and flat, and he wore a pointy hat.

"I am not the Wizard," he said. "Go away."

"You are so," said Billy. "I can tell by your hat."

The Wizard didn't say anything. He was just a picture. After a while, Billy turned the page.

There was the Wizard again. "How did you find me?" he asked.

"Clyde told me you were hiding in the garage," said Billy. He turned the page again.

The Wizard was the same on every page. He had a pointy beard to go with his pointy hat. "That Clyde," said the Wizard.

"Are you really the Wizard of Everything?" Billy asked.

"Turn the page," said the Wizard. Billy did. "And who told you that, my boy?"

"Clyde," said Billy.

"That Clyde," said the Wizard. "You should know better than to pull his string. Turn the page."

Billy turned the page again.

"I'm not the Wizard of Everything," said the Wizard. "I'm the Wizard of Everything Else."

Billy thought about that. "Who are you hiding from?" he asked.

"Who do you think?" asked the Wizard.

Billy turned the page. "I give up," he said.

"The Devil," said the Wizard. "Now put me back in the pile."

"Are you playing with dolls again?" asked Billy's mother. She was standing in the door of the garage.

"No, ma'am," said Billy.

"Come to supper then."

"BILLY was playing with dolls again," said Billy's mother. She was carving the turkey.

"Of course," said Billy's father. "That's because he's a sissy."

"I am not," said Billy.

"You are so," said Billy's father. "Look, I brought you another doll."

BILLY took the doll to his room after supper. It was a baby doll. Billy hated it.

It had a string. Billy pulled it.

"You're a sissy," said the doll.

"I am not," said Billy. He shook the doll and pulled the string again.

"You are so," said the doll.

Billy tied the doll to a pencil. Then he got a book of matches and burned the doll up. He pulled its string so he could hear it scream.

"What are you doing in there?" asked Billy's mother.

"Nothing," said Billy.

"Playing with dolls," said Billy's father.

"DOLLS are stupid," said Billy. It was the next day. He was playing with Clyde behind the garage, where no one could see. "I hate dolls," he said.

"Pull my string," said Clyde.

Billy did.

"Even dolls hate dolls," said Clyde. "I would rather be a little boy like you."

"Really?" said Billy. He hugged Clyde and pulled his string again.

"Not really," said Clyde. "You're a sissy. Would you like to meet the Wizard?"

"I already did," said Billy. "And I am not a sissy."

"How many little sissies get to meet the Wizard?" asked Clyde.

BILLY threw Clyde into the garbage and went to the garage to find the Wizard.

He opened *Today's Wizard*, and there he was in his pointy hat.

"Where's Clyde?" asked the Wizard.

"He called me a sissy," said Billy. He turned the page.

"That Clyde," said the Wizard. "I told you not to pull his string."

"I had no one else to play with," said Billy. He looked around the garage. It was dark and scary. "Can I take you outside?" he asked.

"No way," said the Wizard. "I'm in hiding."

"Why is the Devil after you?" he asked.

"Why do you think?" asked the Wizard.

Billy turned the page. "I give up," he said.

"He wants to steal my hat," said the Wizard. "So he can rule the world."

Billy thought about that. "What does he look like?" he asked. He turned the page.

"He looks ugly and evil," said the Wizard. "Now put me back in the pile. Here comes your mother."

"What are you doing in there?" asked Billy's mother.

"Nothing," said Billy

"Put your dolls away and come to supper."

"GET a load of this," said Billy's father. He was reading the paper. "Wizard Goes Into Hiding."

"He's hiding from the Devil," Billy said.

"He's apparently not the Wizard of Everything anyway," said Billy's father. "So what's the big deal?"

"He's the Wizard of Everything Else," said Billy.

"What do you know about it?" said Billy's mother. "Eat your turkey." They had turkey every night.

Billy and the Wizard

BILLY woke up in the middle of the night. Clyde was standing on his chest.

Billy was afraid. "I'm sorry I threw you in the garbage," he said.

"Pull my string," said Clyde.

Billy pulled his string.

"I'm sorry I called you a sissy," said Clyde. "Now hurry. Come with me! It's an emergency."

"What's the problem?" Billy asked. He pulled Clyde's string.

"The Devil is in the garage, looking for the Wizard. It's an emergency!"

IT was midnight. Billy's parents were asleep.

Billy sneaked out the side door, into the garage.

The Devil was sitting on the floor, going through the magazines. He looked ugly and evil. He had a snout like a dog. He wasn't wearing any pants.

"What are you doing here?" asked Billy. Even though he knew.

"Don't bother me, kid," said the Devil. "Go play with your dolls."

"The Wizard's not here," said Billy.

"You're a liar," said the Devil. "I like that. Now go back to bed and leave me alone. I have work to do."

He started going through the magazines again.

"This is my garage," said Billy.

"It is not," said the Devil. "It's your father's. And you're a sissy."

"I am not," said Billy. "If I had a gun, I would shoot you."

"Be my guest," said the Devil. Then he said something in Latin, and a magic gun appeared in Billy's hand. It was silver. Billy pointed it at the Devil and pulled the trigger but it just went *click*.

"Guess I forgot to load it," said the Devil. He grinned. "It takes magic bullets. And look what I found."

He held up a magazine. It was *Today's Wizard*. "Thanks for the tip, Clyde," he said.

Billy was shocked. "You told on him!" he said. He pulled Clyde's string.

"I'm sorry!" said Clyde. "Pull my string again. But only halfway out this time."

"Don't do it!" said the Devil. But Billy did.

"*Si vis pacem para bellum,*" said Clyde. "*Bibere venenum in auro.*"

The Devil stood up, looking scared. And no wonder: three gold bullets had appeared in Billy's gun.

"I was just about to leave," said the Devil. He held the magazine over his face and tried to hide.

But it did him no good. Billy shot him three times: once in the snout and twice in the heart.

The Devil disappeared. So did the magic gun. Only the magazine was left. Billy picked it up.

It had a bullet hole all the way through it. "Oh no," said Billy. He opened it with trembling hands.

The Wizard's pointy hat had a hole in it, but the Wizard was okay.

"Good going, Billy," he said. "You're no sissy. But how did the Devil find me?"

Billy told him and turned the page.

"That Clyde," the Wizard said. "He can't keep his big mouth shut. Pull his string and let's see what he has to say for himself."

Billy pulled Clyde's string.

"I'm sorry," said Clyde. "The Devil said he would make me a Devil too. Anything is better than being a doll. Almost."

"We all make mistakes," said the Wizard. "So I forgive you. Besides, you saved the day."

"It's true," said Billy. "Maybe the Wizard will make you into a little boy, as a reward."

"Thanks anyway," said Clyde. "I'd rather be a doll."

Billy thought about that.

"Suit yourself," said the Wizard. "I'm out of here."

"What about your hat?" Billy asked the Wizard. "It has a hole in it."

"I have an extra," said the Wizard. He was starting to fade away. "And now I don't have to hide anymore."

Billy turned the page. The pointy hat was still there, and so was the hole, but the Wizard was gone.

"WHAT'S that infernal racket?" said Billy's father. He was standing in the door. "Give me that magazine and go back to bed."

"Yes, sir," said Billy. He handed his father the magazine.

"*Today's Wizard,*" said Billy's father. He threw it onto the pile. "Pointy hats and dolls! You are such a sissy. Go back to bed and take your doll with you."

"Yes, sir," said Billy. He pulled Clyde's string as he went into the house.

"You're the big sissy," said Clyde.

"What did you say?" asked Billy's father.

"Nothing," said Billy. "It wasn't me."

The Magikkers

TERRY DOWLING

If you had the power to perform one—and only one—act of magic, what would it be? Pick carefully, now . . .

One of the best-known and most celebrated Australian writers in any genre, winner of eleven Ditmar Awards and three Aurealis Awards, Terry Dowling (www.terrydowling. com) made his first sale in 1982, and has since made an international reputation for himself as a writer of science fiction, dark fantasy, and horror. Primarily a short-story writer, he is the author of the linked collections Rynosseros, Blue Tyson, Twilight Beach, Wormwood, An Intimate Knowledge of the Night, *and* Blackwater Days, *as well as* Antique Futures: The Best of Terry Dowling, The Man Who Lost Red, *and* Basic Black: Tales of Appropriate Fear. *He has written three computer adventures:* Mysterious Journey: Schizm, Mysterious Journey II: Chameleon, *and* Sentinel: Descendants in Time, *and as editor has produced* The Essential Ellison, Mortal Fire: Best Australian SF *(with Van Ikin), and* The Jack Vance Treasury *(with Jonathan Strahan), Born in Sydney, he lives in Hunters Hill, New South Wales, Australia.*

T WICE upon a time there was someone named Samuel Raven Pardieu. The first to bear the name was a nineteenth-century blacksmith who tried his hand as a toother during the Napoleonic War. In the morning following the Battle of Waterloo in 1815, while collecting teeth from the newly killed to sell to dentists in the big cities, he was spotted by an English patrol and shot as a looter.

The second Samuel Raven Pardieu was that man's great-to-the-fifth-grandson, and on the morning of 24 May 2006, this second Sam, two weeks past his fourteenth birthday, one full month after enrolling in the special classes at Dessida, was sitting in his favourite spot in all of the sprawling Dessida estate when Bettina Anders found him.

"I knew you'd be here," Bettina said in that special know-it-all tone she had. "Haven't forgotten what today is?"

"Of course not," Sam said, as if he could, as if he needed to be reminded. Key Interview Day. His first one-on-one interview with Lucius Prandt, one of the world's greatest magicians.

The real surprise was that Bettina was bothering to talk to him at all. In his four weeks at Dessida, in both the ordinary curriculum classes and the special Magikker classes they shared day after day, she hadn't spoken more than a few dozen words to him. Now here she was, this stand-offish fourteen-year-old, the one the other eighteen students, Sam included, called the Princess behind her back, pretending to be friendly. Pretending. It couldn't be genuine.

Sam was sitting in his special spot, of course. There were twelve stone plinths flanking the old ornamental approach to the front steps of the main house at Dessida, twelve marble pedestals hopelessly overgrown with thorn-bushes and bracken except for this one, the one Sam had cleared himself and now occupied. The large house stood on its rise behind them, overlooking the grounds of the sprawling country estate.

Bettina didn't leave. That was another marvel. She simply stood there, dark-haired and, yes, princess pretty if you thought about it at all, and just seemed to be watching the day.

"Well, I hope it goes well," she said, and astonished him even more.

Sam couldn't fathom it. Bettina Anders saying such a thing. And with it came another thought: what does she know about my Key Interview that I don't? What happens at a Key Interview with Lucius? Should I ask her?

Sam played it safe and said nothing. Why ask only to have her snub him again? He'd been gazing at what lay concealed in the thorn-bushes be-tween the plinths when she'd arrived. Now he looked out over the estate as well, the spacious grounds set amid these rolling green hills under a bril-liant autumn sky. He was determined not to let Bettina Anders know what he'd really been looking at. That was his secret, his one special thing at Dessida.

But she lingered. Against all reason, all sense, Bettina stayed.

"So, do you have your question ready," she said.

"My what?"

"Key Interview Day is also First Question Day, if no-one's told you. Lucius will probably ask you to ask one. He usually does."

Sam couldn't help himself. "A question? What question?"

"Ahhh," Bettina said, which translated as: *So, you didn't know*! "Just what I said. He'll ask if *you* have a question. Do you?"

"*One* question. I've got lots of questions. Like when do the *real* magic classes start. Not just these mind exercises we keep doing all the time."

"You need to be patient," Bettina said, and looked anything but that herself. "It's worth it."

It struck Sam right then that she'd been *told* to come and find him, to say all this. With two months' more experience at Dessida, she was probably following someone's instructions, a script of some kind. Maybe Lucius had sent her himself. It was certainly possible.

"Where would *you* rather be right now, Bettina?" he said, and could see he had surprised her.

"What?"

"This is *my* spot. I love sitting here, just watching the grounds and the house. But you don't want to be here now. Where would you *rather* be?"

The old Bettina defiance was back in a flash. She couldn't help herself. "You're so smart and stand-offish. You tell me!"

Stand-offish! That threw Sam. That couldn't be right. He wasn't the stand-offish one!

"Well, I haven't known you long, but it has to be the top of that tower," Sam said, and pointed back up the hill to Dessida's huge front doors at the end of the overgrown approach promenade. Above that big doorway rose a modest central tower, three storeys tall, with a big bronze bell on an ornate stand at the top and a flag flying on a flag-pole. "Or beside the lake, down behind the trees there. Somewhere away and safe."

Bettina stared at him, not because he was necessarily right in naming either place—how could he possibly know?—but probably because of that final sentence and final word.

The look between them might have been special except that Bettina was guarding, was more protective about some things than even Sam was. His last comment had probably been too close to the mark. She had to say something to deal with the vulnerability it brought with it.

"As if I'd tell you," she said, like "Princess" Bettina on any other day. "And don't think I don't know why you like sitting here. I can see your silly statue down in there." She gestured at the thicket beyond the plinth where Sam sat, then stalked off towards the house.

Sam could have hated her right then, watching her go, but knew that such an emotion was to cover something else, just like Bettina's own sudden outburst. She was guarding, protecting herself. Sam was doing the same.

"It's the only one left!" he might have called after her as she disappeared through the double doorway. But he didn't. He looked instead at the toppled form hidden in the thorn thicket, a figure of dirty white stone, the same old marble as the plinths, toppled and abandoned long ago.

Whatever statuary had adorned the other plinths was long gone. The house itself was maintained well enough, but the grounds of the Dessida estate had definitely seen better days.

Let her tell the other students about the statue. Let her tell their three teachers or the other staff, Lucius himself for all he cared.

And stand-offish! How dare she!

Sam looked at his watch: 9:45. Almost time.

Key Interview. Just him and Lucius at last!

But Bettina had no reason to lie. First Question Day. What would he ask? What did one ask the man who was probably the world's greatest magician, having been hand-picked by him from hundreds, no, literally thousands of other boys and girls across Australia, across the world, if what the Prandt testing officers had said was true? Hand-picked and *paid* to come to Dessida in the Southern Highlands on a Prandt Scholarship to hone his latent skills, become a magician or magikker, whatever that was. It had never been made clear.

That had to be the question.

What's the difference between a Magician and a Magikker?

Sam looked at his watch again: 9:50. And that was when Martin Mayhew appeared in Dessida's big double doorway, happy Martin, always smiling, always happy to be in the world. Tall, blond, and handsome, Nordic-looking and easy in his buff-coloured house fatigues and sandals, greeting every morning with his arms spread wide and his head back, if the stories were true, breathing in the day. Martin was in charge of the household staff, and here he was to make sure that Sam didn't miss his 10 A.M. meeting.

Martin gave a big sweeping gesture of summons. "It's time, Sam!"

"Take care, Rufio," Sam called to the stone figure lying in the thicket, his special name for his secret friend. Then he was up in a flash, off the plinth and up the steps.

"Rufio?" Martin asked as they headed for Lucius Prandt's large office in the north-western wing.

"My name for him," Sam said. "He's the only one left. Do you remember the others?" Sam knew he could ask Martin things like this and be safe about it.

"Sorry, Best Sam. Before my time, I'm afraid. But ask Master Lucius. He'll know. He's lived here all his life. You're allowed to bring up things like that during your interview."

"Anyone else scheduled today, Martin?" Sam had to ask it.

Martin shook his head. "Not today. Today is your day, Sam. Lucius has been looking forward to it."

Then they were at the large oaken door to Lucius Prandt's private office, and Martin was knocking.

"Good luck, Best Sam," Martin said, opening the door for him.

And in Sam went.

It was a wonderful room, Sam saw, a true magician's room, large and high-ceilinged, with bookcases lining most of the wood-panelled walls and fabulous miniature engines of glass and metal working away on a bench top to one side. Against the far wall was a suit of medieval armour with—incredibly!—two heads, two fiercely snouted, visored helmets set side by side on big spiky shoulders. Where could *that* have come from? Sam wondered. How could it be real? There were maps on the walls between the bookshelves: Mercator projections of land after fabulous land with exotic names like Sabertanis Major and Andastaban Arcanus. Small pins with demon heads fastened maps atop others in some places, there were so many.

Lucius Prandt's huge desk was set on a raised dais before four tall lead-light windows that opened onto views of the lawns and forests of Dessida, windows that framed glimpses of rolling hills and held great masses of fluffy cumulus in an achingly blue sky.

So many things sat on that wide wonderful desk, but most noticeable were the three planetary globes Sam had learned about in his Introductions to Magic classes. The closest was the Earth as Sam knew it, but joined by seventeen silver threads to the second, which was the Overworld, set with its spelltowers and mage-points. That orb was joined in turn by red wires to the third, which represented the Underworld, all blacks and reds, with threads of hot bright copper picking out the various Sunder Points.

But Lucius Prandt wasn't at his desk. He sat in one of two big arm-chairs before a fire-place in which was set not a conventional fire but rather a slowly turning image of a burning city.

"Welcome, Sam," Lucius said, standing to greet him, shaking his hand warmly. He wore true-wizard black, of course: soft black woollen top, black slacks, black shoes. None of the star-and-moon robes or mysterious pentagram stuff he wore for his concerts and television performances, not today. His dark eyes glittered under silver-grey hair that swept back like a wave. He was in his late fifties, they said, but others had told Sam that a zero should be added to any age you felt tempted to put him at. Lucius Prandt, they said, had been present at the death of the ancient city that burned forever in his fire-place.

It was difficult for Sam not to keep glancing this way and that, studying some new thing or other that suddenly caught his eye. But at last he made himself sit in the other armchair and face Lucius, who was pouring them both glasses of fruit-juice from a crystal decanter.

"I've been looking forward to this, Sam," he said as he handed Sam a glass. "Your studies have been going well, I hear, and I thought it was time we met properly. We have questions for each other, I know, and you'll get to ask them all over the next few weeks. No doubt you've been told to have a special question ready for me right now, so let's get that out of the way so we can relax properly."

Sam felt a weight go from him. He set his glass down on a side table and didn't hesitate. "What's the difference between a Magikker and a Magician?"

"Straight to the heart of it. Good. That's an important question, and I thank you for it. There have been many true magicians in the history of the world—gifted men and women—but not really that many ever became the fullest quantity meant by that name. Most so-called magicians only ever had bits and pieces of the gift. But I bet you could even name some of the real ones."

"Well, Merlin for a start?"

"Definitely one of the lucky ones, Sam, one of the very few."

"Yourself. Lucius Prandt." It seemed appropriate to say it.

Lucius gave his wonderful smile. "Good of you to say so, but no, Sam. I'm only an illusionist. That's what most magicians are these days—people who create wonderful illusions, learn to be clever enough to use people's perceptions against them. That's nothing compared to real magic, of course, just fakery and fancy tricks, a knowledge of optics and sleight of hand, but sometimes it just has to do. But I *was* a true Magician for a short time, Sam. Seems a lot of us have a bit of the gift, just a bit and just for a short time, some evolutionary holdover from when the mind fired differently. It's almost as if evolution started to take us down a different road, then got side-tracked."

Lucius paused to top up their glasses. "The thing is, most of us lose any traces of this gift by the time we become adults and never even know we've had it. It comes out in crisis situations mostly—a child lifts a fallen tree off an injured playmate. He could never have lifted such a load before. Suddenly he can. Another kid moves a parked car to free a trapped pet. Never knows how she did it. Another pictures the hand of someone buried in a land-slide half a continent away, maybe tells the right people in time. When they check, they find the person still alive, just a hand showing. It's the birthright gift, the power some of us are born with and soon lose."

"But *you* had it."

"I certainly did. For seventeen precious and amazing years. That's an incredibly long time. I was lucky. The memory of it made me become an illusionist. But for a short time I was a *Magician*, Sam! The real thing!"

"And I am?" Sam had to ask it. Why else was he here?

"Straight to it again, Sam. Good. You are—in a small way and for a short time. You may never have known it before coming to Dessida, but you are."

"All those tests at school—"

"Were to prove it. Passed off as aptitude tests and personality indicators, all approved by the School Board and the Department of Education. They never knew otherwise. This year alone we've tested everyone at three hundred and fifty-two schools so far. You're the only one we've found."

Sam was amazed. "The *only* one?"

"Others had bits of a gift but were temperamentally unsuited or had family complications. They were better left as they were, undeveloped and unknowing. For their own sakes, really. I hope you understand."

"So what about my training here? The six months' tuition?"

"You want to be an illusionist?"

"Not if I'm a Magician!"

"Perfect answer! See, we picked well. So let's get back to your question. A Magician with a capital M has the gift for life, just like Merlin and Sancreoch and Quen Dargentis, the Black Mage of Constantinople. But most are what we call Magikkers—people with a tiny bit of the gift, a single burst they can use once and once only, you hear what I'm saying? In magical parlance, we call them singletons. Magikkers."

"And I'm a—a singleton? A Magikker?"

"Sam, you are. You have *one* magic act within you. A single magnificent spell. One big gush of power. It will all come rushing out at once, then be gone."

"Then—then I should wait. I should keep it until I really need it."

"Doesn't work like that. The older you get, the sooner it'll just fade away. It's gone for most Magikkers well before they turn twenty."

"But—but Lucius . . ." Sam couldn't finish.

"Yes, Sam. You have to take my word that this is how it is. I've spent years researching and searching."

"For these—Magikkers?"

"Indeed."

"So you're saying I should use my gift soon."

"You should. And there's an alternative. A suggestion I would like to put to you now."

"What's that, Lucius?"

"Sam, I want you to give *me* your magic."

Sam was amazed. "Give it to you?"

"You have so little—one spell at most, a single act, probably limited in all sorts of ways—but whatever it is, however it is, I'd like you to give it to me."

The request stunned Sam. He felt a new weight settle on his spirit, a new hard emotion surging up. He quickly realised what it was. Disappointment. Disillusionment. "That's why I'm really here, isn't it? Why we're all really here?"

Lucius nodded. "Yes, Sam, it is."

"But it's *mine*," Sam said. "*My* gift. How could I *give* it? How could that be possible?" And behind those words, the unspoken ones: Why should I? How could you ask it?

"I can't help you there, Sam. That has to be your decision. It truly does have to be your decision. I just wanted to let you know how it is and what I'd like you to do for me."

The disappointment Sam felt took all the charm from the room, emptied the excitement and happiness out of the day. He wanted to be gone, needed to be anywhere else. "So I can leave whenever I want? I don't have to stay?"

"Dessida isn't a prison, Sam. You can leave anytime you want. We'll drive you to the station at Milton, even give you a certificate saying you've completed some important vocational training."

"But I'll lose my chance."

"Only to be here with me. Taking our classes. To have us help you use that gift."

"*Give away* that gift." Sam's words sounded bitter. He couldn't help it. "And they're *illusionist* classes. Not the real thing."

"Afraid so, Sam. Once your magic is used up, that's all we have to console us."

"You don't."

"I assure you, Sam, I do. That's why I'm asking for your magic. One illusionist talking to a young man who may one day become another."

"Once my magic is gone."

"Once your magic is gone, yes."

"So you can have another taste!" Sam said the words savagely. He was so angry, so disappointed. This wonderful man, wonderful place, wonderful chance had been ruined in a moment.

"I—I need to go and think."

Lucius stood. "Of course you do. It's right that you do. I wanted to be direct with you about this. But, Sam, please know. Whatever you decide will be the right thing."

Before Sam quite knew it, he found himself out in the corridor again, hurrying back towards the front of the house. He felt numb. He needed to be gone, to be out in the day, somewhere else, anywhere else. He rushed down the front steps and sat on his plinth again, but this time he didn't greet Rufio. He couldn't bring himself to.

Everything was the same. Everything was different. Dessida still stood at the end of its once-grand promenade, still loomed there—an impressive, two-storeyed, nineteenth-century mansion on its gentle rise. But now Sam saw all over again how run-down it truly was: the lawns in need of mowing, the weeds in the gravel of the approach walk. The gardens to either side were overgrown with briars too, not just the pedestals flanking the path.

So much for Lucius Prandt's magic. He couldn't even keep his estate in order, couldn't even manage a "glamour" to hide how it really was.

Sam left the plinth and set off across the lawns towards the estate's western border. Members of the household staff watched him go. Standing with their rakes and gardening tools, they tracked him with their bright curious eyes.

That just angered Sam further. They stood about with rakes and implements like that, yet always seemed to be doing more talking and daydreaming than actual work. Well, let them watch. Let them wonder.

Finally, Sam reached the low wall of grey-brown fieldstone that marked Dessida's western boundary. He leant on the waist-high barrier, glanced at it stretching this way and that off through the trees, then looked out at the world beyond, *his* world, sweeping away in fields and suddenly precious vistas.

How dare Lucius! How dare he!

Sam could so easily jump that wall and be gone. He felt his body tensing for it.

"Hey, Best Sam!"

The voice reached him through the forest, and when Sam turned, there was that gangly, elderly groundswoman, Ren Bartay, heading towards him. She was tall and sun-tanned and was whacking the taller weeds with a stick as she came, a big smile on her face.

"Isn't it just a day?" Ren called, grinning away. "I love this time of year."

And then, when she was right up close: "Thinking of bailing out, eh, Sam? It's an easy leap."

"Seriously considering it, Ren," Sam replied. Why not say it, he figured. Like Lucius had said, it was his choice to make.

"Don't blame you," Ren surprised him by saying. "The magic is all used up here."

"Is it?"

"First Interview Day. You know it is. You're the only one with a bit right now."

"If that's true. If *any* of it's true. What about the others? Bettina and Susan and Crip and the rest? There are eighteen other—"

"Already given. Already gone. Never really had any." Ren set down her stick and started checking that the stones were securely packed atop this section of wall.

"I can't be the only one!"

"Right now you are," she said, turning back. "Lucius would have asked you for it, yes? First Interview Day."

"But if they've given theirs, why do they stay on? How can they stand it?"

Ren looked off through the trees, then pointed to a spot well inside the wall. "Because *how* they used their magic is still here—in almost every case."

"I don't understand."

"Let me show you."

They started walking back towards Dessida together, then made a detour south so they entered the thickest part of the forest.

In the dappled autumn light, Sam saw things—structures—amid the trees. To his left there was a cottage, a full-size picture-book gingerbread house with smoke curling from the chimney, smoke that vanished six metres above the chimney-pot before ever reaching the open air.

"That's Bettina Anders's creation," Ren said. "The Eternal House. How she used her single magic act. Step inside, you'll meet her grandmother Dika, her grandfather Brent. There's always music playing, always something cooking, always a welcome at their table. Couldn't do something like that away from Dessida, Sam. Lucius explained it to Bettina very carefully. You can't bring people back from the dead, put them back in the world, without causing a real fuss. Wouldn't be right. That sort of fix-up needs to be done very discreetly."

Then Ren pointed to a twisted and, yes, *twisting* tower off to the right. It glowed like amber in the soft light streaming through the trees. "That's Sophie Ramage's Living Tower. She would've preferred it in her own backyard, of course, but Lucius made her see that people would gawp and gape and never leave her alone. They'd be forever wanting to know how it was possible, where it came from. She'd never have a moment's peace, what with intruders and souvenir-hunters breaking off bits and pieces. Here it stays intact and hers! She'll be able to come see it anytime she wants."

"And that's what it's all about," Sam said, more annoyed than ever. "Lucius can't do magic anymore, so this way he gets other people's marvels! Talks them out of keeping them."

"Sam, Sam," Ren said, in her wonderful calming voice. "See it another way. These were done by Magikkers who *didn't* give Lucius their magic! The things they used it for have been left here for safekeeping. *Discarded* here if you think about it."

Sam tried to grasp the sense of what Ren was saying. "But Lucius wouldn't be able to convince everyone, surely."

"You're right. So he exercises an important custodial role, a true duty of care, and uses hypnosis. He makes them *forget* that they ever had the gift in the first place. He can't let them go back into their everyday lives and do

294

some outlandish thing or other. Not once they know about the gift. So they leave Dessida thinking they've been given some training in basic illusionist skills, that's all. They go away, and the magic dies in them, then everything's okay."

Sam felt a moment of panic. "*I* still remember all this! He hasn't hypnotized me!"

"You haven't jumped the wall yet."

"What! If I jump it and run away, I'll forget!"

Ren grinned. "Just kidding, Best Sam. Lucius picks his Magikkers very carefully. Mostly it works out fine. He rarely has to resort to mind-tricks. You still have your gift to use. He'd *rather* you use it than lose it."

"He'd rather I give it to him."

"Oh yes. He'd much rather that," Ren said, smiling and, before Sam could ask why, added: "But for a very good reason. One I'm duty-sworn never to reveal."

That made Sam stop and think. He liked old Ren. It made the anger subside a bit. "But how can I give *my* magic to *him*?"

Ren's smile never wavered. "See what a special boy you are, Sam? You said 'how can I' not 'why should I.' That's a nice distinction, especially when you're feeling like you are right now."

"I'm serious, Ren. *How* could I give it to him?"

But Ren just put a finger to her lips as if to say: Can't tell. Can't tell. Keeping a secret! Then she seemed to change her mind a bit. "Well, the Magikkers who worked their spells here certainly didn't do it. Bettina insisted on her cottage. Sophie had to have her tower. Over there you see Kristi Paul's Magical Soda Well and Grant Hennessey's Nifty Golden Treasure Mill. *They* certainly didn't give their magic to Lucius."

"But he would've asked for it."

"Certainly did. First Interview Day every time."

"But if it's *my* birthright gift, *mine* to use, how can I give it?"

They seemed to be in a loop. "Exactly," Ren Bartay said. "How could you give your bit of magic to someone else?"

Then, just like that, without another word, she turned and headed back towards Dessida.

Sam watched her go, saw the tall spry woman stop to exchange a word or two with other household staff doing grounds work—first Carla, then Jeffrey—then saw her hurry on.

What had she told them? What?

No way to know, so Sam turned back to the marvels laid out amid the trees: Bettina's cottage with its endless plume of cookfire smoke and—to hear Ren Bartay tell it—endless happiness within, lost happiness found again; Sophie's miraculous twisting tower, curving on itself like so much settling honey; Grant's mill glinting and cycling away. He heard the fizz from Kristi's well too, heard other wonderful sounds coming through the forest from who knew how many other wonders hidden there? Sam realized he could probably spend hours, days, weeks here exploring what else was laid out among the trees, what years of other Magikkers had chosen.

Because they *wouldn't* give Lucius their magic!

Sam marveled at it. Just how long had Lucius been bringing Magikkers here from all across the world, asking for their bits of the gift?

Which made Sam think further. What single thing did Lucius hope for with the piece of magic Sam carried within him? What was it that Ren—or Martin, or Lucius for that matter—wouldn't tell him?

Sam couldn't fathom the purpose, of course, but suddenly he did realize something. He would know *none* of this, nothing of what Magikkers were and about this gift he had if it weren't for Lucius, weren't for the testing and the Prandt Scholarship that had brought him here.

He owed Lucius for that, and it took the last of the anger out of him.

And blossoming up behind that realization came something else. Sam knew right then *how* he could give his magic to Lucius, and it was so obvious, so simple.

He ran, actually ran back to the main house, making more sudden Sam-commotion in the peace of the day. Grounds staff stood leaning on their rakes or left off sweeping the paths to watch him rush by.

What were they thinking? Sam asked himself as he ran. Here comes the magic boy, the First Interview Day Boy. Best Sam. But what did they think, what did they know, smiling and wondering like that?

Sam saw other students watching him too. Susan and Crip and Hagrib were on the south terrace, Sanford and Nettie by the fountain. And there, there at the top of the tower, leaning on the balustrade, yes, was Princess Bettina, watching from her safe place.

Sam didn't care. He deliberately turned into the old approach promenade, deliberately let her see him run past the plinths and thorn-bushes. He called "Hi there, Rufio!" as he rushed past, just as he'd always done, then he leapt the steps three at a time and plunged into the cool familiar gloom of Dessida's front hall.

Martin Mayhew was waiting for him there, of course.

"Best Sam, what's afoot?" Martin asked.

"I have to see Lucius again, Martin! I need to ask him something!"

"About your interview?"

"About my gift."

"Then I'm sure he'll see you."

And Lucius did, almost immediately. Martin needed only a moment to go in first to explain, then Sam was ushered into the leather chairs, and Martin was once again closing the door behind him.

Sam dropped into the armchair opposite Lucius, just as he had an hour before.

Lucius had already put aside the book he'd been reading. "What is it, Sam?"

"I know how I can give you my magic."

"You do? And so?"

"I want to."

"I thank you. How does that work then?"

"*You* tell me what you want *me* to do. Then I do it for you."

"But I can't," Lucius said.

"What's that?"

"I can't come out and tell you, Sam. It's an oath I took. A condition I imposed on myself. A rule of governance from way back. I'm not *allowed* to tell. It all has to come from you. You're the Magikker-in-command right now. I'm just an illusionist."

"But you can hypnotize me. Plant an activating command of some kind. Then instead of days and weeks of learning how to use an activation spell one time only, you put in a trigger so all I have to do is say what I want. What *I* think *you* want. You can at least do that."

"True. I can. I've done it before."

"I know. I guessed. That's what you're the expert at. Making it quick and easy. Helping it happen."

Lucius smiled. "So how do we proceed, Best of Sams? I still can't say what I want you to do with your gift."

"Lucius, I think I know what you want."

Lucius's eyes glittered with unreadable emotion. "Oh? Yes?"

"So go ahead. Plant the hypnotic cue."

"I planted it earlier today. While you were watching my burning city there."

Sam glanced quickly at the strange shape turning in the fireplace, then looked back. "Then call the Dessida staff together."

Lucius's eyebrows lifted in surprise. "The staff?"

"The three teachers too. All of them. Have them gather out by the front steps."

Lucius turned to an intercom by his chair, pressed a button. "Martin. Dessida One! Ring the bell!"

And moments later the bell in the tower started tolling over and over. Out in the fields, back in the kitchen and service rooms and private quarters, the household staff would be leaving off what they were doing and heading for the front of the house.

They were all assembled there when Lucius and Sam stepped through the big double doorway at the top of the steps. The group stood as if for some anniversary photograph, smiling, attentive, and curious, Martin Mayhew and Ren Bartay among them.

Sam grinned back. He was right. In an instant he'd counted them and knew he was right.

Eight household staff. Three teachers. A total of eleven.

Eleven of the twelve plinths.

Sam gestured then, just as he'd seen magicians and wizards and sorcerers do all his life in countless picture books and movies.

"Make room for number twelve!" he shouted. "Rufio, come out here! It's your turn!"

There was scratching and scrambling in the thicket, then out came Rufio, already in house fatigues, limber and strong and smiling with happiness.

"Welcome to the staff, Rufio!" Sam called.

"Thank you, Best Sam!" Rufio called back with his brand-new voice, and did just that, moved in among the others.

That was when Sam noticed that next to him Lucius was weeping, that tears brightened his cheeks in the late-morning light.

"Thank you, Best Sam. Thank you for this."

"It means I'll have to stay on and become an illusionist now, doesn't it?" Sam said.

"Oh, it does," Lucius agreed. "And I'm sure that's what Rufio and our friends here want more than anything."

The Magic Animal

GENE WOLFE

Gene Wolfe is perceived by many critics to be one of the best—perhaps the best—SF and fantasy writers working today. His most acclaimed work is the tetralogy The Book of the New Sun, *individual volumes of which have won the Nebula Award, the World Fantasy Award, and the John W. Campbell Memorial Award. He followed this up with a popular new series,* The Book of the Long Sun, *that included* Nightside the Long Sun, The Lake of the Long Sun, Caldé of the Long Sun, *and* Exodus from the Long Sun, *and has recently completed another series,* The Book of the Short Sun, *with the novels* On Blue's Waters, In Green's Jungles, *and* Return to the Whorl. *His other books include the classic novels* Peace *and* The Devil in a Forest, *both recently rereleased, as well as* Free Live Free, Soldier in the Mist, Soldier of Arete, There Are Doors, Castleview, Pandora by Holly Hollander, *and* The Urth of the New Sun. *His short fiction has been collected in* The Island of Doctor Death and Other Stories and Other Stories, Gene Wolfe's Book of Days, The Wolfe Archipelago, *the World Fantasy Award–winning collection* Storeys from the Old Hotel, Endangered Species, Strange Travelers, *and* Innocents Aboard: New Fantasy Stories. *His most recent books consist of a two-volume novel series,* The Knight *and* The Wizard, *a new collection,* Starwater Strains: New Science Fiction Stories, *and the long-awaited new entry in the* Soldier of the Mist *sequence,* Soldier of Sidon.

In the strange and evocative story that follows, he takes us into the deepest recesses of a mystic wood and involves us anew in one of the oldest of stories . . .

VIVIANE could understand the speech of animals. That is the thing you must know about her, not the first thing, or the main thing, or the most important thing. Nor is it the only thing. It is the thing you must know. You must know it because you cannot understand it. Viviane—here she comes, the brown-blond not-terribly-large girl urging the dappled mare to more speed—did not understand it herself.

She did not understand it, although she did not put it that way. When she thought about it, she could not understand why other people could not—which is the same thing. That is the way it is with talents. One has a talent for music, another for baseball. One has a talent for acting. (You know her.) Another can fill the whole auditorium with the song from one little ordinary-looking throat. And none can ever understand why others cannot do the things they find so easy and natural.

Viviane understood the speech of animals, and sometimes (quite often, in fact) animals understood her. That last is not equally mysterious. Animals often understand us, and Viviane's talent is not so rare as you might imagine.

The dappled mare jumped a little creek in fine style and came to a full stop without being told; and Viviane, who had been enjoying the song the wind sang and thinking about starting high school next month way over in Rio Colorado, tried to see what had made her stop. Without success.

"That is a drawing-in wood," Daisy said very plainly. "I'm not going in there."

"All right." Viviane made her voice soothing. "I wasn't going there anyway."

"I am not," Daisy said.

It did not quite follow, or so it seemed to Viviane. "You sound," she told Daisy, "as if I said I was. I didn't say that at all. I said I wasn't."

Daisy only tossed her head nervously.

Viviane tapped her with her heels. "This trail doesn't go there, and you've been over it lots of times. Let's trot."

"Let's not."

"Trot," Viviane repeated.

"It's not the same, that wood."

"Trot!"

Daisy trotted, then broke into a thrilling headlong gallop.

This, Viviane told herself, is what getting the right boyfriend—not just any boyfriend, the right one—for my freshman year would be like. A rush and rhythm. A sort of—

Daisy had stopped again, this time as abruptly as the very best roping horse. Viviane was conscious of flying, of spinning, and of nothing much after that.

✳

THEN of lying in coarse grass in an uncomfortable position. For a time that seemed long, she could not think what she might do about it.

At last she sat up and rubbed her head. No bones broken, as well as she could judge. Her watch—a big, tough quartz watch her father had given her for camping—seemed intact, its pink plastic case undamaged, its hands pointing faithfully: 1:27.

"You will be going into the wood," a dusty rattlesnake told her, "and I will come with you and protect you, if you like. I could wrap myself around your right arm."

Viviane spat dirt and a few grass fragments. "You scared Daisy."

"Would you like to be stepped on?" The rattlesnake had coiled itself defensively. "By a horse?"

It had a point, and Viviane decided to change the subject. "I understand animals," she said. "I always have, but they've never talked quite like you."

"Pity," said the rattlesnake.

"Usually it's 'I'm tired,' 'I'm afraid,' or 'I like you.' Snapdragon told me how much she loved her kittens once. Things like that."

The rattlesnake rested its chin on a shiny stone, not quite looking up at Viviane. "Now you may understand us better. It is because of where you will be."

"Where I'll be?"

"Yes."

"Not where I am now?"

"No."

"All right." Viviane's jeans were dirty; so was her denim shirt. She brushed them off. "Where will I be?"

"In the wood. Shall I come, too?"

"No." She tried to make her voice firm.

"If you don't like the wrist idea, I could stretch around your waist, I think."

"If I say no again, will you bite me?"

"I will say it for you," the rattlesnake told her. "No, but remember that you might have had the blessing of serpents." It flowed into the grass and vanished.

Viviane stood, finding it more difficult than usual. The trail stretched before her and behind her, but she could no longer remember where it came from or where it led. The wood—a beckoning wood of pine and scrub oak that stretched up the side of the mountain—promised shade and cool water.

It took her some time to trace the little creek to its spring, a small and secret pool whose outflow was quickly lost among rocks and roots. She had drunk and was perched on a rock wiping her mouth with her bandana when a shrill voice behind her said, "There you are! They said you had come. We need your help. Nod, please, so I will know my speech is not too alien to you."

Viviane turned and stared.

"Oh, nod! Please, please nod!"

Slowly, Viviane did.

"There! I knew you would!" The speaker was a small . . . Woman? With four gauzy wings that fluttered nervously behind . . . Her? "We need your help," she(?) said. "You need your help. Am I making myself clear? When I say we I mean us. Do you understand the Matter of Britain?"

"Sorry I stared." Viviane did her best to look away, with mixed success. "I've never seen anyone quite like—never seen anybody even a little bit like you."

"I understand. If . . . You're not going to attack, are you?"

That took some digesting. Viviane composed several interesting thoughts and rejected all of them; everything, she decided, was already much too complicated. At last she said, "You're afraid of me? *You* are afraid of *me*?"

"Well, you are big. And I am certain you can spring very fast . . ." The wings fluttered so hard that for a moment their owner was lifted off her feet. "If you chose to."

Viviane felt she should show her teeth but smiled instead. "You mean like Snapdragon? Snapdragon's my cat. I call her Snappy."

"Are cats the ones with tails? My name is—is . . . Oh, I forget! I mean, they gave me something to tell you, I know they did. Ariel? Was that it?"

"She's a mermaid, I think. She has lovely red hair." Viviane smiled, recalling the movie. "I'd like to have it on DVD."

"You don't think that's right?"

"I really don't." Viviane shook her head. "You're more of a fairy, aren't you? And you're a girl? Like me?"

"Only not so big."

"So you should have a girl-fairy name. What about Tinker Bell?"

The wings drooped, and their owner looked a trifle downcast. "It is awfully long. I doubt I could remember it."

"Well . . ." Viviane dipped her bandana in the spring and wiped her face with it. "Gee, I read—"

They had been joined by a coyote. It nodded frostily to the (very) small winged woman before addressing Viviane. "This ladybug, or whatever she is, is about to dispatch you upon a mission fraught with danger, my child. You may need the assistance of someone swift, someone with sharp teeth who is not afraid to use them. I proffer my services, gratis. Pro bono, as the expression is. I too have a stake in this matter, you see. Do you wisely choose to accept them?"

"I—I've never shot one of you." Viviane found that her mouth was dry and wished she might drink from the spring again. "I want to say so, first off. It's the truth. There've been times when I could have."

"So you think," remarked the coyote.

"But I—I . . ." Viviane turned to the small woman with wings. "Please— my gosh, I still don't know your name. When I was little I read books about fairies. Now I can't remember them. Wait. Nimue's one. Do you like it?"

"That is you, I believe." The small woman giggled.

"No, I'm Viviane."

The coyote made her a stiff bow. "I am He Who Dismays All Hounds. You may call me Dis."

"I don't *want* to call you."

"You probably like dogs," Dis said, wagging his tail somewhat awkwardly. "You humans do, far too often. I despise them, but I'll be a dog for you. For you alone."

"No!" Viviane shook her head violently.

"As you wish, Viviane." The coyote drew himself up. "You might have had the blessing of the pack. I sincerely hope you will not come to regret having refused it." He turned and trotted away, vanishing (as it seemed) behind the first rock.

Viviane watched until he had gone, then knelt to drink again.

When she stood up, the (very) small winged woman said, "Viviane, Viviane, Viviane! How pretty!"

"Thank you." Viviane dipped her bandana as she had before; the cold water revived her flushed face.

"I will be Viviane, too!"

"That's me. How about Vivien?" Viviane spelled it, and added, "Nobody can tell them apart anyway."

"I was told about you before I came," Vivien said, "but not half enough. Your minds are so, um, like clouds. It makes me awfully dizzy."

Why it's *Alice in Wonderland*, Viviane told herself. That was a good book, and a good movie, too. How did it go? "I'm mad, you're mad, we're all mad here." That was it, or close.

"I am *not* mad at anybody." Vivien sounded as firm as it is possible for a small woman with gauzy wings to sound. "I am hopeful. Very hopeful indeed. We need you. You need you. You called me a fairy. Would you like me to grow the little horn-things?" Her tiny forefingers, smaller than a baby's, wiggled on either side of her forehead.

"Well, those . . ."

"Like a snail, you know? I think I could do it."

"Please don't." Viviane wiped her face with her damp bandana all over again. "I was sort of enjoying this, and I'm afraid it would scare me."

"We almost always do." Vivien hung her head. "We never mean to. Or not usually. But you call us gnomes, brownies, leprechauns, sprites, Martians, pixies, and elves, ever so many awful names we have no title to. And you are afraid of us no matter what you call us."

"I'm *not* afraid of you." Viviane made it as firm as an almost-high-school student and accomplished horsewoman could make it.

"Really?"

"Yes! Absolutely!" Somehow, saying it made it so.

The small woman appeared to draw a deep breath, taking in at least half a teaspoon of air. "You say we steal children. We never do. I promise. I will swear to that by anything you like. By everything."

"I am *not* a child!"

"But sometimes we recruit children. We simply have to. Honestly, Viviane. In the end we will give him back to his mother. Or to you. Whichever comes first."

"I'm sure I don't want him."

"You will. But—but you have got to recruit him for us. The first part. Bring him to us, but make sure he doesn't have any iron on him when he comes. Or steel. Or anything like that. It distorts the field."

"But I've . . ." Viviane paused, looking blank.

"No, you don't."

"Wait! My pocketknife." Viviane thrust her hands into her pockets. "It's gone. It must have fallen out when I fell off."

"See?" Vivien looked pleased. "You're not wearing spurs today—"

"I don't need them with Daisy."

"And the rivets in those blue trousers are copper. The change in your pockets is copper and nickel. You can talk to animals, so naturally you can talk to *me*. And you'll do it. I *know* you will."

"Do *what*?"

A big raven landed between them with a distinct thump. "Take the kid," it told Viviane. "You take, they teach. After that, you keep the kid on track." Its voice was a harsh croak.

The small woman said, "Hello, Nevermore."

"Wait just a minute." Viviane looked from one to the other. "You two know each other?"

"Sure," quoth Nevermore.

"I Ie . . ." The gauzy wings fluttered nervously. "You must understand him. I, well—he . . ."

"He don't work for free." Nevermore cocked his head knowingly at Viviane. "That's what she's tryin' to say."

Viviane nodded. "I've got it."

"Swell. Now you listen up, honey, 'cause I'm only goin' to say it once. I been here before, an' all this she's goin' to get you to do ain't goin' to be half as easy as she lets on. With me on board there'll be two of us, an' I been through the mill a couple times already, see? You want me, fine. We'll talk about it. You don't, I'll split now an' no hard feelin's. Only don't call me when you're in the soup, 'cause I don't carry no cell phone."

"And I'll have the blessing of the birds," Viviane added.

"Blessin' of the flock. That's what we call it. You bet you will. Plus smart advice, an' a pal that's not too goody-goody to do a little spyin' for you. An' this an' that."

"I want you," Viviane said. "How much?"

"You got one of them new quarters on you? A shiny one?"

Viviane fumbled her change from a pocket of her jeans and prodded it with a forefinger. "Here we go." Picking up the coin, she polished it on her shirt. "Oregon, two thousand and five. How's that?"

"Perfect." Nevermore hopped a bit nearer and held out one claw. "Fork it over."

Viviane did.

"Okay. I just accepted your retainer, see? You get my services. I gotta take this to my bank, but I'll be back before you miss me." Transferring the quarter from claw to beak, Nevermore spread black wings of surprising size and flapped away.

"Gone!" A sigh escaped the small woman. "What a relief!"

"Will he come back?"

"Oh, yes. He will find you eventually. They fly awfully high, and they can see for a thousand years from up there. He has a great many contacts, too. The overworld, you know. You did not ask my advice."

Viviane nodded. "I suppose I should have. Are you older than I am?"

"That is neither here nor there. I know how old you are, Viviane, but not how old I am. Yes, you should have. Had you done so, I would have warned you that although he is honest by his own lights—or . . . Or I think he may be. I mean . . ."

"You mean you're not sure." Viviane was getting impatient.

"That although Nevermore is honest by his own lights, his lights are black as his feathers. Shall we go? I will explain what you have to do on the way."

✱

"THIS is the spot." The small woman fluttered above Viviane's head. "It's got to be, or at least I certainly hope it is. See the oaks? Stand in the circle."

"In the fairy ring? All the mushrooms?"

"Is that what you call them? We use them for markers sometimes, in the woods. We like woods."

Viviane nodded. "I'd heard that."

"Now when you appear in this boy's bedroom, you may frighten him. I hope you won't, but you might. He'll see a shimmer on his floor, like a pool of water there. You'll come up through the water—you won't get wet—and it will drain away. Don't watch it. Watch him. If he starts—"

"I know what to do." Viviane stepped into the ring.

"Taking his hand will be the signal. Don't do it till he consents. You may raise your arms now. Or keep them at your sides. As you wish."

Viviane raised them.

It seemed a typical boy's bedroom, dimly illuminated by a night-light. A periodic table was taped to a wall, beside a picture of a president now obsolete by several terms. The small boy kneeling on his bed was dark, with black hair and shining eyes that seemed to see through her.

"Hello!" She smiled. "Don't be afraid. I'm not going to hurt you. Or anybody."

"There was water on my floor," the boy said, "and you came out of it like—like—"

"A swimmer in a movie," Viviane suggested.

"A fish jumping," the boy said. And then, "I'm not afraid. If I were afraid, I'd yell for Miriam."

Viviane smiled again; she had a charming smile. "That's good. Who's Miriam?"

"The sitter. She's watching TV."

"Do you like TV?" A thought had occurred to Viviane.

The boy shook his head.

"Then let me explain things another way. We're going to do introductions, but *different* introductions. First I'm going to tell you my name, and then I'm going to tell you your name."

"Like a game," the boy said.

"Sort of like that, but it's not a game. My name will be my name for real, and your name will be your new name, and your name for a long, long time. I'm Viviane."

To himself the boy said, "Viviane the water lady."

"And you're Myrddin. It's what your new teachers will call you."

"I'll get new teachers?"

Viviane nodded. "I think you'll like them. Do you like the teachers you have now?"

"New teachers are always interesting." Myrddin's expression was unreadable; his eyes were brighter than ever, perhaps with excitement.

"They will be, but the things they teach you will be more interesting than they are. Have you ever wanted to be an animal?"

Myrddin only stared at her.

"A wolf, or—or a hawk." He looked like a fledgling hawk, she thought. A hawk too young to fly. But soon . . .

As if he read her thought, he said, "I'd be able to fly?"

"Yes," Viviane said, "and do lots of other wonderful things." The small woman could fly. Did she like it?

"Why are you giving me this?"

Here it was. In spite of all she could do, Viviane sighed. "Because you're the person who can stop a lot of bad things from happening. You've got a telescope on your dresser."

His eyes darted toward it, and returned as swiftly to her.

"Without you, there won't be any. Not ever. People will still look at the stars, but they won't know what they are. Nobody will work out that chart of the elements. Not ever. Most kids will die of diphtheria and smallpox, now and always. People—"

"When will I start?"

"Now," Viviane said. "Give me your hand, Myrddin."

He offered it, she took it, and they sank until night had gone and broad daylight shone though the oaks, bathing the fairy ring in a soft green-gold radiance. The small woman landed before Myrddin, half his height.

Viviane gestured. "He's in his pajamas. No iron, okay?"

"I know." To Myrddin, the small woman said, "That is why we had to have Viviane fetch you—why we could not come ourselves, Myrddin, though we—would have liked to. Give me your hand? You must, or nothing else will work."

He did, and the two of them walked away, fading out before they would have been lost among the shadows of the trees.

Hearing the fluttering of gauzy wings, Viviane turned around.

"There you are!" the small woman exclaimed. "We need you. Will you come? I know you must be anxious to get home, but—but you *must*. You just *have* to. Really."

Viviane looked at her watch, then squinted up at the sun. "Okay, if you'll tell me something first. Two things."

"I . . . Sometimes I get mixed up."

"I've noticed. Will you try? You've got to be honest if you want me to bail you out."

The small woman looked stricken. "I—well . . ."

"You're always honest and truthful. Except when you're not. I'm trying to be helpful here."

"Well—yes."

"I'm the same way, but I want your promise. Swear you'll answer these, and you won't hide the truth."

"I will," Vivien promised, "if I can. But I may not be able to. I fib when I have no idea, mostly."

"Don't fib this time. If you can't answer, say so."

The small woman laid her hand on her heart. "Only the truth!"

She really needs me, Viviane thought. Great! Aloud she said, "First the time. I got thrown from my horse, and she was gone when I woke up, so I was out awhile. After that, I walked to these woods. That took a while. I had to hunt for a spring, and that took a while, too."

"I understand." The small woman smiled brightly.

"I talked with you and we went here, and I talked with that nice boy—"

"I am *so* glad you like him!"

"And we came back here. Et cetera, right? Well, my watch says its still one twenty-seven, so it's stopped. Only the sun doesn't seem to have moved either. All that stuff had to take a couple hours. Maybe more."

"You wonder about that. Naturally you would. We can, well, do things with time, Viviane. It's an invariable for you. I know that."

"Only not for you."

Vivien shook her head.

"You put butter in the watch." Vivianc sighed. "Or else you never beat Time. When we're through here, will you take me to the Griffin and the Mock Turtle? I always wanted to see them."

Viviane was cheered immensely by the small woman's puzzled look. "I will be happy to show you griffins," she said, "once we are through with Myrddin. Mock turtles . . . ? I really . . . Perhaps I can find some."

"Don't worry about the Mock Turtle," Viviane told her. "We'll get to him later. Here's my second question. Exactly why do you need me this time? The first time was because there was iron in Myrddin's room. But now you've got him, don't you?"

Vivien nodded. "We do. This is, um, quite different. He is, you know. Older."

Slowly Viviane nodded. "Okay."

"More—ah—mature than you are, actually. And we—he objected . . . To continuing his studies, you know. And there's still ever so much for him to learn."

"He wants to drop out."

"I—suppose so. It sounds . . . He—ah . . ."

"What?" Viviane set her jaw. "Tell me, or you get no more help from me."

"Wants to go looking for you." The gauzy wings drooped. "He cannot possibly find you, you see. He must learn much more before he can, ah . . ."

"Can *what*?"

"Search the past for people. For you. So we—it was my idea, Viviane. If you hate me for it, well, you do. We told him that if he studied, the time would come when he would see more and more of you. And—oh, I am so sorry! I never should have. And I will not tell. Not now! He must tell you himself. I . . . I like him, and I know you did, too. You said so. I would be . . . Stealing from him. I could never face myself again. Never!"

"If I go with you, he'll tell me?"

Mutely, the small woman nodded.

"You'll bring me back here after? Soon?"

"Yes! I promise!"

Together, they walked into the wood.

Things changed. There is no other way to say it. The trees Viviane had known all her life thinned out, and soon were no more. Strange new trees replaced them, kind trees for the most part, but secretive. The sky was a shade darker, the sun larger but not quite so bright. The air—motionless, windless air that seemed to await something new and strange—held a delicious chill. "Is this fairyland?" she asked.

At once the small woman shot ahead, turned long enough for a brief smile, and vanished among the trees.

A man's voice shouted, "Viviane?"

"I'm here," she said, and was at once assailed by doubts. Was she? Really? "Are you calling me?"

He ran lightly and silently, but not so silently that she caught no whisper of his coming. Then he was there, dark, hawk-nosed, and scarcely taller than she was. He dropped to his knees before her. "Oh, my lady! My dear, dearest, beloved lady of the lake. How I've longed for this moment!"

She crouched, bringing her face to the level of his bowed one. "You . . . They can do things with time. She said that. Are you Myrddin?"

He nodded. Slowly, gently, he took her hand between soft, long-fingered, brown hands that might have been a pianist's. "I am. I'm Myrddin, my lady, your lover and your slave. Your slave no matter what may befall, and no matter what you or I may do or say."

"I don't want to have a slave, Myrddin." Would he be angry? "I want a friend. A good and faithful friend."

He looked up and smiled, perfect white teeth flashing. "Your slave and your friend, my lady. Faithful always."

Viviane reached toward him, and he toward her, and without her willing it in the least—or not willing it, either—they were in each other's arms.

They kissed, and kissed again, and though neither knew much about it, each kiss was sweeter than the last.

Until at length they sat side by side, she with her sun-brown arm about his waist and her head on his shoulder. He with a more muscular arm around her shoulders and his cheek brushing her hair.

"They promised I would see you again someday," he told her. "If I learned everything. If I studied till I passed every test, I'd see you again."

She squeezed his hand.

"I came to doubt them. Gwelliant I caught and shook till she greatly feared me. Show her to me, I said. Show her to me once, and I'll believe you."

Viviane lifted her head from his shoulder until she could see his face.

It was the face of one who is angry in a dream. "She said she would, and left. Soon she returned. You were coming, and your name was Viviane."

"It is," Viviane whispered.

"A lake arose from my floor. You must remember that. The shimmering water rose, and soon you rose from the water." He sighed. "To me you will always be the lady of the lake."

"I saw you on your bed," she told him, "a little brown hawk, too young to fly. You're bigger now, but a brown hawk just the same. You'll always be that, my brown hawk, small but fierce."

He chuckled, then grew serious. "Even when my beard is white, Viviane?"

"Yes. Even when your beard's white. Even when we're both old."

"You don't know. I see you don't. It's when you're to be mine. When my beard is white."

"Really?" She stared at him. "Is that what they told you?"

He shook his head. "It's what I found out for myself, and it's true. One of the things I've learned is to look with clear eyes on what's past and what's to come. I've combed the years for a time when we'll be together, not for hours but for a time so long that a tree might grow from a cutting. Far in the past, that time existed. When it begins my beard will be white."

For seconds that seemed long, Viviane tried to grasp what he had told her—to truly understand and accept it; but even when she knew she had to speak, she still could believe it true. Haltingly, only because she knew she must say something, she said, "You're going to live a very long time. That's what it sounds like."

"Yes!" His arm hugged her, the hard, firm grip of a man who clings to something precious. "But I haven't told you everything. The rest isn't the crowning part. The crowning part is that once we've saved the future world, we'll be together for many, many years. For decades, it may be."

They kissed again.

"You should know this, too, Viviane. Once you and I are together at last, I'll grow younger as the years creep by. Younger and younger, till at last we're the same age."

"Really? You didn't just dream it?"

"No," he said, "but if I had, it would yet be true. My dreams are no longer the idle fancies of a night. They haven't been for a long while. I'll grow younger, and you older. At last we'll meet. After that, I'll grow younger still. It's hard to speak of this."

"Then don't," she said. "Let's be happy now. I am."

"So am I. But you must know. When I'm a child again, you're to return me to my mother. It will be arranged by them—by Gwelliant and the rest. My mother will never know I've been away. I'll grow up then, like any other child. And you'll call out to me once more."

Somehow, Viviane felt sure it was the truth. "Yes, I know I will."

He shook himself, shivering as if chilled. "We'll win in the end. That's what I've seen, and it's what matters. In this too-short day, we have till moonrise. Let's make the most of it."

✳

THIS was not the stand of pine and oak that Daisy had called a drawing-in wood. Nor was it the strange expectant forest in which she had been so happy. Its towering oaks were familiar, but older than any she had ever seen. And though their upper leaves were bathed in sunshine, the black loam she trod lay in a twilight no sunshine could reach.

"Anywhere in here," the small woman told her. "You may build it anywhere you like. I am no builder myself—"

"Neither am I," Viviane said.

The small woman ignored her. "But if I were doing it, I would try to build it close to the building materials." The gauzy wings fluttered nervously. "I mean, I could not fly carrying an armload of sticks, and I would try to save steps."

"I don't see any sticks."

"There must be some around somewhere, you know. All these trees? There are bound to be sticks. Just build it, and now I have to go."

"Wait!" Viviane reached for her but missed.

"It need not be big." Vivien rose into the air and out of reach. "Have I said that? I feel sure I have." She vanished among the leaves, her voice floating back: "*Two rooms. One big room.*" Very faintly: "*You know.*"

"Oh, my gosh," Viviane said to no one and nothing. Then louder and with increased feeling, "Ohmygosh!"

A raven dropped from the top of one of the surrounding trees to land with a considerable flapping upon a nearby branch. "You ring for me, honey?"

Viviane took a deep breath and found she was smiling—a wan smile, or at least it felt wan. "I," she said fervently, "am very, *very* glad to see you, Nevermore."

"You got a bit of company there." Nevermore cocked his head, regarding her through one bright eye. "You need a nest?"

"A little house," Viviane explained. "A shack, a shed, a hut."

"Same thing."

"The idea is to make this kid Arthur think Myrddin's been living there. Vivien—the other one, the fairy—is going to bring furniture and stuff. My job's to build the house. The nest? Only I don't have anything to work with, and I wouldn't know how if I did."

"Got it." Nevermore spread his wings. "Right up my alley."

"You mean you'll help?" It seemed too good to be true.

"I mean I'm gonna take care of it, honey. First we got to do the Blessin' of the Flock. Stay right there."

Viviane did, watching the black bird as he threaded the moss-robed trees clanging like an iron bell, his deep and solemn croak echoing through the forest.

When he was out of sight and sound, and the forest hushed and hopeless once more, she sat down on a protruding root, put her head in her hands, and thought about home. About meals in her mother's bright kitchen. About lying on the rug in her room and doing homework to music. About cleaning Daisy's stall and bringing Daisy an apple. Her homework had been hard sometimes, and cleaning the stall was hard work always; but at that moment she would gladly have given her new saddle just to be home, with the stall dirty and a theme due in—

A little bird with a bright red breast had flown to the tree nearest her and perched on a twig to study her. It was followed almost at once, with a great deal of noise and commotion, by a flock of swans. These landed (badly) on the forest floor all around her. A pair of partridges came next, and after them a constant whir of wings and far too many birds to count.

The last to arrive was a great golden eagle. Its weight bent a limb just above her as it spread its wings like a canopy over her head.

"When I say down," Nevermore mumbled, "you kneel an' spread your wings like this. Got it?"

Viviane managed to nod.

"Receive now," he intoned, "the Blessin' of the Flock." At the final word, his voice became an urgent whisper: "*Down!*"

Viviane dropped to her knees and bowed her head, and spread her arms wide. The wings of every bird save the eagle were pointed toward her. "Receive the Blessing of the Flock!" was pronounced in a thousand ways by birds of a thousand kinds. Ravens croaked it. Crows cawed it. Warblers warbled it, and ducks quacked it. The swans—mute swans all—merely mouthed it, but gray geese from Iceland hissed it. It should have been a cacophony, and in a way it was. Yet there was a beauty there, the odd, hard beauty of wild things that need not be pretty to please nature (though they often are).

It was followed by a thunder of wings as every bird except Nevermore flew away.

"Now what?" Viviane rose, dusting her knees.

"Now you get your nest, honey." Nevermore preened himself. "We're good at it."

"What'll I owe you?" Once more, Viviane pulled the change from her pockets.

"Nothin'. You ain't used up your retainer yet, see?"

The first whirring of wings came even as he spoke. Eight or ten sparrows had returned, busy and quarreling, with tiny twigs and wisps of straw. After that, the house seemed to grow faster than any bird could fly. Now and then its walls appearing through a seething mass of beaks, claws, and feathers.

"It ain't bad," Nevermore opined, as a patient willow-wren added its finishing touch to the roof. "I coulda done better, only it woulda taken me a lot longer, see? Let's go in an' have a gander."

The door, a door of woven sticks, was standing open. Viviane entered and found she was treading on a carpet of hay, straw, down, and feathers. There were three rooms, each larger than she had expected, each accessible by an arch rather too small. Two boasted little round windows.

"Three openin's, get it?" Nevermore flapped up to land upon Viviane's shoulder. "Three openin's an' three rooms. Most of us can't count higher than that. Me, I can get into the twenties, only it's confusin' after that, so I just say a lot. Most times that does it. Three or twenty-three, they done the best they could. Like it?"

Slowly, Viviane nodded. "It really does look like a wizard might live here, doesn't it?"

"Sure. Like, he might get us to build it for him. Save him some work."

She nodded again. "Right. You're having a little fun with me, aren't you?"

"Me? No way!" Nevermore actually sounded sincere.

"You're allowed to have a little fun after what you've just done, so enjoy yourself. I don't think you could do anything that would make me mad after this."

"Got it, honey. Got it, an' same here. You can jerk my chain, just don't make me fall off my perch."

"In that case, I've got a question," Viviane said. "This isn't a fun question. It's perfectly serious. When all the birds came, I saw two brown hawks, kind of small and plain, but solid-looking."

"Sure. You want their names? I'll try to find out for you."

Viviane shook her head. "I just want to know what kind of hawks they were. Like Cooper's hawk or a red-tailed hawk? I know they weren't either of those, but they remind me of Myrddin, so I'd like to know what they are."

"Pigeon hawks," Nevermore told her. "Only say merlins when you talk to them. It's politer."

Suddenly the whole house was full of gauzy-winged people carrying stools or stepstools, shelves or seashells, tables, tablets, or trinkets, old books or bold banners or a hundred other things, each more miscellaneous than the last. "How do you like it so far?" Vivien asked. She was holding a big glass retort filled with green liquid that bubbled of itself.

"I like the house a lot," Viviane said, "and I hope you do to. But these . . . This clutter—my gosh!"

"The wooden snake?" Vivien positively grinned. "That is a bedpost. There are four, all different."

Nevermore's soft croak was almost soothing. "For the other four kinds, most likely. Birds, snakes, fish, and cats. Number five would be you, only he'll sleep in there, see? So that rounds out the five."

"It's a mess, just the same."

A cracked voice said, "A place for everything, and everything out of place is my rule, my dearest, dearest darling." The speaker was old and bent, his long gray beard nearly white. Advancing with the help of a contorted staff, he took her hand, holding it gently between his. "My lady of the lake," he whispered.

Viviane took a deep breath. "They told me you'd be old, so I expected that. But your eyes haven't changed. They haven't changed at all."

They embraced. No doubt there was a flurry of wings as Nevermore, Vivien, and her gauzy-winged friends departed; but Viviane did not hear it—or indeed, hear anything save his sighs and the pounding of her heart. He kissed her, and one small, hot tear (only one) coursed down her cheek. "Oh, Merlin. . . ." It was less than a whisper. "Oh, my own, my darling Merlin . . ."

When they separated at last, he said, "Sit down. Sit down, please, precious lady. Will you not? To make me happy? For as long as you stand, I shall think you about to desert me."

She did, choosing a small chair curiously carved.

"You're stricken, dear ageless lady of the lake, to see me as I am, a man of many years. I could grow young again before your eyes, but the transformation would be ultimately unreal, and—alas—but temporary. To make it real is past any power of mine. Past the powers of the kind lady I name Gwelliant, as well. And in all truth, lady, her powers are less than mine."

Viviane took a deep breath, drawing in a rich and nourishing atmosphere spiced by the forest and untainted by smoke. "Are you saying you can really, I mean really and truly, do magic with all this junk? I don't believe it!"

Merlin smiled, showing one broken tooth and several discolored ones. "That I am not, dearest lady. My powers are in me. You wish me dentures, and I know it. Watch."

He passed his hand across his mouth and smiled again. White teeth, nearly perfect, gleamed in his dark face. "I have two sets, you see, my lady. Not two sets of false teeth, as you think, but two of true teeth. These are my own, as the others were. And I may display either, as I choose. I have other parts as well, doubled and tripled in a few cases. I cannot display them for you because they are within me, but with them I may do many things. All this . . ." A wave of his hand took in the books, the strange instruments of science, and even the stuffed crocodile hung from his ceiling. "Is but stage dressing."

Tapping his forehead with a long forefinger, he added, "The magic's here. As it always is. Now then. Do you wish to see me change my shape? Or do you wish to change yours, for an hour? We've a bit of time, Gwelliant tells me, ere Arthur comes."

"I . . . Well, I—I'd like to be a bird. A—a dove. Can you do that?"

Viviane did not change at all—or so she felt; but the cozy room of sticks swelled to theater size, and the curiously carved chair on whose seat she perched was far larger than the dining-room table at home.

You are a dove, my dearest.

The voice in her mind emanated from the compact brown bird on the other side of the vast room. She knew that, and did not wonder how she knew, or even how she had been changed. She was a—she had forgotten the word. Still she could fly, and wanted to. Spreading white wings, she fluttered through the doorway.

The brown bird flew after her, far more swiftly than she. *I am a merlin. I won't harm you, but guard yourself if you see another like me.*

Not harm, she thought. Not harm. She flew into a tree, leaving the pile of sticks behind. Landing upon a another stick there, she nearly fell. Once she caught her breath, she would fly high.

The sky was still wide and blue, though the sun was low. Up she flew, and learned to fly by flying.

There are eagles. There are many hawks. Better to hide among the trees. It was the brown bird.

The sky grew darker. When an owl swooped toward her, the brown bird flew at it, keening, talons wide. The owl veered away. *Lower. Follow me.*

Reluctantly, she did.

Lower! On the ground!

The brown bird had vanished.

Down here! Before you die!

She landed, and found herself—found Viviane, in her boots and jeans and denim shirt—crouching on the floor of an ancient forest.

As she stood, a small man with a long gray beard laid a hand upon her shoulder. "Arthur has not yet come, but we must return to my cottage before he does."

She nodded, and as they walked side by side, her hand found his. "It was wonderful," she whispered. "Not as wonderful as I had expected, but wonderful just the same. Thank you."

"You may find yourself a dove again," he told her. "Be careful. Earth or running water will make you think yourself as you are now, and you'll be yourself once more. Have I made that clear?"

"I think so." She spoke so softly that she had to repeat it.

"If you think yourself as you are now when you are high, you will change and fall a long way. Take care."

"And stay low," she murmured. "Sure."

"It will be truly wonderful," he said, "when we are together at last. I will be older then, but being with you will make me grow younger."

Slowly, she nodded. "I heard about that."

"I've years to wait and work." His hand tightened on hers. "I'll work and wait full of joy, knowing what's to come."

The little woman with gauzy wings was waiting for them at the hut of sticks the birds had built for Viviane. "Hello!" she called.

"Hello, Gwelliant," Viviane said. "Do you mind if I use your real name? I like that better."

"You may call me that," the little woman told her, "but we have no real names. Only unreal ones, like Vivien and Gwelliant."

"No real names?"

The little, gauzy-winged woman shook her head. "We don't need them. There aren't many of us left, you see."

"When you were bringing in the books and the round thing with all the pointers it seemed like there were an awful lot of you."

"No." The gauzy wings, drooping already, drooped further. "That was all. Our whole population, and you saw some of us three and four times. We would bring something and look for something else, perhaps for days. When we got it, we would return to the time when we brought the first, and bring that, too. We are very few."

Viviane nodded to herself. "Every time a child says, 'I don't believe in fairies,' a fairy dies. I read that somewhere."

"We are not really fairies either, Viviane. We are—There is no time. Here we are and you must act for us."

"I'm getting really, really tired of it. Is this the last time? Before Merlin and I get together for all those years?"

"Two, but they will be done in five minutes if only you will do them. Stand there."

It was a fairy ring.

"There will be a lake all about you, but you will not get wet. Soon, Arthur will throw his sword into the water. You must catch it without cutting yourself, so take it by . . ."

A fish swam past Viviane, and she did not hear the rest. Looking up, she could see the shimmer of waves. It was broken, as someone flung something long and heavy into it.

It was a sword bigger than she had ever imagined a sword might be, and as it sank by her she snatched its hilt, wetting her hand.

"Good." The little woman's voice sounded in Viviane's ear. "You must not bring it back. It is steel and would distort the field. Feel at your feet. The scabbard is there."

Viviane did. "It's beautiful! Can you hear me? It's really lovely, and all set with jewels."

"We made it." The voice was more remote than as ever. "Thank you for your praise. Pour out all the water, please, before you sheathe the sword."

Water and mud, Viviane thought, but the water that came forth from the mouth of the scabbard sparkled and shone, a river of tiny diamonds. When the last was gone, she sheathed the sword.

"One more, please, Viviane. One more, my dear friend, and all your tasks are done. You will have saved us then—and yourself, too. Yourself, your family, and all you hold dear. Count to five and hold the sword above the water. Let Arthur take it. And that is the end."

When the sword was gone and the lake with it, Viviane stepped from the ring. Walls of stone rose block by block in the distance, higher and higher as she looked. Flowers sprang up at her feet. Not far away, a fountain played. As she walked toward the fountain, a great white tower rose behind it, lifting its proud head until it was far above the tallest trees. A moment more, and crows flew around it—no, black birds too large for crows.

She found him sitting on a marble bench, watching his fountain with rheumy eyes. "You're young still." It was an old man's cracked voice, "I'm old, and Arthur sleeps. *Hic Iacet Sepultus Inclitus Rex Arturius in Insula Avalonia*. I dare not sleep, dearest Viviane. Not yet. And so this." He patted the bench. "Come, sit beside me."

She sat, trying not to sit primly.

"You will not be eager of my kisses," the old man said.

Viviane whispered, "You're wrong."

He seemed not to have heard. "Never fear. Never fear, my darling, you will not have to endure them. Nor these, my words, if you do not wish to. You need not listen, but I must speak."

She nodded. "And I'll listen. I'll listen to all you say, Merlin."

"The Table Round is sundered. Arthur lies with his queen, while its lesser knights war one upon another. Camelot will soon fall to the pagans. All is lost." He sighed. "Except the dream. The dream lives in fireside tales and the musings of plowmen. It must not die. Men everywhere must know that once there was a time of justice, when brave men bent the knee to God and sallied against a dark and evil world. When brave men came forth to do what was right because it was right, though they risked life and lands."

"I know one," Viviane said.

"You're fortunate." That man's palsied hand found hers and clasped it. "I must wait and watch, touching many though I cannot be touched. I must see to it that the flame burns still, however faint, however smoky its light."

He fell silent. Viviane waited.

"You need not linger with me, O Lady of the Lake. You need not, nor will I force you. But I hope . . . I—I wish, please, dear lady . . . I wish . . ."

"Your wish is granted," Viviane told him. "I'll stay."

WHEN it was over, when all the flying years of shared happiness had flown at last, a small woman with gauzy wings guided Viviane back to the spring into which she had once dipped her bandana. "You have helped save us," the small woman said. "We will always be grateful to you."

Viviane nodded absently. "What's your name? I'm sure I used to know it."

"Yes, you did. It is the same as your own. I am Vivien."

"I remember." There was a great deal to remember, and Viviane knew she would never be able to remember it all.

"Do you also remember that I told you we were few? You said that each time a child said, 'I will not believe in fairies,' a fairy died."

"Did I really say that?" Viviane smiled.

"Yes, you did, and in a way it is true." Vivien seated herself on a small stone beside the pool. "We are your future, Viviane, just as we are the future of Arthur's Britons, and of Myrddin's whole family—of his brother's descendants, his sisters' descendants, and his own. If the people of Arthur's day were to stop believing in beautiful things and trying to make them come true, we would perish, becoming less and less probable until we winked out. If the people of your day ever stop, it will be the same."

"I'm going to have to think about this," Viviane said. "Why are you so little, and why do you have wings?"

"We were more once," Vivien explained; her gauzy wings rose in joy as she spoke. "So many that we crowded Earth. We did not want the plants and animals to die to make room for us, so we made ourselves smaller and smaller. When we had become as small as I am, we realized we could fly, if only we had wings. So we gave ourselves these. See them?"

"I certainly do. It's wonderful to fly, isn't it?"

Vivien nodded and rose into the air, her gauzy wings a blur of motion.

"I did it once. He made me a white dove, and I flew." Viviane looked into the pool at the reflection of her own lined face. "I'd be a gray dove now, I suppose."

There was no reply. The small Vivien with gauzy wings had gone.

Viviane sighed, examined her reflection once more, and looked at the thin, blue veins on the backs of her hands. Talking to herself as she sometimes did now, she said, "I suppose I'm sixty. Or older . . . I should've marked the years, but it would . . . I felt . . ."

"You look good, honey."

"Nevermore!"

"Sure. Unless you mean you don't never want to see me again. I ain't easy to get rid of."

Viviane stared, and nodded at last. " 'And the Raven, never flitting, still is sitting, still is sitting, on the pallid bust of Pallas just above my chamber door.' We read that in school."

Nevermore bobbed his head. "Pretty, ain't it?"

"I hadn't thought of it like that, but yes, I suppose it is. The thing that I don't understand, the part I don't understand at all, isn't that raven. It's you, Nevermore. You're a magic animal. He's gone back to his mother—I took him . . ." She wept.

Nevermore waited patiently until she dried her eyes. "You took him back. You did the right thing, honey. You knew it was, and you did it. That's not somethin' to cry over."

"He's gone, and that little woman is, too. So there shouldn't be more magic animals. Not any, including you."

"I got some teachin' to do." Nevermore cocked his head, regarding her

321

through one bright eye. "Only I don't teach for free. How 'bout that pretty watch you got?"

"This?" Viviane glanced at the pink watch—1:27. "It's stopped. It's been stopped for years. I don't know why I put it on this morning."

"Don't matter," Nevermore told her. "I want it."

"Then you can have it." She took it off and held it out. "Will you answer questions for me? For this?"

"You bet I will, honey." Nevermore's bill closed on the strap. He backed away before transferring it to a claw. "Soon's I take it to the bank. It ain't far, and I'll be right back."

She shook her head. "I'm not comfortable here. I don't know why, but I'm not. I know I'm back in my own time. The fairy—I mean that little woman with wings—told me so. I'm uncomfortable just the same, maybe just because I was so happy until today." She looked around, trying to recall the direction from which she had come so long ago.

"That way, honey." Nevermore pointed with one wing. "Go that way, and you'll get out quick. Don't worry about me, I'll catch up."

When he had gone, she walked in the direction he had indicated. She was old now. Old, and there would be no pension for her, no Social Security. Would she starve? It didn't matter, she decided. Her life was over, and she would be better off dead. The world might be right now, as the small woman said; but she was not right for the world, and knew it. How happy they'd been, once upon a time. . . .

"Okay, honey." Nevermore swooped past her head to crash-land on a limb not far ahead. "You got questions? I got answers. Not for everythin', but lots of answers just the same. Whatcha wanna know?"

"I should've been thinking of questions while you were gone." Confronted by her negligence, she felt foolish and helpless. "I didn't, I was woolgathering. What questions would you ask if you were me?"

Nevermore balanced upon one leg to scratch his head. "You said you didn't get it about magic animals. Maybe you could ask about that."

"All right." For a moment Viviane bent her head in thought. "That little woman I assumed was a fairy is gone. Merlin was a great and powerful wizard; but he was a little boy the last time I saw him, and anyway he's gone, too. But you are . . . Well, you know what I mean. Why?"

"I've got clearer questions than that now an' then, honey. So what I'm goin' to do is say it my way. Then I'll answer. You're sayin' there's two of us here an' one's a magic animal. How come? Ain't that it?"

"Fine," Viviane said.

"It's 'cause you're here, that's all. You're the magic animal, honey. Not me. You can turn yourself into a bird. You think I can turn myself into a girl? I can't. I can't build a fire or open a door. I like shiny stuff, just like you. Only I can't make it. I have to find 'em or steal 'em or bargain for 'em like I did. That shirt you're wearin'? I like the buttons, but I can't button 'em. Or unbutton 'em neither."

"I don't believe I follow this."

"Well, try. It ain't tough. Humans are the magic animal, the only one there is. Ask your horse or any dog you run into. You got a cat?"

Viviane nodded.

"Cats catch birds, and there ain't much we can do about it except fly. Suppose they were tryin' to catch you instead. How long you think they'd last?"

"You said I could turn myself into a bird." Viviane looked thoughtful. "I didn't do that. Merlin turned us both into birds."

"He gave you that shape, honey."

"That's what I said."

"So you can use it if you really want to. Once a wizard gives somebody a shape, she owns it. Get me? Like, if he'd given you the things you got on your feet. Once he gave 'em, they'd be yours. You could wear 'em or take 'em off, see?"

"You're saying I can be a bird again if I want to."

"Right."

"This—it used to be a drawing-in wood. Daisy told me." Viviane paused, feeling the wood's rejection. "It isn't anymore, or not for me. If I were a bird, I could get out quicker."

"Sure."

"Then I'd like to be one. Why aren't I?"

"Maybe it's because you got too much sense, honey." Nevermore studied her before he spoke again. "You're goin' to need somebody who knows his way around. You're goin' to need somebody like that bad. I'll do it, only you got to do like I say."

"I will."

"Okay. Stick with me. I ain't goin' to chase you. Fly down below me, all the time. Don't ever get as high as I am. You goin' to do that, honey?"

Viviane nodded. "I'll do whatever you tell me to."

"I'm not goin' to tell you anythin' except what I just did. Look up at the sky, okay. Now close your eyes, but keep on seein' the sky when you do. Spread your wings. . . .

"Now *go!*"

She did, and opened her eyes again as soon as she was on the wing. The black bird rose through the trees until it was higher than the treetops, and she with it.

There was the mountain, with the wood on its flank. There was the trail, a yellow-brown thread winding among the hills. And there—

Someone was hurt or dead, sprawled beside the trail. The black bird had seen it, too, and shot ahead of her, lower and swifter with every beat of its wings. She followed it, knowing it was the right thing to do, though she could not remember why. Here a silver thread crossed the trail—the creek, of course. The black bird was across it already, lower and lower. And she—

Was a wingless girl, hurtling through the air.

THE roar was not just the rush of her blood in her ears. Bruised and aching, she sat up and saw her mother's ATV raising a dust plume as it sped along the trail. Her voice was gone, but there was a damp red bandana about her neck. She took it off and waved it.

"Are you all right, Viv?" Her mother bent over her, and her mother's fear lent a tremor to her mother's voice. "Daisy came home without you, and I've been worried sick."

"I don't know." Viviane cleared her throat and spat. "I—you recognized me, Mom?"

"Of course I recognized you!"

"I don't have a compact. Can I see yours?"

"Your face is bruised, Viv." Her mother sounded more worried than ever. "I wouldn't—"

Viviane spat again. "I don't want your makeup, Mom. I just want to see it."

A badly bruised girl of fourteen stared back at her out of the powder-dusty mirror.

Snapping the compact closed, Viviane returned it and struggled to her feet. "I've got a crazy question. Will you answer, please? Even if it's crazy."

"Yes. Anything."

Viviane held out her right arm. "Am I still wearing that pink watch Dad got for me?"

"It must have come off when you fell," her mother said. "We can look for it later."

"Don't bother," Viviane said. "I never did like it much."

Her mother had begun to search already. "Here's your Swiss Army knife." She waved it triumphantly.

"I think I'm short a quarter. Don't bother to look for that either." Viviane was scanning the trees at the edge of the wood. She accepted the shiny red knife and flung it to the black bird perched there. "Here you go," she called, "and thanks!"

ON the third day of the new school year, sitting in the cafeteria with Joan, she froze.

Joan tried to follow her eyes. "What's the matter, Viv?"

Viviane put down her fork and pointed. "That guy. The little one."

"Him? That's Joe—"

"Never mind." Viviane motioned her to silence. "It doesn't matter what you call him. I know his real name."

She jumped to her feet and waved. "Merlin! Over here! It's me, Viviane!"

The dark, slender boy whirled, eyes wide and bright with hope.

Stonefather

ORSON SCOTT CARD

Orson Scott Card began publishing in 1977, and by 1978 had won the John W. Campbell Award as best new writer of the year. By 1986, his famous novel Ender's Game, *one of the best-known and bestselling SF novels of the eighties, won both the Hugo and the Nebula Award; the next year, his novel* Speaker for the Dead, *a sequel to* Ender's Game, *also won both awards, the only time in SF history that a book and its sequel have taken both the Hugo and Nebula Awards in sequential years. He won a World Fantasy Award in 1987 for his story "Hatrack River," the start of his long Prentice Alvin series, and another Hugo in 1988 for his novella "Eye for Eye." His many short stories have been collected in* Cardography, Tales from the Mormon Sea, Unaccompanied Sonata and Other Stories, The Folk of the Fringe, The Elephants of Posnan and Other Stories, First Meetings: Four Stories from the Enderverse, *and the massive* Maps in a Mirror: The Short Fiction of Orson Scott Card. *His many novels include* Ender's Shadow, Shadow of the Hegemon, Shadow Puppet, Hot Sleep, A Planet Called Treason, Songmaster, Hart's Hope, Wyrms, Seventh Son, Red Prophet, Prentice Alvin, Alvin Journeyman, Heartfire, The Crystal City, The Call of Earth, Earthborn, Earthfall, Homebody, The Memory of Earth, Treason, Xenocide, *and* Children of the Mind. *As editor, he has produced* Dragons of Light, Dragons of Darkness, Future on Ice, Future on Fire, *and* Masterpieces: The Best Science Fiction of the Century. *His most recent books are the novels* Magic Street *and* Shadow of the Giant. *Card lives in Greensboro, North Carolina, with his family.*

In the vivid and compulsively readable story that follows, pure storytelling at its very best (which takes place in the same fantasy world as the Mithermages series, the first novel of which is coming from Del Rey in early 2008), he introduces us to a boy born in poverty who has nothing but his own wits and native abilities to count on in order to survive in an indifferent and even hostile world—and who ends up using those abilities in ways that will not only change his own life, but the lives of everyone else around him.

WHEN Runnel was born, he was given a watername even though there had never been a wetwizard in the family.

In the old days such names were given only to those babies as would be sacrificed to Yeggut, the water god. Later, such names were given to those who would live to serve as priests to Yeggut. Still later, wetnames went to children of families that pretended they once had a watermage in their ancestry.

But now, in the village of Farzibeck, wetnames were given because the mother was fond of a nearby brooklet or because the father had a friend with such a name. This close to Mitherhome, the great city of watermages, it was no surprise that waternames were more popular than any others, even among rude peasants.

Runnel was born to be the rudest of them all, the ninth son and fifteenth child of a farmwife who had the gift of conceiving children readily and bearing them as if her loins were a streambed and each baby a spring flood. Mother had the wide and heavy hips of a woman whose body had reconciled itself to perpetual pregnancy, yet her cheery smile and patient temper still drew men to her more than her husband wished.

Runnel had the misfortune of looking like neither of his parents, so perhaps Father had dark suspicions about the boy's siring. What other explanation could there be for the way Father pointedly ignored him, whenever he wasn't cuffing him or berating him for the constant infraction of being an unloved boy who persisted in existing.

Runnel wasn't especially good at anything, and he wasn't especially bad at anything. He learned the work of a hardscrabble mountain-country farming village as quickly as most, but no quicker; he played the games of children as vigorously as any and enjoyed them as much, but no more. He was too ordinary for anyone to notice him, except that his brothers and sisters could not help but pick up Father's disdain for him, so that he had to fight a bit harder to keep his place when they lined up for food from the stewpot that Mother kept simmering by the fire.

Mother liked him well enough—she liked all her children—but she called them all by each other's names and didn't know enough numbers to take a census and notice when one or two were missing.

Runnel took all these things as his lot in life—he knew nothing else. He flung himself out the door and into whatever day the world presented to him, and came home stinking of sweat from whatever work or play had taken up his hours.

His only distinction, if one could call it that, was that he was a fearless climber of rocks. There was no shortage of cliffs and crags in the vicinity. The children grew up knowing all the grassy paths and steps that allowed them to climb wherever they wanted, with no unusual effort and danger.

But Runnel was impatient with circuitous, gentle routes, and when they all went to play king of the hill or just to look out from one of the lesser crags that overlooked their whole valley, Runnel would go straight up the cliff face, his fingers probing for creases and cracks and ledges and ridges in the stone. He always found them, sooner rather than later—though what was the point, since he rarely reached the pinnacle before anyone else?

His older siblings called him stupid and warned him that they'd refuse to pick up his broken body when it fell. "We'll just leave you for the vultures and the rats to eat." But since he never fell from the cliff, they had no chance to take out their spite on his corpse.

It could have gone on like this forever.

When he reached the age that might have been twelve, if anyone bothered counting, Runnel began to get his man-height, and his face took on the shape it would bear throughout his life. Not that *he* ever saw it—no water in that sloping land held still long enough to see reflections, and he wouldn't have bothered anyway.

Two things happened.

Runnel began to take notice of the village girls, and realized that *they* took no notice of him, though they had eyes for all the other boys of his height. They neither flirted with Runnel nor taunted him. He simply didn't exist to them.

And Father began to be more brutal in his beatings. Perhaps Father thought he finally recognized who Runnel's real sire must have been. Or perhaps he simply recognized that mere cuffings were nothing to Runnel now and it would take more serious effort to explain to him just how despised he was. Whatever the motive, Runnel continued to bear it, though now there were always bruises, and sometimes there was blood.

He could bear the disdain of the village girls—many a man had found his bride in another village. He could bear the pain of his father's blows.

What he could not bear and did not understand was the way his brothers and sisters began to avoid him. Father's constant seething rage against him had apparently marked him in their eyes as someone different and shameful. Their father could not be unjust; therefore, Runnel must deserve the mistreatment. The other children did not strike him—it would have been redundant—but they began excluding him from things and playing mean pranks on him.

On a certain day in early spring, when it was still cold, and old snow lay in all northern shadows, the children took it into their minds to run like a flock of geese for the steepest of the crags they were wont to climb, and as Runnel began his own separate ascent, he somehow knew that this was a joke, that when he got to the top he would be all alone, while the others were off somewhere else.

Yet he continued to climb, thinking: I'm too old to play these games, anyway. I should spend my time like the older boys, lounging around or wrestling near the stream, where the girls came to fetch water, and gape and jape and *try* to draw their smiles or, failing that, their disdain or mockery.

But if he tried, then it would shame him and hurt him if they still paid him no attention. Besides, he didn't think any of the village girls were interesting. He didn't care if they noticed him. And he didn't care that when he got to the top of the crag he was all alone.

The world spread out before him. Mountains were all around, but so high was their valley that this crag was merely one among many, and he could see far and wide over the shoulders of the neighboring peaks.

He saw the pass that led over the Mitherkame—for in Farzibeck they had other names for the other mountains, and only used the sacred name for the great spine of mountains that lined up in a long row like the ragged teeth of a fighting sword—sharp obsidian flakes jutting from between the two halves of a split branch.

The track that crossed it between two of its sharp teeth was called "the Utteroad" if you went west toward Uhetter, and "the Mitheroad" if you went east. That path, the travelers said, would take you down to the great valley of Mitherhome, the city of the water wizards, which was surrounded on all sides by holy water.

On the pass, Runnel could see a wagon moving up the grassy road, though it was so far off that he only knew it to be a wagon because of how slowly and lurchingly it moved. And maybe he could see the animal pulling it, or maybe it was just a blur in the cold sunlight.

He thought, Why am I here, when I could be there?

And with no more contemplation than that, he climbed down the crag on the side toward the Mitheroad, and did not even pass through the village, still less come near the family farm, on his way through the meadows and fields and woods. He came to the Mitheroad just as it began its last ascent over the Mitherkame, and ran easily up the grassy path.

Only when he stood at the very spot where he had seen the wagon did he stop and look back toward Farzibeck. Runnel had never been to this place before, and had never looked at his village from so far away. It took him a considerable time even to find it. As for his family's farm, it was just a brown lump of a hovel in the midst of a meadow. In a week or so, Father would start to break up the earth with his son-drawn plow, and then the meadow would disappear, and bare earth would take its place. But right now, the farm looked no different from countless meadows and clearings. It was as if all their work there amounted to nothing.

I'm hungry, thought Runnel, and he turned away from the vista to search for wild onion and crumbleroot. It was standard spring fare, to help eke out what was left of the winter stores, but of course the travelers now moving along the road would have taken much if not all of the scavenge-able food.

Yet he found plenty to eat, as soon as he started to look, and wondered if this was because crumble and onion grew so thick that it outgrew the travelers' taking, or because the travelers were laboring so hard to get up and over the pass that they did not think of food when they came to the crest.

Or maybe they disdained the biting onion and the bitter crumble. Many did. Mother would add them to the stew in spring, and even though Runnel thought they added a delicious tang, some of his brothers complained that they poisoned the whole thing and made them want to vomit. They never *did* vomit, however, and Mother got them to eat without complaint by saying that crumble was medicinal and would make better swordsmen of them. How they laughed at Runnel, when he was little, for asking when they would start practicing with their swords, now that they had eaten the stew with crumble in it.

Runnel dug up five good-sized crumbleroots and a dozen small onions, used grass to wipe off the dirt as best he could, and then made a basket of his shirtfront in order to hold them. Tying the shirt closed brought it well above his waist, so his middle got cold in the nippy air, even though it was high noon. But better to be cold than hungry, for vigorous walking would make him warmer *and* hungrier by day's end. He'd feel foolish, perhaps, if nightfall brought him to a place with plenty of food to scavenge; but better to carry food he didn't need than to be without it in some lonely stretch of unfamiliar wood, where he would not know which berries and mushrooms were safe to eat, and so have to spend the night with nothing in his belly.

The other side of the pass showed him a world not much different from the side he lived on, except that the peaks in front of him were lower than those behind. As the day wore on, and he walked down one slope and up another, the peaks ceased to be snow-covered. Finally, the road stopped being a track in the thick grass of an endless meadow and became a wide, flat, and gravelly ledge cut from the hills by the labor of men, flanking a stream deep and swift enough that it might have been a river, had there been room enough for one in the narrow valley. The water tumbled around boulders and roared over short but savage falls, so Runnel stayed well clear of the road's edge, for he had no fear of falling from rock, but this water had power that he did not understand.

No wonder the great mages drew their power from water. It was mighty in a way that the mountains could never be. For the water might be smaller, but it was vigorous, while the mountains always seemed to be resting or even asleep. What good was it to be a giant if you never stirred, while small waters raced across your body, cutting canyons in your stony flesh?

And yet it was the mountains that he loved, the roughness and hardness of their bones where they protruded from the soil, and it was the water that he feared. How silly to fear the thing for which you were named, he told himself. I wish they had named me Cobble or Pebble or Rock or Boulder or Crag or Ledge or any other word referring to stone. Then perhaps Father would never have beaten me, for what man would dare to strike stone?

He came to a place where the road veered away from the river and went up and over a hill. But he could hear a roaring sound and had to see, so he left the road and climbed the rocks high above the river until he came to a place where the rock simply stopped.

It was like the edge of one world and the beginning of another. Here he was, as he had always been, in the hard high stoneland of the Mitherkame; there, far below, was a land of soft greens and rolling hills, surrounding the Mitherlough, a huge lake that, for all Runnel knew, could have been the great Sea itself, where Skruplek the Sailor had all the adventures that were told about on winter evenings when the short days left them in darkness long before they were sleepy.

The river flew out from the cliff top and fell into mist that clung like a shy cloud to the cliff's face. Beyond, the great expanse of fields was dotted with houses, all of them obviously larger than his family's hovel; and the villages were far more populous than the few wooden houses of Farzibeck.

Only after he had been looking for some few minutes did he realize that the rocky mount at the right-hand side of the lake was lined with the stone-and-wooden buildings, right to the crest, and high stone walls rose above the treetops in the wild forest that stretched between him and the Mitherlough. It was the city of Mitherhome.

He could see now where the road he had been following emerged from the mountains, far to the right of where he stood, winding its way around the forest and down below the lake, as if it meant to miss the city entirely. That was no good to him. Maybe it joined a road that came back up to the city, and maybe it didn't. But he wouldn't take the chance. It was the city he wanted, and to the city he would go, road or no road.

He swung himself over the cliff edge and began climbing down. It was always harder to descend an unfamiliar cliff; his feet had to find gaps and cracks and ledges that his eyes had never seen. But he did all right, and it took him far less time to get to the bottom of the cliff than it would have taken him to follow the road.

The trouble was that no one else ever used this route, so there was not so much as a path. Which was particularly annoying because the waterfall made so thick a fog at the bottom that he could not see more than a step ahead. But he found a place where a finger of stone spread from the cliff like the root from a tree, and where the stone grew, the trees couldn't, so he made his way easily for some time.

By the time the last of the stone finger plunged under the soil, the air was clear again, and he could see. Not that the trees left him much view, they were so thick; but now he could find deer paths and, as long as he kept within earshot of the tumbling river to his left, he knew he would not lose his way.

Still, it was slow going, and the sun was getting low—no more than two palms above the horizon, he estimated—when he came to the stone wall he had seen from the top of the cliff.

Now he saw that the wall was in ruins. He had thought the wall rose and fell with the terrain, but instead the land was fairly level, and the stone wall had simply collapsed—or been torn down. There was nowhere near enough stone to account for the gaps in the wall. He could only conclude that people had come here and carted away the huge cut stones that were once part of the wall.

The sky was red with sunset when he came to the end of his path. For instead of leading him up to the mount where the city perched, as it had seemed from the cliff top, the river took him to an arm of the lake. Across the water he could see there were torchlights in the city and along what had to be stone bridges spanning the gaps through which water poured from the larger lake beyond into this smaller one.

There was no bridge across *this* river, though. And Runnel, having never seen so much water, also had no notion of swimming; he knew the word only as something fish and geese did. The water of Farzibeck was too cold, shallow, and swift for anything but a barefoot splash in summer; the rest of the time, they used staves to leap the few streams too wide to step over.

Knowing he could not go north, he walked south along the edge of the lake and came to a stone tower. This was not in ruins—indeed, it was surrounded by a goat-trimmed meadow, and the wide stone steps that led from the tower down to the lake were swept clean. Yet no light shone from the tower, and when Runnel thought of calling out to hail anyone who might be inside, it occurred to him that he did not know this place, and perhaps the reason that there were no paths in this wood was that the place was forbidden. For now he saw that this tower was a giant version of the small altars that were erected beside every stream in the vicinity of Farzibeck. What else could he have expected? Such large waters cried out for giant altars—for stone towers like this one.

He realized it was a tower of living stone, all of one piece, as if it had been carved from a natural crag that once stood here—it had not been stacked up from pebbles or cobbles like most little altars.

Runnel moved on along the lakeshore until he came to a place where the lake poured out onto a tumble of stone and down into a steep-walled canyon. There was no crossing here, either. No wonder the huge stone wall behind him had been left to fall in ruins. What need had Mitherhome of a city wall on this side? No enemy could cross this barrier.

Yet on the other side of the rapids more walls stood, even higher than the ones he had passed before, though also with ruined gaps, and undefended. Once this city had felt the need of walls despite the water barrier that protected them. Now, though, they did not, or the walls would not be left in disrepair.

Well, it hardly mattered how permeable the walls beyond this canyon were, for he could not cross it. There was nowhere to go except along its edge to see if it was bridged somewhere.

As soon as he thought of bridges, he saw that it had once been bridged right here. Runnel could still see, in the waning light, the nubs of the bridge that had once spanned the chasm. As best he could tell, the bridge had been like the tower—all of a piece, not made of piled stone or wood. Yet it had broken somehow, and fallen, and Runnel could imagine that some of the boulders over which the water tumbled in the rapids below had once been part of the bridge.

It was growing dark. And though it was warmer here in the wide valley of Mitherhome than it had been up in the high mountains, it was still chilly and would get colder through the night.

And for the first time all day, Runnel thought: What am I doing here? Why have I come? What do I want? I could have been home, warm in the pile of brothers and sisters on the straw floor of our hovel. Not stuck between two rivers and a lake, in an abandoned forest, in sight of ruined walls, with a great city out of reach.

Even if I get to the city, I have no friends or kin there. No one will owe me a meal or a place by the fire.

Tomorrow I'll go back through the forest and climb up the cliff and follow the road home.

Then he thought of his father beating him for having stayed out a whole night, and for coming home weary and empty-handed. "What are you good for?" his father would ask.

"Nothing," Runnel would answer. And it would be true.

The story of his useless journey would quickly spread, and the girls who already ignored him would despise him. He would have even less honor than the none he already had.

He could be friendless and cold here as well as anywhere. And tomorrow I'll find a way into the city.

He untied his shirt and methodically chewed and swallowed the crumbleroot, adding a bite of onion now and then to take away the bitterness. It was not good food, especially because his own body heat and sweat had made it all just a little soggy. But it filled him. He thought of saving some for tomorrow, but he knew the insects would have it before dawn, and he needed his shirt for warmth. He could go a day or two without food if he had to. He'd done it before, in a long winter, when the older children ate nothing at some meals so the little ones wouldn't go without. And other times, when he could not face a cuffing from his father, Runnel would skip his supper and ask for no food when he came in late. Nor, on those occasions, had there been some favorite brother or sister who saved him something.

He hollowed a place for himself among the cold damp fallen leaves near the cliff edge, so he lay on stone, and gathered more leaves to pull on top of himself where he curled on the ground. Others sought soil to sleep on, when they were caught out of doors, but to Runnel, the stone might be cold, but it wasn't damp, and it never left him sore and filthy the way soil did.

At this lower elevation it did not get as cold at night. He slept warmly enough that during the night he cast off some of the leaves that covered him.

In the morning he had nothing to eat, and he could hear few birds through the din of the rapids just over the edge of the cliff. But he had slept well and arose invigorated, and today he did not even think of turning back. Instead he went to the right, mostly southward, skirting the edge of the cliff. The water tumbled farther and farther below, so that even though the ground he walked on sloped downward, it was ever higher above the water.

He came to a wall, which he recognized as a continuation of the ruined wall he had passed through yesterday. Only this wall was not in ruins, and he could hear conversation; it was manned, and though the guards were careless enough to let their chatter be heard, the fact that anyone was keeping vigil meant that there must be something ahead of him that needed guarding.

There was no door or break in the wall here, so there was no point in hailing the guards. Instead, Runnel walked along the woods well back from the wall, looking for a gate.

It was a huge thing, when he reached it, and it was held shut by huge bars. It baffled him: The bars were on his side of the gate. He was *inside* whatever it was protecting. In the middle of the gate was a small door, which a man would have to stoop to get through. But it had the great virtue of being open.

Runnel headed for it. Almost at once he was seized by the shoulder and roughly tripped.

"Where do you think you're going, fool?" said a soft voice.

Runnel rolled over and saw a man standing over him, holding a javelin. Not a soldier, though, for the javelin was his only weapon, and he wore only simple cloth. A hunter? "Through the gate," said Runnel. Where else would he be going?

"And have your throat slit and all your blood drained into the river?" asked the hunter.

Runnel was baffled. "Who would do such a thing to a mere traveler?"

"No one," said the hunter. "It would be done to a fool of a boy who wandered through the sacred forest, thus declaring himself to be a sacrifice, and a right worthy one, in the eyes of them as still think that water needs blood from time to time."

"How would *I* know it was sacred?" asked Runnel.

"Didn't you feel the bones of the dead among the trees? The soldiers who fell here to the bronze swords of Veryllydd still whisper to *me*—I don't forget the blood that made this place holy. But the beasts I hunt for the sacrifice are like you—they don't know it's a sacred wood. They're going about their business when I snare them or pierce them."

"Are you going to kill me, then?"

"I was asked for two hares, and so I'll find hares and bring them. If they asked for a stupid peasant boy from the mountains, *then* I'd truss you up and drag you in."

"All I want is—"

"All you want is to be another useless adventurous lad from the mountains who'll make himself a nuisance to everyone in the city until you give up and go back home where you belong. There's nothing for you here."

"Then I *am* home," said Runnel defiantly, "for home has always been a place with nothing for me."

The hunter smiled a little. "A sharp wit. With that mouth, and that proud look on your face, you'll probably get beaten to death before you starve."

Proud look? How could he look proud, lying on his back in the dirt and old leaves? "Either way," said Runnel, "I'd like to spend some of the brief time I have left inside the city of Mitherhome, but all I find is broken walls and broken bridges and rivers I can't cross."

The man sighed. "Here's what you do if you're determined to suffer more before you go home. There's another gate farther along. *Don't* go near it. Nor should you go near the four houses that are just inside the gate. Skirt wide around them and go on in sight of the wall till you come to a place where the wall is broken down. Go through the gap, then head straight south till you come to the Uhetter Road. Try to act like you just left the road to take a piss and you've been traveling on it all day, instead of traipsing through the holy wood."

"Will the road take me into Mitherhome?" asked Runnel.

"The road will just sit there," said the hunter. "Your legs will take you to Hetterferry, and from there maybe you will and maybe you won't figure out a way to get onto the ferryboat and into Low Mitherhome without your miserable country bumpkin rags getting too wet."

Runnel was curious. "Why are you helping me?"

"I'm not helping you. I'm getting rid of you."

"But I've stepped in the sacred wood."

"I live in it. If the spirits of the sacred dead minded your passage, they would have tripped you with their bones or terrified you with their whispers, and they chose not to. Who am *I* to complain of you?"

"So you serve Yeggut, the water god, and yet you allow me to live?"

"There *is* no water god," said the hunter kindly. "I'm employed by the priests who put on the sacrifices to please the ignorant people who *think* there's a water god. Anyone with even a scrap of sense knows that the watermages do their work, not by praying to some god, but by speaking directly to the water itself."

"So . . . doesn't that make the water a god?"

"It makes the water *water*, and the mages *mages*," said the hunter. "Now go away. And don't even think of asking me for food, or I'll pierce you after all and let them pour you out to give Holy Yeggut a drink."

His mention of "drink" made Runnel thirsty, but he made no request and walked, then ran, deeper into the wood, away from the wall.

He worked his way west and stayed far enough away from the next gate that he saw neither it nor the houses the hunter had described. Not much farther, he came to the ruined wall, and followed it till he found a gap. Then he went back toward the south and found yet another gap, which must have been the one the hunter meant, but it made no difference except a few extra steps. Then he reached the corner of the wall where it turned eastward, and here again was a well-maintained tower with guards in it, looking out over the wood. How stupid, thought Runnel, to have a wall that you can simply walk around, and yet defend one short section of it. Are your foes so lazy you can let most of your wall fall down, and they won't even bother to walk through it?

Soon he reached the road. There was no one in sight. He stepped out and walked east along the shores of a different stream. This one was shallower and broader—it looked like it could be forded. And sure enough, he soon came to a place where wagons on another road from the south crossed the river and joined the Uhetter Road.

No one hailed him, though as he neared the wagons he got some suspicious glances. Not wishing trouble, Runnel skirted them widely and ran on ahead, to make it obvious he wasn't there to steal or beg or whatever it was they feared he'd try. I've errands of my own.

Soon the road ran between houses and shops. From some of the houses came the smell of food, and when Runnel saw that people were going freely in and out of one of them, he concluded it was a roadhouse and he went inside.

He was stopped at once by a burly man, who said, "Have you got money, boy?"

Runnel looked around, confused. "What's a money?" he asked.

The man laughed nastily and shoved him out. "What's a money!" he said. "They come stupider and more arrogant about it every spring!"

So getting a meal would be harder than Runnel had thought. In Farzibeck, any home would open its door to a traveler, and ask no more of him than news or whatever gift he chose to give. Who ever heard of a roadhouse demanding a particular gift—especially one that Runnel had never heard of! How could he have brought a "money" when he didn't know what it was and had no idea where to find one and couldn't have guessed in advance that they'd even *want* such a thing?

Madness. But from the way other people in the roadhouse laughed at him, he could only conclude that everybody here knew what moneys were, and knew the innkeeper would demand it of them. So it was a city thing, and he would have to find out about it. But not here.

Not far into the town of Hetterferry, he came to a dock on what looked to be another lake, though not as large as the Mitherlough. He soon realized, from the conversations he overheard, that this was the river called Ronnyrill, which flowed down in three streams from the lake high above, then on to Ronys and Abervery and other strange, exotic-sounding places. Much good that would do him, though. What mattered to him was that the real city of Mitherhome was plainly visible, not more than a stone's throw away at the nearest point, but the torrent of water pouring out of the deep gash in the cliff made a more impassable barrier than their ridiculous wall.

When he asked a man about the ferryboat, he once again heard the word "money."

"Does everyone here demand the same gift in trade?"

In reply, the man smiled and reached into a pouch tucked into the sash that bound his shirt closed. He pulled out a single half-blackened disc of bronze. "Money," he said. "You get it by working, and then you trade it for things you want."

"But it's so small," said Runnel.

"So's your wit," said the man, and turned away.

At least now he knew how to get money—you worked. That was something Runnel knew how to do. He walked along the dock till he came to a boat that was busy with men carrying crates onto a large raft. A man was standing by a crate, apparently waiting for one of the other laborers to come and carry the other end with him. So Runnel squatted and put his hands under the crate, and said, "Let's do it."

The laborer looked at him, shrugged, and took up his end. Together they carried it onto the raft, which seemed to Runnel to be as big as his whole village. Runnel stayed with the job for half an hour, working as hard as any of the adult men. But when it was done, everybody else got on the raft and pushed off, leaving him behind. He wanted to cry out to them that all he wanted was to cross the stupid river, what would that cost them? But he knew that they knew what he wanted, and they had chosen to take his labor and pay him nothing, and there was nothing he could do about it. Begging wouldn't change their minds—it would only invite their scorn. Besides, the men he had helped were hirelings themselves—they were not the men who could have rewarded him with passage. Runnel had been a fool.

He was very, very hungry now—and thirsty, too. The water of the river didn't look terribly clean, despite having just come out of the canyon. From the look of it, all the waste of the city was dumped into the Mitherlough above and got carried down in the torrent. So he would need water to replace what he had sweated out.

Back home, if you needed a drink, you knelt by a brook or runnel somewhere and drank your fill. It was all clean—there was no village upstream of them. And they left it clean—it was a matter of piety not to dishonor Yeggut by polluting the streams that flowed near them. But they had heard from travelers that the sewers of the great cities flowed right out into the water, as if the god were nothing to them. Now, having heard what the hunter in the sacred wood said of the god, Runnel believed the tale.

That meant he needed to find water from upstream of this town. It would mean leaving again, and it occurred to him that once he set foot on the Uhetter Road he would probably let it carry him all the way back to Farzibeck.

He took a different street away from the dock, and almost immediately found himself at a public fountain, with water gushing from the mouths of three stone fish into three pools into which women were dipping jars and pails to carry back to houses and shops.

Grateful for the bounty, Runnel dropped to his knees beside one of the pools and splashed water up into his face.

Almost immediately, he was once again seized by the shoulder, and once again he was hurled down, though this time he sprawled, not on dirt and leaves, but on the hard cobblestones of the street. A large woman loomed over him, her jar standing on the ground beside her.

"What do you mean, putting your filthy hands right in the water! And then washing the dust from your own face right back into it for the rest of us to drink!"

"I'm sorry," said Runnel. "But don't you dip your jar in? And isn't it standing on the ground right now, getting filthy?"

"But it's my jar," she said, "and I only set it down to drag your filthy head out of the fountain."

"I didn't put my head in," said Runnel.

"Might as well have! Now get away before I call the guard on you!"

"I'm thirsty," said Runnel. "Where else can I get water?"

"Back in your hometown!" she roared. "Or pee into your hand and drink *that*!" Then she picked up her jar, made a great show of brushing off the bottom of it, and dipped it into the fountain, her huge buttocks pointed directly at Runnel.

The stones had bruised him about as well as Father ever did. Runnel knew how to move carefully and slowly until he knew exactly where it hurt most, so he'd know how to get up with the minimum of pain.

"Are you all right?" asked a young woman.

"You mean apart from being thirsty, hungry, embarrassed, and bruised?"

"All right, then, *be* proud," she retorted, and carried her jar to the fountain.

"What did I say?" asked Runnel. "You asked how I was, and I'm thirsty, hungry, embarrassed, and bruised. It was an honest answer."

"And still you have that proud look about you," she said, after a mere glance. "I see you think you're better than anyone."

"I know that I'm not," said Runnel. "And if there's a proud look on my face, Yeggut put it there, not me." For the first time, Runnel wondered if there was something wrong with his face, and that was why his father hated him.

The girl's jar was full. She rocked it up so it stood in the fountain, then turned and faced him, her hands on her hips. She was a girl who worked hard, for her bare arms were muscled and her face was brown. But she was also clean, and so was her clothing. He had never seen a girl in clothes so clean. She must wear it no more than a week without washing.

"You're not mocking me?" asked the girl.

"Why would I mock you?" said Runnel. "You were kindly to me, asking how I was, which makes you the best person I've met so far in this place."

"You say fair enough words," she said, "but your face and your voice and your manner still look disdainful. The god *was* unkind to you. That face should have belonged to a lord or a mage—then no one would mind the proud look."

"No one in my village ever told me," said Runnel. "They must be used to me, having seen this face since I was a baby."

"Oh, and you think you're *not* a baby now?" she said, with a bit of smile at the corners of her mouth.

"Now who's the mocker?" asked Runnel.

"That's different," she said. "You really *are* small."

"I can't help being young. I'm growing, though—I'm taller than I was. I can work hard. I do what I'm told. I can't help my face, but I can bow my head and hide it—see?"

He tucked his chin onto his chest.

"Couldn't get much work done in that position," she said. "But no use asking me for work, I haven't any such thing in my gift. I'm a servant myself, though *not* a slave, thank the god, so I get a coin now and then, and the master couldn't make free with me even if he wanted to, which he's too old even to wish for, thank the god."

"Then let me carry your waterjar for you, and you can let me ask your master for work."

"It's a great household, lad," she said. "You wouldn't speak to the master, you'd speak to Demwor, the steward."

"The what?"

"The man who rules the servants, under my master. The man who keeps the counts. The guardian, the—you've *never* heard the word 'steward'?"

"There's not more than three servants in my whole village, and no house with two of them." Runnel thought of each of them, all of them old, and belonging to houses once headed by men who went off to the wars and came home rich. They had been captured by the men's own hand as spoils of war, which made them slaves by the decision of the gods. Now the men were long dead, and the servants were old, and hardly anybody cared that they weren't free. The only reason Runnel knew was that when he was little, he asked why one of them had never married, and then the whole business of servants was explained to him, and the other two were pointed out as well.

And here he was, volunteering to be a servant himself. Only, like this girl, he intended to be one who was free, and made a—what was the word? A coin now and then.

"If you drop the jar, I'll be beaten for it, free or not," she said. "And no payment for you—I have no coin to spare. Nor kisses neither, in case you thought."

"What?" he asked, dumfounded.

"In *case*," she said. "You claimed not to be a baby anymore."

"I wouldn't just . . . why would I?"

She narrowed her eyes. "And here I thought you weren't really proud," she said.

"I didn't mean . . ." And then he gave up and hefted the jar out of the water. It was heavy. They never used such large jugs in Farzibeck, but that was partly because water was never very far away, and none of the houses used much water, and who could afford a jar *this* big?

He hugged it to his belly, and she eyed him critically. "Get a hand more under it in front . . . yes . . . no, lower, catch under the edge like . . . like that. You don't want it sliding through your arms to land on your feet."

"Maybe I should balance it on my head," said Runnel.

"You might carry a basket of feathers that way," she said, "but you don't have enough of a neck to balance water there. First your neck would break, then the jar."

"Can we start moving?" he said. "Because I can't hold this forever."

The nasty woman who had shoved and threatened him had apparently stayed to gossip with other women. Now she saw Runnel carrying the jar, and she called out to the servant girl, "Ho, Lark, don't you know that fine lordling will take what he wants from you and run away?"

"They only run away from *you*, Wesera!" Lark cheerfully called back.

"Don't know how she thinks I could run anywhere, carrying this," muttered Runnel.

Lark burst out laughing. "You really *are* fresh from the farm, aren't you?"

"Why? What did I say?"

"No, no, I think it's sweet that you don't think that way. You really *don't*, do you? And not because you're too young, either. Now you know my name's Lark, so what's *your* name, since it seems I'm about to introduce you to Demwor and I ought to know it."

"Runnel."

"Is that because you peed yourself all the time as a baby?" she said. "Or is there watermagic in your family?"

"I didn't choose my name," said Runnel, embarrassed and a little angry. "No one mocked me for it where I lived."

"I'm not mocking you!" said Lark. "I've just never—it's the kind of name a man takes when he's joining the service of Yeggut. The kind of name watermages give their children."

"Half the children in Farzibeck have water names," said Runnel. "It shows that your parents are waterfolk."

"It's a good name. It's just that in Mitherhome they go more for ancient names or trade names or virtues. I'm not from here, either—my family farms to the east of here, and northward. I was named for a meadowbird that my mother loves to hear singing. So you can be named for a brook, and it's no shame. I was just surprised."

"Then let's agree never to mock each other," said Runnel, "so that even if it sounds like it, or looks like it, we'll both know that no harm is meant."

"*If* Demwor hires you, which is unlikely, and *if* we have occasion to see each other again—also unlikely—then yes, I agree, I won't mock you."

"Thank you."

"To your face, anyway," she said. Only she was grinning in a way that said that indeed no harm was intended.

I'm going to hide my face from everybody, thought Runnel. *And* my name. People find the one offensive and the other ridiculous. And I had to come all these miles to find out about it.

They walked in silence for a little while. Then Runnel could not contain it. "What's *wrong* with my face?"

"Nothing," she said. "You're not handsome, you're not ugly."

"What makes you say I look proud?"

"Well it's the whole thing. The expression."

"What about the expression?"

"I don't know," she said, sounding exasperated. "You just do. Like you're a statue."

"What's a statue?"

"How can I explain it if you—a statue is made of stone or metal or clay, and it shows a person's face, only it doesn't move, it just stays exactly the same."

"I move my face. I talk. I smile. I move my eyes. I nod."

"Well, stop doing it, or you'll drop the jar."

"Did you have to fill it completely full?"

"Do you want me to carry it now?"

He would not have a girl carry something because he could not. "I can do it."

"You want to know what's wrong with your face? I'll tell you. Right now you were annoyed with me—for filling it so full, then for offering to carry it. But *nothing* showed in your face. You moved your mouth, you moved your eyes, but you didn't show anything you were thinking. It looks like you think you're better than me. Like you don't have to bother feeling anything about me."

"Well, I *was* annoyed. I can't help what my face shows."

"And you're annoyed now, and it *still* doesn't show."

Runnel made a monstrous face. "How about now?"

"Now you're ugly. But it still doesn't look like you mean it."

It was a shocking thing to learn about himself. "Why didn't anybody ever tell me?"

"Probably because they thought you were proud and didn't like them, so why should they tell you anything?"

"So why are *you* telling me?"

"Because I saw you knocked in the dirt by Wesera, and you looked thirsty and miserable. Your *face* looked proud, so I thought that meant you had spunk. Now you say you aren't proud, so that must mean you *don't* have spunk, so . . . no, we said no mockery, so . . . I believe you. I believe you can't help it. But you know what helps? Ducking your head. Makes you look humble. Hides the stiffness. Do that a lot, and people won't want to slap you around."

"Do you want to slap me around?"

"Two answers to that. No, because you're carrying my water for me. And no, because I don't care enough to slap you, and I'm never going to, so if that was your first test to see if you could get close to me—"

He was sick of her assumption that he had some interest in her like that. So he walked faster and moved briskly ahead of her.

"Watch out, slow down!" she shouted. "You'll drop it, you'll break it, you'll spill it!"

Water *was* sloshing and splashing, so he did as she asked, and she was beside him again.

"So you don't like me," she said. "I get it."

"I like you fine," he said. "You helped me. I just don't want anything from you except a chance at a job so I can get some of these moneys or coins or whatever you call them. And maybe, just maybe, a drink of this water after we get it to wherever we're going."

"Well, that would be now, because we're here." She led him to a doorway in a large, high stone wall.

She stopped outside the door and whistled—a bit of birdsong, it sounded like. She grinned at him, and said, "Lark."

The door swung open, and for a moment Runnel thought it was magic. But no, there was a tall stupid-looking man pushing it outward, and Lark flounced through saucily. "Let my boy in, will you?" she said to the man.

Runnel flashed with anger for a moment, but then realized that she was just playing, and besides, just now his only hope of a drink and a meal *was* her. At least she was letting him in. She could have said, Take the waterjar and get rid of this boy, and he could have done no more about it than with the men on the cargo raft. He was inside. That was a good thing. So he said nothing, just followed her through the door and into the courtyard.

She led him to a stone structure about the height of a man and half more, with stone stairs winding around two sides of it. She motioned for him to climb the stairs behind her, and when he got to the top, she had already opened a small trapdoor in the roof of the thing. "Pour it in."

He did.

She took the empty jar from him. "I'll carry it now."

"Now it's empty," he said.

"Believe it or not, *this* is the time when people are most likely to break the jar. Once it's empty, it feels light, and you get careless. Only I'd be the one in trouble, not you. So I carry it down. Now move on down out of my way, Runnel, or I'll mock you."

"Then you'd be an oathbreaker."

"Your back will be to me, so I can mock you without breaking the oath."

"Mock me all you want, I don't care."

He shambled down the steps and headed for the door in the garden wall. The tall stupid-looking man was still standing there.

"Wait," she said. "Are you really angry?"

"I'm not angry, I just need to get a drink of water and a bite of food and a job, and it's obvious it's not going to happen here."

"Why, because I teased you?"

"Because you teased me after you promised not to," said Runnel. "You don't keep your word."

She grabbed his shirt and pulled him back. She was *strong*.

She got right in his face. "That was not mocking. That was friendship. Haven't you ever had a friend?"

He almost made a sharp retort, but then he realized: probably not.

"Mocking you is when I make fun of you in front of people you care about, so it shames you. And I'll never do that, because I took an oath, and because I don't do that to people anyway. How did you get to be this old without knowing anything about people? Were you raised in a cave?"

No, I was raised in my father's house.

She tugged again on his shirt, and he followed her to the other side of the cistern where he had just poured the water.

Down low, so she had to stoop, there was an opening, into which she set one of several beakers that stood on a table nearby. She placed it carefully in the middle of a circle etched in the stone base of the opening, and then pressed on a block of stone beside it. Immediately water started trickling into the beaker. It was steady, and the beaker filled faster than Runnel would have expected from the amount of flow.

She let up on the stone she had pressed, and the flow stopped almost at once. She handed the beaker to Runnel.

Runnel took it solemnly. It was a giving of water, and so he murmured the prayer of thanks, then offered it back to her.

"Oh, I forgot, you come from a pious village," she said. "Look, this doesn't mean we're married or anything, does it?"

"It means I'm grateful for the water." Then Runnel brought it to his mouth and began to sip, letting it fill and clean his mouth before swallowing, making sure not to let a drop spill, not even to dribble down his cheeks. The feeling of slakethirst was so strong it took a while for him even to notice the flavor of the water.

"It tastes like a mountain spring, straight from the rock," he said. "It tastes clean."

"Of course," she said. "The water we pour in above seeps through stone, just like a mountain spring."

"I never heard of the watermages needing stone to purify their water."

"Of course not," said Lark. "But my master won't let them purify his water. He insists that he'll draw his water from the same fountain as anyone, and filter it himself, without watermagic touching it."

"Why?" asked Runnel.

"Oh, you don't know, do you?" she said. "My master is Brickel. The stonemage of Mitherhome." She said it as if Runnel should know all about it.

But the only thing Runnel knew was that there *were* no stonemages in Mitherhome. He said so.

"It's true there are none *in* Mitherhome," said Lark. "You can see we're in Hetterferry, across flowing water from Low Mitherhome. But he's still the stonemage *of* Mitherhome. The one they allow to live nearby, in exchange for keeping their walls and bridges and temples in good repair. Keeping the stone from cracking and crumbling, repairing the damage from ice and snow in winter. Even the watermages of Mitherhome need stonework, and that means a stonemage, if you want things made of stone to last, in the presence of so much water."

"You serve a mage?" he said. "Then why aren't *you* proud?"

"Because," she said, lowering her voice, "he's a *stone*mage. They need him here, but they keep constant watch, lest he start trying to bring other stonemages here. Because they need one stonemage to keep their city in repair, but too many stonemages could bring the whole thing toppling down and break open the sacred Mitherlough."

"Why would stonemages do that?"

"Maybe they have cause," said Lark. "All I know is, people don't get in my way because they know whose servant I am, and that he's a powerful man, and no one dares offend him. But nobody wants to befriend him, either. So . . . nor have I any particular friends in Hetterferry."

"Except among the servants here."

She rolled her eyes. "Oh, yes, we're one big happy family."

"So why do you work here?"

"Because I was an ignorant farm girl when I came here and could find no work. And Master Brickel could find no servants worth anything. I knew nothing, but I worked hard and learned fast. I get coin and I save some and send some home to my family. My brothers are paying a teacher to learn them their letters, from the money I send. So you see? I'm a servant here, and they can hire a servant *there*, and my brothers will have a chance to be clerks, maybe."

"And what will you have a chance to be?"

She looked at him like he was insane. "A servant in a mage's house. You think I don't know how lucky I am to be here?"

The only question in Runnel's mind was: Will *I* be as lucky?

Silently he finished drinking, watching her closely. Watching her face, how she cocked her head to watch him drink, how there were tiny changes in her face reflecting whatever thought she was thinking. He realized that he had always been able to judge other people's moods by what their faces showed. It had never occurred to him that nobody could judge *his*.

He thought of the stupid man at the doorway. How did Runnel know the man was stupid? Because of the slack-looking face, the way his grin seemed to have no purpose in it. From his size, he might have been set at the door to guard it. But from the apparent lack of wit, he was there just to open and close it, this being the full extent of his skills.

What if he wasn't stupid? What if his face simply was slack, and he was actually quite keen-witted?

The stupid man's face showed him a lackwit; Runnel's own face showed him proud and aloof. Lark's face showed her to be friendly, quick-witted, but also earnest.

"So when you look at me like that," she said, "what are you thinking?"

"I'm thinking that I wish I knew how to make my face as clever and generous as yours."

She blushed. "I would slap a *man* if he said such a thing to me," she said.

"Why?" he asked, genuinely puzzled.

"Because when a man says such things to a woman, he wants something from her."

"I don't," he said. He held up the half-empty beaker. "Already got what I wanted."

He felt a hand on his shoulder and immediately began to drop toward the ground, so when this person shoved him down he wouldn't fall so far.

But the hand didn't shove him, and Lark greeted the owner of it with a smile. "Demwor," she said, "I want you to meet this lad. His name is Runnel, he's from the mountain village of Farzibeck, he carried a full jar for me the whole way without spilling any, and he doesn't want to get under my skirt."

"Yet," said a soft, deep voice. Runnel tried to turn to see the face from which it came, and found that the hand held him fast.

"He's a different sort," she said. "I think he might be worth it."

"I think he must be a fool," said Demwor, "to let you talk him into carrying a *full* jar."

Only now did Runnel realize that she must have meant to spill out some of the water before carrying it herself. He glared at her, then realized that perhaps it didn't look like a glare. Perhaps none of the looks he gave people meant anything. What if he always looked the same.

But she smiled benignly at him. "I didn't know you then," she said. "And besides, you *were* strong enough to carry it full, because you did."

"Who told you we were looking to hire someone?" asked Demwor.

"What, are we?" asked Lark.

"No," said Demwor.

"Then it's a good thing I didn't promise him anything except a drink of water and an introduction to you."

So that was it. Another trick. Only now he had water in him, so it wasn't as bad as the first one. Except he was even wearier now, and still had to go out and find a meal and a job.

"You don't like him?" asked Demwor.

"Of course I like him," she said. "Do you think I'd bring somebody I hated? What if you *did* hire him?"

"What I'm asking," said Demwor, "is whether the two of you are going to make a baby here at Lord Brickel's expense."

Lark looked at Runnel with a cocky smile. "I *told* you that's what men always think of."

"Sir," said Runnel, "I work hard, and I learn as fast as anyone, and I keep my word."

"Whom did you run away from?"

"Nobody that will miss me," said Runnel.

The hand tightened on his shoulder. "The name of your master."

"No master, sir," said Runnel. "My father and mother. But I'm the ninth son. As I said, I'll not be missed."

"No mother will come weeping at the gate, complaining we kidnapped her little boy?"

"No one will *notice* I'm gone, sir." Except Father, Runnel thought. He won't have anyone to beat. Still, there was no point in saying *that*. If he mentioned that he had ever been beaten, Demwor would think it was for good reason and assume he was a troublemaker.

"So why did you come here?"

"Because where else does a ninth son go?" he asked. And realized, finally, that it was true. No one had ever explained it to him, but that, as much as his proud face, was why none of the village girls ever looked at him. What did he *have*? The farm would go to one of his older brothers. His sisters would be married out. One of his brothers had married a girl with a prosperous father—the dowry was his farm. But the next brother would expect to get Father's farm, in due time. What would any of the younger boys have? He had known this without knowing he knew it.

Was that why he had taken it into his head to walk over the Mitherkame to this place? It must have been.

The hand on his shoulder relaxed. "It's not a light thing, serving a mage," he said, as Runnel turned to face him. The man was tall and swarthy—a man of the south, like some of the travelers that had passed through Farzibeck.

"So you're no man's prentice?" asked Demwor.

"We're all farmers in Farzibeck," said Runnel.

"No smith? No harness maker?"

"We make our own harnesses. We work in stone and wood. We drink the water Yeggut gives us, and we eat what Yeggut makes to grow from the earth. I've heard of prentices because some of the travelers have them, but I couldn't figure how they were different from slaves."

"The difference," said Demwor, "is that the master pays for the slave, but to take a prentice, the father pays the master to take him. That's how useless prentices are, and why Master Brickel will never, never, *never* take a prentice."

"That's good news to me," said Runnel, "because I'd never want to be taken for a prentice."

"Just so you understand," said Demwor. "We'd hire you as a servant only. Base labor, you understand. There'll be manure, there'll be slops, there'll be backbreaking work with stone, there'll be burdens."

That described the life of everybody in Farzibeck, including the stones, which they had to haul out of their fields every spring, after the winter heaved them up to snag the plow. "I'm not afraid of work, sir."

"Then I have only one more question," said Demwor. "How do you feel about stone?"

Feel? About stone? What was he supposed to *feel* about it? "I'm in favor of it for walls," said Runnel, "and against it for soil."

Demwor chuckled. "You have a proud face," he said, "but a humble wit."

"The face is not my fault," said Runnel. "Nor is my wit, since I was born with both, and both are humble enough, sir."

"What I ask about stone is simple. Have you worked in stone? Have you built with stone? Have you shaped it?"

"Is it required? Because I can learn if you want. But no, I've never worked stone. We just find it and make barriers sometimes, to slacken the floods of spring in a heavy snow year. And the foundations of our hovels are of stone pressed into the earth. But I've never actually helped to build such, since no hovel has been built since I've been big enough."

"It is not required," said Demwor, "and we don't want you to learn it."

"Then I won't," said Runnel.

"Because if you think you can try to learn magic from Master Brickel, I can tell you that you *will* be detected, and it will go hard for you."

"Magic?" said Runnel. "How can I learn magic? I'm no mage."

"Just remember that," said Demwor, "and you won't get this house into trouble."

"The house? Your master *is* a stonemage."

"No, lad," said Demwor. "My master is *the* stonemage. The only one permitted to enter Mitherhome. The only one allowed within this whole valley. And *he* is sworn never to learn new magics, beyond what he knew when he came here. Stonemage he is, but not a rockbrother, and especially not a stonefather. He's a cobblefriend, which is all the power needed for the work he does here. That is why the watermages of Mitherhome pay him so handsomely, and provide him this house—because he hasn't the power to do us harm."

And suddenly it became clear to Runnel. Demwor didn't work for

Brickel, he worked for the Mithermages. Yes, he saw to the affairs of Brickel's household and hired the servants and paid for the food, but he was also Brickel's overseer, making sure Brickel did not break the terms of his oath. Without even meeting him, Runnel felt a little sorry for Brickel.

But not *too* sorry. Because here the man lived with wealth—servants, a garden courtyard ten times larger than the hovel where Runnel's huge family slept, all the food he needed.

"Sir," said Runnel, "my aim in life is to earn enough to eat and a place to sleep and maybe a little of this money everyone wants so much. So Lark is safe, and you are safe, and your master is safe, and your city is safe from my ambition, because I'm little and ignorant and hungry and tired. But if you take care of the hungry and tired, you'll find me big enough to do whatever work you need, and I'll only get bigger, because all my older brothers are as tall as soldiers, and so is my father, and my mother isn't tiny by any measure."

Demwor burst into laughter. "I've never heard such a sales pitch—and from such a serious face, too. I take you at your word, boy. What's your name again?"

"Runnel, sir."

"Start thinking of what you want to change it to," said Demwor.

"I won't, sir."

"We can't have the stonemage's servant with a watername, lest the people think he's mocking them."

"He's not my father, he hired me is all," said Runnel. "So no one with half a wit will think he's responsible for my name."

"But he hasn't hired you, and he won't, with a name like that."

"Then I thank you for the water, sir," said Runnel. "But I didn't come here to be any man's slave, nor to give up my name neither."

"Who said anything about a slave?"

"It's the owner of a slave who gets to change his name, sir," said Runnel. "I know *that* because the three old servants in Farzibeck were given new names when they were taken captive in war."

Demwor shook his head. "So that pride in your face isn't all illusion, is it? Too proud to change your name in exchange for a job."

"Not proud, sir," said Runnel. "But Runnel of Farzibeck won't die here to have a waterless coward rise in his place."

"Waterless coward?" said Demwor. "Farzibeck—it's in the mountains, is it?"

"West of here, along the Utteroad," said Runnel. "Just beyond the pass over the Mitherkame."

"So you're named Runnel out of piety. You serve Yeggut?"

"I come here to find I may be the only one who does," said Runnel.

Demwor put a hand on his shoulder once more, and Runnel flinched, but the hand was kindly this time. "You'll do, I think," said Demwor. "A boy from a mountain village, with a watername that means devotion, not ambition. Yes, that's better. You were right to stand your ground and not give up the name."

Demwor patted his shoulder and walked back toward the house.

Lark wasn't having that. "Is he hired then, sir?"

"Yes," said Demwor.

"What's his wage?" she demanded.

"Same as yours," said Demwor.

"That's not right!" she shouted. "I've worked here two years already!"

"But *he* carried the waterjar full." And Demwor was gone into the house.

Lark was furious. "*Drown* him and all his kittens," she muttered fiercely.

"He hired me," said Runnel.

"At far more wage than you're worth," she said.

"If you like, I'll give you part of it, since you brought me here."

For a moment her eyes lighted up. And then she backed away. "I won't have no man thinking I owe him."

Runnel shook his head. "Your precious treasure is safe from me," he said. "I owe *you*, for bringing me here."

"I thought you'd almost ruined everything when you refused to change your name."

"It turned out all right," said Runnel.

"How did you know it would?" she asked.

"I didn't."

"So you *meant* all that?" She seemed astonished.

"It's my *name*," said Runnel.

"You are the most ignorant person I've ever known. What's a name?"

"You guard *your* purity," said Runnel, "and I guard mine."

Her eyes and nostrils flared and she swung as if to slap him, but then she didn't actually hit him. Nor, however, did he flinch. "Don't you ever dare to compare your *name* with my *purity*, as you call it. Someday I mean to earn my dowry and *marry*, not be some kitchen slut making coin on the side or winning favor from the master or the steward. Purity *is* the only treasure that a poor girl has, which is why I took this job, because people leave me alone, which means I have hope. While your name—it's not famous, it's not important, it's *worthless*. So don't you dare compare them again, ever!"

She stalked away from him, into the house, leaving him to finish his water, which he did.

What's worthless to you might not be worthless to me, he said silently. But he couldn't help feeling disappointed. Somehow he had managed to lose her friendship after all. It would be just like home.

He leaned against the cistern and closed his eyes. He had a job. He would be paid money. He had no idea what money was worth, but he was being paid the same as Lark, and *she* believed it was enough that she could save up a dowry.

She was young, and might be counting on ten years or more to build up what she wanted. But he was even younger, and could work longer before marrying. As a farmer, he had only just started doing men's work, and not yet the full range of that. But here, he would learn everything and grow into whatever jobs were too hard for him.

Lots of hard work. Years of it. Why was he so excited?

It was because he would be with a stonemage. What did he care if he was only a cobblefriend and not one of the higher orders? He might even see magic done.

Meanwhile, there were practical benefits. Like this cistern. He could feel how it worked inside—the water in the tank above seeped right through a porous stone that trapped anything that shouldn't be in it. It was slow for the water to seep its way through the rock, but all impurities were removed—ironic that the purest, cleanest water in Hetterferry should be in the stonemage's house.

The porous stone was a surprise, though. He had never known rock like this, not in any of the outcroppings he had climbed. He wished it were outside the cistern where he could get his hands on it. If only *he* were a stonemage so he could understand how the filtering worked.

Dangerous thought. He must not wish to be a stonemage. He had taken an oath not to become one. If Demwor hadn't made such a fuss about how he shouldn't be one, he wouldn't be wishing he could be one right now.

It didn't matter. Mages were magical people, not ordinary farm boys.

Mages could go out into the world in the shape of their beloved—beast mages as the beast they favored, elemental mages in bodies of stone or wind or water, lightning or sand or metal. They could not be confined, not the ones with real power. Runnel imagined himself as a stonemage like Brickel, his new master. He could walk the earth in a stone body, and then what weapon could harm him?

I hope I can see my master in his stoneshape. Or must he keep such things secret, because Demwor was here to watch?

"Runnel," said an impatient voice. "What are you doing?"

He opened his eyes and saw Lark standing there again.

"Finishing my water," he said.

"Without the beaker in your hand? What do you do, suck it up through your ears?"

Don't be angry with me, he wanted to say. But he hesitated, and she talked again.

"Do you think you're going to live out here in the garden? Come with me. I'm supposed to show you your room."

Runnel dutifully followed her into the house. She walked briskly, so he scarcely had time to notice the different rooms or try to guess what they were used for. His family's hovel was one room, with a chimney at one end. He had no idea why so many rooms would be needed; they did not look convenient for sleeping, there was so much furniture in odd shapes. Tall boxes with doors all up and down them. Tables with cloth covering them, and so bumpy that you couldn't possibly get any work done on them. Until he realized that they were really huge, wide chairs, and the cloth was there to cover the wood so it wouldn't hurt to sit a long time. Cloth, just to dress chairs and make them soft! No one in Farzibeck would even have understood it.

They went up a flight of narrow wooden stairs. "Why didn't we use the wide stairs in the front?" asked Runnel.

She didn't answer.

He sighed. So much for the hope that she might forgive him for what was, after all, an unintentional offense.

"Always use these stairs," she finally said. "The front stairs are for the master, Demwor, and guests. Servants use the back stairs."

So decency and good order had prevailed over temper. She didn't want him getting in trouble because she never told him about the stairs rule. That was almost . . . compassionate.

Up two, three flights, to the very top of the house. And then up another even narrower stairway to a room where the walls and roof were the rafters.

He had never climbed so high inside a building. Farzibeck had only one barn as tall as this, and he wasn't allowed inside it. He had gone once anyway, with a group of his brothers, but they wouldn't let him climb a ladder and he hadn't wanted to anyway. It's not that he was afraid of heights—he could climb as high as he wanted, outdoors. But going up the stairs he felt as though he were climbing right up into the air, leaving the solid earth too far behind him.

Three floors between him and the earth, each one shakier than the one before. He felt as though the house were swaying. He hated the feeling. "We have to sleep up *here*?"

"Too proud?" she asked pointedly.

"Too scared," he said. "What holds us up?"

She looked at him as if he were crazy. "The walls of the house, the floors." She touched one of the heavy rafters. "Huge beams of heavy wood."

"It trembles."

"It does *not*," she said, as if he had just accused her of something.

He tried to think of some rational basis for his discomfort. "It can fall. It can burn. I want to sleep outside on the stone flags of the courtyard."

"Do you want to shame our master by making people believe he doesn't have enough rooms for his servants to sleep in?"

"Who would know?" asked Runnel.

She apparently had no answer, so she glared at him. "Take it up with Demwor. I took you where he said you should go."

She started for the stairs.

Runnel hated that she was so angry with him. "Please, Lark," he said. "If I *do* ask him to let me sleep in the courtyard—"

She answered him scornfully before he could even finish his question. "What do *you* think happens to a servant who makes trouble on his first day?"

Since he had never had a paying job, working for strangers, the fear of being dismissed from his position had never occurred to him. The most he had feared was a blow or two—he knew, from life with Father, that he could easily cope with that. But he could not take the chance of giving up this place.

He didn't even know whether this was a good place to work or not—there were probably reasons why this house did not have enough servants and needed to hire a stray freshly arrived from the mountains. It was his own problem that sleeping three floors above the ground bothered him. Other people did it. He would have to get over being such a mountain boy and learn to live in a town.

As all this dawned on him, Lark's expression showed such contempt for him that it was like a slap. "Whose face is proud *now*?" he asked her.

She whirled her head away from him and went on down the stairs. He could hear the soft sliding of the soles of her bare feet on the wood. It was a sound he didn't like. It made him shiver. Feet were meant to walk on grass or soil or hard-packed dirt or stone, not on trees sliced up and laid out sideways. It was unnatural.

He surveyed the straw-filled tick that was apparently meant to be his bed. Even in the scant light coming into the attic through cracks in the eaves, he could see that there were fleas jumping on it. He had nothing against fleas, he just couldn't imagine how they had stayed alive with no one else sleeping up in this hot space.

Then it all came clear. Someone *had* been living up here until just recently. These were his leftover fleas. If he had happened along just a bit earlier or later, the job would have been taken.

He wondered why his predecessor had been dismissed. He asked to sleep on the ground? Or he tried to learn magery? Or he spoke slightingly of Lark's purity? Any of these offenses seemed near fatal, as far as Runnel could tell.

Since it was still broad daylight outside, and he hadn't eaten anything, and neither had anyone else, judging by the smells coming from a kitchen somewhere on the property, he figured he wasn't meant to try to sleep right now, though he was tired enough. If he was to get along well here, he'd need to show himself a hard worker—that was about the only thing that could ever postpone Father's wrath, so it was worth trying here.

The trouble was, he had no idea what tasks he ought to do. Nor did he want to bother anybody with asking. But unless he asked, he'd . . .

No point in thinking any longer. He headed for the stairs and set his foot on the second-from-the-top step and felt it tremble under him and all at once he was as dizzy as if he'd just spun in circles for a dozen turns, the way they all used to do as little kids, until somebody threw up.

He sat on the top step. There was no railing. Going up had been easy enough—he only had to keep his eyes on Lark ahead of him, a sight that was engaging enough that he hadn't really been aware of the drop-off on either side. Now, though, he had neither companion nor handrail nor distraction, and he was only able to make his way down the stairs by sitting on a tread, extending his legs to a lower one, then sliding his buttocks down to the next step.

The rest of the stairs were much easier, since there was a wall on one side or the other, and a railing as well. But the house never stopped trembling, and Runnel never felt secure until he was on the ground floor.

Which was foolish, he knew, since there was a cellar beneath that floor, so it wasn't truly the *ground* under his feet even now. But being level with the ground seemed to be enough. Maybe it was just that the floor beams rested on stone foundations instead of wooden walls.

How would he find out what work he ought to do? Without asking Lark or bothering Demwor? It was easy to guess that he shouldn't go in search of Lord Brickel.

He ended up following his nose to the kitchen, a stone building behind the main house—far enough that if the kitchen burned down it wouldn't take the house with it, but close enough that hot food would still be hot when served, even after being carried through the coldest weather.

The cook turned out to be cooks: a tall, lean black man and a fleshy woman with slanting eyes. As he approached the kitchen, Runnel could hear him calling her Sourwell—a watername—and her calling him Nikwiz, which wasn't a word he knew, any more than Demwor's name had meant anything to him. Their tones were quiet, and when Runnel entered the fire-dried room—so hot that he thought having an oven was redundant—they ignored him and kept speaking to each other.

"Ready for that."

"Steady with the salt."

"Taste it, you'll see."

"Old.

"But edible."

"Perfect."

If Runnel hadn't been watching, it wouldn't even have sounded like a conversation, but he could see that "ready for that" led to her handing him what looked like a large spoon, but with holes in the bottom so that when he shook it over the steaming pot, white granules came out. "Steady with the salt" was said after he made his second pass with the shaker. "Taste it, you'll see," led to Sourwell dipping a finger into Nikwiz's pot as she passed on an errand of her own; she nodded and he made yet another pass with the shaker.

"Old," she said when she picked up a couple of turnips and eyed them skeptically. He didn't even look—he was busy now mincing an onion—so he must have bought the turnips, because his "but edible" sounded authoritative. By then she was on to the oven, where she slid out a long tray with two round loaves on it—"perfect" was pronounced as judgment on the bread.

Neither of them had yet shown a sign of knowing Runnel was there, but as Nikwiz scattered the onions into a hot pan, making the grease in it sizzle, he said, "If you've come to beg for scraps, no. If you've come to steal, I promise you dysentery."

"I've just been hired, and I came to ask if you've any work for me," said Runnel. "My name is Runnel."

"Can you cook?" asked Sourwell.

"Anyone can cook," said Nikwiz. "You just climb into the oven."

It took a moment for Runnel to realize that this was a joke—Sourwell didn't even break a smile, and yet Runnel could see that both she and Nikwiz were both shaking with mirth at the remark.

"My mother never let me near the cooking. Or knives. My sisters—"

"Fascinating," said Sourwell in a tone that meant the opposite.

"Put the owl on the roof," said Nikwiz, "to scare the birds and mice away."

And they were back to cooking.

I'm supposed to catch an owl? Or is there a tame one?

"Outside," said Sourwell. "Blew off in the last storm."

He went out and walked almost all the way around the kitchen building before he found a carved stone owl leaning against a wall. It was cunningly shaped, and it had been daubed with paint to make it more convincing to birds and mice, though Runnel wondered whether those beasts were really that stupid.

The owl was also very heavy. He realized at once that they expected him to be too small to manage it.

But the end walls of the kitchen were stone all the way up, gables and all, the thatch of the roof resting between them like hay in a manger. The owl must rest on the peak of the stone gable—and now that he looked, he could see that another owl rested on the peak of the other end of the kitchen.

Tucking the owl against his body, Runnel had a tough go of it, climbing up the stone wall one-handed, but with bare feet he managed it well enough, and within two minutes after picking up the owl, he was back down, with the owl perched menacingly atop the crest of the kitchen.

He went back inside. "What next?" he asked.

"We didn't ask you to *find* the owl," said Sourwell. "We need it put atop the roof."

"Did it," said Runnel. "What else?"

As if it were part of her regular routine, Sourwell swept out of the kitchen and in a moment came back in and resumed her cooking. In a perfectly mild voice she said, "Singe my sockets, but the boy must fly."

"Bet he left the ladder outside to rot," said Nikwiz.

"Ladder?" asked Runnel.

Their smooth dance of food preparation finally came to a halt, as both of them looked for a long moment at Runnel, then at each other. "Break eggs much?" asked Nikwiz.

"Prone to spilling things?" asked Sourwell.

"No more than most," said Runnel. "I'm not careless, but I'm not perfect."

"We wanted perfect," said Nikwiz, visibly disappointed.

"Best use me for jobs that can be done by the less-than-perfect," said Runnel.

"Here," said Sourwell, slapping a knife down on a cutting stone and pointing to a pile of peppers. "Don't cut yourself."

For the next hour, Runnel chopped and minced peppers and onions on smooth-cut slabs of granite. He quickly learned not to rub his eyes. He cried a lot and sneezed now and then. His eyes burned. He was useful. He was earning his keep.

Then they kicked him out of the kitchen with orders to wash his hands with soap three times before washing his face—again with soap—to clear the last of the onion and pepper residues from his face. "Scrub," said Sourwell. "Hard," said Nikwiz. "Never a soapmage where you need one," added Sourwell.

"I never heard of soapmages," said Runnel.

"Me neither," said Nikwiz. "Go wash."

He found a washbasin outside the kitchen, made of stone, of course. He rocked the small cistern and filled the basin with water, then lathered his hands with one of the cakes of hard soap. He was scrubbing his face, including especially his closed eyes, when he heard voices.

"Doesn't look like much," said an old man.

"Isn't much," said Demwor. "But he made himself useful in the kitchen this afternoon without being ordered."

"All arse and elbows," said the old man. "And what is he *wearing*?"

"The latest in mountain village fashions," said Demwor.

It had to be Lord Brickel himself that Demwor was talking to, and Runnel wanted to see him, but he couldn't see anything until he rinsed his face, and thoroughly. By the time he was able to towel himself on his shirt and turn around, he could just see them disappearing into the house.

He didn't see him at supper, either. Lord Brickel ate with company in his dining room; Runnel ate at the big table in the kitchen with the other servants, of whom there were only the ones he'd already seen: Demwor, Nikwiz, Sourwell, and Ebb, the stupid man from the doorway. Demwor, Nikwiz, and Sourwell kept up a constant conversation about the business of the house and gossip in the neighborhood. Ebb said nothing, which was what Runnel said as well.

Lark was waiting table tonight so she was in and out of the kitchen, and she certainly didn't speak to Runnel.

"Going to buy the new one something respectable to wear?" asked Sourwell.

"Wasn't thinking of it," said Demwor. "He's not naked. He's not going out on errands for the house."

"He'll have to wear something when she washes his clothes," pointed out Sourwell.

The mentioned "she" had to be Lark. Runnel was sure Lark would be thrilled to know she'd be doing that chore.

"I can wash my own," said Runnel. "If you show me where."

"It talks," said Nikwiz.

"With its mouth full," said Sourwell.

They didn't smile, and nobody laughed, but Runnel knew he was being teased, and with good humor. It felt good.

"Take him to market with you tomorrow," said Demwor, "and buy him something that fits. I'll take it out of his earnings. But if he runs off and takes the new clothes before they're earned out, I'll dock *your* wages."

"Just try it," said Nikwiz.

"When we prepare every bite of food you eat," said Sourwell.

"What kind of household is this?" said Demwor. "Two cooks, one smart-mouthed girl, a mountain bumpkin, and a cheerful dolt."

"You're forgetting Ebb," said Nikwiz.

It took a moment for Runnel to get the gibe; he laughed aloud.

Demwor glared at him. "Don't get the idea that I'll let *you* speak disrespectfully to me, boy, just because I let the cooks do it."

"No, sir," said Runnel.

"And you'll wash those clothes and bathe yourself tonight. With soap! I won't have you bringing fleas into the house."

Which explained why Lark's clothing was so clean. Demwor insisted on it.

"Where do I wash them?" asked Runnel. "Since there's no stream close by."

"The washbasin is at the west corner of the garden," said Nikwiz.

"Carry your own water there," said Sourwell.

"There's a stove out there for heating the water," said Demwor, "but if you break a jar from overheating it or setting it cold on a hot stove, I'll dock you."

Runnel had no idea what "docking" him might mean, but he was sure it was something he wanted to avoid having done either to him or his wages. But that was all right. He had never heard of heating water for washing clothes. And only Father washed in hot water back home, and only in winter.

After supper he found the laundry tub, estimated how much water he'd need to wash and rinse the clothes and himself, and then carried a large jar of water from the main cistern. He stripped off his clothes and put them in the water, then soaped them on the washboard.

"You nasty boy!" said Lark behind him. Her voice was full of revulsion.

"I haven't washed myself yet," he answered.

"I don't care that you're dirty, stupid. You're *naked*."

"Excuse me, I didn't think of washing my clothes with me still in them," said Runnel.

"Do you always do your laundry naked back in Farzibeck?" she said snidely.

"Yes," he said. "It's that or sit naked in the house like a baby while somebody else washes them. Only in Farzibeck, the girls have sense enough to stay away while the boys are laundering, and we boys'd be killed if we walked up on the girls like you just walked up on me." This was not strictly true. When boys got their man growth, they would keep a loincloth on. But Runnel had not started wearing one yet.

"I have laundry to do," said Lark. "For the master."

"Then you can either wait till later, or you can do it with your eyes closed, because I'm not leaving here till my clothes and my body are clean."

"Dry! It'll take forever for your clothes to dry!"

"Dry?" asked Runnel. "Where will they dry, except on *me*?"

"I'm not going to go to bed late because you picked *this* moment to discover cleanliness."

"Demwor told me to wash clothes and boy," said Runnel. "And the reason I was so dirty was because I had just taken a journey along roads and through woods, and slept in leaves on the forest floor. Next time I'll remember to have someone carry me in a litter or pull me in a carriage."

She set down a full basket of white linens.

"The master must wear a lot of white," said Runnel.

"This is his underwear, mountain boy," she said contemptuously. "Obviously you've never heard of it."

It was a strange world, indeed, for a man to have underwear like a baby—and a whole basketful at that.

Lark poured the rest of the water from his jar into the tub and dropped a cake of soap in with it. Then she took the washboard from Runnel's side of the tub and began scrubbing the linens.

"I guess my clothes are clean enough now," said Runnel, getting up.

"Don't stand up!" she said. "Don't you have *any* modesty?"

"You just poured out the rinse water," said Runnel. "I have to get more."

"You should have brought more water in the first place," she said.

"I brought enough water for my body and my clothes to be washed and rinsed," he said. "You brought none." He picked up the empty jar and headed back across the garden to the courtyard where the cistern waited.

The jar was almost half-full when Demwor came up to him. "In this house we wear clothing," he said sharply.

Runnel bit back all his two possible answers: "I'm not *in* the house" would get him slapped or kicked out for insolence. "You told me to wash my clothes when you knew I didn't have any others" was likely to get the same result. So instead he said, "I had to replenish the water so Lark could do the laundry."

"So you were naked with Lark?" Demwor's expression turned furious.

He could not leave that one unanswered. "I was naked alone with a laundry tub! *She* decided she had to do her laundry right then and use up all the water I brought. I had to get more so I could rinse my clothes because not even for *you* am I putting them back on with soap still in them!"

Demwor at first got angrier, but then calmed himself. "You could have left your underwear on until your outerwear was clean."

Runnel just sighed.

"Don't have underwear?" Now Demwor was amused.

"I'm not a baby," said Runnel.

That was apparently the funniest thing of all. But after one bark of laughter, he was back to chiding. "We don't do our laundry in the filtered water." He showed Runnel the tap that drew water directly from the cistern without passing through the porous stone first. It flowed much more readily, and the jar was quickly full.

"He's naked!" said Ebb cheerfully, when Demwor passed him on the way back to the house.

So Runnel had learned something else—people went insane when you took your clothes off. In the village, clothing was for *warmth*. Only girls worried about modesty, and only when they got near that age. During summer, men often worked naked in the fields. It was part of life; during hot weather, a man would strip himself as surely as he'd shear the sheep. What did they do here in the city? *Sweat* in their clothing so it would stink? No wonder they had to wash all the time.

He carried the full waterjar back to the laundry. Lark was still scrubbing linens. He tipped all the water out of the tub onto the stone flags of the washing pit. Lark leapt to her feet with a cry, then began picking up linens. "Now I have to wash them again, you fool! You oaf!"

"You felt free to take my water and the washboard from *me*," said Runnel. "That's how I thought things were done."

"I'm doing the master's laundry!"

"And I'm doing the laundry that Demwor told *me* to do," he said. "You're the one who decided to be mean. If you want to get along with me, then treat me fairly. I'll do the same in return. But right now, I'm rinsing my clothes. And washing and rinsing myself. Then you can do what you like."

Only then did he see that she had already slopped his clothes out of the tub and tossed them, not onto the clean flagstones, but out into the dirt. She saw where he was looking and she blushed. That was all he needed—he knew she was sorry for having caused him extra work.

"Thank you for helping me get this position," he said. "Even if you punish me the rest of my life for saying one wrong thing without meaning any harm, and for washing clothes the way we do it in the mountains, I'll still thank you for helping me get a place here. I'm in your debt, and I won't do anything like pouring out your washwater again. I'm sorry for that. It wasn't right."

As he spoke, he went for his clothes and brought them back to the tub. By now she was pouring water in, her lips set and her eyes downcast. He put his clothes back in the tub and knelt to wash them again. But she held on to the washboard and began scrubbing his clothing herself.

"I'll do it," he said.

But she ignored him and scrubbed.

"I don't want you serving me," he said.

"Go stand behind something till I have your clothes clean," she said irritably. "Pretend to be decent."

He obeyed and leaned against the stone wall of the garden, with a tree between him and her. He thought of climbing the wall to see what was on the other side, but decided that nude wall-climbing wasn't in the spirit of decency that she had in mind. He could hear her wringing out his wet clothes and spattering water on the pavement.

After a while she brought his trousers and tunic and, still averting her eyes, offered them to him. He took the shirt and pulled it on over his head. "I'm covered now," he said.

"Just take your pants," she said.

He took them, but didn't fasten them with the cord; they'd stay up well enough, being damp, and it wouldn't do to tie the cord wet or he'd never get it off. He went back to the washtub as soon as he was dressed.

"Go away," she said.

"Lark," he said. "I don't ask you to be my friend. Just let me help you do your work faster, since I delayed you."

"I do this job myself."

"I can wring out the linens," said Runnel. "I can pour water, even if you don't let me scrub."

In reply, she handed him a pair of underdrawers to wring. He did, and draped it where she pointed, on one of several strings between two tree limbs.

After most of the linens were hanging, she finally spoke to him. "It was a waste of time, you know, putting that stupid owl back up on the kitchen roof."

"Doesn't it work?"

"The mice live inside the kitchen walls and never *see* the owl," she said. "And no birds come here."

"Doesn't that mean that it *does* work?"

"It means no birds come over these walls, whether there's an owl or not."

"Why not?"

"Because they'd expect me to feed them and care for them, and I can't," she said. "So I ask them not to come." She looked up at him defiantly.

He nodded gravely. "You're a birdfriend, then."

"I'm no mage of any kind," she said. "I just get along with birds."

"Birdfriend," he said, "but I won't tell."

"It's one of the reasons it's so hard for them to find servants here. Nobody likes to admit they've got no magery, not even a scrap. First thing people do is show off, or brag if they've got nought to show. Even though birdmagery has nothing to do with stone, and birdmages aren't forbidden to enter Mitherhome anyway. Makes no sense and does no harm, but Demwor won't have a mage of any kind in the household."

"For fear they'll learn stonemagic?"

"It's because of the great war," she said. "When the soldiers of Veryllydd came to try to force Mitherhome to become part of the empire of Yllydd again, and the watermages here said no, for when Yllydd was a great empire, it was Mydderllydd that ruled it, and Veryllydd was subject to *them* then."

Runnel could tell that it was a story she had committed to memory, especially because she pronounced the "ll" of Yllydd in the old way, that hissing sound from the sides of the tongue when it was forming an "L." It was the language of stories. Though he hoped it wouldn't be too long. He was very tired. Also, having drunk much at supper, he needed to pee.

"The armies of Veryllydd had their mages of light and mages of metal, for in those days Mitherhome had only swords of obsidian to raise in battle. Thus in the day, the blood of the holy forest was soaked with the blood of heroes. And at night, the lightmages made the night of their tunnels into day, so they sapped under the mighty western walls of Mitherhome."

Runnel felt a chill as he realized that this was the explanation for the broken walls he had seen, approaching the city from the west. The blood of heroes: That was why the western forest was sacred, and no one built there.

"The elders of the city knew the western approach was their great weakness, so they built the second wall at the foot of the Mitherjut. This, too, the Verylludden sapped, and the doom of the Mitherfolk was plain for all to see.

"Now came the stonemages of Mitherhome, who had once ruled all of Mydderyllyd before the waterfolk conquered them long before. 'We do not wish to be ruled by Veryllydd,' they said. 'We can stop them: Rockbrother and cobblefriend, we shall do it.'

"Then the stonemages went to the peak of Mitherjut, where once their ancient temple stood. They bared again the rocks of the holy place and lay naked upon the stone, and the rockbrothers sank into it as the cobblefriends sang. First their temple arose, new and whole, made not of blocks like the temples of all other folk but of living stone thrust up until rockbrother and cobblefriend were entirely surrounded by their temple, with neither door nor window in the dome. Now they were surrounded by stone, almost as if they were stonefathers who can move within the living rock.

"The Verylludden sappers set fire to the beams in their tunnels, and the inner wall of the city trembled and began to fall. But as it fell, lo! A great cleft opened in the earth, from the Mitherlough to the river below, cleaving the Veryllydd army in twain. Many fell into the great crevice, including all the lightmages, as the waters of the lake swept into the breach, forming a new channel, the Stonemages' Ditch, flowing down to the river, making Mitherhome into an island with water on all sides. Now no need of walls! The portion of the Verylludden on this side of the crevice were pushed back and cast into the cleft; the army on the other side screamed and wept and pleaded as the ground beneath them shook so no man could stand.

"A great bridge grew from the hither side of the Stonemages' Ditch to the yon, and the army of Mydderllydd crossed over to wreak havoc on those who would have destroyed them. Now, with the hearts of the stonemages in them, the stone swords of the Mydderfolk cut the bronze swords of the mighty Veryllydd like new cheese, and their blood flowed like water, until ten times as many Verylludden died there as they had killed before. So many were dead within the broken outer walls of the city that you could walk from wall to Ditch without stepping on the ground." She stopped and bowed her head, for all the world like a traveling talespinner. For such a tale as that, a traveler could earn a meal and a bed for the night; she had told it well.

"I walked that ground just yesterday, and slept there, and woke this morning in that wood," said Runnel in reverent tones.

She looked at him wide-eyed. "Were the bodies there?"

"Covered with leaves and soil, maybe," he said. "I didn't see any. But, Lark, if the stonemages saved the city, why have they been banned? Why are they not welcomed as brothers?"

"That's the sad part of the story," said Lark. "I never like to hear it, but I learned it, if you must have the telling."

"Please," he said.

"The rulers of the city went to the great cleft, and saw the torrent of water that formed a little lake, then tumbled down the canyon to the river below, and they said, 'This new outflow will drain our lake and leave Yeggut diminished so he will no longer bless us.'

"Now it happened that the stonemages had foreseen this, and raised stone on the other side to reduce the outflow there, so the lake level was unchanged. The watermages knew this, for the water told them so, but they feared the power of the stonemages to steal their water. 'Today they were our friends,' said the watermages. 'But tomorrow, what if they remember that Mitherhome was once Mydderstane, built by stonemages and conquered by latecome watermen? They will say, "It is ours by right," and they will destroy us as they destroyed the Verylludden.'

"So in fear of the power of the stonemages, the rulers caused great heaps of wood to be piled all round the solid living temple that contained the great mages who had saved them, and they lighted the fire, which heated the temple until the stone glowed red. Nothing could live inside it. For two days the fire burned, then it died, yet for five more days no man could touch the stone.

"When the rock at last was cool, the rulers of the city caused the dome to be broken open, and inside were found ashes in the shape of each of the stonemages; even their bones were ash. The watermages called water up through the rock and it flowed from the center of the temple, so it became a spring, holy to Yeggut, and not an outcropping of stone.

"Then the temple was broken entirely apart and the pieces carried down and cast into the cleft. The bridge of living stone was broken apart, for it was said that the stonemages had done this to turn the new channel into a tunnel, with living stone all around it. It was decreed that forever no bridge would span that cleft." She broke off the narrative. "That's why Hetterferry came to exist."

"It's a sad story," said Runnel. "And it doesn't make the watermages of the city sound very noble, to murder the very folk who saved them."

"That's not how the tale is told in Mitherhome, I'm sure," said Lark. "But it's how I learned it, back in the—"

"It's a pack of lies," said Demwor.

Runnel whirled to look at him. He was very angry.

"She only told it as she learned it, sir," said Runnel.

"She doesn't need you to defend her," said Demwor. "I see now why she came to work at a stonemage's house."

"No, sir," she said. "I came because the work was good and safe. I learned this story as a child, it's a children's tale."

"Then listen to me well, *children*. Tell this tale no more, not to anyone. It's a slander of the stonemages against our city. They were traitors, that's the truth, in league with our enemies."

"Then why would they make the cleft that keeps the city safe?" asked Runnel.

"They didn't!" shouted Demwor. Then, more softly: "It has always been there. Their plot was to deepen it until it drained the lake and our enemies could get through on dry land. They were barely stopped in time."

"Thank you for telling us the truth, sir," said Runnel. Well he knew that the only way to stave off a beating was to agree quickly with the man who was raging. "We'll never tell it the other way again. Forgive us for being ignorant children from far away, where truth disappears inside extravagant tales." It was something his mother had once said, that bit about truth disappearing inside tales—only she had said it about gossip that had a village girl pregnant by a god, instead of by a traveler who gave her a golden fruit that was full of sweet water.

Demwor peered into Runnel's face, and then Lark's, looking for something—defiance, perhaps. But both of them looked as abject as any ruler could ask, and finally he said, "Your chatter has made you late to bed. I'll have you up as early as ever tomorrow, you understand? And still you must finish washing and wringing and hanging the master's linens."

"Almost done," said Lark. "I kept working while I talked."

"I saw you from the second story of the house, and you were working slowly. That's why I came out here."

Runnel said nothing more, only bowed. He half expected Demwor to cuff him once or twice, just because he had been angry—that was what Father did. Runnel even placed himself between Demwor and Lark, so that if he was one who struck out in his wrath, the blows would fall only on Runnel.

But there were no blows. Demwor walked away, and Runnel and Lark hurriedly finished the rinsing and wringing and hanging. Then Runnel carried what was left of the water back to the cistern, where he poured it back into the top, where it could join the water yet to be filtered. Nothing wasted . . . only the soapy water had been poured out onto the stones; the rinse water was cast into the vegetable garden. "We grow the cleanest radishes and yams," said Lark, but her smile was wan.

"We'll speak no more of your tale," said Runnel. "Your malicious, false, and unbelievable slander. Except to say that I looked down into the crevice, and some malicious, false, and deceptive slanderer has cast stones into the canyon and created the ruins of a nonexistent bridge, just so people will *think* your version of the tale is true."

She smiled at him. "You're a complete fool, Runnel. I forgive you for mocking me even after we took an oath."

"I meant no mockery . . ."

But she was already gone.

Runnel went to the pissery, where urine was saved, and contributed his few ounces to some future slab of soap. Then he went to the cistern and drank again, so he wouldn't waken with thirst in the night. But not too much, so he wouldn't waken with a full bladder.

Mostly, though, he was putting off the climb up those stairs, to try to sleep at the top of a swaying, shaking building. I know how those Verylludden felt, with the ground shaking under them and their bronze swords turning to cheese.

Inside the house, though, all was still. Wherever Lark slept, she must be there; Ebb, he knew, slept by the door in the outer wall. Demwor might be awake but he wasn't on watch on the lower floor.

I can say that I didn't want to wake anybody by climbing the stair as they were trying to sleep.

It was a feeble plan, and he knew it—but having formed the idea, he acted on it at once. He found the steps leading down into the cellar.

It was dark, like a cloudy, moonless night. Even after waiting, his eyes still could not find light enough to make out anything at all.

His toes, though, found the stone flags of the floor easily enough. But there was something wrong—the stones were trembling almost as much as the wood of the upper stories had been. They also gave under his feet, shifting with his weight. Finally he realized: They had been laid across wood.

The watermages are so frightened even of this one stonemage that not only do they have Demwor to keep watch over the house, but also they have cut off the stone of the house from the living rock of the earth.

They're afraid that even from here, Lord Brickel might be able to do some terrible thing to the stone underlying their city—or, more to the point, the channels through which their precious water flowed.

Well, it *is* precious water, thought Runnel. Six hours without water, and I begin to thirst. But when have I ever needed stone to slake my desire? If you have to choose between Tewstan and Yeggut, it was Yeggut who sustained life minute by minute and hour by hour.

Though if Tewstan hated you, where would you be safe from his wrath?

Not here in this cellar. You could put wood between the flagstones and the living stone below, but they could not have done that with the walls of the cellar, because they were holding up the upper floors. Walls had to touch the living stone, or the house could not stand.

Sure enough, the foundation of the great hearth of the common room above was stone that connected fully to the living rock; it was here that Runnel made his bed, his hand touching the stone of the foundation. Here alone the house did not tremble. Here alone he could sleep with the same ease he felt on the packed-earth floor of the hovel he had shared with his family all his life.

Yesternight I slept in the woods among the moldered corpses of heroes and invaders. And only the night before, with my family. So close is my village, almost a near neighbor of Mitherhome. Yet except for the soldiers who went away to the wars, which man of Farzibeck has traveled as far as I, or learned as much as I've already learned?

He could hear Father's voice answering him. "Learn? You've learned nothing, except how to be a slave in a fool's house, where a southerman lords it over you and a girl mocks you and you will grow nothing in the earth, only carry water and pour water, and chop vegetables for others to eat."

"Shut up," he said to his father.

How many times had he thought it, but dared not say the words? He had been slapped and shoved and punched and kicked a hundred times or more, as if he *had* spoken with such insolence. It was about time he finally said the things that he had already been punished for. He could swear at his father every day for a year and not be caught up with what the man owed him.

And as he went to sleep, he thought of Lark, so prudish, but so generous;

so angry, but such a good storyteller. She talks to the birds, and the birds obey her, yet she doesn't think that she's a birdfriend; what could a birdfriend do more than she did, keeping the birds away from the house because she could not serve them well here? A strange world, where someone could be a mage and yet deny it so thoroughly that she did not believe in her own power and therefore could never use it.

It would be wonderful to be a birdfriend, for it was said that beastmages could choose a clant, an animal that was like a second self to them. And having chosen a clant, they could learn to put their soul inside the creature, and see through its eyes, and feel all that it felt, and hear all that it heard. A birdfriend could use her clant to spy on people, or just to soar above the earth, or perhaps to take a hare or rabbit and bring it home, if the bird was a raptor. A birdmage would never have to starve.

But since Lark did not think she was a mage, she would have no clant, and thus would never fly or hunt or spy, but just do laundry and keep the birds away more thoroughly than any scarecrow.

If I were a beastmage, I would ride with my clant every night while my own body slept. I would come to think of my walking hours as a dream, and my sleeping hours as my true life, soaring through clouds or, as a lion or wolf, stalking through the forest or grassland, free and strong and fearless.

With my luck, though, I'd be a mousemage, and spend my clant-hours fleeing from every predator.

He slept and dreamed himself a mouse living inside the walls of the kitchen, scampering out in the darkness to steal food.

And all the night, his palm pressed against the wall of the hearthroot stones, and he could feel the earth beneath, all the deep stone of it, cool and hard near the surface of the earth, but hotter and softer as you went deep, until it flowed like honey, a vast sweet fiery ocean of molten rock a thousand times more voluminous and ten thousand times heavier than the sea. It felt to him as if it were his own blood, and his heart pumped it.

THE awkwardness of the first day soon faded. Each day Runnel arose before dawn and went to the fountain before most of the women of Hetterferry were up. There he filled the jar and carried it back, returned and filled it again, and then again—enough water for most days' work. There were even days when he made only two trips, because the cistern was full.

At first Lark was grateful, for this was her heaviest duty, and since she filled the jar only half-full, she used to take six trips. But after days and weeks of it, she simply took it for granted—as Runnel had meant that she should. Let her work at tasks that required the skill of her clever hands. Runnel had no great skill. The best he achieved was adequacy—but at most household tasks, that was enough.

He continued in the kitchen, because Nikwiz and Sourwell were good and patient teachers. He soon abandoned their expensive metal knives and used the chipped obsidian that everyone used in Farzibeck. The knives were constantly dulled on the cutting stones and had to be sharpened, but the obsidian never seemed to lose its edge, and it fit into his hand more comfortably than any metal blade, however well wrapped in leather the hilt might be.

Lark and he became friends, but not eager ones. When they were together on a task, they worked harmoniously, and even bantered together in a comfortable way. But whole days would go by in which they did not see each other, since Lark's work was mostly indoors, now that Runnel was doing most of the outdoor tasks. Only the laundry brought her out, and Runnel found himself looking forward to laundry days, not because he had any particular yearning for her but because compared to the perfect dance between Nikwiz and Sourwell, which shut out all others, her company was the best to be had in the stonemage's house.

Every week or so, there would be visitors who stayed for a night or two, then went on. Many of them were traders and merchants, and Lord Brickel would dine with them and then keep them company as they went out into the Hetterferry market to trade with the downriver, crossriver, and landbound merchants.

Runnel soon learned that Lord Brickel never did stonework of any kind, not for sale and not for gifts—the Mithermages paid him to work only for them, so that between tasks he was idle. Demwor was ever vigilant.

And yet, when Runnel went down into the cellar during the master's dinners with his visitors, he would press against the hearthroot stones and hear snatches of their conversations, for the stone carried sound that wooden doors and floors hid from hearing. Though the conversations were never clear, he began to realize that their language was guarded. Their laughter was out of proportion to things that were said; answers made no sense in relation to their questions. There must be double meanings hidden in their words.

Why, in the home of the stonemage of Mitherhome, would visitors speak with veiled intent? It occurred to him that these merchants and traders were also worshippers of Tewstan. Perhaps some of them were stonemages themselves.

Runnel's curiosity would not leave him alone. What were they saying? More to the point: What *weren't* they saying?

If only Demwor were not always in and out of the great hall: Conversations never took an interesting turn when he was there. Not that Demwor's spying was inappropriate—perhaps there was some conspiracy of stonemages. But Demwor would never hear of it, not the way he was going about it. Nor would Runnel ever hear the conversation of mages.

The only hope of it was to get Demwor out of the great hall. And Demwor would never stop spying . . . unless he had another spy.

Runnel began to find excuses to be in the kitchen during dinner, then took any excuse to carry this and that into the great hall. This way he could see the visitors, even though he heard less than he did when he listened in the cellar. Gradually, he transformed his own role until he waited in the room throughout the meal, ready to carry messages, run errands, or carry away finished bowls and platters. He remained absolutely silent, except when he had to deliver a message from the kitchen.

At first Demwor seemed irritated with him, until Runnel came to him one morning and began to ask him about the things Lord Brickel's visitors had spoken of the night before. In the process of asking him questions, Runnel made it obvious that he had memorized most of the conversation— and his questions were about the very things that seemed to be hinting at stonemagery. "Come to me anytime with your questions," said Demwor.

So Runnel was now welcomed in the great hall—by Demwor, anyway. The more Runnel was able to repeat the conversations of the night before, the more Demwor left him alone in the room with Lord Brickel and his guests.

Runnel's weekly coin was doubled.

He felt guilty for his double betrayal. For he was, indeed, spying on Lord Brickel. But he wasn't spying as well as Demwor wanted. He always reported the kinds of things Demwor himself used to hear. But he never reported when Lord Brickel and his visitors slipped and revealed more than they meant to. So he was taking Demwor's coin under false pretenses.

As Demwor began to let Runnel do all his listening, Runnel would catch Lord Brickel gazing at him now and then, studying him. Each time Runnel tucked his head into a properly servile position, hiding the arrogant expression that he now knew his face always bore. Runnel assumed that Lord Brickel knew he was Demwor's spy; he also guessed that Brickel was pondering just how stupid Runnel might be and how much could be said in front of him.

Gradually, as Runnel's reports to Demwor omitted anything unusually incriminating, Lord Brickel grew more candid with his guests. They would glance at Runnel, but Lord Brickel would only smile. He could never speak aloud about Runnel's new role as ineffective spy, in case Runnel was not an ally but merely obtuse; still, it was clear to the guests that Lord Brickel did not regard him as much of a danger.

As high summer came, the visitors became more common, sometimes two or three in a week, and sometimes overlapping their visits. Meanwhile, Demwor was often out at night, pursuing his own business, relying on Runnel's report the next morning to tell him what was said in the great hall.

One of the guests was a dealer in marble named Stokhos, and it was plain he was important—the other two visitors and Lord Brickel himself attended to his every word, and he was full of inscrutable sayings that must be codes that only stonemages could understand. If Demwor had been in the room, the very meaninglessness of their conversation would have made him suspicious, and Lord Brickel's interview with him the next day would have been difficult. Runnel would report none of the oddities. But he would remember them, and try to make sense of them later.

In the midst of the conversation, Stokhos arose from the table to piss into the fireplace; with Demwor gone, they all did this, as if it were some kind of offering to the stone, or perhaps just marking themselves as belonging here, like dogs that peed their way around the fields and fences of Farzibeck. But when Stokhos rested his bare hand against the hearthstone, he suddenly stopped, dropped his tunic back down to cover himself, and turned to face the others.

"When did this come to life?" he asked.

The words were too plain, and Lord Brickel glanced at Runnel nervously. Runnel tucked his chin and looked at the floor.

Footsteps told him that the guests were all going to the hearth and touching it.

"Alive all the way down to the heart," said Stokhos. "I didn't think you had it in you, friend."

They called Lord Brickel "friend," and Runnel had long since guessed that by this they were giving him his title cobblefriend, the lowest degree of stonemage—but still a true mage, and not just a worshipper of Tewstan.

"Currents hide under still water, brother," said Brickel, who alone seemed not to have risen from the table. The title "brother" implied that Stokhos was a rockbrother, the middle degree of stonemage.

"So you do your work under the very gaze of the birds of heaven?" asked Stokhos—which, Runnel guessed, meant, You practice stonemagery here in the house with Demwor watching?

"The nest is twigs, but the bird still builds it in a sturdy tree." To Runnel, that meant: I have to live in a wooden house, but that doesn't mean the stone parts can't be connected to the deepest living rock.

The trouble was that Runnel knew the hearth was not alive. Or at least it hadn't been. It *touched* the earth, with no wood under it like the flagstones of the cellar floor. Small stones linked it to bedrock. But Stokhos was saying that it was living rock—all of one piece.

"Clever," said one of the other guests. "It all looks loose from the surface, but yes, it *is* all of one piece, deep inside."

"Subtle," said another. The admiration in their voices was obvious.

"You were never that good a student in school," said Stokhos, chuckling—but the chuckle was artificial. He was genuinely surprised.

"A man never stops learning," said Lord Brickel.

"But a wise man does not show his enemies what he has learned," said Stokhos. Runnel understood: You risk being discovered.

"The fish sees only what's in the water," said Lord Brickel. Meaning: The watermages of Mitherhome can't tell what's going on deep inside the stone.

"But when the spring flood rolls loose cobbles down the stream, the fish sees *that*." Meaning: What if they tried to repair or remove some of this stone and found it was no longer loose?

"Living stone doesn't roll with the flood," said Lord Brickel. Meaning: Why would anyone repair this hearth when living rock will never need repairing?

"Well," said Stokhos, resuming his seat, "a bird like me can tell if the tree is sound before building his nest—but such as I cannot heal a dead tree and bring it back to life."

Did that mean that Lord Brickel had leapt past the level of a rockbrother to do work that only stonefathers could do? No wonder Stokhos sounded surprised. A true stonefather was rare; a fathermage was rare in any of the houses of magic. That's why in Lark's story of the great battle with the Veryl-ludden, the stonemages had been only cobblefriends and rockbrothers, and had to work together to do what a stonefather could have done alone. There might not have been a stonefather in all the world, or not one close enough to get to Mitherhome in time to save it.

From things he had heard all his life, he had always believed that magery was a combination of what you were born with, what you learned, and what you earned. The stories of wolfmages that alternately terrified and fascinated the children of Farzibeck talked of how a child would find that dogs were always drawn to him, then his parents would fear he might be a wolfmage, and kept him away from dogs. In the stories, the child always found a wolf pup out in the forest and fed and protected it, and thus gained in power among the wolves, not just because of his inborn ability, but also because he took risks and spent many hours serving and saving a wolfkin. But the stories all implied that a mage could never surpass the level of ability born in him.

Even if greater power could be earned, how could Lord Brickel have earned it when he was expressly forbidden to serve the stone? Of course, under that circumstance, it might be that any small service he gave could be magnified by the risk. That must be it.

What surprised Runnel most, however, had nothing to do with Lord Brickel. It was when Stokhos said, "A bird like me can tell if the tree is sound." To Runnel, this clearly meant that only a rockbrother could sense whether stone was living or not.

But *I* can do that.

The idea of this took his breath away. He was like the wolfmages in the stories. He was like *Lark*—having a mage's power without realizing it. He had thought that at most he might be a pebbleson, a person who liked stone but had no power over it. After all, wasn't he a worshipper of Yeggut, like all his village?

And how had he ever served stone? How *could* you serve stone, except to bring it back to life when it was dead? And since that was a thing that only a stonefather could do, how could stonemages earn any increase in power? Yet Lord Brickel had done it.

Then it dawned on him. If he was indeed a rockbrother, or at least had one of the powers of a rockbrother, then when he came to this house, perhaps the power of two stonemages—one trained and one raw and untrained—combined so that the trained one, Lord Brickel, could do things beyond his ability alone.

I'm serving here in ways that I hadn't even guessed, thought Runnel. It made him proud to be useful, not just in the housework but in the magery itself.

The meal went on, but the conversation shifted to safer subjects—or else the code was more obscure, and Runnel didn't know how to understand it. No matter—they began to send him out for more ale and finally for a second round of food, which he knew would irritate Sourwell, though Nikwiz never seemed to mind. It was a late night, and when Demwor came home and saw the dinner was still going on, he sent Runnel to bed. "I'll tend them myself till they finally notice it's late," said the steward. "I'll tell the master myself if I have to—he has much work to do tomorrow."

"Can I go along?" asked Runnel.

"Ebb will be glad of the help in carrying the master's touchstones." It was the first Runnel had heard of "touchstones," so he was all the more eager for morning. He would learn something about what stonemages actually *do*—he had only realized his own magery just in time to realize that he could profit from the learning.

As always, Runnel "went to bed" by climbing up to his attic room and sitting in the middle of the floor, practicing controlling his dread of being so far from stone. Tonight he managed it easily, for now he understood why he needed the stone so much and why he feared being in structures that to other people felt safe and solid. Here he would wait until the house was fully quiet, then creep down to the cellar to sleep. It never mattered to him that he got less sleep than anyone. As long as he could sleep with his hand touching the stone of the hearthroot, then he could get his full rest in only a few hours and awaken refreshed long before light. But if he slept away from stone, then his rest was fitful, waking often, and in the morning he felt as though he hadn't slept at all.

Because I'm a stonemage!

He wondered how Lord Brickel managed to sleep. There was no channel of stone from *his* bedroom down to the earth. The master slept on a wooden bed, which rested on a wooden floor, which rested on wooden beams and joists.

Runnel lay down on the attic floor and closed his eyes as he listened for the sounds of the house to quiet down.

He awoke in darkness and silence.

The floor trembled under him. He sprang to his feet. How had he slept?

That had never been possible before on this high wooden floor. But maybe he could do it, now that he knew why he feared being away from stone.

The things he had learned tonight flooded back into his mind. He felt ridiculous.

I was even more blind than Lark, he thought. She knew she *might* be a mage, and refused to believe it. It never even crossed my mind about myself.

He was hungry to get down to the cellar and feel what Stokhos had felt in the hearthstones. Lord Brickel must have bonded the stones into a living whole during the day yesterday, or surely Runnel would have felt the change the night before. It must have been a great undertaking.

But Lord Brickel had been out at the dock of Hetterferry most of the day, keeping company with his visitors and greeting Stokhos, who only arrived that afternoon. How could he have done it in the few hours he spent at home?

Because he was so excited, Runnel found himself being careless and making a bit of noise on the stairs. That was no problem on the way down to the main floor—he could always say he was going out to pee. But then he really *would* have to do it, and put off going down to the cellar till later. Better not to waken anyone. So he was extra careful going down the rest of the stairs.

There were still a couple of candles guttering on their sconces on the main floor, but they were nearly gone. To his surprise, going down the cellar steps, there was a light ahead of him. Someone was down there, but by now his feet were visible. He had been seen. So there was nothing for it but to continue, and decide what lie to tell based on who was down there. If it was Demwor, he could tell him that he was looking for him to report to him now, since they'd be busy in the morning.

It was Lord Brickel himself, holding a candle and pressing the other hand on the hearthroot stones. As soon as he recognized Runnel in the dim light, he set down the candle and beckoned.

When Runnel was close enough that they could talk in whispers, Brickel took him by the shoulder and brought his lips close to Runnel's ears.

"What are you doing to me?" he asked.

Runnel thought he was asking about the things he told to Demwor. "I never tell him anything that you didn't used to say in front of him."

The hand squeezed harder. "Where did you study?"

Now Runnel was confused. "I never studied anything, sir."

"To do this—I tried to dislodge a stone down here, any of them, an easy thing. Dislodge it, pull it out, push it back in—it's what I do. Only I can't. The stones are all of a piece. They're alive, as Stokhos said. And don't pretend you don't know what I'm talking about. I know you understand us. I *trusted* you."

No point in pretending now. "It wasn't alive when I first came down here," said Runnel.

"So you can tell which stones are living and which are dead?"

"I didn't know that it was magery," said Runnel. "Nobody told me."

"You can't be that stupid."

Runnel grew angry. "I grew up in a village that's faithful to Yeggut. Who would teach me anything about stone?"

"It's not just the hearthstones, it's the flagstones, too. They underlie the floor with wood, but you bound all the stones together into a continuous sheet of living stone. Do you think they won't be able to tell? All he has to do is *walk* down here and feel how they don't spring back up under his feet."

"He" had to mean Demwor. "He sends me down here," said Runnel.

"But one day he won't. You'll be on another errand, and he'll come down himself, and he'll realize what you've done. Only he'll think *I* bound them together, and I'll lose my position. And if he realizes that it's *living* rock, I'll lose my life."

"But *didn't* you do it?" Runnel reached for the hearthstones, then shook his head. "My lord, these hearthstones are no different from the way they were when I got up this morning. I mean yesterday morning."

"Why would you have checked them yesterday if you didn't know something was changing with them?"

"I didn't *check* them," said Runnel. "I sleep down here."

"So you can't tell if these stones are living rock?"

Runnel pressed his hand against the stone and deliberately traced the stone inside, to find where it ended . . . and it didn't. It kept going down into the earth, in a single column. It never rested on hard-packed earth. All the tiny stones that had once formed a thousand chains down to bedrock were now a single great sweep of stone that grew out of the bedrock and soared through soil till it came out here as hearthstones and flagstone, creased where they had once been separate pieces, but now fused inside, where it was hidden from view.

"I didn't . . . I didn't *look*," said Runnel. "I never noticed a difference. It felt the same every day."

"You've been sleeping down here?" asked Lord Brickel. "Show me."

Runnel lay down where he always did, and pressed his hand against the stone.

"Aw, Tewstan, what a fool," said Brickel. "A natural mage sleeps every night with his hands in the stone."

"Not *in* the stone, my lord," said Runnel.

"Of course your hand is in the stone, and the stone is in your hand. You've been pouring your life into the stone, and the stone has been pouring strength into your body. Look at your face; I should have seen it, it's half stone already."

Runnel touched his hand to his face. It felt like ordinary flesh to him.

"And Demwor tells me you can carry full water jars without ever stopping to rest, and I don't even *wonder*? I deserve whatever happens to me."

"Why should anything happen to you, my lord?" asked Runnel.

"Because I swore an oath that I was nothing but a cobblefriend, and by Tewstan it was the truth. But they'll never believe that it's sheer chance that brought a . . . a *stonefather* here to my house."

"A what?" A thrill went through Runnel. He wasn't sure if it was fear or joy. Both, probably.

"What do you think, that cobblefriends and rockbrothers can do this? You slept your way through the stone—of course it joined to the bedrock, to the whole globe of living rock on which the oceans and the continents float. You're ignorant, you know absolutely nothing, that much is obvious, but you have power. The stone loves you. Don't you see it? Hasn't it shown you its love all your life?"

Runnel thought back to his rock-climbing and realized: The reason I could find cracks and handholds and toeholds where others couldn't was because the stone opened up for me. Because it loved me.

And I love the stone. Like the child wolfmage in the story loves the wolf pup. All my life, I've loved the feel of it in my hand. I've worked with it, built with it, cut with it, climbed it, slept on it when I could. And it never occurred to me that this made me a stonemage.

"It has," he said to Lord Brickel. "But I didn't realize. It was part of being alive, to hold the stone, to climb it."

"And you didn't feel yourself connect with the stone below?"

"I thought it was my dream."

"If you had gone to school in Cyllythu, you'd know. Dreams like that must be told to a master. You would have been known for what you are."

"I can't be a stonefather," said Runnel. "I'm . . . Runnel."

"Well, you're *not* a stonefather. You have the power of one, but you have no skills at all. You don't even know what you're doing. You can't control it. You can't keep yourself from doing it."

"Teach me."

"Impossible. Not here. Don't you think Demwor would notice? No, you're getting out of here, while I try to take these stones apart one by one."

The thought of dividing the rocks again struck Runnel like a blow. "But . . . it's alive now."

"It shouldn't be. It *wasn't* till you meddled."

Now he registered what Lord Brickel had said before. "Where will I go?"

"To Cyllythu, of course. Go to the temple of Tewstan and tell them what happened here. Stokhos will vouch for the truth of it, and they'll test you and you'll be fine, I promise. But you're getting out of here tonight."

"I don't know the way. And the soldiers of the guard will challenge me."

"They won't see you. Don't you understand? Just press yourself against the stone walls of the fortress and they'll never see you."

"I've never—"

"I don't have time to argue. You are getting out of here tonight."

"Why can't I wait for day?"

"Because if Demwor challenges me, I will betray you, do you understand? It's the only way to keep him from thinking *I* did all this. So yes, I'll tell him the truth about you—that you clearly didn't know what you were doing, that it was an accident. But do you think they'll care? A stonefather, here in Hetterferry, at the very base of the Mitherjut."

"What will they do?" asked Runnel.

"What they do to stonemages: drown you, then burn your body to ash and stir it into the living water."

"And you'd let them do that to *me*, just so you don't lose your job?"

"Stupid boy, it's not *my* job. It's the only connection the stonefolk still have with the Mitherjut. Even if they don't kill me, they'll never let another stonemage into this whole valley. My only hope of keeping trust is to denounce you myself. Now get out of here, out of the house, out of the garden, onto the street, while I take apart the mess you've made down here."

The "mess" was living stone, and it made Runnel sick at heart to think of it.

"I can't go," he said. "I can't let you do it."

"What?" demanded Lord Brickel.

"I can't let you kill the stone."

"And yet you will," said Lord Brickel.

Brickel laid his hand on a stone and Runnel could feel what he was doing—feel the cracks growing where they had originally been, the stones separating. Dying.

And without even trying to, Runnel flowed the stone back together again.

"Tewstan!" whispered Brickel. "I said get out."

"And leave the stones to die?"

"Stop being such a child," said Lord Brickel. "These stones would gladly die, for the sake of the stonemages someday returning to Mitherjut. I'm not *killing* them, I'm helping them make their sacrifice. Now go, upstairs, out. We've talked for far too long."

Runnel tried to make sense of it all. He could feel the death of the stones under Brickel's hand; yet he could also understand that it might be necessary. Didn't cobblefriends work with dead stone all the time? Weren't streets cobbled with it? And didn't those dead stones feel warm and good under Runnel's feet? Dead wasn't *dead*, not the way people died. A stone could be cut off, but it could then be put back and joined again to the living rock, and it would live again itself. He must let this happen.

I'm a stonefather. I must do what's good for all the stone, the way the packfather in the story willingly died in his clantbody to save the pack.

He went to the stairs and climbed to the main floor. He owned nothing; there was nothing to take with him but the clothes he wore. And maybe a single obsidian knife from the kitchen.

Runnel walked quietly across the floor to the back door that led out to the kitchen. When he opened the door, Demwor was standing there.

"What are you doing up?" asked Demwor.

"Had to pee," said Runnel.

"Where were you?"

"Asleep," said Runnel.

"I went to the attic. You weren't there. I came out looking to see if you were peeing. I wanted to talk to you about last night. About our *guests*."

"I *am* peeing."

"Where were you when I looked in the attic?"

Where could he claim to have been that would put him inside the house now, still needing to urinate?

Runnel raised his voice a little louder as he stepped out onto the stone steps leading down into the garden. "Lord Brickel wanted to talk to me about tomorrow's work," he said.

He pressed his feet into the stone and felt the connection of living rock all the way to the hearthroot where Lord Brickel was working. He found a section that was still alive and pushed it, squeezed it out so it bulged. Surely Lord Brickel would see it and realize it was a warning.

"He wanted to take me instead of Ebb," said Runnel, loudly enough that if Lord Brickel would just come up from the cellar, he'd hear. "To work in the city."

"You *asked* him, didn't you?" said Demwor.

"Why would I, sir?" asked Runnel. "You already told me I'd bear half the burden of touchstones."

Demwor glowered. "Why would he want to *talk* to you about it? You'll do what you're told."

"He doesn't know me that well, but I'm . . . well, quicker than Ebb. Or at least he wanted to make sure of it. Maybe there are things he needs that Ebb has never been able to do. I don't know, sir. I just do what I'm told."

"What did they talk about last night?" demanded Demwor.

Suddenly Lord Brickel was in the doorway behind Runnel. "What did you just ask my servant?"

Demwor clamped his mouth shut.

"Are you spying on me, Demwor?"

What, thought Runnel, was that a secret? No, it was a pretense that he was just a steward. Now the pretense is broken.

"Is this how the Mithermages treat me? Have I not performed every service and kept faith with every term of our agreement?"

"You have these visitors," said Demwor.

"I'm allowed to have friends come to see me," said Lord Brickel. "It's in the terms."

While they talked, Runnel was continuing Lord Brickel's work, separating the stones in the hearth, in the hearthroot, on the cellar floor. He did it more quickly than Lord Brickel had, and he didn't have to be touching the very stone he was working on. An hour ago he wouldn't even have known to try what he was doing, but having seen Lord Brickel do it he now knew what it felt like, and how to show the stone, how to flow through it and make the separation.

And Lord Brickel was right. The stone did not groan; it accepted the separation. It knew that Runnel was doing right, protecting it by this separation. It had loved him for joining them together, but it did not hate him for separating them now.

"You're not allowed to bring stonemages here," said Demwor.

"Exactly," said Lord Brickel. "But who do you think my friends *are*? All pebblesons, at least, worshippers of Tewstan."

"A worship that's forbidden here."

"And we don't *worship* here," said Lord Brickel patiently. "But you know that just as puddlesons have a bit of power clinging to them because of their service to Yeggut, so do pebblesons because of their service to Tewstan. If you've detected some sort of power in them, that's why. But no *mages*."

"I've seen the links between you and them," said Demwor.

So he was key—not really a mage, but able to find magical links.

"Of course," said Lord Brickel. "But never when I'm working. I do no magery for the city when such links are present. If you're what I think you are, then you know that. You *know* I've never bound myself to stone except when the Mithermages ask me to."

Runnel realized that was a warning. If Demwor really *was* a key, he would sense Runnel's connection to the stone beneath his feet the moment he looked for it. So he stepped back up over the wooden sill and onto the wooden floor, and held the wooden doorframe.

In case Lord Brickel had not heard what he said earlier, Runnel chimed in. "I *told* you he wanted to speak to me about what we'd do tomorrow," he said. "Now can I go pee?"

"What *will* you do tomorrow?" Demwor asked Lord Brickel.

"My duty," said Lord Brickel. "As of this moment you are not my steward. If you stay here, then it's as a spy, and as long as they have a spy with me, they're in breach of the contract."

As Runnel headed into the bushes where he routinely peed—he saved the private house for other uses—he could still hear the argument.

"Well, then, you know I was using the boy as a spy," said Demwor. "So is he going as well?"

"If you aren't here to ask him, whom will he tell? He works hard and he's ignorant. *You're* the one who's leaving. Now. We'll put your things out the front gate in the morning."

"Where am I supposed to go at this time of the morning?" asked Demwor.

"To your masters, to report on me," said Lord Brickel. "Tell them that their bridges and arches can all fall down, now that I know I've been serving oathbreakers."

"You knew I was a spy."

"I wondered," said Lord Brickel. "*Now* I know. Get out."

What have I done? thought Runnel. I never meant for any of this to happen.

When he got back to the house, Lord Brickel and Demwor were both gone—presumably to the gate.

Runnel ran down into the cellar and quickly finished the work of separating the stones. He tried not to think of it as killing them. Someday I'll make you whole again, he thought over and over, promising Tewstan, the stone god.

If you think of it as stone, how can you talk to it? But if it's Tewstan, a god, then you can pray, and hope to be heard.

Yet he felt a twinge of guilt, for he had grown up with the worship of Yeggut, the god of water, the master of all things, who brings life to the desert and tears down mountains.

How did I become a stonemage, when all my thought was of Yeggut?

It is not the rituals of worship that please the gods, he realized. I worshipped Yeggut, but I climbed the stone, I put my fingers into the rock. There in the mountains, it was the stone heart of the world that made me who I am, no matter who or what I prayed to.

THE wetwizards of Mitherhome came for Brickel when the sun was halfway to noon. The day was cool and bright, so many of the people of Hetterferry came out to watch the procession. Lord Brickel wore an elaborate costume that Runnel thought looked ridiculous, but it seemed to impress everyone else. What does clothing have to do with magery? But the watermages were also in fancy headdresses and bright-colored robes, and there were boys carrying banners and pipes and drums being played as they walked down to the dock.

There was a raft there waiting for them. It reminded Runnel of the raft he had once helped to load, his first day in Hetterferry. If the raft had carried him to Mitherhome that day, would he ever have discovered his ability? Then again, if he had never discovered his power, would he be more or less happy?

Of course, as far as anyone knew he was only the stonemage's boy, carrying on his back a heavy load of many different kinds of rock—small samples of each, but in the aggregate, it felt like he was carrying a wall. Yet he *could* carry it, and he wondered if it was because the stone was somehow lighter for him than for other people. Or perhaps there was enough stone in *him* that he was sturdier and could bear more of a burden. That would explain why he could carry a full waterjar, even though he was not a full-grown man. Maybe everything about him that mattered came back to the stone in his heart.

They were poled across the water to Mitherhome, and then began the long trek up the endless stairways to the upper level of the city. Their course wound around the steep slopes of Mitherjut, and as Runnel's bare feet trod the stone steps he could feel a throbbing inside the mountain, not like a heartbeat, but rather like the slow fluttering of a huge bird that was trapped and could not get free. He thought of trying to find the source of it, but Lord Brickel had warned him to do nothing, seek nothing, *think* nothing about stone. "It's too dangerous," said Brickel. "Look what you did to the stones of this house—in your sleep, without even meaning to."

So Runnel did not explore the stone. Instead, he trod the steps upward, upward, with the well-maintained city wall on one hand and the buildings clinging to the steep slope on the other.

They came to a gate in the wall and went through it. In only a few steps they were at the brink of a cliff—not the steep drop-off of the Stonemages' Ditch that he had seen on his first day, but a natural channel cut by water. A stone bridge with a single arch led across the water. It was this bridge that Lord Brickel had been brought to strengthen. And without even trying to, Runnel could see why. All the vibration of carts and pedestrians crossing the bridge had vibrated the stones, making them rub against each other, shrinking them. The arch was sagging, putting outward pressure on the stones near the edges. They were going to break free, and the whole bridge would come down as the loss of a few stones weakened the rest. Maybe in a year. Maybe in a month. But the bridge was not strong.

Lord Brickel walked out onto the bridge and knelt, then lay on it, face-down, as if he were staring into the stone. Runnel stood by him, the bag at the ready. Brickel raised a hand from the surface, and Runnel brought the mouth of the bag to his hand. Brickel rummaged through it and came out with a cobble of granite and another of quartz. These he now held in each hand and pressed them into the stone.

He's not doing a thing, thought Runnel. This bridge is failing, and he's doing nothing but making a show. It's fakery.

When it falls, people will die.

But if Runnel fused a few of the stones together, right in the center of the bridge, so they were one piece, no one could see from the outside, but the stones would no longer rub against each other, and the pressures would return to being vertical instead of horizontal, as the bridge was designed. As long as he was careful not to let the fusing go right to the living rock at the ends of the bridge, the stone would not come to life.

It was so simple, so subtle, to link stone to stone.

But it got away from him. Runnel hadn't the skill or self-control to stop himself in time. The fusing went beyond his intention. The bridge linked to the living stone at both ends of the bridge.

Lord Brickel raised himself up on his elbows, and cried out, "No!"

Underneath the bridge, the water suddenly roiled and splashed, as if it were angry.

"What have you done!" cried one of the watermages.

"He's tunneled the stream!" shouted another.

At once they reached down and dragged Brickel to his feet. One of them made as if to drag him to the edge of the bridge and cast him off, but the others held firm and did not let him do it.

"You're no cobblefriend!" said the leader of the watermages. "You roofed the stream with living rock! You made a tunnel of it! Sacrilege! All along you've lied to us. You're a stonefather!"

Lord Brickel looked long into Runnel's eyes. But he did not say, It wasn't me, it was this boy. He said nothing at all as they dragged him from the bridge, back through the gate, and on up the stairs into the city.

Runnel followed, carrying the bag of stones, cursing himself for a fool. It did not help Lord Brickel that Runnel had made the fatal error by accident. Nor was it an excuse that he did not know that water hates to be roofed and tunneled, that it constantly struggles to break free. And how, above all, could he have known that the watermages would sense the moment the bridge became living rock?

It would do no good to declare himself to be the stonefather, Runnel knew. For then Lord Brickel would be charged with knowingly allowing another stonemage to practice in the city, and the penalty would be the same. They would both be punished then.

I have to free him, thought Runnel. I did this to him by disobeying him. It's my responsibility now to get him out of it.

Runnel followed until they came into the main city, which clung to the southwest shore of the Mitherlough. Most of the city was outside of the walls, which ran much higher up the slope of Mitherjut. They took Lord Brickel to a single tower that stood at the far point of a stubby peninsula that projected into the lake. When Runnel tried to follow them inside, one of the watermages stopped him.

"I belong with my master," said Runnel.

"Where he's going, you don't wish to go," said the watermage.

"What will you do to him?"

"What he agreed to by the contract he signed when he first came here," said the watermage. "He knew the penalty."

Runnel wanted to shout that Lord Brickel was *not* a stonefather, that he had only discovered Runnel's abilities last night, that there was no way he could have known or prevented Runnel's foolishness. I'll undo it, Runnel wanted to say, I'll make it back the way it was. But that would accomplish nothing—except to get Runnel inside the tower, subject to the same penalty that Lord Brickel was now facing.

He thought of going back to the stonemage's house and asking Lark's advice. But what would that accomplish except to take him farther from Lord Brickel? Lark wouldn't know what a stonefather could do, or ought to do.

He thought back to her story of the stonemages in the great war. What had she said? "They bared again the rocks of the holy place, and lay naked upon the stone, and the rockbrothers sank into it as the cobblefriends sang." He had no cobblefriends to sing for him, nor did he have any notion what their songs might have been. But he was a stonefather—if the rockbrothers could sink into the rock, so could he. Sink into the rock of the tower wall, and come out the other side—the inside, where Lord Brickel is held. I can bring him out again the same way, or tear open a door if I want to.

He walked around the tower to a spot that was not observed and pressed his hands against the stone. But this was not living rock. He could climb it, and gaps would open for his fingers and toes, but he could not merge with it, as he could with living rock.

Just as well that he had failed, for as he leaned against the wall, someone walked around the tower into view. Demwor.

"I wondered where you'd got to," said the former steward. "See what your fool of a master has done now?"

"I don't know what he did," said Runnel.

"He revealed himself," said Demwor. "And he'll die for it. Now come with me—I'm to dispose of all the stonemage's property."

"I'm not his property," said Runnel. "I'm a free man."

"Man?" said Demwor. "You're a boy, and barely that. But a free one? That's your choice. A *free* boy will have nothing to eat and nowhere to sleep. You can eat the stones in that bag, for all I care. Come with me now, and you still have a place; stay here, and I'll have you ejected from the city under the vagabond laws, for you have no place here, neither a master nor kin." Demwor reached to take Runnel by the shoulder.

Runnel dodged away, then reached into the bag and pulled out a cobble of sandstone. "Don't make me throw this at your head," said Runnel. "I don't miss."

"Are you threatening a citizen?"

"I'm protecting myself from a man who wants to lay hands on me," said Runnel.

Demwor backed off one step. "Is that how you'll have it, then? Fine. When I return, it'll be with soldiers, and you'll be ejected from the city by *them*. I don't have to lay a hand on you."

As soon as Demwor walked away, Runnel dropped the bag and began to run. Back the way he had come, till he was through the walls and up to the highest point of the road that led around Mitherjut. But instead of continuing down to where the bridge was, Runnel scrambled up the steep slope, away from the road, up toward the peak.

It might not have been the smartest move. For he soon discovered that near the peak, a spring gave birth to a stream, and it must have been a place very holy to Yeggut, because the stream was lined with the huts of sacred hermits, who would come out several times a day and immerse themselves in the stream, letting it flow over them until they were so cold they could barely move. And around the spring there were the houses of priests, and several temples, and a constant stream of visitors coming and going.

But it was the very peak that Runnel wanted, not the spring or the stream. And at the peak, there was just the ruined stone circle that had once been a dome of living rock, in Lark's story. Here it was that the bodies of the stonemages were burned alive inside that stone oven, as their payment for saving the city. A place of treachery. Mitherhome had first been built by stonemages; the watermages dispossessed them and ruled over them, then, when the stonemages might have thought they'd earned the right to be brought back into equality in their own city, they were murdered.

There was no one here in these ruins. It was not holy ground, as far as the watermages were concerned.

But it was to Runnel. He could feel the throbbing again here, stronger than ever. *I have found the heart of the mountain. Maybe the heart of the world.*

Following the words of Lark's story, Runnel took off all his clothes and lay down upon the living rock, right where one of the rockbrothers must have lain, back when the battle was raging, and there was no hope for the city.

The sun shone down on him—it was afternoon now, and despite the coolness of the air, the sun was bakingly warm. Runnel realized, now that he was lying still, that his own body was trembling. *What have I done? Brickel told me to do nothing, and I thought I knew better. I thought I was saving a bridge, and instead I've cost him his life.*

The throbbing under him grew stronger.

He began to sink into the stone.

I'm not doing this, he thought. *I'm not pushing myself into the stone. I'm just lying here, and the stone is welcoming me.*

He sank; the stone closed over him. He lay in darkness, but he could still feel the sun beating on his skin. No, not on his skin—on the stone above him. The stone of Mitherjut, that was his skin now. He sank into the stone, but the stone also sank into him. He could feel the whole Mitherjut as if it were part of his body.

And he was not alone.

"Stonefather," came a whisper. It was repeated, again and again, until two dozen at least had called to him.

"Who are you?" he asked. Only he did not move his lips—could not move them. Yet he heard his own voice as if he had spoken aloud.

"You know who we are," said one of them. "We have waited long for you."

"Are you the rockbrothers who created Stonemages' Ditch? The ones who won the battle and then were burned?"

"They burned our bodies," said one of them. And another, and another. "Our inselves died. But our outselves were wandering in the stone, shaping

391

it. That is all that lives, and we are fading. We have waited for a stonefather to come. Now you are here. Save the city, Stonefather!"

Save the city? What was *that* about? "*You* saved the city," he said. "From the Verylludden."

"Long ago," said the voices. "And they were only men. It is from the flowing stone we save the city. Feel how it wants to rise."

It was as if they led him, for even though his body did not move, he was traveling through the rock. "Is this my outself that you lead through the stone?" he asked them, and they said, "Yes."

They took him down under the Mitherjut to where a thick dome of cold rock pressed down as under it a hot dome of seething, flowing magma pressed upward. "The blood-stone wants to flow. It wants to burst free. We have held it down all these years, but now it grows stronger, and we grow weaker. Soon it will break free."

"What can I do?" asked Runnel.

"What we have done. Hold it down. If it breaks free, the Mitherjut will disappear, the city will be utterly destroyed, the lake will become a mere river, and all this good land will be covered in ash and new basalt."

"They killed you. Why don't you let them be destroyed in turn?"

"Mitherstane was built as a partnership of stone and man. What if the watermages rule for this moment? We cannot let the holy city be destroyed."

"I'm supposed to stay here for the rest of my life? Holding down a volcano?"

"Inside the stone your life will be long and longer. Till another stonefather comes."

"I can't. I have to save my master, Lord Brickel."

"He's only a cobblefriend. He can't help in this work."

"You don't understand. It's my fault that he's in trouble. They're going to kill him. I have to set him free from the prison he's in. I have to do it now."

And with that he wrenched himself free from the gentle pressure of their company and began to wander alone through the living stone. It was hard to imagine, deep in the rock, where he was in relation to the city above. Only when he brought his outself near the surface could he feel the cobblestones of the streets and the great buildingstones of the city walls, and the pressure of the heavy buildings as they pressed down into the earth.

He found the tower out on the peninsula and fused the stones of the tower to the bedrock on which they rested, making it a place of living stone. He did not bother to preserve the outward facade of separateness; he knew that the tower would no longer appear to be made of many stones, but of a single, smooth sheet of it, rising straight up out of the earth. Let the watermages see something of his power; let them wonder how it could be happening. He grew stone over the doors of the tower. No watermage could get in or out.

Now that the walls of the tower were alive, his outself could rise up into them, and now, as naturally as if he had been doing it all his life, he formed a body for himself out of the living stone. He gave it eyes, so his outself could see; legs and feet, so it could walk. He pulled his new stone body free of the wall and began to walk the downward-spiraling corridor of the tower.

Watermages and guards tried to stop him—they broke their puny weapons on his stone body, and cast their spells, but there was no water in him to obey them, and he brushed them aside and went on.

At the base of the spiral ramp there was a pool of water, at the same level as the lake. Out in the middle of the pool, on a raft of reeds, floated Lord Brickel, tied down, unable to move.

Runnel took his stone body—his clant, for now he knew what he had created—to the edge of the water and knelt. His knees grew into the living rock of the ramp, and drawing on the stone he was once again a part of, he extended his arms, longer, longer, until one of them completely bridged the pool, passing just over the raft on which Brickel was bound. Then with his other hand, he broke open Brickel's bonds.

Brickel climbed onto the bridge that Runnel had formed and walked over the pool to safety. "Runnel," said Brickel. "What good will this do? You should have let them kill me."

Runnel did not know how to make his clant speak. But he pressed his head against Brickel's head, and spoke inside his mind, as he had spoken to the outselves of the rockbrothers. "It's time to undo an old injustice," he said. "Be my voice. It's time for the stonemages to return to Mitherstane."

"That's our dream, but we're not ready."

"You have a stonefather now," said Runnel. "Tell them."

Runnel's clant, his stone body, led the way back up the ramp, to where the wetwizards and soldiers were clustered around what used to be a door.

"Let us out!" they cried. "We won't harm you."

Lord Brickel stepped around Runnel's clant. "Do you think I care about saving myself?" he said. "I bring a message from the stonefather whose clant you see before you. This is the city of Mitherstane, built by stonemages at the beginning of time. You are the children of treachery, who slew the stonemages who saved you from your enemy. This is the day of reckoning."

"What can we do?" cried the wetwizards.

But then Runnel felt something terrible and strange. The living stone of the tower was being attacked by something that chewed through the stone and turned it into tiny bits of dead dust. A gap opened in the wall, and through it stepped one, then another, then a third creature made of water.

The wetwizards cheered. "The waterfathers bring you your answer, stonefather!"

The three waterclants strode to Runnel's stoneclant, and the moment they touched him, he could feel them wearing away the stone of his skin. He tried to replenish himself from the living stone beneath his feet, but there were three of them, and he could not keep up.

So he flowed his clant back down into the living stone of the floor.

Once again, he had left Brickel at the mercy of the watermages.

I was a fool, he thought. I felt all this power, and forgot that the watermages have power of their own. They defeated us before; why did I think that I alone could defeat them now?

"Forget them," murmured the rockbrothers. "Help us suppress the flowing stone."

But Runnel was not going to forget anything. He thought: What can I do to hurt them? How can I make them release Brickel?

He thought of the porous stone in the cistern back at Lord Brickel's house. There, it served as a filter. But here, that kind of stone could serve another purpose entirely.

Runnel sent his outself through the stone that underlay the lake. Starting with a little outcropping of rock surrounded by water, he expanded the stone by making it as porous as the filterstone in the cistern. He expanded it more, with larger holes and channels, and it filled with water. He spread the porousness through more and more of the lake-bed rock, and took it deeper and deeper. As the stone expanded, it rose higher, toward the surface of the lake; the water level fell as the water soaked into the stone.

Until finally there was no lake. Just a single sheet of porous rock, with all the water held inside.

He could feel the flow of the water down the channels as it came to a stop. The water flowing into the lake from the streams and rivers that fed it soaked into the stone as fast as it arrived. There was no lake. Below Mitherjut, there was no river.

Where will you draw your power from now, waterfathers?

He returned to the tower, to the pool in the middle of it, and there, too, he made the stones of the tower porous, so the water was soaked into the floor and walls. The pool was dry. Runnel formed another clant out of the newly porous stone of the walls and returned up the ramp. The waterclants were no longer there. No one was there.

Where had they taken Brickel?

He emerged from the tower through the hole the waterclants had made. Outside, the streets were deserted. He could see that the sun was low, nearing the horizon—it had taken him longer to swallow up the lake than he had thought.

Where were the people? There were a few, kneeling at what had been the shore—the docks now hung over bare stone. But not the watermages.

Of course, he thought. They've gone to the holy place. To the spring near the peak of Mitherjut.

"It's working," said the rockbrothers. Runnel did not know what they meant—nothing was working.

Runnel's stoneclant strode up the steep, rocky slope and walked directly over the spot where his real body, his inself, lay buried in stone. He could feel his clant tread over him. Then it went down to the spring.

There they held Brickel in the flow of the stream. Brickel was gasping.

The watermages shouted at Runnel's clant. "We'll sacrifice him! We'll drown him if you don't return our water!"

In reply, Runnel turned the streambed porous and soaked up all the water there. The spring ceased to flow.

The watermages wailed.

Brickel rose to his feet. To Runnel's great admiration, Brickel immediately resumed his role as spokesman for the stonefather.

"It is time for you to abide by the ancient treaty," he shouted. "When first the stonemages allowed the waterkin to settle here, you made the vow that stonemages and watermages would dwell in peace here together, in a place holy to us both. You were the ones who broke that vow! You were the ones whose treachery murdered the best of us a hundred years ago! No more will a single cobblefriend live like a prisoner in order to tend the ancient walls and bridges that were built by ancient stonemages. Either we live here together in a place of stone and water, or it remains as it is now, a place where only stone can live."

"We will!" answered the leader of the watermages. "But only if you give back the sacred Mitherlough."

"When you have taken the solemn unbreakable oath in the treaty tower," said Lord Brickel.

"How can we get there from here?" said the watermage. "The Stonemages' Ditch blocks the way."

"Only because you broke down the living bridge we made there."

"It was a tunnel!" said the waterfather.

"It was a bridge!" roared Brickel back at him. "We all know what a tunnel is—it's where your water is now, in millions of tiny tunnels through stone! A bridge that leaves many yards of air between the water and the stone is no tunnel! We will have bridges wherever the stonemages wish to have them. Bridges of living stone that will never break down!"

With that, Runnel began to walk his stoneclant down the dry streambed, and Brickel followed him. When he reached the broken-down wall that had once been the inner defenses of a peninsula, and now marked the edge of the Stonemages' Ditch, Runnel led them along the wall to the place where once a living bridge had crossed the canyon—where soldiers had poured over the bridge to slaughter the Verylludden.

While his clant stood on the surface, Runnel himself reached into the living stone and extruded a wide bridge that reached out over the open air and finally met the stone on the other side. Then he walked out onto it with his clant, Lord Brickel following him, and all the watermages after. They walked on through the forest until they reached the tower that Runnel had seen on the first day, when he was trying to find his way into Mitherhome. This was the ancient temple of the treaty, which had long since been converted into a temple of Yeggut.

Runnel reached into the tower and made it, also, a thing of continuous, living stone.

Then he turned and looked out over the sheet of stone where once the little lake had been. To his surprise, he could not see the stone at all. Instead, thick steam rose from the whole surface.

What is happening?

The rockbrothers answered him: "You brought the water down to the flowing stone and cooled it. We are turning it to granite, deeper and deeper, by pouring the heat of the magma into the water."

"I didn't know it would do that."

"The flowing stone is already far below where it used to be. Soon we will need no one to keep it from bursting through. You have saved the holy city."

But at the treaty tower, the watermages saw the steam and wailed. "You're making our holy water vanish!"

"Will the rains not come?" said Brickel. "When the stonefather restores the stone of the lake bed, will the rivers not flow and fill it again? Now in your hot blood and mine, the mixture of water and stone that flows in all of us, we will sign again the treaty that you broke."

The ancient document was sealed under clear quartz; Brickel did not need Runnel's help to separate the quartz from the surrounding stone and lift it off. There he and the watermages opened their veins and dipped pens in blood and signed their names again.

When it was done, Lord Brickel replaced the quartz and fused it again to the granite pedestal.

"Now give us back our lake!" they said.

Runnel first restored the sacred spring and stream that flowed down the slope of Mitherjut. Then he worked his way from the farthest edge of the Mitherlough, shrinking the stone of the lake bed so it was no longer porous. But he did not release the water from the stone; instead, he guided it to flow down to the magma, ever deeper, cooling it more and more. "Yes," murmured the rockbrothers. "It will be as if the stone had never been hot. The flowing stone is deep again, where it belongs."

As the lake bed sank back down, the steam continued to rise. It was not until well after dark that the entire lake bed had been restored. Now the waters of the inflowing rivers flowed out onto the stone, and slowly the lake began to form itself again. It would take many days to refill the lake as it had been. But it would refill.

"Move my household into the city," said Lord Brickel. "We will have a new home in the shadow of Mitherjut, near the walls our ancestors built. I will invite as many stonemages to come to the city as you now have watermages. One for one, our numbers equal. We will sit on your councils in exactly the same numbers as you. We will have an equal voice in the making of the laws. All according to the treaty we have signed today."

And the watermages said yes, for they could see that their lake was coming back to its place.

Runnel flowed his stoneclant into the rock of the treaty tower.

High above, at the crest of the Mitherjut, his body of flesh rose upward out of the stone.

But it was not the same body that had sunk into the stone earlier that day. For he had been too closely bonded with the granite of the mountain, and now his skin was hard and flecked; there was stone in him, all through him. He moved as flexibly as ever, but he could feel that his feet would never grow tired from walking, and only the sharpest obsidian could cut his skin. He was not pure stone like his clant had been, but neither was he pure flesh and bone.

He put on his clothes again and made his way down the way he had come. No one noticed him in the gathering night. He was just a boy walking the streets.

When he got to the low port across from Hetterferry, he only had to tell the ferryman that he was Lord Brickel's servant. After the events of this day, that paid for his passage, for everyone feared the stonemage. After all, they believed that it was Brickel who had done all that was done today. They could not afford to cross him by offending his servant.

At the stonemage's house, Demwor was already there, but his errand had changed. Instead of disposing of the stonemage's wealth, he was supervising the move to the upper city. Runnel immediately began to help with the work, and if anyone noticed that he was now carrying loads far heavier than anything Ebb could bear, they said nothing about it. In the darkness, no one could see how his skin had changed.

All night they worked, carrying everything to the ferry. On the other side, a team of puddlesons lifted everything onto their backs and carried it up the long stair.

By dawn, Lord Brickel's new house was ready, and, exhausted, they all fell into bed and slept well into the next day.

Except for Runnel, who was not weary. He lay down on the stone of the new cellar floor and fused the stone walls of the house together into living rock. This was the home of a stonefather—it would look like it.

Lord Brickel came to him late in the morning.

"What were you thinking?" he said softly.

"Isn't this what you and your friends were working for?" asked Runnel.

"Were you planning this, then? All of it?"

"None of it," said Runnel. "I didn't have the faintest idea what I was doing." Then he told Lord Brickel about the rockbrothers, and the near volcano that the water of the lake had cooled. "I didn't know the water could do that," he said.

"It was Tewstan that guided you," said Brickel.

"Look what it did to me," said Runnel.

He led Brickel up the stairs and stood where the light shone through a window.

Brickel touched his skin. "You are part of the Mitherjut now," he said, in awe. "I've heard of such things, a man taking the stone inside himself. But I've never seen it."

"Will it go away?"

"No," said Brickel. "Not if the lore is true."

"I don't know anything," said Runnel. "Will you take me as your apprentice? Will you teach me?"

"Me? Teach *you*, a stonefather?"

"Is there a stonefather somewhere in the world right now who can do it?"

"No," said Brickel.

"Then what you know, all the lore, all the secrets, I have to learn it. Will you teach me?"

"Of course."

"And let the watermages go on believing that you're the stonefather," said Runnel. "I don't want to be Lord Runnel Stonefather."

"You have no choice," said Brickel. "Among stonemages, that is your name, though we shorten it. 'Runnel Stanfar.'"

"But my common name, here on the streets of the city. Let me be . . . Runnel Cobbleskin. Your apprentice. Your servant. Let this skin be known as something that you did for me, to make me strong and tough."

"You really don't want to take your rightful place of authority?"

"I'm a child," said Runnel.

"You were man enough yesterday, to steal the lake from the wetwizards and burn it into steam." Brickel laughed. "Once I stopped being so terrified myself, it was really funny."

"If I had known what I was doing there at the bridge, I would never have done it," said Runnel.

"You should have obeyed me. But it turned out well."

"I'll obey you now," said Runnel.

Brickel laughed. "Except when you think I'm wrong."

The days and weeks and months passed by, and Runnel's new stoneskin did not stop him from growing taller, till he had a man's height. Stonemages came to the city, many of them to live there and take part in the government of the place, but many more merely to meet the young apprentice who had restored them to their holy city. Runnel went with them and stood in the circle when the leading rockbrothers built back the dome of living rock that had once enclosed the bodies of those who saved the city from the Verylludden.

They showed no outward sign of his prominence among them, lest the watermages realize that Runnel was their stonefather. But they all knew that it was Runnel whose power did most of the stoneshaping; that it was Runnel who drew up to the surface the fading outselves of the dead rockbrothers. He fashioned for them bodies of stone, which stood around the inside wall of the dome, their feet fused to the living rock. As long as their outselves persisted, they would have the use of these bodies; and when they faded, these would be their memorial.

When Runnel Cobbleskin was eighteen years old, by the nearest reckoning he could come up with, he went to Lark, who had long since come into her own as a birdfriend, keeping doves at the crest of Mitherjut that carried messages far and wide. He took her into his arms, and she held him close.

"Lark," said Runnel, "I want to hold you forever, the way the living stone holds the waters of the Mitherlough."

"I'm only a weak-skinned girl, and mostly water," she said. "You're too hardskinned for me now, Stanfar. How can I take a stone as my husband?"

"Gentle can be as good as soft," he answered. "And there's no burden I cannot lift for you."

"I have flown with my birds high above the earth," she said. "But I will make my nest with you."

CREDITS